MW01254159

# GHOSTS

## OF

# INNOCENCE

# GHOSTS

# OF

# INNOCENCE

## Ian S. Bott

Dark Sky Press

This book is a work of fiction. All the characters in this book are ficti-tious, and any resemblance to actual persons, living or dead, is purely coincidental.

Copyright © 2014 by Ian S. Bott

All rights reserved. No part of this publication may be reproduced, distributed, or transmitted in any form or by any means, or stored in a database or retrieval system, without the prior written permission of the publisher.

Published by Dark Sky Press, an imprint of Ian S. Bott, Writer and Artist. Visit our website at www.iansbott.com

Book Design by Jim Bisakowski    BookDesign.ca
Cover illustration by Ian S. Bott

Library and Archives Canada Cataloguing in Publication

Bott, Ian S., 1960-, author
        Ghosts of innocence / Ian S. Bott.

Issued in print and electronic formats.
ISBN 978-0-9937242-0-6 (pbk.).--ISBN 978-0-9937242-1-3 (html)

        I. Title.

PS8603.O9183G56 2014        C813'.6        C2014-902878-4
C2014-902879-2

Printed in the United States of America

First Edition: June 2014
10 9 8 7 6 5 4 3 2 1

To Ali,

Loving and supportive

And batshit crazy to be putting up
with the likes of me

Mouth dry, Shayla Carver swallowed a sour taste at the back of her throat. An orbiting battle station, one of many surrounding the Emperor's home planet, Magentis, filled the nearest viewport of *Chantry Bay's* forward lounge. A mushroom forest of defensive batteries, domes blackened by centuries of conflict, studded the outward face of the fortress. The Imperial crest was barely visible on its dulled and scarred flank.

As it receded behind them, Shayla murmured a mantra to ready herself for action. But she couldn't rid herself of the unwelcome thought: that station was too damned close. They could blow us to Space and beyond when they realize what's happening.

No. The mission planners had discussed this possibility. The big plasma cannons were all facing away from the planet. They can't threaten us now.

Shayla forced her head back against the hard wall of the lounge, feeling the roughness of the hangings behind her. A tiny knot in the fabric pressed into her scalp. The pinprick pain helped steady her thoughts.

She breathed deep and surveyed the lounge through half-closed eyes. She counted at least sixty passengers scattered in groups amongst the benches and circles of stools and armchairs cluttering the coarse, grey carpet. People of all ages and races, resplendent in uniforms or formal dress denoting their professions in readiness for landfall.

Excited chatter barely masked growing tension as they approached their rendezvous with an orbiting reception base. A round-faced woman, wearing the crimson headdress of a planetary ambassador, paced the length of the lounge and brushed yet another imaginary speck from the sleeve of her robe. Even such a dignitary wasn't exempt from stringent interrogation before setting foot on Magentis.

But the knot in Shayla's stomach had nothing to do with security screening. Once more she mentally rehearsed her movements, awaiting her cue.

A diamond-bright spark separated from the expanding disk of the planet. The reception base.

According to the schedule, starhopper *Chantry Bay* should have slowed and docked.

It didn't.

A few puzzled gazes followed the sunlit jewel of the base as it flashed past the viewports. Shayla saw the first glimmer of comprehension in some faces. Decades of terrorism had sensitized the public psyche to unannounced deviations from schedule.

A coterie of scribes and administrators on the other side of the lounge looked up from their scrolls and notepads and stared at each other, styli wavering in their hands. External communications had died. Right on cue.

The lights flickered, then failed. Through the lounge's forward viewpoint, the daylight side of Magentis flooded the cabin with an aquamarine glow.

An eerie silence fell, the ever-present hum of machinery now deafening by its absence. Shayla closed her eyes, barely breathing. In the back of her mind she'd started a countdown at the first flicker of the lights. Eight and a half minutes until they hit atmosphere. Unless the navy caught them first.

Shalya squeezed her eyes even tighter shut, counting steadily, as bedlam erupted.

"Sabotage!"

"Terrorists!"

"The Insurrection!"

A wet crash and a shriek. Someone had toppled the samovar bubbling in the center of the room.

A groan and a sour whiff of curdled milk told Shayla that the jolly, mustachioed bureaucrat opposite her had brought up his lunch. He'd spent the last hour enthusing over his duties in the Office of Corrections, in charge of the public punishment stalls for the eastern end of the Bay of Jorka. His dedication to human suffering had made Shayla sick.

A hand squeezed her knee through the heavy embroidered textile of her robes. She opened her eyes a crack to see a worried face gazing at her. Not Scolt again, she groaned to herself. Not now.

She glanced around the lounge, then took his hand in hers. Scolt had taken unwelcome interest in her for the whole week-long flight. Another time, in another life, she might have returned the interest, but even out of uniform the emerald tattoo on his forehead and his preening arrogance had marked him out as a member of the Imperial Color Guard. Not a good bedfellow for a woman with treason on her mind.

Shayla had no time to waste. She gazed into his eyes, smiled, and finally did what she'd been longing to do the whole flight.

She broke his fingers.

As he shrieked in pain, Shayla slipped around the end of the bench and into the main corridor leading from the back of the lounge into the depths of the ship.

She squeezed into a crush of people jamming the short ramp up to the command deck. The captain, face ashen in the planet's ghostly light, faced the scared and angry crowd, trying to restore calm. Shayla felt a twinge of pity. The crew must have been shocked when the normally-secure door to the command deck had opened. The malicious code she'd inserted into the ship's command system had been designed by her twisted genius brother. Shayla was confident it couldn't be bypassed, but her mission planners had figured that the crew could do with some distraction to hamper any attempts at troubleshooting or communications.

She pressed her back against the wall and pushed past the edge of the crowd.

A figure in the gloom caught her eye. A young girl, eyes wide, clutched a stuffed toy lion tight to her chest. *Shit! I thought this ship was for Imperial staff only!*

Shayla glanced back towards the lounge. Through a gap in the press of bodies she saw that Scolt was already on his feet, his face twisted into a snarl. Damn, that was quick. She would have only moments more to get away from him.

Leaving the planet-lit lounge behind her, Shayla felt her way in lengthening shadows down the ship's central passageway. She melted into the deeper gloom of a doorway as someone stumbled past, then continued on her way.

She reached the door to the master kitchen. It was sealed, but its keypad accepted Shayla's command to unlock.

A hoarse voice called through the opening, "At last! What's going on?"

Half blinded by the brilliance of a hand-held glowtube, Shayla aimed a straight-fingered jab at the sweat-soaked chef who'd been trying to open the door from the other side. She slipped through the door as he crumpled with a wheeze, windpipe crushed. She kicked the glowtube aside and turned to lock the door again. The lamp's light spilling into the corridor would have been visible the length of the ship.

The door snapped shut, cutting off a shout and the sound of running feet. *Scolt! That was close.*

Shayla ducked and rolled, robes flapping, as a skillet clattered off the wall above her head. She counted two more figures in the dancing shards of light and mess of reflections off polished metal and ceramic.

She dispatched the nearer crewman as easily as the first, and focused on the one remaining occupant. *Military training?* He faced her in a fighting crouch. He was the pan-thrower, and now he'd found a broad and heavy kitchen knife. *Out of practice though.* He looked worried, backing into a corner, knife wavering in front. No match for an assassin trained in the Firenzi Special Service.

Shayla approached quickly, forcing him to act. When he lunged, she moved with the speed of a striking mantis, catching his knife hand and using his own momentum to draw it safely past her. She pivoted away, his forearm gripped tight in front of her, and brought her hip hard onto his outturned elbow. A loud crack told her the knife arm posed no further threat. She released it and continued turning, whipping around behind him and breaking his neck.

Shayla returned to the door. It sounded quiet outside. She pulled out her notepad and accessed *Chantry Bay's* command system. The security logs showed Scolt's identity alongside the Imperial seal and the insignia of a Lieutenant Colonel. So, he *had* tried to open the door to follow her, but her lock had held.

For now.

The command deck was disabled, communications blacked out, all guidance under her control bringing the ship onto a carefully planned course. But freezing the door codes was a last minute detail, and Shayla now wondered how secure those locks were. What if Scolt had higher level access codes?

She retrieved the glowtube and checked the kitchen for any unwelcome surprises. Empty.

She checked the doors and hatches to the servery. Still sealed, but the logs revealed that Scolt had tried here too. Damn him. He was proving to be too smart and persistent by half, even for a member of the Imperial elite.

No time to do anything about it. She had to get into position.

Shayla hurried to the far end of the kitchen and into the rows of storage lockers behind. She counted down the doors, then opened one and felt inside. She pulled out neatly stacked packets of rice, tossing them aside, until she found a backpack fastened to the locker ceiling just within reach. The agent on the ground crew had done his job well.

She continued through the storage section till she came to a service hatch. The hatch led into a narrow corridor, a steep companionway, then a cramped loading bay.

Breathing a sigh of relief, Shayla threw off the bulky clerk's robes and tunic that concealed a skintight pressure suit. She buckled the pack onto her back and double-checked the fastenings. She clipped her notepad to the straps across her chest, and donned gloves, helmet, and visor. The head-up readings from the ship's systems reassured her that she still had a few minutes to go.

And she was still alive. They hadn't been blown out of the sky. The downward trajectory had been chosen with care to aim for a vast and unpopulated area of swamp and forest. *Chantry Bay* would be tracked, and when she veered off course someone would have to decide whether or not to destroy the ship. Shayla had judged that they would elect to let it crash into the middle of nowhere rather than risk deflecting it onto one of the surrounding cities.

There was a tiny control pad on the shoulder strap below her left collarbone. Shayla fingered the touch pads. A cascade of silvery fabric tumbled from the pack to the floor behind her, half supported by a network of veins woven into its thickness. The veins merged into ever thicker branches converging on a pair of hand grips, then flowed around behind her to join onto the pack.

She took the grips in her hands and flicked the shimmering robe out behind her, then stepped backwards over the hem and sat on the fabric with her back to the outer loading hatch.

*Two minutes to atmosphere.*

Shayla drew her feet close in and folded the robe loosely around herself. She tapped the controls at her shoulder. The edges of the material slowly zipped shut in front of her. She had a working knowledge of the molecular processes in play, but the sight of the fabric smoothing and sealing itself into an airtight bag fascinated her.

From the strap at her other shoulder, she pulled a mouthpiece on the end of a short tube. There was a tiny scrubber and oxygen generator built into the harness. She kept the mouthpiece in her hand, and crossed her forearms in front of her, curling up closer still.

*Time to say goodbye.* In her mind, Shayla performed the brief ritual of release that she always used when switching identities. Libby Hollis, the clerk in the Imperial logistics corps that Shayla had been impersonating for the last week, was laid to rest. Now she was simply Shayla Carver again. For a while, at least.

*One minute.*

An alarm flashed in the corner of the visor.

Shayla fumbled the notepad from its clips in the confines of her bubble, and unfolded it, flipping the stylus out of its holder in one smooth motion.

The captain was using his access codes to override her locks. She activated a jamming agent. Secrecy was no longer relevant. *Just disrupt them for a little longer.*

Too late. The door was open.

A blow sent Shayla reeling. A yelp told her that her assailant had come off worse. His fist had connected with her helmet. She held tight to her notepad, but she'd dropped the stylus.

"Hold her! We need her alive." *Scolt's voice.*

Shayla groped beneath her for the stylus.

Arms tried to pin her, fumbling for purchase on the slick folds of fabric. She kicked, aiming by guesswork, and connected with something soft.

*Got it.*

Once more, encircling arms restricted her movements.

Shayla jabbed the stylus upwards over her shoulder. A curse, and she was free again.

*Do it now!*

A voice somewhere in the back of her mind screamed at her: *we're too high up.* But the sensible faction had already lost out to the tyranny of the immediate. Acting without conscious thought, stylus tracing brief stokes across the notepad as if with a will of its own, she overrode the planned sequence and activated the launch command early.

Shayla curled into a ball, notepad clutched to her chest, and ignored the hands trying once more to pull her to her feet.

Ship's telemetry showed the outer hull temperature already soaring. A distant clangor echoed through the hull. White noise rose to a rushing roar, smothering all other sounds.

The loading bay door blew outwards. Escaping air propelled Shayla into the upper stratosphere. Her gauzy shroud snapped taut into a luminous bubble under the pressure of the air trapped inside. She resisted the urge to gasp in agony at the sudden decompression, and forced herself to keep her mouth open and airway clear while her lungs vented. After a few seconds she clamped her mouth tight around the rebreather and let a trickle of oxygen diffuse back into her lungs.

Her suit absorbed most of the pressure change, but she felt as if her eyes were going to burst.

*How high am I?* Black dots clouded her vision as she tried to read the display on her visor.

Burning agony pierced her shoulder. Shayla twisted her body away from the pain and glanced around. A tiny needle of white fire lanced through the air in front of her eyes. *Dammit!* The stylus must have pierced the fabric. The material was tough, but if the hole spread she was dead.

In her supine position, Shayla secured the notepad back in its clips, careful to keep her arms and legs tucked away from the walls of her cocoon, and away from the torch hissing past her ear.

The plasma of re-entry glowed through the veined skin as she plunged through thickening air. The inside of the bubble was like an oven.

*This is madness!*

Shayla rehearsed her next movements. Before she had time to reconsider, she reached for the handgrips, her shoulder once more in the path of the intruding fire. Trembling fingers squeezed the controls on the grips. The trailing edge of the bubble split open and eased outwards, spreading to slow her descent and revealing a dazzling circle of blue above her.

A thin shriek escaped her lips around the mouthpiece as she kept hold of the controls, braking her fall as much as she dared.

When she could stand the pain no longer, she relinquished her grip and curled into a tight ball, allowing gravity and friction to do their work.

The stench of charred flesh recalled childhood nightmares, and the flight from her doomed home on Eloon twenty three years ago.

*As you sow, thus shall you reap.* An ancient text came to mind. She blinked away tears and set her mouth in a grim smile.

Weak and nauseated, Shayla felt the roasting temperature subside. Watching the speed, altitude, and temperature displays, she breathed more easily, still relying on oxygen from her mouth unit but thankful for a gradual return to a livable pressure.

Her visor display clocked down the altitude.

At twelve thousand feet she removed and stowed the breathing unit. She flexed her limbs, testing the mobility in her tortured shoulder, and took hold of the hand grips.

Ten thousand. A shock wave buffeted her. A low, drawn-out rumble told her that *Chantry Bay* had hit the ground some miles away.

Five thousand. Still arrowing downwards like the piece of meteoric debris she was trying to emulate.

At two thousand feet she spread the canopy further to stem her speed.

At five hundred feet she squeezed and twisted the grips. The support structure woven into the fabric flexed. The re-entry bubble split open like a flower and reformed into flight configuration, flipping Shayla over onto her front. She cupped the wings spreading out on either side and slowed her descent to a shallow glide, skimming the upper reaches of the forest canopy.

A multi-colored whirling of wings erupted from a nearby tree as Shayla's scream echoed through the forest. The outstretched wings tugged at her burnt flesh.

She panted hard, and then clenched her teeth against the pain. She had a small medical kit in her backpack. Inaccessible unless she landed, and then she had no way to get airborne again.

She had no choice but to continue. She had to distance herself from the crash.

Keep sight of the mission. For every agent the Insurrection placed on Magentis, another twenty died on the way. And of those, only one in twenty survived their first month.

Shayla angled the wings, hugging the treetops.

It took years to establish credentials solid enough to pass border security. She didn't have years to spare, but she did have a plan. The Leading Council said it couldn't be done, but they had nothing to lose. And she was here!

A maneuver to catch an updraft yanked at her shoulder. Shuddering, Shayla swallowed back the urge to vomit.

One in twenty.

*I am not some damned statistic.*

## Chapter 2

S entries on either side of the door to the security operations center came to attention. Imperial Chief of Security, Chalwen ap Gwynodd, straightened the tunic of her uniform as she approached. Red-rimmed eyes peered briefly back at her from a rough and ruddy face mirrored in the armored plastic of the door before it slid aside.

Chalwen's massive silhouette eclipsed the light from the corridor, hushing the buzz of conversation in the cavernous room ahead. She pursed her lips and surveyed the terraces of desks and lecterns rising towards the back of the room. She, in turn, felt a hundred and fifty pairs of eyes assessing her. Measuring her mood.

She paced, slow and steady, to the nearest aisle and began to climb.

A whisper behind her didn't quite escape her keen hearing: "Essence of Unity, this is going to be rough."

Chalwen paused near the top of the aisle, and turned, ignoring the quaking personnel nearest to her. Vast wall displays stretched in an arc across most of her view. A map of Magentis to the left. To the right spread the inhabited worlds of humanity. In between was a schematic of planetary border security.

Chalwen glared at the livid starburst denoting a security breach. Lips pressed tight and nostrils flaring, she pointed a stylus at the starburst and watched information flow across the face of her notepad. Starhopper, inbound from Tinturn, fifteen crew and one hundred eighty three passengers.

Impotent fury rekindled in the back of Chalwen's mind, the same fury that had greeted the news brought by an attendant fifteen minutes ago. But, for now, her rage boiled inside a prison of cold logic and determination.

She continued up the aisle, each heavy step echoing through the expectant hush.

Her office dominated the apex of the operations room, with broad windows giving a panoramic view of everything below.

When Chalwen entered, her personal aide, Florris, turned from preparing tea and bowed low. Her division chiefs were already there, standing at attention. She locked eyes with each in turn. Paul Malkin, border security. Fleur Trixmin, intelligence. Henri Chargon, internal affairs. Each returned her gaze, unflinching.

Still without words, Chalwen watched Florris pour tea for the four of them. When she finished, Florris stepped back, hands clasped in front of her, head bowed but upturned eyes on Chalwen, waiting. A curt nod from Chalwen, and Florris backed from the room, closing the door.

"At ease," Chalwen growled. She threw herself into a deeply cushioned chair, ignoring its ominous creaks.

Her inner circle of commanders took their cue and relaxed. Safe from disapproving scrutiny, the normal management culture of Empire was temporarily suspended. Paul settled in another easy chair. Fleur perched on the edge of Chalwen's desk, legs kicking idly. Henri picked up a cup of tea and stayed standing, turning his back on the rest of them and gazing out of the window across the expanse of the security operations floor.

Chalwen pursed her lips and eyed her commander of border security. "Paul? This is your patch. Speak to me."

"Routine flight inbound. You've got all the stats, point of origin, complement and so on."

"Notable dignitaries?" Fleur said.

"A newly-appointed ambassador from Kallis."

Fleur sniffed. "Poor farming community. Nobody the Emperor would be interested in."

Chalwen's eyes narrowed. "The governing body there has been notified?"

Paul nodded, then took a deep breath. "Perimeter clearance okay, then *Chantry Bay* broke contact and diverged from approved flight path. Mai bin Mellion was the duty officer for that quadrant. She followed protocol and called all available units to bear, including ground-based batteries. When she got the trajectory plot, she took the call to let her crash instead."

"What's the heaviest unit we have up there right now?" Chalwen said.

"Inside the perimeter we have five *Implacable*-class. Lots of smaller units, but nothing with firepower to completely vaporize a starhopper in that short time. There would have been lots of debris, some of it big."

"I don't like having our planetary space so bare. I said it would be a problem. I'll seek an audience with Admiral Kuvar and insist he pull back a couple of *Sword*-class ships."

"He won't like that." Fleur's voice gave the impression that everything in life amused her. "They're his favorite tool for showing the flag around the provinces. There's nothing like a *Sword* hovering overhead to remind people how grateful they are to their Emperor."

From the corner of her eye, Chalwen saw Henri frown. Fleur's tone would have earned anyone else a public lashing, but she routinely delivered insolence with such disarming innocence that it was simply accepted as her way with words. And her loyalty and competence were beyond question.

"So, she came down in Horliath," Chalwen grunted. "Nothing of value there. Fair call."

Paul grimaced. "Assuming she was powered down and without guidance, yes."

"You don't look happy. This was something other than a technical failure."

"There's a lot to this that doesn't make sense, but we can be certain this was not accidental failure."

"Explain."

"Tracking telemetry showed she was not without power."

"Go on." Chalwen's voice was a low growl.

"Drive and guidance appeared to be merely inactive, not dead. They still had a grav field running. And communications were being aggressively blanked."

Chalwen nodded and relaxed slightly now she knew she had a human adversary to pursue. Accidents were always so much more difficult to explain than an honest conspiracy.

A fly buzzed across the room in front of her. It flew towards Fleur. A lightning movement, and the buzzing stopped.

Chalwen tore her gaze from Fleur's clenched fist. "So. Sabotage then. And of course you've got investigation teams out picking up anything that might give us a clue as to the cause. But I sense something more than just bringing down a ship."

"Just as we lost contact," Paul said, "she made a small course correction that brought her around to Horliath. Mai managed to backtrack her trajectory and project the original point of impact. Before *Chantry Bay* broke contact, she was approaching straight at Henriss Garden."

For a few seconds there was complete silence. Blood drained from Chalwen's face. *Henriss Garden.* Seventy million people. And the home of the Emperor's favorite winter palace. Fingers of blackness crept into the edge of her vision. "Was that the intent? Use the ship as a missile against a city?"

"I said it didn't make sense. If that was the target, why change course?"

"Maybe the captain regained some kind of control," said Fleur. But her expression said she didn't really believe it.

Chalwen sat silent, trying to regain her focus. A wingless fly struggled across the polished surface of her desk. "Unlikely," she said at last. "But if not, that leaves us with the equally unlikely idea that someone deliberately laid waste to a hundred square miles of equatorial rainforest."

She broke off and her eyes swiveled to Paul, simmering anger showing for the first time. "What fucking moron—"

"Authorized such an approach path?" Paul interrupted wearily. "The docking controller in question is under investigation. No space-side approach is supposed to pose a direct threat, but approved paths can sometimes mean costly diversions for incoming ships. Controllers are always under pressure to cut corners."

"Cut corners?" Chalwen's voice shook. "Not on *my* watch, mister. I want an audit of the last six months' records. Any bad practice to be disciplined." She pursed her lips, then added, "I suspect this was just sloppy work with no real connection to the crash, but make an example of this controller. Ten lashes. In public. How could he think to let a ship approach straight at a major city?"

"Understood," Paul said. "I'll continue investigations, with Henri's help. I want to be sure there's nothing deeper here. It's not unheard of for people to take bribes. That approach line might not have been accidental."

"And then again maybe we've been spooked by co-incidence. Maybe the ship itself was the only target after all." Chalwen stood and stomped over to the sideboard where her tea sat neglected. "We can speculate all day but we need to know the how, the who, and the why." She took a sip and returned to her seat. "Fleur, any of this show up on your radar?"

"Not a hint." Fleur's voice was uncharacteristically grim. "I have a whole team working round the clock going over all sources with a nit comb. There might be something we missed, or some correlation which will only become clear after the fact."

She slipped off the desk and bowed low, "I will of course tender my resignation ..."

"Cut the crap, Fleur."

"What, no ritual disemboweling?" Fleur pouted, but settled back on the edge of the desk. "Okay, nothing concrete I'm afraid, just specula-tion so far. Paul's right. There's a lot that makes no sense. On the sur-face this has the hallmarks of the Insurrection. They've brought down three ships in the last three months, but all in outlying systems. Nothing this close to home. This could represent an escalation, but ..." She frowned and shook her head. "This is too subtle for them. They have the resources but usually go for brute force. Planting a pulse bomb, or blinding the ship with a plasma beam. This kind of sabotage has always been beyond their reckoning. It just doesn't *feel* right."

Chalwen grunted. Fleur's irreverent manner concealed a mind like a scalpel. Her instincts proved sound nine times out of ten.

Fleur continued, "One of the Grand Families might have the know-how to subvert a ship's command systems, but they have no interest in destroying ships. They target individuals for leverage."

"Could we be looking at some kind of alliance then? My brains and your brawn kind of thing?" Paul wondered.

"Not on *my* watch, mister!" Fleur's return to characteristic flippancy told them she was on firm ground again. "That's always been our big-gest nightmare, and we pay minute attention to who's getting into bed with whom. Besides, the Insurrection are as ideologically opposed to the Families as they are to us."

Fleur's mouth twisted and her brow creased. She shook her head, baffled. "This has the feel of something new, some player in the game that we haven't met before. But believe me, I intend to become acquainted."

"I have another item to consider, that may or may not be relevant." Henri Chargon spoke for the first time, his voice little more than an oily whisper. "One of my own agents died on board. Last week he reported suspicions of one of the passengers. He only filed a preliminary report. I understand he had nothing specific to offer, just gut feeling, but he was in the process of following up discreetly."

"Does this passenger have a name?"

Henri consulted his notepad. "Libby Hollis."

"Could this passenger have compromised the command systems?" Paul asked.

"Are you suggesting a suicide mission?"

"Makes more sense than remote or pre-programmed sabotage. This looks like a command system breach, but those systems are completely secure and checked before departure. I'm confident they can't be broken into from outside. It must have been someone on board."

"Agreed," said Chalwen. "But again it might be nothing more than co-incidence. Follow up on Libby Hollis, Henri. See if there's anything to implicate her in this. And interrogate the service crew at Tinturn. Thoroughly." They exchanged knowing looks. "If anyone tampered with *Chantry Bay* before she set off, that crew are either involved or incompetent."

Chalwen stood abruptly and paced the office. Her division chiefs eyed each other. They knew better than to interrupt her train of thought. Eventually she turned to face them.

"Henri, here is the official line. *Chantry Bay* was sabotaged and intended as a missile against the Palace of Butterflies at Henriss Garden. Whether this was a suicide mission or rigged remotely I'll leave to your discretion. The captain regained enough control to divert to Horliath. He died a hero. Your official investigations have three days to reach this conclusion."

Chalwen scowled. "Find someone involved in this. Positive proof preferable, otherwise a plausible connection. If all else fails draw on your archives for someone we've left on a long leash up to now and bring them in. We need a show trial and some public display of closure." Her voice turned hard and grim. "Then we can conduct a proper investigation without everyone watching us."

The three took their cue and snapped to attention. As they turned to leave she muttered under her breath, "The Emperor will expect some public executions for this."

The clearing in front of Shayla was unnaturally level, its true purpose revealed by occasional mounds of crumbling masonry around its perimeter. Massive dressed blocks, some carved with bas-relief glyphs, jostled with less brutish remains of more recent construction. A temple in some form or other had stood on this site for over ten thousand years. A nearby half-buried dragon's head, cloaked in lichen and the height of a man, bared foot-long fangs at Shayla. She gazed past it at the emptiness of the clearing beyond.

The sun blazed high in the sky, blanketing the forest in suffocating heat. Even in deep shadows under the trees the air was stifling. Sitting on her pack, sweat tickling her spine, she squirmed and eased her shoulder into a more comfortable position. The burning agony had taken days to subside to a dull throb through a veil of medication.

Her hasty exit from *Chantry Bay* so high up had thrown her way off her intended course. She'd used her wings for as long as she dared, first seeking thermals to rise high enough above the trees to spot key landmarks. When vapor trails appeared overhead, she hugged the treetops, mingling with the birds thronging the air. Eventually the tell-tale glint of sun on faraway metal told her the navy was overhead. They would be scanning the ground with far more than human eyes. And so, reluctantly, Shayla abandoned the aerial highways for hard slog through the undergrowth.

That was five days ago. Much too long. She was dangerously behind schedule, and wondered if her accomplices had already abandoned the rendezvous.

Hot, dirty, scratched to shreds from days of bushwhacking, Shayla listened to the forest, small animals foraging, birds calling. Dragonflies with jeweled wings a foot across patrolled the clearing. Shayla charted the sounds in her mind's eye, noting a region of stillness to her right. Someone else was waiting.

That was according to plan, but she had to be sure there wasn't yet another party watching the watchers. What was the chance that her local contacts had been followed here?

She scanned the edge of the clearing for signs of danger. She detected nothing but the sounds and movements of the forest.

At last Shayla decided to move. The hidden observer could either be friend or foe. There was only one way to find out. She checked the skies once more for signs of air- or space-borne activity, then stepped out from cover. She hurried to the centre of the clearing and found what she was looking for. On a worn section of paving that had not yet succumbed to creeping vegetation, four sticks were laid out in a square. Shayla stooped and picked up two of them. She rearranged them in a cross between the two remaining sticks. The pattern formed a crude hourglass shape.

She stepped back to face the side of the clearing where someone lay hidden. She waited once more, all senses straining.

*So exposed!* Shayla bit back irritation at the recognition protocol chosen by the local Insurrection cell. It required her to show herself out in the open while her contacts stayed safely hidden. She breathed deeply and reminded herself that her contacts faced risks of their own, hiding out for days, watching for her to show up, and wondering if she herself was bringing the Empire in her wake.

She didn't have to wait long. A tall and gangly man stepped out to meet her. He looked young, barely into his twenties, with dark hair braided into a complex basket around his head. He kept his eyes on Shayla as he approached, relaxing slightly when he glanced down at the pattern of sticks on the ground. He picked up the two that Shayla hadn't moved and kicked the other two aside.

He held the sticks out with a bow. "Cobra," he said.

Shayla accepted them, also relaxing at his correct response, and bowed. "I am Shark."

Cobra glanced up to the sky. "We must get under cover. Most of the debris from that ship landed well south and east of here, but damage teams are scouring the region."

Cobra led them back the way he'd come. Shayla noticed that he was always careful to keep to one side of a line between her and the bushes cloaking the base of a tree on the edge of the clearing. *Not complete amateurs then. Good.*

As they reached cover, Shayla stopped. "You may as well join us," she said to the bushes. "If I wished you harm, your weapon would be of little help."

Cobra grinned. "C'mon, Tiger," he called. "They said she was good."

The bushes hesitated, then rustled. A woman emerged, scowling. "You're late!" Her hand rested on a holstered pistol. Small. Precision beam weapon. Deadly in the hands of an expert, but it took an expert to use it properly.

Shayla bowed low. "Shark, at your service."

"So you say." Tiger glanced at Cobra.

He shrugged. "She followed protocol. She knew the rendezvous. If she's a spy with that knowledge, we're finished anyway."

Tiger's scowl softened. She nodded and bowed. "Tiger. I welcome you. We'll talk more later, but we must get going." She gestured to Cobra, who led them into the forest at a breakneck pace.

Shayla hurried to follow him. "I was hoping to make better time, but the air got busy quicker than I'd wished," she called over her shoulder to Tiger, who brought up the rear.

Tiger grunted in reply as she toiled to keep up.

Cobra led them through the dense undergrowth that had hampered and exhausted Shayla for five days. She marveled at how he found paths through. Walls of green parted in front of him. Subtle trails, discernible only to an expert eye, eased their passage. Shayla followed his footsteps as precisely as possible. More than once, she strayed slightly only to feel the familiar tug of thorns on her clothing and vines snagging feet. She learned to watch where Cobra placed his feet and how he twisted his body. The curtains of branches and leaves seemed to respond, to admit her without resistance as though she'd uttered some secret password.

From the sounds behind her, Shayla deduced that Tiger was having a much harder time of it. Shayla felt a warm glow of satisfaction, which she hastily quashed. She sensed a deeper hostility, an instinctive dislike, beneath Tiger's natural suspicion, but Shayla was not prepared to let personal feelings interfere with the mission.

They emerged into a small clearing, barely reached by the sun. An almost perfect circle of huge boles framed a shallow depression. The trees soared high into the air before the first branches spread out, arching, meeting, and interleaving overhead. The ground in between was mercifully free of vegetation, and floored with leaf litter flattened by the passage of animals.

A shrunken figure, swathed in a grubby, threadbare cloak, stood to greet them.

"Eating again, Weasel?" Cobra said with a laugh.

Uneven teeth flashed through straggly whiskers. Shayla realized there was a faint smell of cooking hanging in the air, reminding her stomach how little food it had seen recently. Her pack held a small supply of concentrated rations, enough for minimal sustenance, woefully inadequate for a body stressed by long hours of hard slog.

"Shark, meet Weasel," said Cobra. "He doesn't say much, but he is very useful to have around."

Shayla bowed. Weasel bobbed his head and leered at Shayla. He looked unclean and disheveled, but Shayla noted the recently-used cooking plate already folded, and a small carryall, presumably holding provisions and utensils, neatly packed at his feet. He must have heard them coming and cleared up in a space of time that bespoke forethought and discipline.

Shayla grimaced as she shrugged her pack and cloak from her shoulders.

"You're hurt," Cobra said, concern in his eyes.

"My descent was never going to be easy." She tried to keep her tone casual, but she saw Weasel tense, oafish demeanor gone, and Tiger's face darken into tight-lipped anger.

Cobra reached out and peeled back the collar of her shirt, exposing the edge of the field dressing she'd applied.

"I have a vial of sprayskin in my pack," Shayla said. "I could use some help applying it properly."

"What use is an injured assassin?" Tiger's beam pistol was trained on her. "We should kill her now and return home while we still can."

Shayla studied Tiger's stance, and assessed the speed with which she'd drawn her weapon. *I could take her, I think, but…* "I'd be happy to prove my ability to you, but this mission requires stealth. If I need to fight, it will be because I've already failed."

Cobra pursed his lips, then nodded. He gestured to the side of the clearing. "We travel by boat. The river network extends right up to the edge of Horliath."

Shayla peered into the gloom. Dark water glinted, framed by over-hanging boughs. A long and narrow boat lay half hidden, prow pulled up on the muddy bank of the inlet. "We'll be able to travel freely?" she asked. "I have no ID until we reach Hawflun. We can't afford to be stopped."

"Don't worry," said Cobra curtly. "We got your instructions and we know this territory. There are hundreds of tribes scattered through the wetlands. The Empire pays them no attention. As long as we look like tribesmen from above we'll be okay." He looked Shayla up and down. "Your cloak is fine, but you'll need to keep your head hooded. That mess of straw's a dead giveaway."

While Cobra spoke, Weasel picked up the cooking plate and car-ryall and clambered down to the stern of the boat.

Cobra gestured to Shayla to follow. She stepped into the boat, crouching low to steady herself as it wallowed in the water. From his perch in the stern, Weasel nodded encouragement. He flashed a crooked grin and pointed to one of a series of seats built across the width of the flimsy craft. Shayla sat, and stowed her pack under the seat. Tiger followed and sat facing Shayla. Cobra pushed the prow clear of the bank and leapt lightly aboard, stooping to avoid a low-hanging branch.

The boat surged backwards. Shayla turned to see Weasel twist-ing the throttle of an impeller, guiding the craft down the meandering waterway.

Cobra guided them with occasional hand signals to Weasel. Even though Shayla had studied the terrain in preparation, she was soon lost in the labyrinthine bayous.

Eventually the trees thinned overhead, and they emerged into the open. Shayla couldn't tell whether they were on the edge of a narrow lake or a wide river. The far side looked to be about a mile away. The water seemed unmoving, oily surface disturbed only by myriad dancing insects.

Weasel kept the boat close to the near shore and headed north. Tiger and Cobra scanned the sky constantly. After half an hour, Cobra held up his hand and Weasel cut the motor.

Cobra pointed to a smudge of deeper shadow amongst the trees on the far shore. Weasel nodded and angled the boat out into open water. Afternoon heat closed in like a vice, amplified by the heavy air and sunlight reflecting off the water.

"Keep your head well covered," Cobra called to Shayla. "We'll be exposed to view for some time."

Shayla pulled her hood close about her head, tucking telltale strands of blonde out of sight. She wondered why they were moving so slowly. She was sure the boat had the power to cross in a minute.

Cobra seemed to anticipate her thoughts. "We must behave like one of the river tribes if we don't want to attract attention. Their boats are not as fast as this one."

Tiger muttered a warning. Shayla heard a low growl above the soft hiss and suck of water. She wanted to turn her head to see the approaching air cruiser, but she caught Tiger's warning glance and slight shake of the head under her hood. "The river folk ignore Imperial craft. Just sit still."

Shayla closed her eyes and concentrated on the sounds around her. The growl filled the air. Above it, she discerned a faint hum of machinery. The craft moved low and fast. It sounded like it would pass some way off. She listened for any change that would signal a change of course.

For the first time, Shayla felt keenly the dangers of capture. She knew she would likely die before giving information away under interrogation, not from choice but from deeply implanted conditioning. And in Imperial custody, the road to death could be long indeed.

*I will not be taken.* Her fingers closed around the grip of a needle gun under her cloak. She glanced at Tiger, and saw the thin set of her lips and a small movement as she also loosed her pistol in its holster.

The sound faded. The ship continued on its way without wavering from its course. Shayla relaxed. She saw Tiger heave a deep and unsteady breath, but Cobra still looked tense.

"If we were stopped before, the three of us could have bluffed our way out," Tiger explained. "We all have credible IDs. But your presence amongst us would be a death sentence for us all."

They resumed their vigil as the boat crawled across the expanse of water. It could only have taken a few minutes, but it felt like an hour. As they slipped into the shade once more, Cobra finally smiled again. "Tiger's right. We always live with the possibility of discovery, but we've spent so long establishing decent credentials and living normal lives most of the time, we're kinda used to that possibility being a bit more remote."

"Well, right now we're on a mission, so better get used to it," Shayla retorted. "We have a war to take to the enemy, in case you hadn't noticed." *But if only you knew we aren't on quite the same mission.*

She had quoted almost directly from the Insurrection's propaganda handbook. The words seemed to galvanize Tiger and Cobra.

"Heh! That was some firework display you put on for us!" said Cobra gleefully.

"One hell of an entrance," Tiger added. There was grudging admiration in her voice.

"And a shipload of stinking *Magisters* down too." Cobra spat the honorific like a curse.

"They were nothing but clerks and civil servants," Shayla said. "Hardly something to celebrate."

"Propping up the Empire. All as guilty as each other." Tiger's tone was dismissive. She scrutinized Shayla with sudden suspicion. "You going soft on us, *assassin?*"

Shayla couldn't say what it was about this exchange that made her feel sick. She could scarcely argue with Tiger's assessment. It was the same she'd used herself to ease her mind over the killing of nearly two hundred people. They were all Imperial servants. All part of the machine. All fair game.

But a face haunted her. A young girl half seen in ghostly light. She wiped the image from her mind and set her expression to match Tiger's harsh stare.

"I do what I have to do of necessity. Not for fun, and certainly not for your *entertainment.*" Shayla's voice dripped acid. She was glad to see Tiger taken aback. "None of you are native to Magentis." Tiger looked even more unhappy at Shayla's matter-of-fact tone.

*Surprised I could see that? And you try so hard to blend in.*

"So, let's see, you probably started with an offworld cover, then worked your way into a suitable position in some useful organization. Something that would eventually make a move to Magentis perfectly natural, and with some history behind it to satisfy security checks."

*Why am I so upset?*

Shayla took a deep breath and eyed Tiger coolly. "How long did it take you to get here?"

"Three years."

"Fourteen months," Cobra interrupted cheerfully. He wilted under Tiger's fierce glare, and added, "I had an ID already prepared, but it still took time to get it sound enough to use here."

Weasel simply grinned, teeth gleaming in the shadows under the wide brim of his hat.

"So you know full well that nothing but Imperial craft land on the planet," Shayla said. "No cargo lands unopened. No person gets near here without the toughest border checks in the known galaxy. Hours of interrogation at a reception base in orbit, with the most gifted truth-sensers. Personal details, biometrics, and genetics cross-referenced to official records. Passkey audited for forgery or tampering."

She realized she was nearly shouting, her voice thankfully lost in the muffling blanket of the forest. Tiger, eyes wide, leaned back, distancing herself from the ferocity of Shayla's outburst.

She paused to calm herself before continuing. "I don't have years or even months to spare, but nobody has ever successfully infiltrated Magentis by impersonating an Imperial citizen. Not in the last century, anyway. It was easy enough to board a starhopper under a stolen identity, but I couldn't afford to be seen leaving it again here. I had to disappear with no chance of being noticed or missed."

*Who am I justifying myself to?*

"So tell us more," said Cobra. "We've been going mad guessing how you managed to bring that starhopper down." Tiger frowned at Cobra, but he ignored her and pressed on. "I can't see any way other than taking over the command system. But I didn't think our technoprats had the know-how."

Shayla closed her eyes. She could do without this kind of questioning. "I had help, obviously. And you're right about our abilities. I was able to contract in some specialized expertise. I can't say more than that, the Executim doesn't take kindly to excessive curiosity."

Tiger grimaced then nodded with a resigned expression. Cobra frowned. He didn't look satisfied, but Shayla was spared further explanation by a tap on her shoulder. Her good one, fortunately. Weasel handed her three small cartons.

Cobra's face lit up. "Of course! Well done, Weasel." To Shayla he said "He's always thinking of his stomach, but for once I suspect it's appropriate. I guess you haven't eaten much recently."

Shayla shook her head as she passed two of the cartons to Tiger and Cobra and turned her attention to her own. She opened it out and felt her stomach snarl eagerly as a tempting aroma filled the air. There was meat. Real meat. Her tongue rejoiced in almost-forgotten flavors. Shayla was unconcerned by the fact that she couldn't identify the animal in question. It was small. Maybe caught here in the forest. Its roasted carcass was wrapped in leaves and lay on a bed of pulses, again of indeterminate origin.

Shayla picked the bones clean and tossed them over the side, following Weasel's example. He managed to beat Shayla's voracious feeding even though he had one hand on the controls of the boat.

They raced through a maze of narrow waterways, with occasional directions from Cobra in the prow.

"This will be a long journey," said Tiger, consulting her notepad. "We plan to reach the waters of Wasanni before nightfall. We'll be able to travel round the clock then, and make up some time. I suggest you get some sleep while you can." She curled up in the bottom of the boat and covered herself with her cloak.

"Go ahead," said Cobra. "Weasel and I will take us through these swamps, then we'll need all eyes on watch through the night."

## Chapter 4

Henri Chargon perched on the edge of his seat, upright and seemingly alert, but the red around his eyes and his grey complexion betrayed his fatigue. Imperial Chief of Security, Chalwen ap Gwynodd, knew she looked no better. She reached into a pocket and pulled out a nicodyne spray. She directed a short squirt into her mouth and drew the vapor deep into her lungs, closing her eyes for a moment as she felt the drug lift hot fog from her mind.

Henri gazed blankly at the spray when Chalwen offered it to him, then shook his head. "Too much already," he muttered.

"Then let's keep this brief, Henri. You need to rest."

Chalwen heaved a deep sigh and settled into a chair, cup of tea in hand. She looked at Henri over the rim of her cup as she sipped the scalding, bitter drink. She'd insisted that he sat for once, too tired this evening to cope with his endless pacing.

They faced each other across a low table. An antique lamp on Chalwen's desk glowed rainbow colors, opalescent panels depicted hummingbirds feeding at a cascade of vibrant fuchsias. The light glittered off the panoramic windows, now darkened to shut out the round-the-clock brightness and hum of activity in the operations centre beyond.

There was a long pause while Chalwen marshaled her thoughts. "So, we have four sacrificial lambs."

Henri nodded, gazing at the floor.

"But we still have no real information."

Henri looked up. His face sagged. "We interrogated the entire service crew at Tinturn, not just the crew that handled *Chantry Bay*."

"You are certain about this—" Chalwen consulted her notepad "— Bernhardt Maas?"

"No doubt. He was previously unknown to us, and his background checked out okay, but during interrogation it became clear he was part of the Insurrection."

Chalwen frowned, but left questions unasked for now.

Henri continued. "He had no connection to any known cell. It looks like he was in deep cover, waiting for instructions."

"You reported his mid-term memory had been suppressed."

Henri shook his head. "Wiped."

Chalwen gave Henri a puzzled look.

"Looks like he did whatever he needed to, then took animastin."

"Are you sure?" Chalwen was aghast.

"The sweep team found a trace on the floor of his apartment."

"*That* wasn't in the report!"

"They've only just identified it. They weren't looking for it at first, and he cleaned up very carefully. He must have incinerated the vial somehow, and anything he used to take it. But he must have been nervous; he spilled a drop."

"I don't blame him." Chalwen was silent for a few moments. *Animastin! Who willingly tampers with their mind like that?* "So. Not a *temporary* memory block then. He knew something that he was desperate to keep from us."

"Then why not just kill himself?"

Chalwen cocked an eyebrow at Henri. "How long did you spend interrogating the whole base before you realized who he was?"

Henri blinked, then nodded slowly. "He bought time." He rolled his eyes to the ceiling. "He interviewed well on the preliminary scan. It was only when we went back over details more carefully that the interviewers suspected something wasn't right."

"He was working from a script, wasn't he?" Despite herself, a slow smile spread from the corners of Chalwen's mouth.

Henri nodded. "He must have written it before taking the drug, to fill in weeks, maybe months, of memory that he was about to destroy."

"And he'd have had a whole week to learn it while the ship was in transit."

"It must have been crafted to brief himself on what he needed to do, and enough facts of his recent movements, without giving away any unwanted details. When we finally broke him, he knew he'd done some-thing momentous, but we could extract no clues as to what or why."

"And he still had all his faculties?" Chalwen shuddered at the thought of the mental impairment that often went with the drug.

"Enough to still pass as a member of the service crew. And he kept enough of his training to resist intensive interrogation for two days."

Chalwen whistled under her breath. "What about the others you pulled in?"

"From an unconnected cell. I'm convinced they knew nothing of this plot. And they knew nothing of Maas either."

Chalwen grunted and scowled. "So what's the schedule?"

"The trial is set for the end of next week. Executions two weeks later."

"Why the delay?"

"We need a public spectacle around this one." With dainty move-ments of long fingers, Henri straightened his untouched cup of tea. "But the Emperor's new Master of Circuses isn't here yet."

"They appointed a replacement weeks ago, didn't they?"

"Someone from local government in the Provinces. I understand she had affairs to tidy up and religious duties to observe."

Chalwen's scowl deepened. She detested religion getting in the way of civic duty. On the other hand, the more devout members of staff were usually more predictable in their loyalties. She made a mental note to speak to Fleur about this new appointee's affiliations.

"Have you spoken to old Scottin recently?"

Henri's question broke her out of her black mood. She gazed wist-fully at the jewel blue-green hummingbirds on the lamp. "Still in ther-apy. Barking mad, but happier than I've seen him in years."

"Well, he always was a bit loopy. I guess that's what made him such a good M of C. Once, anyway."

"Our dear Emperor has been getting very difficult to please, hasn't he? Enough to drive anyone mad."

There was a long silence. Chalwen drained her tea and set the cup down. Henri jumped at the sudden clink.

"Go, Henri. Get some rest. *Proper* rest," she said firmly when Henri started to protest.

He hesitated, mouth hanging open in mid word, then bowed his head and heaved himself upright. He paused again. "But I need—"

"You need a clear mind," Chalwen barked. "And don't think I'm concerned for your welfare. There is something bigger and more subtle happening than we thought. You have other lines of inquiry to follow, and I need you functioning at full capacity!"

Chalwen watched him leave, then she hauled herself from the depths of her chair and plodded stiffly to her desk.

They might not have much real information, but Henri's investigations had revealed one crucial fact. Whatever had happened to *Chantry Bay* was no simple act of sabotage. The Insurrection would not have sacrificed a valuable field agent for anything trivial.

The room around Chalwen blurred. An old specter haunted her: a faceless opponent taunting her, too clever for her, and her many enemies within the Palace gloating behind half-closed doors, peering around curtains, waiting for her to stumble ...

She snarled and snatched a pair of heavy gel balls from her desk. She squeezed them, the rhythmic movement cracking her knuckles, until she felt her mind's focus return.

She was sure that something was yet to happen. Here, on Magentis.

She needed to speak to Paul Malkin, her chief of border security. There must be something about the crash that they'd missed.

She had a long night ahead of her.

## Chapter 5

Shayla leaned against the cliff wall and surveyed the landscape through a gap in the trees. A cascade of treetops tumbled down the mountain flank in front of her. The green carpet of Horliath unrolled to the horizon, broken here and there by glittering slashes of water cutting through the forest.

Their boat had carried them almost to the foot of the mountains in little over a day. Somewhere in the tangle of greenery far below they took their leave of Cobra, who disappeared back into the forest waterways with a cheery wave. Tiger introduced Shayla to their guide for the remainder of the journey. Raven. His dark hair, rounded features, and red skin marked him as a native of Chensing Province. The contrast between Cobra and Raven was stark, and not good from Shayla's point of view. Where Cobra was open and friendly, Raven was sour and taciturn. He also seemed to share Tiger's open hostility towards Shayla.

*What is it with these provincials?*

Weasel handed Shayla, Tiger, and Raven small, leaf-wrapped parcels of food. They took cover under an overhanging rock face while they ate.

Shayla worked her shoulder gingerly. Cobra had stripped off her field dressing and tended the burned flesh. He'd done a good job. The sprayskin and fresh dressing should last for weeks. By then, she'd either have completed the mission, or be in need of something more than a new shoulder.

Despite her confident words to Tiger, she knew she'd be hard-pressed if it came to a fight. Stealth was the key to this mission, but Shayla was used to having more than just stealth to rely on.

She watched a vapor trail trace a hair-thin scratch across the sky in the distance. By now, she would have expected the search to be tailing off. It was clear there could have been no survivors. But, although it was difficult to be sure now they had left the crash scene so far behind, the activity overhead seemed to have intensified again.

"What's the plan from here?" Shayla asked. She had let them lead the way up to now without asking too many questions, but she was starting to feel a need to take some measure of control.

Raven glanced at her, but finished eating without replying. Shayla persisted. "I can see we started off heading almost straight towards Hawflun, but we've veered some way south since yesterday. This isn't the route the mission planners discussed. I need to know how we're going to reach Hawflun on time."

"Time we move," Raven muttered. "Watch the sky. The Imperials are everywhere."

*And I'm not some dumb piece of baggage either!* "We're not done here!" Shayla snapped. "Is this how you honor the Leading Council's wishes?"

Raven jerked his head like he'd been slapped. He looked to Tiger for support.

Shayla turned her back on him and faced Tiger. "Remind me what your orders are."

"To deliver you to Hawflun Temple, and help you to switch places with the Magister bitch on her way to the palace at Prandis Braz."

"And ...?"

"We are to follow your orders," Tiger said, every word an effort.

"I am responsible for the mission, but I understand you are in charge of the ground operation here and I commend myself to your expert care." Shayla's tone was matter-of-fact, with no trace of sarcasm.

Tiger's expression softened slightly.

"All the same, I need to share your plans. It could be the difference between success and failure if we get separated."

Tiger chewed her lip, looking at the sky, then nodded. "Very briefly though."

Raven snorted. "We have no time for this. We must move on."

Tiger ignored him. "We've come this way because the river is navigable much deeper into the mountains here, and close to a town on the other side. Because you're so late, we had to change plans and risk a route through some larger towns."

Shayla's throat tightened. "We were supposed to avoid major centers of population. My ID—"

"We have no choice," Tiger snarled. "This is now the only way to deliver you in time. We have two days hard march to Skerrin Brethwyn, then a day by public transport to Hawflun."

Shayla steadied herself against the rock face. "What if we're stopped by a patrol?"

"Once we are on the pilgrim route, the papers of Meditation we've obtained should be the only ID you'll need around here."

"So, those papers, and the clothing I asked for ...?"

"Stashed on the other side of the pass."

"Thank you, Tiger." Shayla gave Raven a curt nod. "Let's move."

———————

The path wound high into the mountains. They had left the trees and the last vegetation far behind, and now felt perilously exposed. Weasel went ahead, whistling tunelessly to himself. Looking completely in keeping with the wild and untamed landscape, he presented the least conspicuous choice to scout the path ahead. Raven followed at a short distance, ready to deal with whatever threat Weasel might signal. Tiger and Shayla brought up the rear, scanning their surroundings and the skies.

The climb was uneventful. The track, for so long hugging the mountain side with precipitous drops to one side and towering cliffs to the other, leveled off and meandered through a wilderness of bluffs, boulders, and splintered rocks. Icy wind sighed around them, hissing through ravines down from jagged peaks clawing the cloudless sky above.

Shayla became aware that Weasel had stopped whistling. He now moved silently, a ghostly shadow amongst grey rocks. Everyone else grew tense as Weasel signaled them to stay put. He edged forwards, then stopped, head cocked to one side. Eventually he inched his way back, then disappeared into a gully. He rejoined them a few minutes later, and motioned them to retrace their steps a hundred yards or so.

"Patrol?" Raven muttered, when they had taken shelter under an overhang. Weasel nodded. He picked up a shard of stone and started sketching in the dust at their feet.

Raven grunted. "I half expected it. You stirred up a right storm here. You know that," he said to Shayla.

*Is that your problem?* Shayla wondered. *Upset your comfortable wait in hiding?*

Weasel continued drawing in the dirt, swiftly and neatly. Shayla recognized the path as far as she had been able to see, and she was sure the rest had been rendered with equal precision. There was the unmistakable outline of a small air cruiser straddling the path at the head of the valley. It looked like the ground was clear and level for at least a hundred yards in front of it. Towering cliffs closed in behind, leaving a narrow canyon climbing up to the pass beyond.

*Well positioned!* Shayla felt fleeting professional admiration.

"Crap. We can't get past that!" Tiger snorted.

"Won't be easy to sneak up on them either," said Shayla. "Too much open space around."

"How many soldiers?" asked Raven.

Weasel held up three fingers. He looked at Shayla with glittering eyes and pointed out a route alongside the path. From his depiction of contours and obstacles, she reckoned it would provide cover most of the way to the cruiser.

It was the 'most of the way' part that bothered her.

"Diversion?" she asked. Weasel heaved a silent laugh, face crinkling around his eyes, and tapped his nose with a grubby forefinger. Shayla nodded and reached under her cloak, pulling out her needle gun. She inspected the magazine and selected a fast-acting nerve poison from her chemical armory.

Tiger drew her own pistol.

"Put that away," said Shayla. "The navy's still patrolling up there. They might pick up a beam discharge."

Tiger looked ready to argue, but Raven said, "She's right. Last resort only."

"OK, Shark," said Tiger grimly. "Time to see what you can do. You and Weasel take care of them."

Shayla nodded to Weasel. "Lead on."

He leapt to his feet, grinning maniacally, and started back up the path whistling again under his breath. Shayla took one last look at the map at her feet, then scuffed it out with her foot and hurried after him. Before the path came within sight of the waiting patrol, she ducked off to the right, around the back of the boulder from which Weasel had surveyed the route. He was waiting for her, and gave hand signals for her to take position and wait.

This gully would take her a fair distance away from the path, leaving maybe twenty or thirty yards where she would be in plain view of anyone looking her way. After that she should be hidden by the contours of the ground alongside the track.

She had no idea what Weasel was planning to do, but she needed to be ready to take advantage of any opportunity he might arrange. She climbed up a loose scree slope, careful not to dislodge anything. Any sound in this confined space would echo and travel. But Shayla soon realized she needn't have bothered. Hoarse chanting whispered up the ravine behind her. Weasel!

She reached firmer ground and sprinted in a crouch when the gully opened out, until she could see the three soldiers in the distance. They stood, staring at the bizarre apparition on the path in front of them. Weasel must have discarded his hat somewhere out of sight. His tangled hair streamed out like grey flame, whipping back and forth across his face as his head shook in a frenzy. He held his arms outstretched on either side, hands quivering, and danced erratically along the path, chanting and mumbling all the while.

Shayla took her cue. She crouched low and glided from rock to rock, taking advantage of every small piece of cover to conceal her approach. She saw one of the guards move towards Weasel. The other two drew weapons.

They were out of sight again. Shayla sprinted hard, charting her progress against her memory of Weasel's sketch map.

*This should be close enough.*

She angled closer to the path, dropping low as she heard mumbled conversation ahead of her. She reached the top of the shallow rise between her and the path, and dropped to her stomach, inching forwards until she had a clear view of the tableau below.

The soldiers hadn't moved far from where she'd first seen them. Their eyes were still on Weasel, but they were arguing amongst themselves, clearly unnerved by his antics.

He was seated cross-legged in the middle of the path, eyes closed, face uplifted. It looked like a meditation pose.

"Move him on. He gives me the creeps," muttered one of the soldiers.

"Looks like a religious type to me," said another. "Hermit, or somesuch?"

"Could be a shaman or monk or something," said the first.

"We're supposed to check the ID of anyone who passes here." It sounded like the third soldier was balancing duty against fear.

"Well, he hasn't actually *passed* yet, has he?" the first pointed out with rather tenuous logic.

"And we're supposed to be careful dealing with monks and priests. Remember how touchy the locals are about their temples." There was a murmur of agreement.

Shayla studied the scene from where she lay, biding her time. This would be a tricky shot. The soldiers' body armor left few areas of skin exposed to her needles, and she needed to down all three before any of them could raise the alarm.

She also needed them to separate a bit to get a clear shot at each.

At last, Shayla's patience was rewarded. "He's no priest. Just a mad old man. Go check him out," the dutiful one ordered. "Make it quick. My food's getting cold."

With a nervous glance over his shoulder, the first soldier moved towards where Weasel was still seated. Weasel muttered an incantation under his breath. The guard looked back at his companions, pleading in his eyes.

Shayla studied the second and third soldiers intently, waiting for her chance. *C'mon, move apart a bit.*

The one in charge rolled his eyes skywards. He grunted to his companion and motioned him to help.

*Always trust an Imperial to lead from behind!*

She aimed. The commander dropped. Before his body hit the ground she picked off the second, and turned to where the remaining soldier had almost reached Weasel. She wasn't quite quick enough. He must have heard something, and turned again. He let out a cry, cut short as Shayla's third needle buried itself in his cheek.

"Fuck it!" Shayla's exasperated curse echoed down the valley. His hand had reached the stud of a lapel transmitter. Weasel was already on his feet and switched it off, but the damage was done.

"We don't have much time," she shouted to Tiger and Raven as they hurried forward. "Someone will be along to investigate that broken transmission."

Raven and Weasel grabbed the nearest soldier between them and lumbered up the path with their burden.

Tiger nodded to Weasel, who grinned his sly and crooked grin and bobbed his head back at her. She gestured to Shayla. "Help me get this one into the cruiser."

Shayla helped Tiger bundle the commander up the ramp and into the cramped cabin. They cleared all signs of human presence from the temporary encampment while Raven and Weasel loaded the third guard.

Without a word, Weasel leapt into the air cruiser and took off, arrowing low across the ground and up into the mountains.

"He'll dispose of the craft somewhere and meet us in Hawflun," Tiger explained. "With a bit of luck it'll buy us some time while they try to figure out what their border guards were chasing a few miles from here."

"We still need to put distance between us and this place, yes?" said Raven. "The sooner we can lose ourselves in a crowd, the better."

They picked up their packs, temporarily discarded while they completed the clean-up, and set off at a trot. Shayla's lungs burned, and she felt her legs weaken under the continued exertion in this thin air.

The canyon climbed steeply then opened out into a desolate wasteland dotted with tiny, brackish tarns. The path became lost from view, their route marked only by lichen-cloaked, irregularly-spaced cairns. They crossed as fast as their weariness allowed. This would not be a good place to be discovered.

Soon a pair of more carefully built cairns marked the start of the descent.

The path took them into a crease in the slope, that deepened to an almost-vertical gully plummeting hundreds of feet down the face of the mountain. Large boulders formed a giant, treacherous staircase down a dry stream bed.

Raven led the way, dropping from one rock to the next. Shayla and Tiger followed.

Muscles burned in Shayla's calves and thighs. Dry, cold air seared her throat. One slip, and she would tumble, unable to stop herself, to the distant scree slope. She divided her attention between keeping her footing and scanning the ribbon of sky above.

Below her, Raven shouted a warning and ducked behind a rock, working his way into a crevice in the side of the gully.

Shayla stopped and looked for somewhere to hide.

Tiger clambered onto the ledge next to Shayla, then let out a cry.

Without pausing for thought, Shayla reached for Tiger's outstretched hand as her feet slipped from under her. Shayla fought to keep her own footing, feeling with her free hand for a handhold in the gully's walls. She bit back a shriek as the dressing on her shoulder gave way.

Tiger gasped as the edge of the ledge caught her across the stomach.

She scrambled for purchase on the smooth rock.

She froze.

A low growl and hum of machinery filled the air.

## Chapter 6

The Imperial cruiser appeared far below, traversing the mountainside. It disappeared past the lip of the gully, then reappeared moments later. It began to climb towards them.

Tiger groaned, still clinging to Shayla's hand. "They're following the path up to the pass."

Shayla blinked back tears of pain. She gritted her teeth and looked around for cover. There was nowhere to hide from the approaching cruiser. "I'll haul you up," she muttered. "Looks like we'll need to fight our way out."

Options were already forming in her mind. They'd have surprise on their side. If they could take out the pilot with a clean shot, they might have a chance.

Tiger grunted in reply.

Shayla pulled.

Just as she regained the ledge, Tiger's feet dislodged a fist-sized stone.

The stone rolled over the next ledge and clattered down the gully, gathering speed. Tiger and Shayla watched, helpless, as it plunged towards the cruiser.

Would the crew assume it had been dislodged by the vibration of their own craft?

The stone skipped off an outcrop which sent it sailing out into open air, just feet past the flank of the cruiser. Shayla counted the seconds until a faint rattle, barely audible above the sound of machinery, told her it had come to rest.

The cruiser continued its steady climb. Shayla could now make out the helmeted heads of two soldiers through the canopy. They were scanning the slope ahead of them. If either of them looked up, they couldn't help but see them.

Tiger had her pistol ready.

"Do you think that will penetrate the canopy?" Shayla asked.

"Raven has a more powerful weapon," said Tiger. "I'll leave the pilot to him and try to pick off the comms array."

Then how long before the electrical noise of beam discharges brought the rest of the army?

But Raven, crouched a few yards below them in his hideout, hadn't drawn a weapon. Instead, he concentrated on a small comms scanner in his hand.

Without warning, the cruiser wheeled away from the ravine and sped out of sight.

As the sound receded, Raven said, "Weasel has drawn them away."

They leapt from rock to rock down the rough staircase, all caution gone in their haste. Only when they had slipped and slid the last hundred yards over a loose scree slope and gained the relative safety of the first outposts of trees did Tiger finally call a halt.

Shayla heaved deep breaths and massaged her muscles.

Tiger's breath rasped in her throat, and it was some minutes before she indicated readiness to move on.

Only Raven looked unaffected. He was on his feet, scrutinizing the path in either direction, and the sky above. Evening was starting to darken to night. "We must keep moving," he said. "Half an hour, then there is a safe hide for the night."

———•◆•———

Raven led them to a hidden clearing, set back from the path and screened by trees and dense undergrowth.

Shayla watched him spread a gossamer fabric above their heads, unrolled from a bundle no bigger than his index finger, and suspended from overhanging branches.

He smirked when he saw her studying his preparations. "Impressive, no? Will keep us hidden from thermal imaging tonight."

Shayla nodded, feigning appreciation. She wondered what he'd think if he knew she had a tiny bundle of the same material in her flight pack. She also wondered if the Firenzi Special Service knew that the Insurrection had acquired this material.

While Raven continued setting up camp, Shayla shrugged off her robe and felt around to her shoulder. Her hand came away sticky with blood.

Tiger hissed, then reached into her own pack. Shayla tensed, remembering how Tiger had reacted on first hearing of Shayla's injury, but Tiger pulled out a medical kit. She peeled back Shayla's tunic. "This'll hurt." Shayla clenched her jaw as Tiger ripped off the remains of the dressing in one clean movement.

"You'll have to be more careful until this skin has a chance to knit." Tiger's voice was terse.

"You'd rather I dropped you?"

Tiger didn't answer. She worked in silence for a few minutes, then, "This burn goes deep. Doesn't look like a beam discharge. How'd it happen?"

From the corner of her eye, Shayla saw Raven turn. His gaze pierced her.

"I used a re-entry shield to escape from the ship."

Raven scowled. "A *personal* shield? I know not of materials light enough for that."

Shayla jerked her chin towards the thermal fabric cloaking the camp. "You think that is the only material we've acquired recently?" She wondered just how much Raven knew of the Insurrection's capabilities. The organization's paranoid secrecy was supposed to shield her from such questioning, but the same secrecy meant she had no idea how high up the hierarchy these agents were.

When Raven hesitated, Shayla continued, determined to steer the conversation. "It's still on evaluation." She caught his eye. "Need I say more?"

Raven pursed his lips. "There were problems?"

"A small leak. My shoulder happened to be in the way."

Behind her, Tiger sucked her teeth. "Why would the Leading Council agree to untried technology on a mission like this?"

"Nothing to lose," Shayla said. "I put myself in harm's way for the cause."

"A bigger leak and you'd have saved the executioner some trouble."

Images of bright fire haunted Shayla. She gazed at the darkening forest, trying to stem a flood of childhood memories.

"You hate Imperials that much?" Tiger's words broke the spell.

"Only one," Shayla whispered to herself.

———•+•———

Shayla tried to settle into what she called 'mission sleep': that dreamless twilight world where part of her rested, while part remained alert to her surroundings.

Instead of watchful rest, she watched an eleven-year-old girl throw clothes into a backpack. Next door, Mother roused Shayla's younger brother, Brandt. Her throat tightened at the strained edge in Mother's voice.

The young Shayla grabbed a bag of kibble and stuffed it on top of her clothes, then snatched up a travel basket. Matiki eyed her from his pillow at the foot of the bed, spat at the sight of the basket, and darted for the door. Shayla was quicker. She caught the struggling cat by the scruff of the neck and shoved him into the basket.

Mother hurried Shayla and Brandt through the family quarters. Servants appeared in doorways and around corners, open-mouthed, rubbing sleep from their eyes.

Confusion…unasked questions…cold sickness as familiar surroundings swept by. Stumbling out into the night. *Nobody ever lands a cruiser on the front lawn!* Yet there it was. Mother, grim-faced in the open hatch, beckoned them while scanning the horizon as if watching for an approaching storm.

*Adult Shayla stirred, ears tracking the sound of a small animal scrabbling through the underbrush.*

Acceleration pressed young Shayla into her seat. Instead of descending back to the planet, blackness beckoned. A ship loomed, squat and ugly. A hangar door yawned.

Shayla stood, dumbstruck, at the sight of the cramped and shabby stateroom. Mother, cold and aloof, had never shown any hint of emotion that Shayla could recall, but Mother's evident fear rubbed off on Shayla and Brandt. And now *this*. Shayla had never imagined such squalid surroundings. Crowded corridors, stained walls dripping with condensation, the smell of sweat and hot machine oil.

Minutes later, so it seemed, Mother was shaking her and Brandt awake. Shayla huddled on the bed, cradling Matiki's basket, nose pricking with the whiff of bleach from the grey bedding.

"Come. You need to see this." Mother's grim tone banished all fatigue from their minds.

Hurrying once more through the starhopper's corridors, joining a stream of passengers filling a wide, low-ceilinged lounge.

People perched on meager belongings, eyes downcast. Others milled around the lounge, exchanging nervous glances. Conversations hurried and hushed. A mother nursed a baby, tears flowing openly down her face. Nobody paid her any attention.

Mother pushed Shayla and Brandt before her until they had a clear view of the lounge's walls.

Mother's hand gripped Shayla's shoulder like a raptor's claw. "Watch the Empire at work."

The wall lit up and showed a familiar coastline. The Sea of Trayn. Shayla's mouth hung open. They seemed to be flying downwards, though she knew they had long since departed Eloon's space. Sunlit streamers of cloud parted over the planetary capital, Torremis. Around the lounge, other aerial views adorned the walls like vast paintings in a gallery.

Voices behind Shayla muttered.

"Remote drones."

"They want the galaxy to have a good view."

"Bastards."

Mother's grip tightened.

The sprawl of the city, nestling between encircling mountains, resolved into avenues, blocks, and parks, then into individual buildings as the view closed in.

*Pappi is there, on business.* The gulf separating Shayla from her father, from her home, wrenched at her.

The only sound was the muted thrum of machinery.

Blinding light seared Shayla's eyes. She shrieked and blinked to clear black dots clouding her vision.

The unmistakable shape of the planetary parliament buildings glowed briefly, then collapsed into a pool of incandescent slag.

Shayla's knees weakened. The cityscape was gone. An expanding circle of devastation filled her view as the shock front engulfed the outskirts. Far beneath their remote vantage point, masonry exploded in tiny powder puffs that sparkled in the ballooning wall of plasma. A furnace heat seemed to bathe Shayla across the light years. Her whole body trembled with the ferocity of the attack.

Next to her, an elderly woman let out a sob and buried her face in her husband's shoulder. His mane of white hair hung almost to his waist. The ruddy glow of the distant inferno glinted off tears streaking his cheeks.

*Our home is gone! Pappi!* Shayla glanced up at Mother, who gazed at the unfolding destruction, face impassive. The same blank mask she always wore when she had to scold her children. An expression all too familiar.

Everywhere around the lounge, city after city succumbed to unseen tongues of hellfire.

Somewhere at the end of a long tunnel, a young girl screamed. Shayla recognized her own voice. Her mind analyzed the emotion, not yet ready to feel it. Facts clicked into place from half-forgotten history texts. Planetary cleansing. Vast warships gathering around a doomed planet. A few refugees — *us* — allowed to escape, to spread the word, spread the fear.

One thought blazed clean and clear through the roiling confusion in her mind. This was no random act. Someone *chose* to do this.

Only the Emperor in person could give such an order.

Shayla shuddered and unclenched her fists. Fingernails drew bloody crescents in her palms. Mother's hand lay on her shoulder but there was no comfort there. Instead, Shayla put an arm around Brandt and hugged him close.

## Chapter 7

They were up with the first glow of dawn tingeing the clouds that had gathered during the night. Raven pulled out replacement packs he'd hidden earlier.

Shayla opened hers and took out a brightly colored cloak. She changed and pulled the deep hood over her head. It was like looking out on the world through a tunnel, but her face was completely concealed. She was also thankful for the extra warmth. After the muggy heat and stillness of Horliath, they had climbed high through the mountains. The border towns of Chensing were at some considerable elevation, and the air was clean and bracing.

She looked around and saw that Raven and Tiger had also changed. The richly-embroidered cloaks and leather packs Raven had supplied were entirely authentic. "Good work, Raven," she said. And she meant it.

"Now we are pilgrims, no?"

"Now we are pilgrims indeed," Shayla replied quietly, checking through her pockets and stuffing her wing pack into the capacious journey pack.

They were on their way while the sky was still barely light, anxious to get off this path and onto a larger road where their presence would go unremarked. Until then, they kept close together and under cover as far as possible, watching for any signs of scrutiny. Simply being seen on this path would arouse interest. It led nowhere but up the mountains and into Horliath. No Vantist pilgrim would have any business being here.

Raven's scanner would alert them to any craft passing nearby, so aerial observers were easy to hide from. All they had to worry about was the chance of other travelers or ground patrols.

Only when they were hidden, an hour later, in a thicket overlooking a crossroads did they stop to discuss the next move.

Tiger surveyed the road and skies. "I see no signs of activity. With any luck, Weasel managed to draw them well away from here."

"We journey north," Raven said, pointing out the route to Shayla. "We pass a few dwellings, but say nothing to anyone. Don't acknowledge anyone."

"The codes of meditation," said Shayla, nodding agreement. "Strict observance. Silence. I understand." She looked hard at the other two. "And we must take this charade further. Fasting during daylight hours. Faces covered at all times, even when we are alone. We must stay in character. We can't afford a slip."

Raven pursed his lips, eyes widening at Shayla's emphatic tone, then he nodded. "We travel singly from here. Pilgrimage is solitary activity, no?"

Tiger continued, "Shark, you go first. Raven and I will follow at a respectful distance. If you get into trouble we can close the gap to assist without arousing suspicion. Stay to this road. Some time this afternoon we'll reach a fork. Turn left to Skerrin Brethwyn. Seek lodging there. We will meet tomorrow in the main square. Look out for my cloak and follow me."

Shayla had already studied the striking and highly individual patterns on the robes. Recognition would not be a problem.

"Remember," said Raven to Shayla, "if a patrol stops you, keep silence if possible. I've provided you with papers confirming you are on a pilgrimage of Meditation. If they ask you to remove your hood, refuse. We will not be far behind."

"Most of these soldiers are locally born and superstitious as hell," added Tiger. "If you get challenged and have to speak, righteous indignation and quoting some passages from the Book of Unity or the Pillars of Duty are better than any official ID for a traveler on an Exalted Meditation."

Raven nodded emphatically.

"I can do that," said Shayla. She'd had plenty of time on her journey to study the Vantist holy books in preparation for this task.

"*Kestrel* was the closest vessel tracking *Chantry Bay*." Paul Malkin talked rapidly, transferring a series of images onto the wall of the darkened conference room. "Fifteen hundred miles out. The captain recorded as much debris as possible to aid search efforts and investigations. Thanks to his data, we recovered a lot of evidence from the forest that we'd never have found otherwise."

"Your point?" Chalwen scowled at the list of the day's appointments and tasks crowding the surface of her notepad.

"Getting there." Paul shuffled more images glowing on the desk in front of him. He pointed his stylus at one and dragged it across to the wall to join the growing collage. "One of the analysts spotted this." He enlarged the image and closed in on some tiny specks near one edge of the screen.

Paul's pale eyes locked with Chalwen's. His intensity stilled her impatience. She glanced at her other senior security chiefs. They, too, were alert with expectation.

"This was right on the trailing edge of the plot, amongst some debris that came off very high up. Mainly external structure breaking up." Paul ran the recording forward. The image was blurred and jittery. Specks of white drifted across the screen against a sea of green. "There!"

"What?" Chalwen, Henri, and Fleur responded as one.

Paul smiled, thin-lipped and humorless. "I thought you might have been quicker than the analysts. Watch again." He replayed the sequence. This time, one of the fuzzy specks, tiny and almost invisible, was circled.

Henri hissed between his teeth. "It changed course."

"It could have caught a gust," said Paul. "Some of the pieces were odd shapes. Some tumbled, got deflected, did odd things on the way down. But this looked different. Worth following up."

"Can you enhance this?" asked Chalwen.

Paul shook his head as he pulled more images across the conference room desk. "That was the best we could get. We projected a course from these few seconds before it went off the edge of the plot. *Brazen* started low level sweeps of the area a few hours after the crash, so I got a team of analysts picking through every frame along that projection. They found this."

Henri stared at the new scene, breathing deeply. "At last. The missing piece." He looked around at the sudden silence. "One of them, anyway."

"Yes!" said Fleur, eyes sparkling at the tiny, blurred image. At first sight, it looked like a bird, long and slender wings outstretched on either side. But in between was the unmistakable outline of a human being.

"Libby Hollis," Henri announced.

"Aww. Let me tell them." Fleur pouted. "Purrleeez!" Without waiting for an answer, she continued. "Henri and I followed up on Scolt's interim report on Libby Hollis. Her background checked out. No connection now or ever with any terrorist group or associates thereof. So Henri went into the psyche-profiling side, and I went digging for dirt. Scolt reported that she rebuffed all attempts to get close to her. Now I've seen his picture, and I wouldn't kick him out of bed."

"Fleur," Chalwen growled.

"This testimony is relevant, Yer 'Onour. All reports suggest that Libby Hollis was a shameless gadabout. A flirt. She clocked up Guardsmen like trophies. Miss a chance to bed a Lieutenant Colonel of the Imperial Color Guard? Especially a gorgeous hunk like that? Not bloody likely!"

"There were other indicators as well," Henri interrupted smoothly. "Scolt observed her as closely as he could, and recorded everything meticulously. Her actions do not match the profile of Libby Hollis."

Fleur snorted. "Never mind the psycho-babble! I've learned that Hollis was addicted to exnet game feeds, and she was a devoted follower of the Jivers ground-race team. There was a sector level race meet on Derrin during the flight. Libby Hollis would have known about it, and Libby Hollis would not have missed the live transmission. Apparently our Libby Hollis stayed in her cabin that evening, and transmission logs show that she watched an opera instead. She had to be an imposter. I'm sure she had something to do with toasting the ship."

Henri nodded. "The evidence is suggestive. Plus there were the signals that alerted Scolt in the first place. Subtle signs of extreme tension, very well masked. Signs of an agent at work. This was not some lowly clerk returning from an offworld vacation.

"But here's the thing that stumped us." Henri leapt to his feet and paced up and down in front of the wall screen. "Scolt reported none of the markers that would indicate a suicide agent. She was up to something, but she was not facing imminent death. Not as far as she knew, anyway. We've been trying to reconcile that problem. One possibility is that she was entirely unconnected to the ship's destruction. She was on some other mission, and happened to pick the wrong ship to be on."

Fleur grimaced. "Neither of us liked that idea. Too much of a coincidence. And two separate missions that I didn't get wind of?"

"So here's the answer." Henri gestured to the picture. "One mission. One agent on board, with no intention of dying."

"So," said Chalwen, frowning, "our mystery guest crashed a ship just to get herself down to the planet undetected."

"We had no hope of accounting for the occupants," said Paul. "The identifiable body parts we recovered would hardly fill a bath tub."

"I don't suppose anyone can explain how she managed to get off the ship without frying?"

"Theories only. We're working on it," said Paul.

"Hmm. Put that in the 'nice to know' category for now. Point is, she did, and she's on Magentis. Somewhere. More important to find out what she's doing here." Chalwen leaned forward, eyes glinting, galvanized by the first distant glimpse of her quarry. "I need a list of targets. Things that someone would go to all this trouble to reach. Things that one person could make a material difference to."

"Looks like she was heading north, towards the Solven Plateau," said Paul. "That's the centre of ground-based defenses for the whole continent of Traplinki. Plenty of military targets there."

Chalwen nodded slowly. "But she could just be making for a rendezvous. The Insurrection and all the Families have networks of agents here already. What's so special about this one? An ID would help. Track back on Hollis's movements prior to boarding the ship. Who did she come into contact with? Was she ever alone with anyone? Any other oddities or uncharacteristic behavior that would suggest when a switch might have been made?"

Chalwen thought for a few moments. "And have any unidentified bodies turned up on Tinturn recently?"

Chapter 8

The innkeeper prattled on merrily, to no-one in particular. "The Provost told me — my brother-in-law is the Provost of Skerrin Brethwyn you know," he said for the fourth time that evening. "Anyway, he says a patrol's come a cropper up on the pass to Changoon."

Shayla wanted to hear more, but bit her tongue and simply nodded, hoping he'd keep talking.

She needn't have worried. His was almost the only voice in the room, and he clearly deemed it his mission to fill the silence on behalf of his devout guests. Bright cloaks crowded the long tables, heads shrouded and bent over bowls of a thick and aromatic broth.

"Nasty spot at this time of year," said one of the locals seated in front of the crackling fire. "Still lots of ice about. What're they doin' up there?"

*Changoon?* Shayla's mind raced. She had seen that name recently, but she couldn't risk taking out her notepad here. Trawling for information would be seen as communication beyond the bare essentials allowed under the strict codes of meditation. She closed her eyes and pictured the map of the region she had studied. There it was. Changoon. A small town some way north of here on the road to Hawflun. A high and narrow pass led from there to join the path they had taken out of Horliath.

"Watching the border," the innkeeper said.

"They bin doin' a lot of that, haven't they? Ever since that ship crashed over the hills."

"But last night, they found this patrol cruiser. Up on the mountain. All burnt out."

"Accident?"

"Now, there's a question, Brevin. There indeed is a question." The innkeeper paused, knowing his mysterious tone had captured the undivided attention of his mostly mute audience. "And it's not for me to say one way or another, but the Provost told me they suspect foul play."

"Bloody Insurrection!" growled Brevin. There was a mutter of agreement from the handful of regulars, and even from a few pilgrims, breaking their vows of silence.

*Shit! I wish I could ask questions!* Shayla wanted to hear how many bodies they'd recovered, but the rambling monologue had moved on to travel restrictions, the number of soldiers patrolling the border towns these days, and the market price of beans.

All the same, she felt elation at what she'd heard. And, more importantly, what she hadn't heard. There had been no mention of a captive or a fugitive, something the innkeeper would surely have heard about. Weasel had either perished or escaped. And he seemed to have successfully drawn attention away from them.

*He's more useful than he looks.* It dawned on Shayla that Weasel had taken the cruiser along their direction of travel, rather than the more obvious course away. They would have to pass through Changoon tomorrow, but the guards there would not be looking for pilgrims on the road from Skerrin Brethwyn. Any self-respecting terrorist who had gotten this far would surely be heading away from, not into, the scene of the crime.

———◆———

Alone in her room, Shayla assumed a pose of meditation. Even alone, she was reluctant to let down her guard. Surveillance here, in this unassuming backwater, was unlikely, but she was taking no chances.

After a few minutes she stood and pulled out her notepad from under her cloak. She flipped it open and set it down on the bedside table, her stylus gliding casually across the surface.

Soft music filled the room. Complex rhythms played against each other, tantalizingly irregular. If there were any hidden onlookers they would see nothing remarkable as Shayla sat once more, her stylus twiddling idly in her hand.

But Shayla's actions had more purpose than it seemed. The music was no aid to meditation. It was the outward face of one of the many secret features buried deep in her notepad under layers of security. The broken rhythms spoke to her in a language of their own. As her spinning stylus scanned the room, the music told her that the place was free from electronic eavesdroppers.

Satisfied at last, Shayla returned to the table. Her movements now swift and purposeful, her stylus traced another path across the labyrinthine face of the notepad.

Eventually she was ready. One of her software minions connected itself to the communications port in the corner of the room. It left no hint of its presence. There would be no record of this activity. Shayla knew it would be working its way through the planetary net, worming past the many defenses and eavesdroppers, building a secure and untraceable path from her to the outside world.

This much she knew, and no more. The details of the ethereal phenomenon she'd just unleashed were strictly the province of her dear brother Brandt, who had spent many painstaking years equipping her notepad with its electronic arsenal. Shayla's own interest lay in people, not in machines. People: what made them tick, and how to stop them ticking.

She sat. She waited. *Wonder what time it is on Chevinta?* But whatever time of day or night, she knew Brandt would not be far from reach.

After twenty minutes, subtle tones in the music that was still playing announced another presence in the room.

"Hey, brother." Shayla fought to keep the excitement out of her voice. The room was not being remotely watched, but it would not do for a passer-by in the passageway outside to hear voices. Besides, they had a job to do. "Are you following me okay?"

"You're not exactly easy to miss." His voice, small, and distorted from light years of travel across a hundred hacked networks, sounded amused. "Security forces are frantic, as expected. Though, as far as I can tell, you yourself remain invisible."

"Good. Plenty of background noise, and I want them on edge." Shayla took a deep breath. "And the navy?"

Brandt chuckled. "*Wrath of Empire* took up an outlying orbit around Magentis yesterday. It's not common knowledge yet. And comms traffic suggests there's another *Sword* on its way."

*Two Swords!* Visceral dread almost eclipsed Shayla's satisfaction. She exhaled slowly. "That will suffice."

"I guess your local contacts have told you already, but your target was in Hawflun on schedule."

*No, they didn't. Why doesn't that surprise me?*

"You have time still, but you realize you're cutting it fine."

"I know. This whole mission is balanced on a high wire. But that's a chance we chose to take. We've never had an opportunity like this before, and I can't see another one opening up in our lifetimes."

"Shayla, one more thing. Looks like our beloved Lady Jasmina Skolax is getting ready for another *excursion*."

The back of Shayla's neck prickled. Mother? What's she up to now?

Cold and distant, Mother lived her own life quite separate from her children. Shayla unclenched her fists and took a deep breath. Mother traveled often, but Brandt only used the word 'excursion' when he recognized the signs of more secretive preparations.

"You going to try tracking her again?"

Brandt was silent.

"Only the Firenzi Special Service and Imperial Security have ever been able to lock you out."

"I know."

Unease gnawed at Shayla. For her to evade Brandt's surveillance, Mother must have powerful friends somewhere. The timing was too coincidental. *No! Surely you're just keyed up from the mission.* All the same…"Brandt, I've got a funny feeling about this. Please keep a close watch on her."

"I'll do my best. If I find out anything I'll let you know." He didn't sound hopeful.

"This is probably the last chance we'll get to talk before I reach the Palace."

"Remember, I can't break into the Palace net from the outside."

"I'm disappointed!" Shayla's teasing tone belied the words.

"Not without setting off alarms, anyway." He sounded hurt.

*That still bugs him!* "Brandt, you've already worked miracles. I'm content with miracles, I don't expect omniscience."

"Hmph! Well, it's a lot easier to tunnel out from the inside without detection. When you get a chance, set an agent with your signature showing."

"I know the routine."

"Once your signature's out on the exnet, I'll find it and follow it back to you."

"Just remember, I'll be under round the clock surveillance in there. Not like here. We won't be able to talk in plain speech without someone picking it up."

"I know, you'll have to watch your movements and keep in character. If I have anything to pass on to you I'll use *Chirple*."

*Chirple!* Shayla suppressed a snort. *How did we stick with that daft name all these years?* But she just nodded to the empty room. "Agreed." Their secret musical language was limited, she knew, but it would allow them to exchange essential intelligence if the need arose. "For Father, and for Eloon."

"Death or glory."

"And probably both." Shayla completed the childhood mantra and closed the connection.

———•◆•———

Shayla stood in the main square, her breath forming clouds in the opening of her hood. She surveyed the comings and goings of pilgrims and townsfolk. And soldiers. Lots of soldiers. Last night when she'd arrived, the place had been quiet. The guard at the gates had admitted her with no more than a cursory glance at her papers before disappearing back into the warmth of the gatehouse.

Overnight, the town had been transformed into an army camp. They must be widening the search for whoever had ambushed the patrol.

At last she spotted Raven's cloak in the crowd. He crossed from the other side of the square. He must have seen her, but he gave no acknowledgement as he passed. He joined a line of cloaked pilgrims waiting to board a ground transport in the middle of the square. It squatted like an iridescent green beetle amongst the milling figures. Down the side, in between two rows of steamed-up windows, were the words 'Temple Travel'. A makeshift sign hung from its side read, 'Hawflun centre. 10 francs'.

Shayla searched her pockets for money. Ten francs was an outrageous sum to charge for transport. Especially a vehicle as crowded and uncomfortable as this one looked. But the fat and jolly-looking woman standing at the bottom of the entrance ramp seemed to have plenty of takers.

She hesitated a while longer, allowing a few people to line up behind Raven. As she joined them, Tiger approached from another corner of the square.

The line moved slowly. Two soldiers stood next to the transport owner, checking papers and questioning everyone waiting to board. Shayla was relieved to see that they mostly answered with simple nods or shakes of the head. No-one was asked to remove their hoods.

At last, Shayla found herself face to face with the younger soldier. Heart thumping, she handed him her worn and grubby documents of attestation.

"Meditation of Atonement, eh?" He sneered at Shayla. "Wotcha bin doin' to deserve that then?"

She bowed her head as if in shame.

"Summat bad I'll bet. Hey! Corporal! Wotcha have to do to earn five days atonement these days?"

A few muffled sniggers sounded from somewhere back down the line.

Shayla gritted her teeth. *I'd like to meet you down some dark alley one night ...*

The older soldier, long beard turning to grey, handed documents back to the figure in front of Shayla and turned his attention to her.

"Now then, Cox," he said mildly, "let's see what we've got here then."

He took Shayla's papers from the grinning guard and glanced over them. "All the way up from Creech, eh?" Shayla nodded. "Walk this far, have you?" Shayla nodded again. "See anyone behaving suspiciously on the road?" Shayla paused for a moment as if in thought, then shook her head.

He looked Shayla up and down, pursing his lips.

In a moment of panic, Shayla realized that her cloak was far too clean. She must look out of place amongst these road-weary travelers. Her hand slipped under her cloak and rested on the hilt of her needle gun. The narrow opening in her hood restricted her view of the square too much to plot an escape route. She half-closed her eyes. Time slowed as she took in the sounds around her, the swish of robes, the scrape of boots on flagstones. From memory, she charted the outlines of the square, the alleyways leading out through the town, the positions of soldiers.

But the bearded guard simply grunted and handed Shayla's papers back to her. "Looks like you managed to find decent lodgings on the road, at least. Dangerous place right now."

With an inward sigh, Shayla handed the transport owner ten francs.

She also eyed Shayla's cloak. "And five francs security surcharge. These good gentlemen are providing a valuable and expensive service in these times of trouble."

Shayla bit back a retort, and let her shoulders sag in submission. She fumbled in her cloak for another five francs and dropped it into the chubby, outstretched hand.

The old soldier winked at Shayla and turned to the next person in line.

On her way to the stairs at the back of the transport, Shayla passed a door leading to latrines. By the odor wafting out of the door they were either blocked or out of water.

As she wormed her way into a window seat on the upper deck, she wondered how long the journey would last. It was two hundred miles direct to Hawflun, and much further along the road.

The morning wore on and the transport filled slowly. At a rough count, Shayla reckoned there must be seating for about two hundred people. The original seating had been removed and replaced by rows of hard benches crammed together. The transport would have once been equipped with a small kitchenette and servery, but that must have been removed to make way for more seating. There was no need for catering facilities on this journey. They were all supposed to be fasting. Shayla was glad she'd had the presence of mind to fill a small water bottle before she left the inn.

Using her pocket knife, Shayla popped the latch on the window and let in a welcome draft to dispel the damp heat of the press of people.

From her vantage point, she watched the line of waiting people dwindle. The owner paced up and down at the bottom of the ramp, stamping her feet against the cold, and looking around for any last passengers to fleece.

She evidently decided it was time to move. With a last few words to the soldiers, and a round of hearty laughter, she heaved herself up the ramp.

A low vibration thrummed through the vehicle, and it lurched across the square towards the main street. They passed the gatehouse. A sleepy outpost last night, it was now a hive of activity. Soldiers with weapons drawn shepherded a row of southbound travelers into line in front of a desk, where they were questioned by a stone-faced sergeant. He had a scroll unrolled in front of him. It looked like he was checking papers far more thoroughly against central records.

As they passed, Shayla noted a black-cloaked woman, thin faced, long hair plaited down her back. She stood behind the sergeant, watching his questioning intently.

*They have a truthsenser on duty now? Holy shit! We were lucky to get in last night when we did.*

As they gathered speed on the open road, it was clear that the ancient suspension had seen better days. Shayla wedged herself tightly into the angle between the seat and the window, and hung on to avoid being bounced around.

It was midday when they reached Changoon. If Skerrin Brethwyn had looked like an army camp, this tiny town was a fortress. A field alongside the road had become a military airfield. Three hulking transports squatted low. Alongside one was an encampment. Bristling communications arrays sprouting alongside long tents suggested a command post. A constant stream of soldiers came and went, running or marching briskly.

Shayla felt mounting anxiety battle with curiosity. *Why would the loss of one small border patrol excite so much attention?*

Her heart sank further when a patrol flagged them down. A long line of vehicles of all descriptions stood idle by the side of the road. Soldiers moved slowly down the line, inspecting each one carefully. Drivers and passengers were lined up alongside under the watchful eye of more guards.

Shayla watched the leading soldier speak to the driver below through her open window. She strained to catch the conversation.

"We need to check everyone's papers. You'll have to wait in line back there."

"That could take hours. This is a regular transport run. I've a full load of pilgrims to deliver to Hawflun by nightfall."

The guard chewed his lip, looking up and down the crowded road.

"They all carry proper documentation." The driver must have seen his hesitation and pressed the advantage. "Your people checked them all this morning. Surely there's no need for you to go through all that again? Looks like you've got enough to do already."

He looked back towards the airfield, and along the road again. When he spoke, his voice was low and urgent. "Come straight from Skerrin Brethwyn, did you? No stops or anything? Nobody got on or off in between?"

Shayla didn't hear the reply, but he stepped away from the noise by the side of the road and fingered a lapel microphone. After a few minutes he returned.

"The guard house at Skerrin confirms they checked everyone boarding. You can go through. I'll send a squad with you to carry out a quick inspection on the move. Apart from that, nobody gets on or off. Understand? Otherwise you'll have to pull in for a proper check."

"Understood." The jolly tone had disappeared. There was only standing room left on the transport, but Shayla wondered if the woman had intended to pick up more passengers here.

A few soldiers moved around the front of the vehicle to the boarding ramp. After a few seconds the leader nodded and waved them on. The transport lumbered slowly past the line of waiting vehicles and through the gates into Changoon.

They were through in a matter of minutes. Two soldiers appeared briefly on the top deck and wandered up and down the aisle before disappearing again. They stopped outside the northern gates to let the squad disembark, then they gathered speed once more.

Shayla breathed a sigh of relief, and gazed out at the passing countryside in the eerie quiet.

They passed isolated farms and a few hamlets. A couple of hours out from Changoon they were stopped briefly by a patrol. A cordon of air cruisers sat either side of the road, and armed guards watched carefully while their comrades carried out a door-to-door search.

In the distance, airborne cruisers swept slowly back and forth across the farmland. Shayla studied the advancing line of craft. *This must be the boundary of the search.*

———•◆•———

Rolling farmland petered out into rough grassland and increasingly dense stands of trees. The thickets merged to hem them in with towering forest broken occasionally by long glistening lakes.

When the road emerged once more into the open, blue-grey mountains clawed the skyline ahead of them. Occasional glints of white topped the range. The road twisted and turned as it started to climb.

Mercifully, the transport slowed as the road became rougher and more sinuous. After an eternity, without warning, buildings appeared around them. They were in Hawflun.

In a few minutes, they pulled up to one side of a wide square. Passengers stood and stretched. There were a few sighs and quiet groans, but none of the chatter that normally greeted the much-anticipated arrival at a destination.

Shayla joined the stream of people walking stiffly down the ramp into the square. The town was already in shadow, the sun had long ago disappeared behind the mountain looming over them to the west. She spotted Raven and Tiger in the thinning crowd, and followed discreetly.

Raven led them away from the main square, back down the southbound road. After a few hundred yards he turned off onto a side road, which led between shabby apartment blocks.

It wound through a huddle of tiny chalets clinging to the rising skirts of a sharp and snow-capped peak soaring high over the town. Raven stopped at the end of a row, outside one furthest from the town. Shayla and Tiger caught up with him.

Something was not right. Shayla touched Raven lightly on his sleeve, and held a finger up to her lips, deep in shadow under her hood. Raven nodded. Shayla surveyed the front of the chalet, taking in the rough-hewn sidings and shuttered windows.

*Someone cared for this place once.* The shutters were a sad echo of former gaiety. Paint, cracked and peeling, faded to shades of off-grey.

Window boxes hung, sporting nothing but weeds and a few desiccated stems.

There were no signs of life, but still the hairs at the back of Shayla's neck bristled. She reached under her cloak for her gun, and pushed gently on the door. It opened with a creak. *Shit!* In a blur, Shayla rolled forward into the room, eyes scanning her surroundings as she did so. Peripheral vision decoded shadows within shadows in the gloom. In an instant she was up on her feet, the snout of her needle gun already homed in on the figure in the doorway on the far side of the room.

Tiger and Raven had followed her in, weapons drawn, but Shayla lowered her gun. "Hold your fire," she whispered urgently.

"Well met, Weasel," Tiger said quietly, also holstering her gun.

Shayla finally worked out what had alerted her. The smell of cooking! She frowned. *That could have given us away.* Irritation swelled, then died as she thought more carefully. Only her ever-vigilant senses had picked up the clue. She relaxed and chuckled. "I guess it is close enough to nightfall," she said. "I'm starving!" She sobered quickly. "But we must be careful to stay in character around here. No slip-ups now."

Raven switched on a light and checked the shutters carefully. He then slipped his hood back from his face. "Keep up pretence if you want to, but I'm sick of tunnel vision, no?"

"Don't know why these religious nutters put themselves through this," Tiger grumbled, also removing her hood. "Nice work with that cruiser, by the way," she said to Weasel. "Had them all stirred up, but looking in completely the wrong direction."

Weasel grinned broadly through straggly whiskers.

"How did—" Shayla started.

"Don't even bother asking," said Tiger. "He just has this knack of sorting things out then turning up like nothing out of the ordinary'd happened."

Weasel's grin turned to a lopsided leer at Shayla, and he gave her a wink that made her skin crawl.

## Chapter 9

Brynwyn bin Covin paused to catch her breath. The path wound along the mountainside ahead of her and was soon lost to sight, but the summit was not far now. She had trodden this path every day for the last week. The climb had been hard at first, the path was steep and the air was thin, but she was getting used to it and was making good time today.

Today, she would complete the Meditation of Thanksgiving. Tomorrow, she would join an Imperial escort and resume the journey to Prandis Braz and a future in the service of the Emperor himself.

*I give thanks for the honor.* The homage came automatically to mind.

She pulled the heavy pilgrimage cloak tighter against the chill wind keening across the exposed path. Patches of snow, late to melt, clung to the slope. A few figures toiled up the path far behind Brynwyn, cloaks bright against the barren face of the mountain. Morning sun melted the shadows below and struck fire from the rooftops nestled in the valley.

A faerie tinkling caught her attention, barely audible over the moaning wind. The noise came from a small shrine slightly off the path up ahead. Streamers fluttered, some bright, some faded and tattered — tokens or prayers left by countless pilgrims.

Brynwyn had passed many such shrines on the way. Normally she scorned such ostentation, preferring the solitude afforded by the labyrinth of cells and cloisters of the summit temple. But today ...

*Why not? I've earned a small indulgence.*

She left the path and clambered the few feet down the slope to where the shrine clung to an outcrop over a dizzying drop. A dilapidated pergola straddled a walkway, supporting rainbow festoons of streamers. Some had tiny bells attached, producing the musical chimes striving to be heard above the ever-present wind.

Brynwyn walked under the pergola and into the shrine. A dais in the centre offered a seat for meditation. The floor around it was inlaid with a mosaic of a serpent eating its own tail — a symbol of the circle of life. Stone columns supported the roof. The sides were open to the elements. Brynwyn peered over the balustrade. The town of Hawflun was laid out like a map some three thousand feet below her.

Beyond the town, the far side of the valley climbed high into the sky. A snow-laden peak clawed through wisps of cloud and seemed on the verge of toppling towards her.

She retreated to the dais, a few feet from the edge. She squeezed her eyes shut against the beckoning drop and focused her thoughts.

*I give thanks to the Emperor for this call to service.* Brynwyn repeated the calming mantra over and over.

After a few minutes, the inner peace of true meditation washed over her. She saw her world, and her past, as if from a distance. She felt like she was a spectator, a stranger, watching her own life pass by.

*But I am a stranger now!*

It was an uncomfortable realization. Brynwyn had never set foot outside Chensing, and had never expected to. The far continent of Prandiski might as well have been the other side of the galaxy. Her family, her whole life, belonged to a time and a place that was now behind her. She was alone, a stranger, about to enter a world she had never imagined inhabiting.

But when she looked back, she saw that this was little more than a natural progression in her life. From helping out at her family's fish packaging plant at Stoon Barza, Brynwyn had soon found herself, still only a young girl, looking after the accounts, then procurement, and finally becoming the unofficial works manager. Her flair for organization had come to the attention of the town officials, and she soon flourished in a new life as a public servant.

Moving to the provincial administration at Toomin Barza had been a big step. At the time, it had seemed unbearably final. She'd never been so far from home before. But that, too, she'd taken in her stride and she'd blossomed in the intrigue and politics of provincial government.

The call from the Mosaic Palace had come out of the blue. When she'd sought an audience with the High Provost to tender her resignation, nervous and shaking, he didn't seem surprised. He had always taken an interest in her career. He'd said more than once that she would move on to higher duties.

Brynwyn had taken time to wind up her affairs in Chensing. The little coastal town of Stoon Barza had turned out in force to wish her well. She doubted her duties would take her there again.

This retreat in meditation was the final severance from the world she left behind. She belonged to the Emperor now.

———•◆•———

Emperor Julian Flavio Skamensis strode up and down the Office of Deliberation, face purple, mouth working silently.

At last he found his voice. He whirled round to face Chalwen across his desk. "An intruder? Here? On Magentis?" he thundered.

This was hardly remarkable, Chalwen thought as she stood silent against the tide of fury. All the enemies of the Empire, and all our friends too for that matter, have agents here already. Many — most, she hoped — were known to Chalwen's team, and watched discreetly.

"It was bad enough the Insurrection sabotaging a ship in our home space, but are you telling me that…that…*outrage* was nothing more than a ploy to land someone here? Making a mockery of all the security we have in place?"

Chalwen gazed steadily in front of her, still saying nothing while the Emperor ranted. She felt the eyes of the room's other occupants on her. *Bet you're enjoying this!* But she knew that she could do nothing but ride out the storm.

Beyond the Emperor's desk, a broad spread of tall, arched windows overlooked the Fountain Court, an oasis of light in the dark night. True to its name, the hexagonal courtyard was dominated by a circle of dancing fountains. Each fountain, lit such that ice blue radiance seemed to emanate from the depths of the cascading water itself, played into a wide pool. Around the edges of the courtyard, beds of roses offered a spectacular display of regimented finery.

Chalwen looked longingly at the manicured borders. *When did I last have time to tend my own garden?*

At last, sensing a lull in the tirade, Chalwen returned her attention to the Emperor. "They went to great trouble and enormous risk to land this agent. Whoever it is must have some particular skill or be bringing something of vital importance with her."

The Emperor breathed heavily, outburst over, but anger clearly far from spent, eyes leveled at Chalwen now cold and calculating. "For something this brazen, the prize must be of great value."

"Does this in any way affect the trials due to start tomorrow?" Supreme Judge Abraham Crode's words caught Chalwen off guard.

She pursed her lips and glared at him while her mind raced. Crode was just one of many powerful figures waiting for her to stumble. Waiting to pounce. Where was this leading?

When Chalwen spoke, she tried to put confidence into her voice. "Why should it?"

"I want to be reassured, my dear ap Gwynodd, that you've gleaned whatever intelligence you can from these miscreants." He cackled. "Nothing missed? Before it's too late?"

"My staff have been thorough."

"The same staff who let this agent slip in before their very eyes?" He laughed again and continued before Chalwen could frame a retort. "I know you can't be everywhere and watching everyone. But if this agent is as important as you claim, these prisoners must surely know something."

The Emperor looked expectantly at Chalwen. He needed analysis, not bitching. She shook her head. "We have extracted everything possible from them. There is no reason for me to keep them any further, Crode. They're all yours." What's left of them.

She turned to the remaining person in the room. "And the communications we prepared for public consumption still hold true. There's nothing to be gained by advertising the presence of another agent here, and I don't want them getting wind of the fact that we know about them. This matter stays between the four of us and my own staff."

Eloise Spinflower, Minister of Public Knowledge, nodded.

"To get back to the point," said Chalwen, "we need to discuss possible targets."

The Emperor snorted. "There's no shortage of targets here. Bases, cities, the seat of Government itself…where do you intend to start?"

"By ignoring the obvious for now. This intrusion carried enormous risk. It has a feeling of haste, almost of desperation. Bases and cities have been standing for centuries. What is the hurry now?"

"You have some suspicions?"

"Some. But right now one in particular stands out. Your Imperial Majesty is entertaining the Heads of Family next month. Such a gathering would make an attractive target for the Insurrection."

"The Palace of Butterflies?"

"That is a very real possibility. I am stepping up security around all engagements while our visitors are here. We are still not discounting a military target, and we're looking for other possibilities, but right now the Festival of Fountains at Henriss Garden is the most obvious risk."

———•◦•———

Tiger and Weasel watched silently while Shayla sorted through her pack, transferring essential items to pockets in her jacket and cloak.

Raven arrived with news of their target's movements. "She set off thirty minutes ago. Usual route."

"She will complete her devotions. We can rely on these religious types for something at least," Tiger said. "You managed to tag her?"

Shalya looked up from her packing, senses tingling. An edge in Tiger's voice bespoke danger. The tension felt wrong, beyond normal pre-operation nerves.

Raven nodded. "We've carried out the instructions we were given. But Tiger, you know this is insane." To Shayla he said, "You're picking her up too late. She was cleared and registered weeks ago. The Palace security codes are all locked into her passkey by now, and tied to her biometrics. You should have switched with her before that."

Tiger and Raven both drew pistols. "I agree with Raven. This plan makes no sense, Shark. It's your turn to share information."

Weasel had a knife in his hand. They all faced Shayla.

"We're going nowhere until you answer some questions," said Tiger. "We've been trying to get into the Palace for decades. The agents we do have there took time and planning to place. And then last month the only assassin we've managed to get in was betrayed and killed."

"We think," muttered Raven. He caught Tiger's look. "We don't know what has become of him."

"He's in Chargon's hands. As good as dead. Better off dead," she snarled.

"Point is, who the fuck are you to just stroll in and do what we've been struggling to do for so long?" Raven's voice was harsh with suppressed rage, resentment in every line of his face.

*Crap! This is not good.* Shayla was acutely aware that she couldn't complete this switch without help.

Tiger continued more calmly but with no less hostility. "You're holding back on something. You may have hoodwinked the Exec, but as far as I can see you're either an Imperial agent sent to trap us, or you've got access to something we don't know about."

"In the first case, you'll die very slowly indeed. *Keep your hands in sight!*" Raven was quick. Shayla had barely moved. "I don't care how good you are, there are three of us. Tiger and I are not totally useless and Weasel's as good as they come."

*Guess I can't argue with that.*

"You only live now because I'm curious and I'm giving you the benefit of the doubt," said Tiger. "Because if you really can do this, it's too good an opportunity to miss. But first you have to satisfy me on how you plan to achieve the impossible."

Dammit. These field agents were supposed to follow orders and not ask questions. The Insurrection was notorious amongst its own members for paranoid secrecy, with one cell not knowing what its neighbors were up to. She had been expecting unquestioning obedience, not this inquisition. They could not know the whole truth, so how little could she get away with?

"Impersonation," Shayla said, simply. *Worth a try.*

Raven snorted. Tiger's eyes narrowed. "Don't mess with me, Shark. You might get away with a stolen ID and a bit of make-up out on the offworlds, but that won't work here." She leveled her gun more pointedly at Shayla's head. "Landside security here is nothing like border control, but it's still tight. And I know for a fact that the Insurrection doesn't have the know-how to fake a passkey well enough to fool Palace security."

OK, *maybe not*. Shayla's mind raced. How to convince them to help? Tiger must be far more senior in the Insurrection's ranks than she had thought. It looked like a simple 'don't ask questions' approach was not going to work. She quickly ran through her options. Anything that linked her to the Firenzi Special Service would be a quick path to a slow death. And yet Tiger was right, she was making full use of technology the Insurrection should know nothing about.

Shayla sighed. *The best lie is one cloaked in truth.* She raised her arms slowly, careful to keep her hands in sight. The other three stiffened, weapons ready, but Shayla simply lifted her hood away from her face.

She tensed herself for action as Tiger gasped. "But…you're not …"

There was a blur of movement and a soft hissing sound. Two heads thumped to the floor followed by two crumpling bodies.

## Chapter 10

Weasel grinned at Shayla, who had stepped smartly back to avoid the arcs of blood. She glimpsed a cold line of blue fire winking out as Weasel sheathed his knife. *A shimmerblade.* That was how he'd managed to behead the two of them so effortlessly.

"They were getting too curious for comfort." Weasel spoke for the first time. Shayla was taken aback by his voice, rich and firm, and completely at odds with his raggedy appearance. "I'm quite sure you could have talked them round eventually, but probably not without mentioning things that were best left unmentioned. That would have left some loose ends to tie up later. Besides, we are now very pressed for time."

Shayla holstered the needle gun she'd drawn at the first movement. She tried to process what had just happened. She got no sense of threat in Weasel's manner, and one fact stood out above all else: a shimmerblade was a Firenzi weapon.

Weasel smiled. A true smile this time, not the evil leer Shayla had become accustomed to. Deep lines around his eyes vanished and his face glowed with timeless age. "Finn Probey, at your service." He bowed low.

Shayla stifled a gasp. "Shayla Carver. The honor is mine."

"Nice transformation, by the way."

"Thanks. But...*the* Finn Probey?"

"You know of another?"

Shayla shook her head, still slightly bemused. Finn Probey. One of the most feared and renowned assassins living. A legend in the Firenzi school.

She looked on the wiry and disheveled man in awe. He seemed to have grown six inches in stature. The sly and oafish facade evaporated and he now radiated competence and authority. He gave the impression of a man who could stand unmoved in the face of a hurricane.

"We must move." His voice was firm, and brought Shayla back to her senses.

"Yes. A moment." She took her notepad and studied her reflection in the bathroom mirror, comparing it with the images she'd been given to work from. Finn was right. The transformation was very good, considering she'd been working while traveling. Shayla suppressed a smile while she checked herself over for any last adjustments. She had made full use of the obligation to keep her face hidden during the journey, allowing her to remodel her features in private. The mimetic implants under her skin were a jealously guarded Firenzi secret. She could understand Tiger's confusion. Tiger would have seen emerge a different person from the one she had met a few days before.

Her face had plumped out to match the biometric data stolen from local Government records. Skin tone darkened and reddened. Hair transformed from straw blond to glossy black. She would probably not fool a close friend or relative, but she wouldn't need to. This target had been chosen with care, and would be far from home. This was close enough. Shayla was relieved. Morphing the bio-implants took huge amounts of energy, and she was exhausted.

Shayla finished sorting the contents of her pack. She carried no truly personal items, only props and equipment needed for the mission.

There was her notepad. Outwardly standard, it concealed a wealth of useful — and spectacularly illegal — software.

She ran her fingers over a worn Book of Unity, the Vantist holy book, an ancient relic from the days of print. Except that this was no ancient relic. The forgery was perfect, the patina of age and use painstakingly recreated. This tiny book hid a small but deadly toolkit worked into the thickness of its spine and cover. A blow tube, darts, and a carefully selected armory of drugs and poisons.

She'd keep her needle gun for now, but would have to discard it before long. Such weapons were not common in the Empire; it would certainly not be carried by a member of the public service. A low-performance beam weapon wouldn't attract any comment, but Shayla regarded them as rather less than useless. She could kill or disable more effectively with her bare hands. And beam discharges could be detected and tracked from miles away.

Her pocket knife was another matter entirely. Looking perfectly commonplace, it was a shimmerblade like Finn's. When activated, the vibrating crystalline edge could shear effortlessly through anything short of military grade vehicle armor.

Finn watched her preparations patiently.

"I'll leave you my pack to dispose of. This mustn't fall into Imperial or Insurrection hands. You know that?"

Finn nodded. "Whatever the Empire covets, it has wealth enough to acquire."

Shayla recognized the passage from the Assassins' *Book Of Enemies*. "The best defense against envy is ignorance," she added from the same passage. "And obviously it won't burn. You'll need a high grade plasma or better to destroy it."

"No problem." Finn smiled shrewdly. "I have just the thing. I don't want these bodies to be identified either."

———•◆•———

Satisfied that she had everything she needed, Shayla left the chalet with Finn and walked back to the main square of the town.

Occasional moans and screams greeted them from the row of punishment stalls in front of the town administrative buildings. There was the usual small crowd of people gathered around them. Shayla instinctively gave the stalls a wide berth. She knew all too well what she would see there: a row of miscreants, shackled, placards in front of them announcing their misdemeanors to the world, left to the mercy of the populace to mete out punishment as they saw fit.

Coarse cheers and a ragged shriek drifted across the square as someone dropped a coin into one of the slot machines, delivering a measured jolt of torment to one of the prisoners.

On the other side of the square, ground cars and air cruisers jostled for space. There were a few scheduled transports, departure times and destinations blazoned across their fronts. Others offered rides to the top of the mountain. Drivers vied for custom, calling prices and striking deals with travelers unwilling to complete the trek on foot. The transport they had used the day before was nowhere to be seen.

Finn and Shayla hurried past the transports with the disdain of true pilgrims. A few hundred yards from the square, a large signpost pointed the way up the mountain. A narrow road wound past the last few dwellings, then climbed steeply up the hillside.

They soon found themselves alone on the rough path, and panting for breath from their exertion as they climbed a towering staircase cut into a sheer cliff.

Once they were well above the town, they paced their ascent. Eventually, Shayla broke the silence, still struggling to overcome her awe at her companion. "Finn. Can I ask a delicate question?"

"You want to know why I am not performing this task myself?"

"Yes," she replied, slightly flustered at his prescience. "How did you guess?"

He laughed quietly. "The truth is, I would have relished this chance maybe thirty years ago. Now, I am too well known. No matter how I disguise myself, I'd never penetrate Palace security. This is a job for an unknown."

"But you're not here by chance, are you?"

"I've been making myself useful to the Insurrection for years now, in various capacities. The local cells have grown soft. Most of the Insurrection's work is directed at the offworlds, so the agents here see precious little action. When they do, they prefer to have people like me to do the dirty work."

Shayla could hear the contempt in his voice.

"When news of your mission came through," Finn continued, "I made sure I was in the right place at the right time to accompany the local ground force. I'm here to help you succeed. I'll be watching out for you in Prandis Braz. If you need help on the outside, I'll be there."

There seemed to be no resentment in his voice, which puzzled Shayla. "But you've done so many incredible things. How can you stand to be on the outside while some newcomer has all the fun?"

"Nowadays, the only work I *can* do is on the fringes. Even so, I'm finding it more difficult to stay ahead of Security. This will be my last assignment on Magentis."

Finn slowed and stopped, settling on a flat rock at the side of the path. He feigned weariness, all too believable at this altitude. Shayla sat beside him, genuinely thankful for the rest, but wondering why he'd stopped. She realized that another couple of travelers were slowly catching them up, and guessed that Finn wanted them to pass and be gone. They had conversed in low voices. The sound would not have gone far above the keening wind but it would not do to be heard talking.

The pilgrims passed without acknowledging them. When they were a safe distance away, Finn turned to Shayla. "I hear the implants are something of a mixed blessing."

"They have their limitations, but they offer the most effective disguise available."

"You know what I mean." Finn's tone was stern.

She hesitated. *Is he testing me?* The memory of the implant process left mental scars, even after six years. Strapped to a bed to stop her from scratching herself to shreds, while fungal filaments wormed their way into her body and invaded every inch of her skin. The physical pain, like a thousand insects invisible and untouchable, crawling and burrowing, was nothing compared to the primal revulsion that the deliberate infestation evoked.

But Shayla shook off the feeling. She knew exactly what Finn meant. "Maintaining the disguise is physically demanding, and I've never had to morph them so much and so quickly. It's tiring, but nothing I can't handle." She sounded more confident than she felt, hoping that Finn had no more than rudimentary mastery of truthsense. She was acutely aware that this elderly man was still a feared assassin. He might have orders to terminate the mission if he judged she wasn't up to it.

Finn took a deep breath and nodded. "Time to pick up her trail." He handed Shayla a thin translucent strip about an inch across and a few inches long. "You know how to use a nose."

It was not a question.

Shayla took the strip and placed it across her eyes. It stuck to her skin and held itself in place. To outward appearances, this might have been nothing more than a fashionable sun visor. Perfectly reasonable in the high altitude glare.

Through the hard but flexible material, she could just make out the outline of the path. Her vision cleared when she squeezed the topmost of a row of tiny protrusions at each end of the strip, and a luminous display hovered in her line of sight. Shayla fingered the bumps along the edge, tuning the device in to the chemical signature that had been planted on their quarry. This was another secret from the Firenzi materials laboratories, but one which the Insurrection had known about for decades.

"Got it." A hint of fluorescent violet hung in the air in front of Shayla. "Raven managed to plant the tracer OK."

"Good. You follow the scent. I'll be our eyes and ears."

They set off again more slowly. The last mile to the mountaintop temple was steep and rugged, with many steps cut into the rock. Here and there, they passed small shrines and memorials. Most of them were occupied. Robed and hooded figures sat, looking out over the valley in silent meditation.

"Looks like she stopped here," Shayla muttered, as they passed one shrine commanding a clear view of the town below. "Moved on again some time later." The scent resuming up the path was noticeably stronger.

At last the path turned back across the face of the slope and leveled off. The walls of the temple rose ahead of them, completely enclosing the broad mountain summit. An imposing gatehouse was the only visible way in.

A flattened landing field by the side of the road was a hive of activity, with cruisers of all sizes arriving and leaving, surrounded by milling crowds of people.

"Bloody tourists," Finn drawled softly in mock disdain.

"I must have 'sucker' writ large across my forehead," said Shayla. "I didn't realize that arriving on foot was only for the serious pilgrim."

"Which is exactly why we've maintained this pretence," said Finn. "We don't have to meet too many people, and the local guards are skittish about challenging obviously serious pilgrims."

They joined the stream of people, some hooded but many in street clothes, heading for the entrance. Inside the walls, Shayla found the press of people overwhelming, almost obscene, after the isolation of the last week.

Just inside the gates, market stalls huddled close together. Smells of cooking drifted and mingled across the road, cruel temptation for those travelers observing a strict fast.

"Crap! I'm losing the trail in all this lot," Shayla hissed, voice barely carrying over the babble.

"Keep moving. I doubt our target would have dallied here. She'll have made straight for the temple cloisters."

The crowd thinned. The road ahead led to the main temple building on the highest part of the summit. Most of the movement of people was in this direction, but Shayla soon spotted a wisp of violet leading up a wide flight of stairs to a pillared portico set back from the main road.

They followed, into the echoing splendor of a marbled atrium.

Finn stood patiently by her side, turning slowly on the spot as he pretended to study the vast tapestries encircling the higher reaches of the room.

Shayla could see the trail, faint and patchy, leading up to a lectern where a balding, stern-faced monk in a plain hemp robe sat. A steady trickle of people approached the desk, and scrawled briefly on the surface of a wide scroll unrolled in front of him.

*Checking in and out.*

But where did she go from here? Shayla scanned the atrium. After a minute she realized the monk was casting irritable glances their way.

"Yes?" he said at last, clearly out of patience.

*There it is.* "Through that far archway," she muttered to Finn. "We need to get past that desk."

Finn stepped forward. "I beg forgiveness for my tardiness," he said. "I was simply lost in admiration at the magnificence of this place of worship."

The monk's face softened slightly. "Meditating or visiting?" he asked.

"Just visiting, this time," said Finn. "My niece and I are looking for a suitable cloister for a Meditation of Charity. We are practicing the disciplines in preparation."

Irritation left the monk's face, his expression became bland and unreadable. "Well," he said, "let me see...Thirty francs will gain you access to all grounds and cloisters."

Finn reached into his robe.

"Each," the monk added.

Finn hesitated, then dropped a few coins into the monk's outstretched hand.

"Enjoy your visit," he said, handing Finn two plastic slips.

"Sixty francs?" Shayla hissed once they were past the desk and safely out of earshot. "I've killed for less than that! We're already supposed to be on a Meditation. We could have just presented our papers."

"And had to sign in," Finn murmured. "And out again."

"Oh." Shayla suddenly felt rather foolish. "I'm sorry. That would have caused some difficulty."

"No problem." Finn sounded amused. "Thinking through all the details on the fly is a hard art to master. I've made enough mistakes in my time."

"All the same, that was an outrageous price to charge."

"This State-sanctioned religion is as rotten as the State itself," he snorted. "And examine your robes. Pilgrimage is essentially anonymous, but these were chosen to display a moderate measure of wealth. We felt that ground patrols were less likely to question someone who might turn out to be in a position of power. But that makes us fair game for corrupt officials on the take. You don't want to know how much we paid for that miserable chalet."

They emerged onto a paved terrace running along the far side of the mountain summit. Behind them rose the walls of the main temple buildings. Ahead, they looked out over a maze of roofs cluttering a thin strip of moderately level land. The buildings ended abruptly where the mountain dropped away to meet the wide western plains of Sho Min.

Shayla led the way along the terrace. The low wall on the western side was broken here and there where flights of stairs led down into the warren of shrines and meditation cells.

The chemical tracer painted a course down one such staircase. The trail wound along narrow streets, across courtyards, through archways, and down shaded galleries. Some streets were crowded, others empty. The whole temple was eerily quiet other than the muffled shuffling of feet and distant tinkling bells. At length, they entered a square cloister enclosing a graveled yard. The gravel had been meticulously smoothed and raked into an elaborate series of swirls and geometric patterns. They surveyed the yard from the shadows of the archway where they had entered, mid way down one side of the square. Another archway opposite showed a dazzling patch of blue. They were close to the far side of the plateau, looking out over the western plains.

On either side, the cloister gave shelter to a row of openings leading to meditation cells set back in the wall. Tiny copper bowls sat by each opening, some by the wall to one side, some in front of the entrance to show the cell was occupied.

From where she stood, Shayla followed the trail to where it led into a cell. The bowl was in the middle of the entrance.

"She's here. Fifth cell on the right."

Finn nodded.

"Picking up any signs of surveillance?"

"Not a blip," Finn murmured. "This is supposed to be a temple, y'know."

Shayla, puzzled, looked sidelong at him around the edge of her hood. "So? Do you think the Emperor's Security service would respect that if there was something here they were interested in?"

Finn smiled from the shadows of his hood, and Shayla realized he was teasing her.

Shayla checked up and down the cloister. While Finn stood watch, she slipped into an empty cell. She whipped off her cloak and turned it inside-out. The dazzling colors of pilgrimage were replaced by unadorned off-white hemp.

She emerged again and walked along the cloister to the fifth cell. The figure seated in the shadows looked up, startled, then relaxed at the sight of the plain robe of a monk.

"Pardon the intrusion, Daughter of Unity," Shayla murmured. "I have an urgent missive for Daughter bin Covin. Please show your face."

The figure lifted its arms and pulled back the hood of its cloak. Shayla's needle gun spat softly.

Eyes gazed at Shayla in shock as the drug took hold. "Please lower your arms." Brynwyn bin Covin obeyed, powerless to resist Shayla's instruction.

"You will sit quietly while I scan you. I strongly advise you not to make any voluntary movement." Shayla sat opposite her. "Trylex is a very powerful drug. You have no choice but to obey my instructions. Any resistance will cause you severe and quite unnecessary pain."

Shayla flipped open her notepad and passed her stylus up and down Brynwyn's body. She needed to connect to the passkey implanted into Brynwyn, somewhere. This was not something you could normally do from a personal device like a notepad.

*Where is it?*

You could usually point your stylus at any device — other scrolls and notepads, public wall displays, information and communications panels in buildings and vehicles — and make a connection. Whether you were granted anything more than a handshake was another matter entirely, but such devices were at least visible to you.

Imperial passkeys were different. They used their own protocols, jealously guarded by the Empire. But not quite well enough. Shayla's notepad carried the recognition protocols and a wealth of tools to decode them. Simply possessing such tools was a capital offence. Naturally she kept them well hidden.

Shayla scanned methodically. Chest cavity. Abdominal. Sometimes the tiny device was buried in an arm or a leg, but that was rare.

A faint signal pinged on the notepad.

*Gotcha!* Buried deep, just in front of a kidney. Shayla confirmed the connection, and dispatched her illicit agents to work unwrapping the security codes, layer by layer.

A shadow passed by the entrance behind Shayla, momentarily blocking the dim light in the cell. She knew Finn would be somewhere outside, keeping guard. If anyone else passed by, all they would see would be a monk instructing an acolyte.

Minutes ticked by. This was not something you could hurry, and Shayla would only have this one chance to strip out enough information to successfully pose as Brynwyn.

She watched graphics unroll across the face of her notepad, charting the agents' progress. *Damn, this is going slowly.* The security codes were more complex than anything she'd seen before. They must be getting twitchy at the Palace.

Feet crunched behind her. "Who are you?" The voice was male, thin and reedy. "You don't belong here. I need to see your ID."

## Chapter 12

Shayla rose in a fluid movement, pulling back her hood to show compliance and buy herself a few moments. She turned, hand reaching beneath her robe. The monk's mouth opened as he took in the two identical faces before him.

It was all the hesitation she needed. She fired from the hip. The needle buried itself in the fleshy folds of the monk's chin. *Thank Space for well-fed clerics!* She drew the needle and inspected where the fine point had pierced the skin. Only someone knowing what to look for would have a hope of spotting the wound.

Shayla's mind raced. She had hours yet before she could afford to leave the temple. This man mustn't get the chance to raise the alarm, or identify her later, yet she couldn't leave a dead body behind.

Finn appeared in the doorway. He had also reversed his cloak. "Trylex?"

Shayla nodded. "Someone must have seen something suspicious. This may not be the last to investigate." She pursed her lips, recalling the layout of the temple grounds from plans she'd studied. "I need more time with her to complete the transfer, but I need to deal with this fellow first. Meet me on the North Walk, and be ready to pass the parcel there." To Brynwyn she said, "Cover your head. Follow this man and do as he says."

Finn hurried from the cell, with Brynwyn obediently in tow.

Shayla thumbed the selector on her pistol's magazine. Animastin. This would be harder to disguise. A heavier needle, and the drug had a nasty habit of raising a welt. She parted the monk's robe and lifted his tunic, aiming into the depths of his navel.

She removed the needle and stepped around behind him while the memory-erasing drug took hold. Mouth dry, Shayla listened for signs of movement outside while her mind ticked off minutes. Possibly the monk himself had seen Shayla enter an occupied cell, and decided to investigate, but someone else could also be watching.

*Blast! I should have swapped robes with Brynwyn while I had the chance.* What were the odds that someone would recognize Finn and Shayla together? Would anyone notice that Finn temporarily had a different partner? Slim, she decided. Besides, Brynwyn had just left with a monk, not with Finn, and she still needed to get close to Finn again herself, so maybe it was best that she still had her own cloak. Her head ached, and she cursed herself for not thinking it through and making a reasoned choice.

At last, she judged the drug would have done its work. The monk would be confused now, with no recollection of how he'd got here, and likely with a blinding headache from trying to move while still under the influence of trylex.

"Turn to face the door," she whispered, disguising her voice. While the monk complied, Shayla circled him, keeping out of sight. "Sit. Close your eyes." That would deal with any chance of recognition or raising an alarm. A slow grin crept across Shayla's face as she hooded her head. "When the gong signals the end of meditation, stand and walk to the centre of the courtyard." With luck, any odd reports now would be ascribed to this monk's eccentric behavior.

Forcing herself to keep a sedate pace, Shayla left the cell and set off in the opposite direction she'd seen Finn depart. She would head for the rendezvous when she was sure she wasn't being followed. She ducked into an archway, and emerged the other side with her cloak reversed once more. Vibrant pilgrimage colors replaced monk's off-white.

On the ramparts of the North Walk, amongst sparse knots of people braving the bitter wind whipping off the mountain slope, Shayla spotted Brynwyn standing a few feet apart from Finn, who had also swapped his cloak back. She strolled past and leaned on the balustrade next to Finn.

"She's been instructed to follow you now," he murmured.

Shayla inched closer. "Take my needle gun. I'm done with it now and you'll need to keep her dosed up. When I'm finished, take her and wait for me at the bazaar at four-thirty. Follow me out closely. We must pass through the gate together. Brynwyn's passkey will probably be clocked there, so Brynwyn must be seen leaving at the same time in case anyone matches up video to security logs later on."

Shayla turned and headed back into the warren of streets. From the corner of her eye, she saw Brynwyn follow. She knew Finn would not be far behind. Warmth enveloped her in the shelter of the huddled buildings. Wood smoke and incense pricked her nose.

Three monks appeared around a corner, striding towards her. Their faces were hidden, but the set of their shoulders spoke of determination. Time slowed as Shayla readied herself for action. She was so intent on planning the quickest way to deal with the threat while drawing the least attention to herself, that they were past before she realized it. She chanced a backward glance to check on Brynwyn. The monks ignored the startled pilgrims in the street and hastened down a side alley towards the courtyard Shayla had recently left.

Ahead was a sign for a public washroom. She entered, breathing a sigh of relief when she saw it was empty. Brynwyn followed and stood, awaiting instructions. In a matter of seconds, Shayla removed both their cloaks and swapped with Brynwyn. Outside once more, Shayla worked her way back towards the main temple walls.

At the top of the stairs leading onto the paved terrace, Shayla turned towards Brynwyn. While gazing off into the distance, she murmured, "Go and sit on that bench, beside that pot of pink thornflower. Wait for further instructions."

Finn strolled by without acknowledging her. As he passed, she whispered, "When I leave this place, she's all yours." Without a glance at Shayla, Finn crossed the terrace and sat next to Brynwyn.

Shayla walked along the terrace a little way. She settled on another bench where she judged she would still be in range.

With a quick glance up and down the terrace, Shayla half-opened her notepad, keeping it concealed in the folds of her robe. She aimed her stylus at Brynwyn, probing once more for the passkey. The agents still working inside the grain-sized device responded, and resumed transferring data to her notepad.

After thirty minutes, Shayla decided she had unraveled enough to pass routine checks. Most security challenges would only go as far as asking for identity, though when she got to the Palace she would need to be able to withstand closer scrutiny. The decryption could go on for hours yet, but she didn't need Brynwyn near her for that as long as she'd found and copied every last word buried in the passkey. Shayla checked the scavenging agents. It looked like they'd picked through everything.

Without a glance towards Finn or Brynwn, she stood and walked to the far end of the terrace, seeking another bench away from the human traffic streaming to and from the temple entrance.

An hour passed. Two hours. The codes revealed their secrets one by one. Shayla waited patiently. All need for urgency was gone. Brynwyn's time was Shayla's now, and she had to complete the devotion Brynwyn owed the temple before signing out.

Shayla shivered and drew her cloak closer around her. Cold seeped into her limbs, but it was nothing compared with the emotional chill this mountaintop retreat instilled in her. Pots of plants set between the benches did little to lighten the bleak stone. The hush was unnatural. Even the wind seemed to mute its cries under the stern gazes of hemp-robed guardians.

The austerity reminded Shayla of Mother's estate on Ploorbellin. She'd spent the remaining years of her childhood there before joining the Firenzi military at the first opportunity. Her mind drifted further back, to the contrasting warmth and joy of her father's home on Eloon. Shayla swallowed past a sudden constriction in her throat.

At last, a gong sounded from atop the wall behind her. Moments later, a distant shout echoed over the rooftops. Shayla grinned. Her drugged monk was still following orders. She waited a few minutes before rising and returning to the atrium. The desk was still guarded by the same surly monk. She shuffled in line as people approached one by one to sign out.

Behind her, running feet clattered through the atrium. Shayla resisted the impulse to turn. Voices grew louder.

"Daughter bin Covin!" The voice was thin and rather shaky.

## Chapter 13

S hayla turned. Adrenaline surged as she recognized the monk who'd accosted her in Brynwyn's cell. The dose of trylex must be wearing off. His face was white, brow pinched in pain, but he looked sheepish. There was no hint of accusation in his eyes.

Facts and deductions clicked into place. "Brother William." The Insurrection had managed to get only the name of the monk assigned to oversee Brynwyn's Meditation, and that only at the last minute. "You look ill." Her voice oozed concern.

Relief flooded the monk's face. "Deepest apologies, Daughter, I don't know what happened today."

"Brother William was found in the Court of Five Circles," one of his companions said. "Utterly entranced."

"He may have received a vision," said another. "But he can't remember anything."

"Only voices," said Brother William, with a twist of his mouth.

"Weren't you meant to meet Daughter bin Covin there?" The monk behind the desk pierced Shayla with an accusing glare.

Brother William looked puzzled. The dose of animastin should have wiped out several hours of memory. Shayla siezed her chance. "I completed my Meditation on the main promenade, as we arranged this morning. I wondered why I didn't see you there."

The monk at the desk looked from Shayla, to Brother William, and to the line of intrigued onlookers. "So, can you, or can't you, attest that Daughter bin Covin has completed her devotions?"

Brother William chewed his lip. "You have been a model student."

*I'll bet she was!*

"Did you reflect on the honor that has been bestowed on you, like we discussed?"

Shayla's mind raced. *Duty with humility.* She bowed her head. "It is but a worldly honor. I remain an unworthy vessel for His eternal grace."

Brother William's face creased into a smile. Shayla's heart missed beats as she signed out, giddy with relief.

------------

At the bazaar, Shayla tarried, pretending to browse the stalls offering trinkets and souvenirs. She was careful to keep the road in sight at all times. At four-thirty precisely, she recognized the cloaks of Finn and Brynwyn in the milling throng. She brushed off the stallholder trying to interest her in a lapis lazuli pendant, and moved to join the steady exodus.

She kept close, without being obvious, and passed through the main gate, not looking at the guards posted on either side.

*Loosen up!* Outside the gates, out of the claustrophobic crush, she unclenched her fists and rolled her shoulders.

Most of the stream of visitors headed for the landing field and the luxury of transportation off the mountain. Technically, she had completed her devotions and could afford to take the easy way out, but Shayla knew Brynwyn would have seen this through properly. No short cuts for her. And Shayla herself needed privacy before she reached the town again.

She left the landing field behind her, moving slowly to give Finn time to distance himself as he led Brynwyn down the path. She stopped briefly at a viewpoint, and surveyed the peaks across the valley, snow glowing like fire in the setting sun.

Shayla felt elated. Light-headed. Another hurdle cleared. Each step took her deeper and deeper into enemy territory. Closer and closer to the seat of Empire, and to realizing her lifelong thirst for revenge.

But evening was drawing in, and she still faced a long climb down the mountain path.

------------

The shrine where Brynwyn had stopped on the way up was empty. Shayla looked up and down the path, then walked under the pergola and sat on the dais.

*One last task to complete.*

Screened from the path, she took out her notepad and scrawled instructions with quick, economical movements. The decryption was still in progress, but there were now enough layers unraveled to pass any checks she was likely to meet between here and the Palace.

Shayla pointed her stylus at her own abdomen with practiced aim, and located her own passkey lying dormant inside her.

This was another piece of illicit technology, and key to her plan. Tiger had been correct to say that they lacked the ability to fake a passkey. The electronics were subtle and sophisticated. Imperial technologists had put a lot of effort into patterning the transmission fields in ways that nobody had yet been able to duplicate. Some came close, but all failed when examined closely.

Shayla's response to this hurdle some years ago had been simple. She'd stolen one.

*No!* she told herself, *I simply found someone who no longer had need of a passkey.* The fact that she had, not two minutes prior, been instrumental in relieving that someone of their need didn't bother her. That wasn't theft. To Shayla, that was simply business.

That had left the problem of breaking the security layers that locked the personal information held within. But that was a hurdle that lay within Shayla's reach. Or rather, within the reach of her brother, Brandt.

Brandt lived a life of academic reclusion, in the relative safety of the university Freeworld of Chevinta. His academic knowledge areas were wide-ranging. They included abstruse and sophisticated techniques in topological number theory.

They did not officially include designing and breaking security codes.

Officially.

Unofficially, Brandt had equipped Shayla with the most sophisticated security armory in the known worlds of humanity.

He had provided the tools to subvert a ship's command systems amongst other things, and to reprogram a passkey. With these tools, Shayla could teach her passkey to mimic anyone's identity. Unraveling authentication codes from their biometric profile, and re-encrypting with her own, Shayla Carver could assume their identity well enough to pass the most stringent of automated checks.

Shayla set to work transferring the security codes stolen from Brynwyn into her own passkey. She would still be in trouble if anyone chose to question her too deeply, or sought to verify biometric data against central records, but that kind of rigor was generally reserved for the border checks on the orbiting reception bases. Once on the ground, the movement of people was too great to go to such trouble, and the security forces had great faith in the unbreakable validity of the passkey.

Shayla had no intention of enlightening them.

With her own passkey now mimicking Brynwyn's identity, Shayla resumed her lonely trek down the mountain path.

When she reached the town square again, she sought out the inn on the corner of the square where Brynwyn was staying. Raven had given her a detailed brief on Brynwyn's lodgings. The layout, the names of the staff, the room where Brynwyn slept. He had even unearthed valuable information like the fact that Brynwyn gave no tips. In her eyes, the staff were paid to do their duty — what more could they want?

Shayla mounted the steps at the front of the inn and entered the warmth of the long entrance lobby. The concierge behind the desk glanced up at her. "Good evening Lady bin Covin," he said, rather distantly, before turning his attention back to the screen on his desk.

Shayla slipped the hood from her head with a sigh of relief.

The concierge looked down his nose at her. "The mountain air agrees with you, my Lady." Slight surprise registered in his voice.

Shayla puzzled for a moment. She was confident that Brynwyn would not have shown her face in the past week. The concierge could not have seen her for days. All the same, she had not been able to study Brynwyn's true appearance properly in the gloom of the meditation cell. She was sure her features were a good match, but maybe her complexion was off?

Shayla dismissed the thought. She could detect no undertones of suspicion, just disdain. "The spirit nurtures the body," she said, "but I will eat now."

"It is not quite dark." The concierge tutted. "We take pride in helping our guests observe their duties."

"And I have completed my Meditation." Shayla tried to keep calm. *Who's the friggin' customer here?*

The concierge sniffed. "As you wish." He muttered into a microphone, and waved Shayla towards the door of the dining salon.

## Chapter 14

Shayla Carver — Imperial lackey! She smiled at the incongruity of it as she checked her appearance in the wall mirror.

Her ruddy skin tone had grayed slightly overnight, and her plump cheeks sagged. She squeezed her eyes shut and willed her implants to correct the signs of fatigue. After a few minutes, Shayla opened her eyes and staggered back to sit on the edge of her bed. She took deep breaths and wiped a sheen of sweat from her face, but the face that gazed back now radiated calm and confidence befitting her station.

Brynwyn had left a clean set of traveling robes hanging, ready to wear. The Imperial crest and official insignia announced her status in the higher echelons of the Palace staff, someone of high standing indeed in this provincial backwater. It looked like Brynwyn had intended to make a dramatic exit after the anonymity of her Meditation.

She must have been proud of her new position.

The thought left Shayla with a bitter taste, but she would have to play the part to the full. She took a few minutes to clear her mind and review her notes. The facts had long ago been committed to memory and rehearsed endlessly. But the time had now come for more than mere recollection.

She had to *become* Brynwyn bin Covin.

She took another deep breath and finished packing Brynwyn's belongings. During the night, Shayla had unpacked everything in the small pile of trunks in the room, familiarizing herself with every item.

This was her life now. For a short while, at least.

As Shayla walked down the stairs and rounded the corner to the entrance hallway, she saw the same haughty concierge who had been on duty last night. In front of the desk, a soldier stood, at ease but alert. He wore the formal traveling uniform of a corporal of the Imperial Palace Guard.

"Here she comes now," said the concierge, glancing up from the desk. His face held a trace of barely suppressed glee, and Shayla had to fight back the knotting of her stomach as she reminded herself that she was *supposed* to be meeting an escort here.

The soldier turned and came to attention. "Magister Brynwyn bin Covin?"

Shayla nodded.

"Corporal Kurt Weiler, at your service, Magister Summis."

The concierge's face fell as he took in the cut of Shayla's robes, the insignia, and the Imperial crest. "B-b-beg pardon for my inattention, Magister Summis." He hurried round from behind the desk and bowed, hands wringing.

With sudden insight, Shayla realized that this man and his staff must have been making Brynwyn's stay here miserable. Her profile reported an unassuming humility, in keeping with her strict attention to duty. And her religious observances would have allowed her no latitude to assert her status.

She ignored him and spoke to the soldier. "Corporal Weiler, I assume you've brought transport?"

"I have a ground car waiting around the corner. I apologize for the inconvenience, but I'm sure you've heard the news by now. Air travel in this region is reserved for military purposes only while they continue the search for terrorists." Kurt chattered on amiably. "But the car is comfortable, and fast. We'll head north and pick up the Toomin Sho Min highway. From there it's about six hundred miles at full throttle. We'll be in Sho Min Barza by mid-afternoon. I've held seats on a scheduled shuttle …"

Shayla tried to determine whether he was overly eager to please, overawed by her status, or just naturally garrulous. She held up a hand to stem the flood. "Thank you, Corporal. I'm sure the arrangements will be acceptable." She glanced down at the fawning concierge. "Have my baggage loaded into the car."

"At once, Magister Summis." He scuttled away.

While they waited, Shayla and Kurt stepped out into the crisp morning air.

"You know," said Shayla, "I think that odious little man thought you were here to arrest me or something."

"I was wondering. He seemed rather keen for me to find you."

"This is the first time I've worn these robes." *Why am I explaining myself to this man?* But Kurt was nodding, and she realized she'd unwittingly hit the right note.

"'If you should seek to serve me, first you must leave your pride at the door,'" he quoted. "Many in your station would have made it known before now."

"Duty with humility," she whispered. She looked across the square to where a fleet of cruisers busied themselves ferrying people to and from the mountain top. "Corporal, I thought you said all air travel had been restricted."

He followed her gaze, and sniffed. "I hear the temple has dispensation from the local security commander."

"The temple has much influence in these parts." *Which is why I chose this path into the Palace.* Shayla fought to keep her expression neutral to hide a surge of contempt. *Bad idea to let religion compromise security.*

They walked on in silence for a few moments. Kurt looked across the plaza at the punishment stalls. The hungry glint in his eyes turned her stomach. He caught her eye, hesitant, seemingly on the verge of asking something. She anticipated the question and nodded in the direction of the stalls. "Go ahead."

Kurt grinned and strode across the plaza, rummaging in his pockets.

Shayla followed at a more sedate pace, swallowing back acid. She knew what would be expected of her.

The sparse crowd, mostly pilgrims on their way to the temple, parted before her.

When she caught up with him, Kurt was moving down the line slipping a small coin into each slot in turn. Moans and screams followed him.

He stopped near the end, turning out his pockets with a frown.

"Run out of small change?" Shayla asked.

He nodded, the corners of his mouth downturned.

She tossed him a few coins.

He looked surprised, then delighted. "Eternal thanks, Magister Summis," he spluttered.

"Tribute to the Emperor, vengeance to the Almighty," Shayla intoned, showing that she felt it to be nothing more than her duty to help him.

By now, the onlookers had closed in behind Shayla. Talk stilled, as if in anticipation of sport beyond run-of-the-mill torture. She felt eyes burning into the back of her head as she approached the line of prisoners. She felt alone. Exposed. It was not like an assassin to be the center of attention like this.

She tried to ignore the stench of urine and excrement while she thought. How would Brynwyn behave here? She was sure that Kurt would be taking note of her actions. He may appear to be genial and bumbling, but she had felt him observing her. Who might he be reporting to back at the Palace? If nothing else, people there would be curious about her. She was an unknown from the Provinces taking up a senior public appointment. Whatever she did here, whatever she said, every word, every gesture, would find its way to attentive ears in time.

Shayla started at the far end of the line, scrutinizing each prisoner and reading the placards in front of them. Some met her gaze. Some looked away. Expressions a mixture of pleading, defiance, resignation.

*Theft from a market stall…Insulting the personage of the Emperor…* All petty crimes. One in particular caught her eye though. *Stealing from the Temple collection box.* Brynwyn would not approve of that. She looked at the young woman standing, naked and manacled, before her. She ignored Shayla, murmuring instead to two young children clinging to her.

Shayla sorted through her money and selected a small silver coin. This would be a heavy jolt. Prisoners occasionally died from neural stimulation, despite the safety limits built in, but her briefing notes had been very clear regarding Brynwyn's harsh views on duty and discipline. She had to stay in character.

"Leave my mommy alone!"

Shayla looked down, surprised, at the tiny bundle of fury pummeling her with minute and ineffective fists.

One of the duty guards pulled the child away. He raised his fist to cuff the young boy, but Shayla held up a cautioning finger. The guard bowed his head. "As you wish, Magister Summis."

"You have courage, my son. Be strong," Shayla said. The boy glared back, hatred in his eyes, tears streaking his grimy cheeks.

The woman looked up from the girl, no more than three or four years old, still clinging to her. "I have sinned, My Lady. I am ashamed. But my children need to eat."

Shayla nodded. She studied the woman, noting the sunken cheeks, grey complexion, and ribs showing through her skin. *And so do you.*

A hush descended on the square.

Struggling to quell a tremor running through her whole body, Shayla dropped the coin into the slot.

A dreadful scream rent the air. It tailed off into convulsive sobs, joined by a chorus of wails from the children.

Shayla felt the square spinning around her. She was almost overwhelmed by revulsion at the coin-operated torture she had just inflicted. She gritted her teeth, trying to twist her grimace into thin-lipped satisfaction. *Immerse in the character! Brynwyn was a self-righteous prig.*

A few people cheered. One man stepped forward with a coin in his hand, but stopped short when Shayla whirled round. "Shame on you!" she spat. "All of you!"

It took Shayla a fraction of a second to realize her error. Wouldn't Brynwyn have approved of further punishment? Yes, but Shayla couldn't let this continue.

The crowd fell silent once more, faces showing anger and confusion.

*No! This can work, and remain in character too.* Her mind raced as she saw a way forward. "How can you stand to see this? A woman resorting to stealing to feed her children? This is a holy town. A site of worship. You of all people should help your poor. The collection box at the temple is supposed to be there to help people like this, so they don't need to steal to live."

She surveyed the circle of faces, staring down anyone who dared meet her eyes. "This woman has sinned. She has been punished."

Shayla called the Overseer, who had been hovering at the edge of the crowd. She whipped out her notepad and scrawled briefly on it, then pressed a handful of coins into his palm. "See to it that these children are properly fed and clothed."

He looked blankly at the handful of money.

"I have just lodged a pledge that this gift be used appropriately in the spirit in which it was given," Shayla continued, "witnessed by all people present here. The timestamp will tally with surveillance records. You will ensure that this pledge is honored." The man didn't look overly dishonest, but it never hurt to be sure.

He bowed. "It shall be done, Magister Summis."

"And mercy to the children, for they are your future judges," murmured Kurt, as they walked back across the plaza, completing the quote Shayla had used a few minutes before.

"Amen to that," said Shayla, taken aback. "I'm impressed. That was from the original Mikhael Avantis edition."

Kurt nodded. "Most people misquote it as 'for they are your future.' It rather loses its meaning like that."

"Go and see if the car's ready," Shayla said. She didn't want to get into a religious discussion right now. "And make sure that heathen wretch of a porter has loaded all my baggage safely."

Shayla fought to catch her breath as she stepped from the cool of the large air cruiser into the midday furnace heat of Prandis Braz.

True to his word, Kurt had driven them at breakneck speed to Sho Min Barza to meet a commercial cruiser. They'd spent the last ten hours chasing the sun, hopping from city to city along the Bay of Jorka. In the perpetual noon sleep eluded her, despite the prime seating her privileged rank had secured for her.

Sleep-deprived, half-crazed from the effort of maintaining her disguise, the short drive from the landing field on the outskirts of the city was a confused jumble of images. Two massive defensive batteries, part of a ring encircling the city, loomed over opposite corners of the field. A long avenue, pools and fountains playing down the center. Narrow and crowded streets, buildings pressing in on either side. A bustling market.

The car emerged into a wide and almost empty plaza. The abrupt transition was unsettling, the scale of the space difficult to gauge at first. Shayla squinted, and decided that the plaza must be a mile from end to end, and half that in width.

She cursed herself for allowing her attention to lapse.

The walls of the Mosaic Palace stretched across the far side of the plaza, a geometric facade of pillars, arches, and windows. The hypnotic rhythm of fine detail was punctuated by three wide balconies, each a hundred and fifty yards across, hanging valleys in mountains of masonry. Through these gaps in the mathematically precise arrangement of the frontage, a glimpse of walls and angles, jumbled roofs and domes, hinted at a less orderly plan beyond.

In the middle was the State Balcony, from which the Emperor greeted his subjects on holidays and special occasions. Seeing it in person, it looked at once bigger and yet less impressive than the media images, plain stone, empty, unadorned by trappings of pomp and the Imperial presence.

Shayla dried her hands on her robes. Sweat tickled the small of her back.

At either end of the square, two porticos towered above the surrounding buildings. Each was a colossus of columns and polished granite. Kurt angled the car towards the eastern portico. "Staff entrance," he said with a grin. "Guests to the Palace use the west gate half a mile thataway." He waved a hand towards the other end of the Palace.

The archway loomed a hundred feet or more over their heads, flanked by smaller openings, and framed by the massive bases of soaring pillars. As they drew level with the Palace walls, Shayla glimpsed a deep trench separating the walls from the vast and empty expanse of the plaza. A high balustrade kept people safely away from the drop. Along its length, blackened focusing domes of particle beam weapons rose like a row of silent, helmeted sentries.

As they entered the shadow of the archway, an armored sergeant strode out to meet them and Kurt stopped the car. While Kurt conversed with the sergeant, Shayla studied her surroundings. They were in a tall tunnel a hundred yards in length. Daylight beckoned at the far end, but heavy blast doors ahead and behind could be dropped in seconds. The walls were lined, not with stone, but with a dull, burnished refractory material.

The nape of Shayla's neck prickled. She recognized a defensive killing field when she saw one.

She knew her passkey would be scanned. The challenge this time would be thorough, not the superficial checks she'd passed so far. This was the first serious test of her adopted identity, and there would be no escape if she failed.

The sergeant stepped back from the car. His eyes narrowed as he fixed Shayla with a cold stare. He cocked his head slightly to one side, seeming to be listening to some private conversation.

*They must be scanning me.* Shayla fought to control her breathing and heartbeat. She was sure that remote monitors would be checking her life-signs as well as her electronic identity.

*I must stay in control.*

Shayla cleared her mind and focused on the memory of her home world. Cold fury calmed her — a feeling familiar from many years of careful nurturing. She met the sergeant's gaze, and felt a small measure of confidence return when he looked uncomfortable and lowered his eyes.

She breathed a silent sigh when the sergeant saluted Kurt and signaled him to drive on.

*I'm in!* She could hardly believe it. So much planning. So many dangers along the way. But another milestone passed. Another step closer to her goal.

After the dense bustle of the streets of Prandis Braz, and the eerie emptiness of the plaza in front of the Palace, this was another world again. Busy, but not crowded. Activity calm and purposeful, rather than frenetic. Every person a tiny cog in a vast and well-ordered machine.

This place reeked of millennia of tradition. Architecture and decoration unlike anything she'd seen outside of history texts. Some of these buildings may well have been standing even before Eloon was populated. Guards in the latest armor brushed shoulders with servants in costumes so antiquated that Shayla had to stifle a giggle.

She couldn't tell for sure whether they drove on a street, or through a long and irregular courtyard. They passed walls and buildings that seemed to have been strewn across the ground. Towering walls closed in, then opened out again as they turned a corner. Alert once more from the rush of adrenalin, Shayla drank in the details. Hiding places, escape routes, points of ambush.

It was a few seconds before she realized that Kurt was giving her a running commentary as they drove. "That's the back of the State apartments, where high ranking guests are housed," he was saying. "Looks a lot more impressive from the other side." They passed under an archway. "And over here's the barracks, where lowly guards like me live." The open courtyards closed in again to become a maze of narrow alleyways. Shaded canyons in cliffs of stone. "Store rooms…staff quarters…that's for junior staff. Your quarters are further on and much more comfortable."

At last Kurt pulled over in front of a flight of steps leading up to a wide porch.

"Palace kitchens over there," he said, pointing to the building opposite. "Very important. Worth getting to know the folks in there if you value your stomach." He leapt out of the car and opened the door for her. "Palace administration offices. Your new boss gave me instructions to bring you straight here." He started up the steps.

Shayla hesitated, half out of the car. "But I'm still in my traveling clothes. Shouldn't I at least bathe and change first?"

"No time. 'Straight here,' she said, and I'm not one to argue with Mabbwendig ap Terlion."

Shayla cursed inwardly, but was careful not to let her feelings show. She was hot, tired, and dirty from her journey, something her employer would have been well aware of. This was a deliberate and clumsy attempt to disadvantage her and put the poor provincial girl in her place.

Well, she would give these Imperials a lesson in dignity.

She stepped out of the car, straightened her robes, and squared her shoulders. With her face expressionless and her head held high, she walked steadily up the steps behind Kurt.

At the top of the steps, a row of huge glass doors stood open, leading into an echoing foyer. Bare stone seemed to soak all warmth out of the air. The center of the floor was inlaid with the Imperial crest, over thirty feet across, colors muted, stones polished and worn from the passage of countless feet over many centuries.

Their feet clattered across the floor, and although the space imposed a sense of calm it was not entirely silent. An undercurrent of noise and distant activity enveloped them. A faint whisper of a hundred conversations. Robes swishing, footfalls, doors opening and closing, and a low hum of machinery.

Straight ahead, a wide flight of stone stairs rose, then split left and right to join the lowest of five galleries running around the walls. Looking straight up, Shayla saw a circle of tall windows admitting shafts of light high overhead, surmounted by the inside of a plain white dome.

Kurt waved at a surly commissionaire prowling behind a shining rosewood counter that ran almost half the length of the left-hand wall. "Magister bin Covin for Magister ap Terlion," he called. The commissionaire nodded and waved in the direction of the stairs.

At the top of the stairs, a row of archways separated the gallery from a long corridor running into the depths of the building to their right. Shayla had no time to register anything more than a fleeting impression of polished oak floorboards, statues and vases in the distance, and stern portraits looking down at her, before hurrying after Kurt.

She followed him past two stone-faced sentries into a brightly-lit office. A receptionist glanced up from his desk as Kurt approached and spoke in a whisper. He nodded and turned his attention back to the notes he was scribbling on the desktop.

Kurt stepped back alongside Shayla. "We wait."

*More mind games.* Shayla had half expected something like this from her experience so far.

Shayla and Kurt stood patiently for half an hour. To her right, three clerks kept their heads down, studiously busy. A wide archway opened out to another office where at least a dozen more clerks worked. They stole occasional glances her way before resuming work. Their uninterested manner told Shayla that this treatment was nothing more than standard practice. She quelled her elation at this insight. So far, her deception was working.

At length, the receptionist looked down at the corner of his desk and nodded at Kurt. Kurt stepped forward and threw open the doors to the inner office. Shayla followed at a sedate pace. *Two can play at this game.*

A small robed figure sat hunched over a desk. The top was cluttered with scrolls, ornaments, a pile of oldworld books, and a tray of dishes holding the remains of a meal. The office was large, a good fifty feet square, but it felt small and cluttered despite the light flooding in from windows along two sides. Mismatched chairs and tables were strewn around the floor. A tall bookcase stood along one wall, crammed with volumes of all descriptions. Huge and ornate pots, overflowing with greenery, turned the far corner behind the desk into a veritable jungle.

The oppressive atmosphere was heightened by the heat in the room. After the cool of the foyer and outer office it was like entering an oven.

Tiny movements caught Shayla's eyes, and she turned to see a pair of white cats slink around the end of the desk. More cats curled up or stretched out on a chaise longue and several armchairs, in various states of feline repose. Shayla counted at least eight.

The woman still didn't acknowledge her. *So, what was so urgent that I had to be brought straight here?* But Shayla simply said "Brynwyn bin Covin, reporting for duty."

Mabbwendig ap Terlion looked up at last. She slipped out of her chair and stalked around her desk to stand in front of Shayla. She peered close, wrinkling her nose as if Kurt had brought her something deeply distasteful. Shayla gazed coolly back.

She was a diminutive figure, short and wiry. Her dark and deeply lined skin, her long grey hair, tied back from her forehead and gathered in thick braids down her back, bespoke great and unguessable age. But her eyes glowed fiercely and she seemed to radiate boundless energy. She prowled around Shayla, examining her minutely as she went.

Shayla held herself still. Not stiffly at attention, but exuding calm self-control. She followed the tiny scarecrow figure as best she could without moving her head.

"Duty, is it?" Mabbwendig rasped. "Is it duty that keeps you in the provinces so long? You are needed here. Not hobnobbing with wastrel monks."

Shayla knew this would be an intolerable insult to the devout Brynwyn. She stiffened, but kept silent.

Mabbwendig carried on muttering to herself as she continued her inspection. "Now Artur Stiles knew about duty. Gave his sanity in service to his Emperor, he did." Finally she stopped in front of Shayla again and glared up at her as if she were the root of all the Empire's problems. "So this is the great bin Covin? The one the High Prefect of Toomin Barza recommends so highly? The provincial upstart who will teach us city folk how to organize things?"

Shayla decided it was time to break silence. "If you are recanting your own good judgment, then I will gladly return to Toomin Barza forthwith in favor of someone more fitting for Imperial service," she said, in cold and aloof tones. She was rewarded with a brief flicker of panic in the depths of Mabbwendig's eyes, and pressed home the advantage. "I was informed that my first engagement would be the entertainment for Heads of Family visiting next month. That left ample time for fitting observance to the higher power that vests the Emperor with his holy authority."

"Have you not heard the news?" Mabbwendig looked shocked. "Terrorists at work, here on Magentis. Dark days, dark days," she muttered.

"I had heard of such," Shayla said distantly, as if such things were beneath her concern. "What of it?"

"But they have been caught. There will be a burning next week."

Shayla kept her surprise to herself. *Who do they think they've caught?*

Mabbwendig's eyes were shining again. She continued prancing around Shayla, talking rapidly. "Much work to do. Yes, yes. Emperor will expect a grand show to celebrate his greatness. Oh yes. Much celebration for his triumph over the darkness that surrounds us. Little time. Very little time. You work."

She stopped in front of Shayla once more. "All the briefing material is waiting for you in your Palace workspace. Little time. You must go. Attend to your duty."

She turned to Kurt, doing her best to look down her nose at him from a clear foot disadvantage in height. "Scriven, show the new Master of Circuses to her office." Kurt showed no expression at being addressed in such a derogatory manner. Mabbwendig sniffed. "Then show her to her chambers. Much in need of cleaning before she sullies these offices further, I think."

She turned her back on them with a dismissive wave. Shayla took her cue, and turned to leave with just the merest bob of her head in deference to protocol.

⸻

Kurt led them along the corridor, past the row of arches leading back to the entrance lobby, feet clacking on the hardwood floor.

"You've just been inducted by Mad Mabb," he said cheerfully. "Don't read too much into it. She gives all newcomers hell, just to make it clear who's boss."

*You don't say!*

They passed another corridor to their left, with daylight in the distance, then doors on either side. An open stairwell to the right. More doors.

"This is your domain," said Kurt, leading them around the corner at a T-junction. Shayla glanced over her shoulder as she followed, catching a glimpse of another bewildering perspective of light and shadow vanishing into the distance. "The offices of the Master of Circuses." He stopped outside a door at the end of the passageway, and gestured to Shayla to enter.

She took a deep breath and pushed open the door. As she entered a long and windowless anteroom, an elderly man hurried round from behind a desk to meet her. The sound of voices drifted in from a sliding door, half open, to her right. They seemed to be in heated discussion, now raised, now hushed and urgent.

Kurt stepped to her side. "Magister Brynwyn bin Covin, allow me to present your personal administrative aide, Colin Bandolini."

"Magister bin Covin, I am honored to offer my services," he said, bowing. While he waited, he puffed his cheeks and pursed his lips, making his long waxed moustache and pointed beard quiver.

Shayla tore her eyes from the dancing streamers of glistening hair. She ignored the door where the sounds of argument had suddenly stilled, and strode over to an open door to her left.

"Your office, Magister," said Colin, leaping forward with arms flailing in his rush to usher Shayla through the door.

She suppressed a smile at the sudden animation. "Thank you, Colin."

Shayla froze. Behind Colin's desk, the wall was a patchwork of images, feeds from a number of vantage points in the Palace, together with reports, graphs, figures, and newscasts. One of them caught her eye. It showed a scene she recognized, the town square at Hawflun. She pointed. "That feed. Quickly!"

Colin fumbled with a stylus and the image expanded to cover the wall. The accompanying audio filled the air around them.

"Last night a massive explosion demolished a group of chalets on the outskirts of Hawflun," the story summary announced, before cutting over to the live commentary from the scene.

"... Completely incinerated. There is no firm death toll at this point, but early estimates are in the region of fifty. Recordings from street monitors will help establish movements in and out of the area and allow a firmer figure to be reached, but this will take some time."

The camera drone lifted and panned, giving a panoramic view of the town. It homed in on the south eastern quarter of the town, where Shayla had stayed three nights ago.

"Security forces have so far refused to comment on the possibility of an escalation in terrorist action right here on Magentis, or on speculation that this involves the Insurrection."

The whole street was gone. Shayla noted the surgical precision of the hole in the ground, still glowing in the pre-dawn gloom. A conventional explosion big enough to blast that hole would have flattened every building in sight and littered the whole town with debris. But just along the road were more dwellings, scorched, windows blown in, but still standing.

It looked suspiciously like the aftermath of a quark detonator. Outwardly, she let her face register the same shock that both Kurt and Colin were showing, but inwardly she smiled to herself. Finn said he had something special in mind.

The reporter was still prattling on about an explosion, willfully oblivious to the evidence in front of his eyes. Not surprising with a State-controlled media. The Security forces would have already briefed them on how to portray this, and Shayla could understand why. In the public imagination, where there was a quark detonator, there would be a quark bomb nearby. A device like that would have vaporized a large part of the mountain and sterilized half the province.

Possibilities like that could make a population edgy.

"Shocking business," Colin muttered.

"But…isn't that where …" Kurt stammered.

"Where you just escorted me from?" Shayla finished for him. "Yes, it is."

She noticed that they had been joined by three more people who had come from the next room.

"I understand there was an Insurrection outrage in Horliath just as I was preparing for Meditation. But that was so far away, and Hawflun is a most holy site. I thought that, at least, would be safe." She shook her head, her face a mask of sadness and disbelief. "There have been many awful things happening on that continent recently. I am happy to be out of there."

Colin tore his eyes away from the scenes of destruction. "Ah! Magister bin Covin, please allow me to introduce some of your members of staff." He waved them closer. "Jojo bin Duvin, the master of event planning, and Willem Skimlok, in charge of event security. And this is one of Jojo's assistants, Colleign ap Scoth."

The three bowed.

"Jojo has made a start on the arrangements surrounding the executions next week. We are all glad you are here to give much-needed guidance."

Jojo was a massive man. Hands twisted in front of him, sweat glistened on his bald scalp, tiny eyes in his smooth face looked pleadingly at Shayla. She was more intrigued by Willem's murderous glare at Colin as he spoke.

"Thank you," Shayla said. "I am pleased to meet you. I understand I have some reading to catch up on, and we have urgent work to do. After the shock of the news we've just heard I need some time to myself, but I would like to see all my senior staff here in two hours time."

They exchanged nervous looks.

"Colin, summon my direct reports for a briefing." She paused, taking a few moments to catch up with the local time zone. "And order food to be brought here from the kitchens. People can't think on empty stomachs."

Colin's eyes widened slightly. "As you wish, My Lady."

———•—•———

Kurt led her back the way they had come, through the echoing hallways of the administration offices. Before they reached the entrance foyer, he turned down the corridor that Shayla had noted before. The daylight at the end flooded in from double doors, standing wide open, which led out onto a bridge. The aerial walkway carried them over a courtyard from the offices and into an adjacent building.

"This is the living quarters for all the senior Palace staff." They passed an airy atrium, then more corridors. These were plush and deeply carpeted. Oak panels, stained with age, and soft yellow lighting added to an air of faded opulence.

Kurt stopped outside a door. "Your quarters, My Lady." A yellowing ivory sign on the door was engraved *Master of Circuses*.

Shayla entered a long sitting room. Tall arched windows at the far end looked out over another courtyard. A solitary fountain played in the middle, surrounded by worn flagstones.

Shayla's baggage had already been brought up, and stood in a neat pile near the doorway.

"If you need any assistance, please let me know. You can reach the Palace net from here and send word to me. There's a ton of reference material to help you find your way around."

"Thank you, Corporal. You've been a most excellent guide and escort." The warmth in Shayla's voice was genuine.

Kurt's neck reddened. As he made to leave, he paused, then turned back to Shayla. "Magister bin Covin, it's not my place to say such things, but…old Scottin was highly regarded by many people in the Palace. His will be a hard pair of shoes to fill. And there may be some who will resent any who would fill them."

Shayla nodded. "Thank you for the warning." She thought a moment. "Kurt, I've heard that Magister Stiles left through ill health, but I've heard nothing more than that. What happened to him?"

Kurt frowned, and when he spoke, it was clear he was choosing his words carefully. "The pressure of this job grew too much for him. Let us say, he found himself trying to serve two masters."

He turned and left before Shayla could ask any more.

## Chapter 16

E xactly two hours after she left Colin, Shayla approached the door
to her office once more. She had timed the walk through the staff
quarters and administration building, intending to set an example for
precision and discipline.

She'd spent the two hours skimming her briefing notes while she
freshened up from the journey. She couldn't accuse Mabbwendig ap
Terlion of exaggeration. There was indeed much to do.

A buzz of conversation stopped as she strode through the sliding
door from the antechamber. She paused on the threshold to survey the
room.

Six people sat around the near end of a long conference table. Three
of them she already knew: Colin, Willem, and Jojo. She was glad to see
her orders had been obeyed. Covered platters and steaming tureens sat
on a side table. Three kitchen staff stood ready, and a surly senior waiter
scowled at the wall opposite.

The wall in question was plastered floor to ceiling with plans, charts,
maps of all scales — the Palace, Prandis Braz, the Plaza — schedules,
lists of instructions, calendars and timetables. Shayla's mind reeled as
she tried to take in nearly a thousand square feet of brightly colored
detail.

She walked to the head of the table, and sat.

"I am Brynwyn bin Covin. By the grace of his Imperial Majesty,
newly appointed Imperial Master of Circuses." She took a deep breath.
"You have your own professional standards and procedures. I have my
own rules. The first rule is this: do not, under pain of instant dismissal,
compare me to Artur Stiles. I am not he. My methods are not his. I
cannot replace him, nor do I intend to."

She scanned the table, looking each person in the eye. Her face was stern. Smiles of greeting faltered as they, each in turn, concluded that this was not someone to cross lightly.

"I've met some of you already. Colin, please complete the introductions."

Colin Bandolini, sitting to her right, jerked upright. "Yes. Yes, of course," he flustered.

He gestured to the woman opposite him, almost knocking over a tall glass with his elbow. "This is Bo Branson, public relations. Bo works with Public Knowledge, and all the media channels. Whatever message needs to go out, Bo will find the right way to get it to the right people at the right time.

"Willem Skimlok you know. Works closely with the Palace Guard, planetary forces, and the Security services to ensure we don't get any unwelcome surprises.

"Jasmine Trove, client relations. If you want to know what Charlotte di Brugui likes for breakfast, or Scipio Firenzi's taste in women—" a few muffled laughs sounded around the table "—ask Jasmine. Likes, dislikes, alliances, enmities, protocols, modes of address, who not to sit next to whom, it is for Jasmine to know, or Jasmine to find out.

"Then we have Jojo, who you've also met. Jojo's office plans everything we do. From menus and seating for banquets, routes for processions, entertainment. Anything that needs planning, buying, arranging, scheduling. Most of the mess on the wall belongs to him."

He turned his head. "Finally, this is Marcus Halley, stage manager, though that title hardly does justice to his role. He has the unenviable task of bringing Jojo's planning to life and making it happen."

Colin looked at Shayla, moustache twitching.

"Colin," she said, "you still have some important people in this room to introduce."

He looked blank. Shayla nodded past his shoulder to the kitchen staff standing patiently at the side of the room.

He turned, eyes wide. "Aah, yes! Of course! Let me see. This is Luke Frendis, in charge of our catering this evening. And...and ..." he stammered, face beaded with sweat.

"Johns, Chartwell, Tipoli," growled Frendis, coming to his rescue. The three waiters bobbed their heads as they heard their names.

"Thank you, Master Frendis," said Shayla.

She clasped her hands and lowered her head in prayer. From the corners of her eyes, she saw her companions give each other startled looks before, one by one, they followed her example.

"By the grace of his Imperial Majesty, the worldly essence of Unity, we give thanks for the food we are about to partake of. We thank Master Frendis and his staff, and the unseen Many who have brought this gift to our table. May the nourishment of the body nourish the soul."

She looked up, and nodded to Frendis. At his signal, the waiters uncovered the dishes and began ladling soup into bowls.

While food was being served, Shayla brought her staff's attention back to the business at hand. "I see we have guests arriving at various times for the Festival of Fountains. The first are due in six days' time, and they will need to be entertained. The highlights are at Henriss Garden starting in a little over two weeks from now. The Conclave of Families, the State Banquet, and, of course, the Festival itself."

Shayla looked around the table again. "I assume routine arrangements are already in place for the minor events. I will be interested to see what ideas you have for the main spectacles." Embarrassed expressions and averted eyes told an unpromising tale. She sighed. "In between times, I see we also have a big celebration to arrange, at short notice, around the executions due to take place in just over a week."

---

*Shayla looked down at Matiki, his sleek grey head cradled in the crook of her arm, amber eyes gazing back at her. She knew Matiki was sick, dying, suffering. It didn't seem to matter how she knew, she just did. And she knew she had to end his suffering. The exact logic of it escaped her, but that, too, didn't matter. She just knew. And the knowing made her feel sick.*

*"Be strong," she heard herself say, "I must do this."*

*Matiki looked at her with love and infinite trust, as if he were saying "I know you mean well. I forgive you."*

*Tears streamed down Shayla's cheeks as she picked up the hacksaw ...*

Shayla's eyes flew open. She took a few moments to still the pounding in her chest. The darkness of the room was broken by the softly luminous filigree of a wall clock hanging opposite the open windows.

One of Brynwyn's possessions, and one of the few to show any touch of luxury or ornament. Shayla gazed at the glowing symbols woven into an intricate geometric background. At first, the alien words in provincial dialect failed to register, and she felt a wrenching disconnect from her surroundings, as if she were still struggling from a dream state.

Her mind scrabbled for a fingerhold on time and place, seeking stability in a sea of uncertainty.

*Calm!* Shayla ran through a quick litany she'd used for many years to anchor her self-identity while working under cover.

There was Shayla Carver, the bedrock, the core of her being, hidden under so many layers of subterfuge. She mentally reconstructed those layers, like applying theatrical makeup and costume.

Shayla the Firenzi assassin, a small cog in the machinery of one of humanity's most powerful families. Trained to work under cover. Trained to kill. Placed by the Firenzi Special Service into the ranks of one of their deadliest ideological foes as ...

Shark, the Insurrection agent, in turn posing as Brynwyn bin Covin, loyal Imperial servant.

Shark was assigned to worm her way close enough to the Emperor to kill him and turn the reins of power over to the Insurrection. Shayla the Firenzi was supposed to subvert that plan at the last minute and hand the Emperor over to her masters to force an abdication. And Shayla Carver? She had her own plans for revenge. The Emperor would die, but first he had to understand what was happening to him and everything he had built.

Her mental edifice whole once more, the symbols on the clock became familiar and meaningful.

*Sheesh! How long since I last had that dream?*

For three years after the burning of Eloon, Shayla's nights had been the stalking ground of ghosts and phantasms, of endless dark labyrinths and impossible acts of cruelty. Many were so extreme as to be almost laughable in the light of day, but the worst were those that verged on terrifying reality, almost normality, with some sick twist of dream-logic to tease her sleeping awareness.

She had known that Brandt, two years younger, was equally tormented. They often talked about it in the long nights, comforting each other. How many times had she and Brandt pulled each other back from the brink of insanity?

Then she and Brandt made a pact. Impossibly foolhardy, the stuff of childhood fancy. Together they would take on the Empire.

The nightmares stopped.

———•—•———

The first blush of dawn crept through the windows behind Shayla. Her office was unlit and cold. Enormously thick walls of the ancient buildings soaked up the worst excesses of the sub-tropical glare of day. At night, any residual warmth drained from the air. She had been sitting here for an hour, cloak drawn close around her, gazing into the darkness.

As the first blinding sliver of pink flared across the wall opposite her, Shayla tapped a stylus on her desktop. The polished ceramic surface cleared.

*I need to gain the Emperor's trust, and this appointment is my way to reach him.* Shayla frowned. *But to do that, I have to make a success of this appointment.*

That first evening had seemed promising enough, there were plenty of ideas for the long program of events they had to stage. But she'd spent the whole of yesterday pushing past the superficial gloss, the high level plans, looking for substance. Again and again, arguments broke out over ideas, details, practicalities. Differences and divisions ran deep, both between her senior staff and amongst their own subordinates.

*Crap. This isn't going to be so easy.*

Her whole staff was in a shocking state of disarray. Right now, they were incapable of planning anything. They worked with a will, but utterly ineffectively.

Shayla's stomach felt like ice. Did Brynwyn understand what she'd taken on?

She shook her head in irritation, then kneaded throbbing temples with her fingertips. She'd forgotten how tiring it was to keep up a disguise with her implants.

She blinked furiously and focused once more on the empty desktop.

*If I can't turn this mess around, I'm done.*

Had this pushed Stiles over the brink of madness? It must be hard satisfying the whims of a tyrant when every tiny decision was a protracted battle.

*No pissing around here. I need to stop the rot.*

Shayla scrawled names randomly across the desktop — Colin Bandolini, Jojo bin Duvin, Willem Skimlok, Marcus Halley, Bo Bransom, Jasmine Trove. Around them she clustered assistants and subordinates, those she had met or heard of, anyway. She started drawing lines between them, colored to show events, moods, relationships, alliances, and conflicts. Plenty of conflicts.

She heard movement outside and stiffened, then relaxed as she recognized the voices of Colin and Jojo in the outer office.

The spiders web grew. One name stood out, enmeshed in angry red. She was not surprised by the picture it painted, but the clarity was startling.

"Colin!" she called.

Colin Bandolini appeared in the doorway, ungainly arms flapping as he balanced on the balls of his feet, performing a remarkable impression of a man teetering on the brink of a cliff.

"Good morning, My Lady. I didn't realize you were here already. Shall I order coffee for you?"

"In a minute," Shayla said, trying hard to conceal a smile despite her fatigue. "First have a look at this."

He stood over the desk, rocking back and forth on his feet, cheeks puffing. "Interesting technique. I've seen pictures like this before ..."

Shayla waited. "Please tell me if I am jumping to conclusions here," she prompted at last.

Colin Bandolini looked troubled. "Security is a most important part of any event we stage. The safety of many important people are at stake. For all his faults, Willem does know his job."

*And even you are scared of him!*

———•+•———

Willem Skimlok stood in front of Shayla's desk, fidgeting.

Shayla reclined in her chair, gazing at her notepad.

He coughed. She pretended to ignore him. *You are too sure of yourself for my liking.*

Shayla recalled Kurt's words about Artur Stiles. How had Skimlok behaved towards him? Was he one of the factors that had driven Stiles out of his mind?

A low growl of exasperation and a tiny movement seen from the corner of her eye. Without looking up, Shayla barked, "I have not dismissed you, Skimlok."

"As you wish, Magister." His tone oozed insolence.

She let him stew a few more minutes. Then, "I've been studying your record." The statement was flat, no hint of either approval or censure. Shayla turned and looked him in the eye. "You are a competent security supervisor."

"Thank you, My Lady."

"But you are not content with that."

He frowned. "I don't follow."

"You are undermining and disrupting the work of every other member of this office. You are off my team."

He snorted. Then he laughed, shaking his head. Strands of greasy hair plastered themselves across his cheeks. "You don't mean that."

"Yes, I do."

The laughter died. He scowled, leaning over Shayla with balled fists planted on her desk. "I don't think you quite understand how things work around here."

"Quite frankly, I don't care." She whipped out of her chair, brushed one hand away, unbalancing him, and pinned him to the desk. He struggled briefly, then stilled as the keen edge of Shayla's knife grazed his neck.

"You think me a naive Provincial, don't you?" Shayla's mind raced as Willem mumbled a denial. *Shit! I'm too tired for this.* Her heart sank. She had reacted instinctively as Shayla, not as Brynwyn. Again. *I don't have time to fuck with this creep.*

In less than a heartbeat, she knew what to say. "Life is hard in a northern fishing town. You learn to look after yourself and to take no nonsense from bullies. I have a duty to my Emperor and you will not stand in my way." Shayla's voice was cold. She leaned close. "You've already given me more than adequate cause to have you tried for treason," she murmured. "Learn this well. I am *not* Artur Stiles, and *this* is how things work around here now."

———•—•———

The summons came quicker than Shayla expected. Barely an hour after Skimlok had left, muttering threats under his breath, she was back in Mabbwendig's office.

The air was as stifling as it had been two days ago. There was no waiting in the outer office this time. Mad Mabb was in too much of a hurry to bother with the niceties of psychological abuse.

"You prance in like the Shal-heil ..." Mabb spluttered. Shayla puzzled for a second, searching her mind for the undoubtedly insulting reference. Shal-heil? The evening desert wind? Flighty. Hot. Bringing no relief from the day's sun. *Aah! Late and useless!*

"Make Mabbwendig and whole Palace wait on your precious *meditations.* You have no respect for Palace. Nor Emperor, I think. What Grand Duke saw to recommend you, I know not."

*Hmm. What interest does the Emperor's uncle have in Brynwyn?*

"Ten thousand years these walls have stood. Traditions old beyond your paltry wit to understand. Who you think you are? Red-faced *fishlander,* coming here upstart-nose-in-the-air to teach us new ways like we know *nothing?*"

Shayla wondered how long Brynwyn would have put up with this. *Big conflict between pride and duty.* A part of her felt the turmoil in Brynwyn's character. *Good. Gives me plenty of leeway while still appearing natural.*

"We have *rules* here. Not some lawless backwater."

*Just give me the right opening.*

Mabbwendig prowled up and down in front of Shayla, momentarily lost for words. Shayla had remained silent throughout the tirade, conscious of the unseen audience beyond the still-open office door. She was sure Mabbwendig had deliberately arranged for it to be left open. Public humiliation seemed to be her stock in trade, but that suited Shayla fine. She allowed the silence to lengthen, awaiting her chance.

"You not been here but two days. How can you possibly make such judgment in such short time?"

"Do I, or do I not, have authority to make staffing decisions within my own department?" Shayla's voice rang clear as a bell through the momentary lull.

At once Mabbwendig sensed her mistake. "Yes, of course, but ..."

"Then I will not waste your valuable time with further discussion. You have no need to remind me how much there is to do in such a short time, and I'm sure you are equally busy."

Shayla turned on her heel and strode out of the office, leaving Mabb spluttering behind her, mouth working in rage.

———•◆•———

Back in her office, Shayla sat at her desk deep in thought. Colin was right, she needed an event security manager. She had also upset one of the most powerful people in the Palace, next to the Emperor himself.

She wondered about Mabbwendig's reaction. It seemed out of all proportion to a simple case of overstepped boundaries. Mabb was a bully and a despot. She liked to hold the reins of power over every aspect of Palace staff life, and yet Shayla had been careful to check that she was exercising her prerogative.

*Skimlok was Mabb's spy in the camp!* The revelation hit like a plasma bolt. *That's why he held such sway in this office.*

It also explained why Mabb was so furious at his dismissal. That made up Shayla's mind. She needed more than a security manager. She needed a friend. And she needed someone who would not be intimidated.

"Colin," she called, "please send word that I would speak with Corporal Kurt Weiler of the Palace Guard."

## Chapter 17

Shayla joined a flood of people streaming into the cavernous staff dining room. A wall of sound, the voices of hundreds of people, seemed to squeeze her chest. The air was heavy with the remnants of the day's heat and the scent of cooked meats steeped in pungent sauces. The senses combined to form a suffocating blanket around Shayla's head.

*Am I doing the right thing?* Her eyes burned from fatigue, but there was no turning back. After Shayla's brush with Mabbwendig yesterday, she knew she could no longer put off this moment.

She emerged half-way down one side of the vast hall. Three rows of long tables stretched away left and right, broken by an aisle ahead of her which led to the center of the room. Three more rows of tables filled the far side. To her right, a more lavishly appointed table sat apart, under the frowning portrait of Emperor Julian Skamensis.

Colin Bandolini had explained why Shayla's request to have food brought to the office on that first evening had been met with surprise. Although there was officially nothing against it, she had breached another unwritten rule of Mad Mabb's regime. There appeared to be no order to the seating in the thronged dining hall. Robes and uniforms showed a mixture of ranks and professions. But each place setting on the top table was labeled with a faded card. Shayla knew there would be one that read 'Master of Circuses'. Brynwyn bin Covin was *expected* to be there.

Shayla spotted the rotund figure of Jojo bin Duvin on the far side of the room. She turned her back on the high table and walked over to him. As she crossed the open space in the center of the room, the hairs on her neck prickled. A lull in conversation seemed to follow her.

That she had continued to eat in her office these past two days had been a simple matter of practicality. There was too much work to do. To the ever-observant Palace gossip mill, it had appeared an act of defiance, but to persist would soon be seen as an act of fear. That last piece of analysis had come from Kurt. She needed to face Mabb once more on Mabb's own turf.

As she sat next to Jojo, she looked around and caught glimpses of hastily-averted eyes. She also noted that many of her own staff had congregated in this corner, as far from the high table as possible.

Bo Branson sat across from Shayla and Jojo. Kurt Weiler approached from the other side of the room and sat next to Bo.

A bell chimed, and a hush descended on the gathering.

"Now the fun begins," Jojo muttered to Shayla.

The diminutive figure of Mabbwendig ap Terlion, Master of the Emperor's Domestic Household, appeared in a doorway near the far end of the hall. As she took her seat in the center of the top table, one of her Heads of Staff leaned over and whispered in her ear. Eyes turned towards Shayla.

Mabb smiled, slow and predatory. "So, Master of Circuses finally graces us with her presence." Her eyes glittered in the light streaming from windows set high in the wall behind Shayla. "Methought our company too poor for Her Provincial Highness."

Muted laughter swept the room; angry warmth crept up Shayla's cheeks. She remained silent, but half-stood and bobbed her head in Mabb's direction. The minimal show of deference would not be lost on the Palace functionaries.

Mabb's nostrils flared, but Shayla had not quite given her cause for a public reprimand. Instead Mabb clapped her hands and shrieked, "Food!"

Shayla recognized the senior waiter, Luke Frendis, standing behind Mabb's table, looking like he'd bitten a lemon. The serving staff watched Luke, clearly waiting for his signal. His eyes were on Shayla. He tilted his chin slightly at her.

*Dammit! What's he playing at?*

The silence deepened, broken when Mabb twisted her head around and yelled, "Scriven! Start serving." Spittle flew from her quivering lips.

The slap of Shayla's hand on the table broke the silence. All faces turned towards her as she stood. She knew what Brynwyn would do here, what Luke Frendis was waiting for, but her stomach knotted as she thought how Mabbwendig might react.

"Are we all swine at a trough?" Her voice carried to every corner of the room. "Is gratitude so impoverished here?"

She bowed her head and clasped her hands in front of her. Without waiting to see if anyone followed her lead, Shayla said, "From sea to cloud to rainfall, from field to crop to table, we take from the earth and we give back to it. In the circle of life we are united, and we offer thanks for the life-giving gifts brought to our table today. May the nourishment of the body nourish the soul."

She glanced at Luke Frendis, who gave the tiniest nod. As one, the army of serving staff began weaving in and out of the tables with heaped platters.

As she sat, Shayla glimpsed Mabb's flushed face and gimlet glare.

*I can't afford all-out war, I just need to show I won't be intimidated.* But with quickening pulse Shayla realized this battle was far from over.

She picked at her food, appetite gone, while she took stock of her situation.

Following Skimlok's dismissal yesterday, and her clash with Mabbwendig, she had called her staff together. Nearly fifty people had crowded into the conference room. Others had been woken, or had work or meals interrupted, to view the proceedings from site offices around the planet while she announced what had happened that morning.

At first, she had been met with a mixture of disbelief, trepidation, and some anger. Who was she to march in and make such changes? *Only the new boss, that's who!* But, unlike Mabbwendig, she needed these people on her side.

Despite the almost impossible deadlines looming, she had set aside all thoughts of work for the day. She had spent the remainder of the day and long into last night reviewing how her staff worked. Each individual in the room, the planners, designers, researchers, and assistants, had talked through their role, what they contributed and what they needed from each other.

Shayla said little, asking questions occasionally, but otherwise content to let them talk. As the day wore on, she felt the mood in the room start to change. The fear, the dread of failure, evaporated to be replaced by an undercurrent of excitement at the task ahead.

Today had gone well. Up until now.

They still had a Herculean challenge to meet, but the team had their directions and were finally starting to make progress, free from the poisonous influence of Willem Skimlok. But if Mabbwendig chose to interfere, all this progress could be for nothing. Once more, Shayla questioned her decision to venture into this snake pit.

From time to time, Mabb's voice rose above the hubbub. "Yama, hair looks like rats' tails."

A wide-eyed girl looked like she'd been slapped. She stared at Mabbwendig, lower lip trembling. A lustrous river of immaculately-groomed hair hung to her waist.

"Shave it off." Mabb waved her hand dismissively. "Farouk, rose beds in Fountain Court are a disgrace. Tomorrow, you personally inspect and groom each plant. Emperor must have beauty to look on while he works."

A few minutes later, "Shiveh, any little ones to bless yet?" Mabb's voice dripped honey.

Bo Branson grimaced. In response to Shayla's questioning look, she whispered, "Shiveh has just miscarried."

"Again," Jojo added. "Mabb would have known that."

A waiter removed Shayla's barely-touched plate, and returned with a dish of mousse molded in the shape of a swan.

"Is it always like this?" Shayla asked Jojo.

He frowned. "She normally picks on more people, but her barbs cut unusually deep tonight."

Mabbwendig looked up from her plate. Her eyes roved across the sea of faces like a hawk surveying a meadow. "Time for music, I think." Her face creased into a smile. "Tanya."

Jojo groaned under his breath. "Poor Tanya. Not again."

A young woman at the next table stood. Shayla's eyes narrowed. She recognized her, a clerk from Colin's staff. Her red skin and rounded features suggested a Traplinki provincial. Like Brynwyn.

Even from where she sat, Shayla could see her tremble. Tanya faced the head table, tears welling in her eyes.

"What? New Master of Circuses not taught you to sing yet?" Mabb shook her head. "Sad times. How she make spectacle fit for Emperor when own staff not sing?"

Shayla looked along the rows of people filling the hall. *Is nobody going to speak out?* Some faces showed glee or anticipation. Some people whistled and stamped their feet. But many eyes were downcast, haunted, shamed. Relieved not to be the focus of attention themselves.

"Or maybe voice hoarse today?" Mabb's mouth twisted in glee. "If you want out, I set a bail at—" she pursed her lips "—fifty francs."

Some people gasped. Others cheered. The bestial din grew.

Shayla turned to Bo Branson. "Can she pay that?"

"Her husband died last year. She has young children. She cannot pay."

"She can't sing either," Jojo whispered.

Tanya edged into the center of the hall, one reluctant step after another, each step accompanied by jeers and catcalls.

"Hold!" Shayla stood. With a jerk of her head, she motioned Tanya to sit. "If my staff's talents displease you, I pay this *bail* from my own purse."

Mabb snarled as Tanya scuttled back to her seat. "*Fishlanders* swim together, hmm?" Her lips formed a thin line. "We still need entertainment, Master of *Circuses.*"

"That, I will provide." Shayla leaned across the table to Bo Branson. "Access the public music library for me."

Bo's scroll appeared from the depths of her sleeve. She unrolled it on the table.

"Find 'The Serpent's Passing' from *The Dragon Prince.*"

Jojo smiled. "My favorite opera."

"Be ready to send it to the dining room's public address when I say so." Shayla removed her boots and threw off her heavy robes, to reveal leggings and a close-fitting tunic.

A lieutenant sitting nearby in full ceremonial regalia leered at her. With a murmured "Thanks," Shayla leaned over and relieved the startled soldier of his short sword. She held it in her right hand, appraising the balance. The gleaming weapon was anything but ceremonial. With her left hand, she drew her own knife.

Shayla strode to the center of the hall, and nodded to Bo. She stood, barefoot and head bowed, with the blades crossed over her heart.

The first chords of the aria filled the room like a distant lament carried on the wind across a wilderness of ice.

Shayla slowly slid her left foot up to her thigh, while spreading her arms wide, blades outstretched.

All grace and perfect balance, her raised leg extended behind while her arms closed in again, drawing the points of the weapons down her body.

Shayla had chosen one of the more dance-like routines in her martial repertoire. It would not do to advertise her full mastery of the Shohan Calinda, but she hoped this would not arouse comment. *The Palm Tree...lean forward into the Hawk, then the Cobra, back to the Hawk...* She recited the set poses, letting the sequence unfold from years of training as the lyrics sang of the poison coursing through the doomed Serpent's veins, and the agony of his awakening.

*And hold...ready for the acrobatics ...*

Three forward flips and Shayla planted her feet in a wide fighting stance. The languid grace of the stylized poses gone, she was now the hunter, circling the room. Her blades were fangs seeking their prey.

*Slash left, slash right, right again...* The sword and the knife weaved patterns about Shayla's body. She was oblivious to her audience now, fully immersed in the dance, and the story of betrayal and quest for revenge.

The music's tempo quickened. The sword spun in the air above Shayla's head while the knife pointed an accusing finger of steel at Mabb.

Shayla leaped and pirouetted from one side of the central aisle to the other. She whirled ever closer to the high table, blades an almost invisible blur about her face. She now danced mere feet from Mabb, who sat wide-eyed with palms down on the tabletop as if she were pushing herself away from the dervish in front of her.

As the music climaxed, on the final beat, the knife and the sword flew from Shayla's hands and buried themselves an inch from Mabb's outstretched fingertips.

Mabb flinched but, to her credit, didn't snatch her hands away.

Shayla stood, head bowed once more, breathing hard. The healing wound in her shoulder screamed at her in protest. She swayed, fighting to bring the room back into focus.

A handclap echoed through her mind. Another. And another, slow and rhythmic.

She squeezed her eyes shut. She was being mocked. Her throat tightened.

"Bravo!" She recognized Kurt's voice behind her. Other pairs of hands joined in, growing, filling the air with a thunderous cadence. *In this culture, a slow handclap is a sign of respect.* Shayla's mission preparation reasserted itself. All the cultural differences she'd absorbed settled once more into the forefront of her awareness. She breathed again and lifted her head.

As Shayla leaned forward to retrieve the blades, Mabbwendig murmured, "You full of surprises, Master of Circuses."

"The Knife Dance is a holy and private meditation," Shayla whispered. "You know traditions. You must know that to commission it for public spectacle commands a blood price."

Mabb opened her mouth, then closed it again and swallowed hard. As Shayla pulled the weapons from the tabletop, Mabbwendig's veined hands trembled.

———•◆•———

Shayla slumped at her desk and rubbed her eyes.

She opened them to see Colin Bandolini standing opposite her, lips pursed and cheeks puffed. Her heart pounded against her ribs, and it took an effort of will to keep her hand from drawing her knife. *How in Space did he creep up on me like that?*

"I see you've introduced yourself to the heads of the Palace administration."

"Yes." Shayla had spent many hours prowling the labyrinth of the office buildings. "Thank you for your guidance on who's who in the hierarchy."

She'd also started to find her way around the sprawling Palace itself. Centuries of expansion, renovation, and rebuilding had established a warren of buildings clustering around courts and gardens, and filling in the spaces between ancient landmarks. After her performance last evening, her public clash of wills with Mabbwendig, Shayla took careful note of people's reactions to her. She watched their faces, their body language, and especially their eyes.

Many were distant, reserved. She was a target for Mabbwendig's wrath and dangerous to associate with.

Some tried to hide calculating hostility beneath excessive charm. Mabbwendig's allies. People to watch.

But the most interesting reaction was from her own staff. They seemed energized. The offices in her corner of the administration building hummed with activity today.

She tapped her stylus on the desk. The surface cleared. A sheaf of progress reports appeared. Shayla skimmed them. "Colin, let the staff know that, from now on, anyone working late is welcome to dine in the conference room."

Colin's moustache twitched.

"Please make the necessary arrangements with Master Frendis."

The merest hint of a smile played across Colin's face. "Yes, My Lady."

Shayla crossed the plaza away from the Palace. The bustling warren of Prandis Braz engulfed her, yet the crowds parted magically in front of her. Her clothing announced her rank, and the inhabitants of the city were endowed with a keen sense of self-preservation.

Watchful soldiers in Imperial livery patrolled the streets. Stalls of all kinds lined the edges of the broad thoroughfares. Produce, fish, meat, trinkets, clothing, furniture. Everywhere had an air of moderate afflu-ence. But off the main streets, Shayla noted dark and cluttered alley-ways, narrow, heaped with garbage. She fancied she could smell rotting vegetables beneath pungent spices and citrus tangs. The gloss on this city was only skin deep.

Occasional ground cars inched their way through the crush of people, reminding Shayla of her arrival with Kurt.

Not for the first time, she wondered about her decision to appoint him. Since her dance in the dining room, he'd been a goldmine of infor-mation about everything to do with the intrigues of Palace life.

Yesterday evening, Kurt had given her a tour of the public rooms bordering the northern sides of the famous Fountain Court. They tra-versed the echoing vastness of the Green Throne Room, peeked inside the Concert Hall, the Banquet Hall, and some of the lavishly appointed State and Drawing Rooms. They returned to the administrative building through a network of underground passageways. "Don't try this without a guide," Kurt said with a grin. "You could be lost for days before you find your way back to the surface."

Shayla decided this was not the time to mention that she'd already studied and memorized the schematics of huge sections of the subter-ranean labyrinth. She felt she could have found her way around this region in the dark.

Kurt's appointment seemed to have been a good choice, but for once Shayla had trouble explaining what led her to it. It seemed obvious. Instinctive.

*Instinct is good…*Shayla had lost count of the times her instinct had saved her life…*but it's colored by emotions.*

*I must detach myself. He's as dead as the rest of them.* Shayla shook off the cold knot that had formed in her stomach. It seemed like she'd been in the Palace for months, but when she counted back, she realized it had been only five days. She was enjoying what felt like a return to real life for the first time since her arrival here.

And she had work to do.

She checked the directions on her notepad, and found Frendis Avenue cutting a swathe through the market stalls.

A little way along, aloof from the hubbub of everyday commerce, Dognoty's coffee shop stretched for a hundred yards along the avenue, with tables and parasols spilling out into the street under the spread of cherry trees.

As Shayla stepped into the tiled foyer, a uniformed waiter spotted her robes of office and hurried forward to meet her.

"Please to follow me, Magister Summis," he fawned, ushering Shayla into a roped off section in the centre of the frontage. "I don't believe we've had the pleasure of your custom before."

*Observant!* But not really a surprise. Shayla was sure the staff here would know all the ranking members of the Imperial hierarchy.

She just nodded in reply, deciding it was probably beneath her station to make small talk with servants like this. She settled into an easy chair in what was obviously a prime position reserved for high rank and nobility. She was seated in welcome shade, overlooking the street. A few tables around her were occupied. A judge. A group of richly-dressed merchants. With a shock, Shayla recognized an outspoken member of the Imperial Assembly at the next table.

The waiter hovered nearby, hands clasped at his waist. Shayla looked surreptitiously for a menu, momentarily at a loss. The tables on the other side of the ropes all had menus on display, but here they were conspicuously absent.

*I guess my wish is your command then? Or am I supposed to have memorized what you have on offer? Okay, let's give this a try.*

"A pot of Solven Gold, steamed cream, and a dish of pastries. Chef's choice." Shayla kept the uncertainty out of her voice, feigning just the right level of disinterest. A voice accustomed to unquestioning obedience.

The waiter smiled and bobbed his head.

"And I would speak with Elmer Dognoty."

The waiter bowed and scurried away.

Elmer Dognoty was a member of the Insurrection, and was almost certainly known to the authorities. This place was bound to be under close surveillance. And yet, its very conspicuousness was an effective camouflage. Dognoty's was frequented by Palace staff at all levels. The sergeant at the Palace gates had recommended it to Shayla and given her directions. If questioned later, he would even be convinced that it had been entirely his idea.

Shayla sat back and watched the endless procession of people pass by in the street beyond. After a few minutes, a man approached, hands twisting together in front of him. His round face was unusually pale.

"Elmer Dognoty at your service, My Lady." He bowed low. Shayla noted the obsequious manner didn't extend to his eyes, which were coldly appraising.

"Brynwyn bin Covin. Imperial Master of Circuses."

The eyes widened. "Your coffee will be a few minutes brewing. We may talk while you are waiting."

"I understand you offer the best selection of coffee and baked goods in town. I would like to discuss terms for a regular supply to my staff."

"Please, allow me to show you around my establishment and let you see for yourself what we have to offer."

Shayla inclined her head and stood to follow. "I understand your Creme Julian is the best in the Empire."

"Nobody else can match it." There was the merest hint of a tremor in his voice.

"An old family recipe?"

He nodded. "And a perfect accompaniment to our finest coffee."

"I find it goes better with the sharpness of black tea."

The pre-arranged exchange completed, Elmer Dognoty led Shayla into a corridor, then through a door to a small but comfortable office. The aroma of cinnamon pervaded the room. As soon as he had closed the door behind them, his manner changed. No longer the suave businessman, he looked scared and alone.

"You can speak freely here. Enough sensitive conversations take place in this establishment that we have some influential help in keeping it free from eavesdroppers."

Shayla nodded, but she took out her own notepad anyway and scanned the room for signs of communications devices.

"So ..." he began, nervously. "You've made contact at last. You must understand that the Leading Council is deeply unhappy."

"With what?" Shayla said, looking affronted. "I've infiltrated the Palace. Everything is going according to plan."

"But we lost an entire cell in Hawflun. The Council suspects a betrayal ..."

*Thought they might. Finn's handiwork was bound to raise questions.*

"I heard the news," Shayla interrupted, voice low but furious. "An explosion? Pah!" she spat. "I saw the pictures!"

Elmer Dognoty stood, speechless at the sudden ferocity.

"What the hell were they doing playing about with a fucking quark bomb?" Shayla continued. "They were supposed to be aiding me! Nothing else! Not pratting about on a little side venture of their own." *Nothing like a bit of credible indignation to deflect suspicion.*

"They had no other plans that we were aware of."

"Then they must have been following their own agenda. I approve of local initiative, but quark detonators are touchy things and need expert handling, otherwise accidents happen. How dare they endanger my mission like that? You tell the Council to rein in their loose cannons."

Dognoty's jaw hung open at this, eyes wide. It was unheard of for field agents to criticize the workings of the Council in this way. He was completely on the defensive now, all thoughts of betrayal swept aside by her tirade.

"I will be in touch shortly with further instructions," Shayla continued, "once I've assessed the state of security from within the Palace. Meanwhile, send word out as planned. Ready all agents to rise up and overthrow local guards as soon as I have the Imperial family."  ʻ

Raw terror showed in the depths of Dognoty's eyes. Shayla remembered what Finn had said about these agents' state of readiness.

"Your arrival here has stirred up a wasps' nest," he stuttered.

"And all looking in the wrong direction."

"But now we've got *Swords* up there ready to crush any uprising!" His voice was almost a wail. "*Swords!*"

*Grow a backbone, please! I need you ready to carry out your orders.* "They will not trouble us with the Imperial family dead. And what if they do? Have you forgotten your pledge? Have you lost the will to die for the Cause?"

His pale face turned white. Sweat trickled down his cheek.

"You've been removed from action for too long," Shayla hissed. "Sitting pretty here. Lying low while others fight. Four of our brethren from Tinturn are going to die next week. Was that in the plan? No. But it was a risk they willingly took for the Cause."

"But I've spent over twenty years establishing myself here. The Council would surely not risk exposing me now?"

"How long have we fought to bring down the Emperor? Have you ever managed to get an agent this close? I am almost within striking distance. Do you want it on your head if this opportunity slips by?" Shayla's voice dripped saccharine. "Do you think the Council will approve of your stance if that happens?"

Elmer Dognoty slumped into a chair, chewing the knuckle of his index finger.

*Aah! Found the right lever at last. You fear your own masters even more than the Empire.*

————•••————

Guards stood at the doors and at intervals around the walls of the Office of Deliberation. None of them had weapons drawn. The nearest was a good twenty feet away. Shayla stood alone in front of the desk, scant feet from the Emperor himself.

She regarded him with a mixture of loathing and curiosity, masked under an expression of bland obeisance.

*I could kill you here and now!* The feeling was overwhelming. It would be so easy. She could end it now, and she didn't care what happened to her afterwards.

But she submerged the burning rage under glacial determination. *I don't just want to kill you. I want to destroy you!*

Emperor Julian Skamensis leafed unhurriedly through a sheaf of documents floating across the surface of the desk. He spent a few seconds reading each one, scrawled notes on some, signatures on others, oblivious to the simmering hate standing opposite.

*Patience.*

To calm herself, Shayla forced herself to gaze past the Emperor's shoulder and through the tall windows behind him. Fountains played in the courtyard outside. Rose beds formed a blaze of regimented color. Her hammering heart slowed. Her eyes followed the tracery between the window mullions. High glass panels glowing in afternoon sun depicted scenes of Imperial conquest; she suppressed a grimace, and instead followed the plush folds of green and gold drapes.

At last, the Emperor looked up from his desk. "Master of Circuses."

Shayla bowed her head. "I am honored to be called to do your bidding, Magister Summis."

"The first of the Families arrived this morning." He pushed himself away from the desk and leaned back in his chair, stretching his arms above his head. "There is a lot of work to do over the next two weeks. My security advisors are in a state of great agitation. They believe some sort of attack is imminent. They warn me of something big coming, and I would be a fool to ignore them."

The casual warmth in his voice surprised Shayla. Shoulder-length black hair hung loose around his face. He wore a simple, faded tunic with no insignia. His manner suggested he was discussing the day's news with an old friend.

She remembered protocol, and stayed silent.

"If Commander ap Gwynodd had her way, she would have me cancel this meeting of the Families altogether."

Shayla thought she saw a shadow pass over his face. For an instant he seemed grey and tired, then the moment passed.

"The Conclave is of the utmost importance to me, and to the Empire. I expect to reach agreements that will cement our position in the galaxy for many years to come, and nothing can stand in the way. I will not allow the heightened security to dampen the mood, so your part in this is all the more important.

"My most honored guests will be inconvenienced by the strictures of the necessary security. Their movements will be restricted. They will be shadowed everywhere by an army of guards. Although this is for their own protection, they will find these precautions irksome, even threatening. I am relying on you to keep them in good humor. You will take especially good care of my old friend Josef Firenzi and his entourage."

He looked Shayla in the eye. She looked deep into iron grey eyes set in a mask of stone.

"I am expecting great things from you. Do not consider disappointing me." The Emperor pulled his chair back to his desk and looked down, resting his hands on the surface.

"Preparations are well in hand, Magister Summis," Shayla ventured.

He looked back up sharply. "I did not ask for a briefing. I set expectations. It is up to you to deliver on them."

He turned his gaze back to the documents on his desk with an irritable wave of his hand. As he picked up his stylus and resumed work, Shayla bowed and backed her way out of the office, fuming at her lapse of judgment.

## Chapter 19

Shayla glared at Jojo bin Duvin across the table in the darkened conference room, and tried to keep the anger out of her voice. "You showed me our budget only two days ago. How can we be short now?" Possibilities raced through her mind. *Accounting errors? Embezzlement? Is someone trying to set me up?*

A deep dread had been gnawing at her ever since Jojo called her and her department heads together at this late hour. It was hardly lessened by the explanation Jojo now offered.

"The Exchequer has cancelled all special budgetary provisions for your office." Beads of sweat trickled down his cheeks. "As of today, we have only the bare operating stipend to work with."

The words made lexical sense, but Shayla struggled to understand their meaning through a fog of fatigue. A quick glance around the table told her this was serious. Bo Branson and Jasmine Trove's mouths hung open. Colin's whiskers twitched like worms on a hook as he chewed his lips. Kurt's eyes narrowed. Marcus Halley's brows were drawn together, brooding over a clenched fist pressed to his mouth. Shayla sensed more storm clouds gathering there, but she needed to understand this threat properly first.

"Explain," she said. "Keep it simple. Assume I know nothing."

Jojo gulped. "We have a basic budget set by the Treasury Committee of the Exchequer. It covers only routine expenses, staff salaries and suchlike. All special events need special provisions approved by the Secretary to the Exchequer."

A glimmer of light dawned. "Events like the executions, entertaining the Emperor's guests, and the Festival of Fountains?"

"Exactly."

"But those provision were already in place." Shayla pictured the financial planning models Jojo had shown her. She remembered seeing many annotations labeling the headings and columns of figures with special provision vote numbers. At the time, she hadn't questioned what this meant, but it made sense now.

"They have been withdrawn." Jojo's voice was a choked whisper.

Marcus's fist slammed into the table. Shayla glanced at him, but his head was bowed. She turned her attention back to Jojo. "Why?"

Her mind traced through the labyrinth of office politics. Motivation was one thing, but she was already leaping ahead to understand how this affected her personally, and her mission. If her office couldn't function, it would take longer to gain the necessary standing with the Emperor. She needed to clear up this mess first.

Jojo seemed on the verge of answering, but Kurt leaned forward, eyes blazing. "The Secretary to the Exchequer is a long time friend of Mabbwendig ap Terlion."

*Aah!* "Can the Secretary do that? And why would Mabbwendig cripple one of her own departments? Surely this will reflect badly on her?"

"It is the job of Office Heads," Jojo inclined his head towards Shayla, "to negotiate budgets for their needs. The funds we've been working with were agreed with Artur Stiles. The Secretary to the Exchequer feels no obligation to extend any agreements to Artur's successor."

"Is this normal behavior?" Shayla looked from Jojo to Kurt, trying to judge where the best information would come from.

"It is within his prerogative." Jojo screwed up his face, eyes almost vanishing behind round cheeks. "But the Secretary would normally allow a new official time to re-negotiate special provisions."

"It's a calculated vote of no confidence," said Kurt. "In you, personally."

"So, Mabbwendig is distanced from the fallout." Shayla's gut heaved. "All she needs to do is wait for a visible sign of failure ..."

"Admitting she made a mistake in appointing you will be a small price for her to pay," said Kurt, "and she will save some face by acting swiftly and severely."

"There's more." Marcus broke his silence at last. "I thought I had problems of my own to report, but it's clearly part of a pattern. Many of our suppliers have suddenly found themselves—" his mouth twisted

"—challenged to meet our orders. Either out of stock entirely, or prices doubled, even tripled."

Shayla sat back, her face blank. Given what she'd already heard, this twist came as no surprise. "Belt and braces," she muttered.

*Options…options…*Shayla immediately dismissed the notion of making up to Mabbwendig. Mad Mabb was out to see Shayla gone, and she was not the forgiving type. She'd love to see Shayla crawl, begging. She'd draw it out, gloat, before dropping the axe.

Equally, Shayla guessed that an appeal to the Secretary would bear little fruit. Oh, she was sure he'd go through the motions of negotiating, but results would be too little, too late.

She had to stave off disaster long enough to finish her mission. The Emperor seemed to care nothing about the office politics beneath him, only outcomes, so she needed a delaying tactic to keep her department operating a little while longer. Mabbwendig and the Exchequer weren't the only ones playing games.

The short term arrangements demanded immediate action. She would have to dig deeper into the rats' nest that passed for working life here, but meanwhile, "I believe I've established some measure of standing with Elmer Dognoty."

Jojo and Marcus exchanged glances. Jojo said, "How can a coffee merchant help provision events on the scale we are talking about?"

"He has an extensive network of contacts. More so than I think you realize." Shayla grinned to herself. *Let's see how Mad Mabb fares against the unseen fingers of the Insurrection.* "Mention my name. Remind him he needs my help to see some business ventures reach fruition. He will know what I mean."

Marcus's bleak expression lightened.

Shayla looked around the table. "This discussion stays between us. If Mabbwendig gets any sense that we are fighting back, she will find other ways to hurt us. Jojo, we need to make at least a decent job around the executions, and keep the entertainment for the Emperor's visitors on track. We have no special funding right now, so run the remaining operating budget dry while I sort out this mess. Make sure nobody else has access to our accounts to see the hole we're in."

Kurt leaned forward. "It occurs to me that Mabbwendig might relax her efforts if she knew how far we were draining our reserves to keep up appearances. It's a sign of desperation."

Shayla stared at him. *For a humble guard, he's remarkably tuned in to palace politics.* She blinked. "Can such rumors reach her in such a way as to arouse no suspicion?"

Kurt smiled. "Leave it to me."

Jojo nodded, but still looked unhappy. "That will only last us a matter of days. I can keep the accounts secret for a short while, but the quarterly audit is due in four weeks. Everything will come out then."

Four weeks? That was less time than Shayla had planned on, but an idea began to form in her mind. "Colin, make contact with the Secretary's office and make an appointment. Make it clear I will only see the Secretary to the Exchequer in person."

---

"These are all stills from security monitors in Hawflun."

Chief of Intelligence, Fleur Trixmin, studied the proffered pictures.

"You see these two pilgrims here? They are seen coming and going in the quarter where the explosion was."

Fleur gave a curt nod, trying to conceal her distaste at the young but balding man standing over her desk. Some newcomer, recently transferred into her division. It wasn't his perspiring face or wisps of greasy hair that offended her, she was more than accustomed to everything repulsive the human body had to offer, it was his manner. Over eager. Sycophantic. He had something to tell her that he was convinced would lead to exquisite pain for some other party, and he was barely able to suppress his glee.

*Sadistic.* That was what bothered her. Delight in someone else's pain was her prerogative, and she resented anyone else treading on her turf.

"This is a sequence from the Temple gates," he continued, oblivious to her disgust. He pointed out two figures amongst the flow of people.

Fleur compared the images. No faces were visible, but the robes all bore distinctive patterns. Assuming the brightly colored markings really were unique, then the two figures were the same as in the other pictures.

"So?" This young upstart had bypassed the line of command and insisted on seeing her personally. This had better be good.

"Here are security logs corresponding to this point in time. You can see that some of these people carried passkeys. These were all in close proximity to the two in question."

One name in the list was highlighted. Fleur sat up straight, her interest piqued.

*Looks like this odious little man has earned his keep after all.*

She frowned in concentration, then sat back.

*This is a dangerous situation.*

She regarded him through half-lidded eyes, feigning only moderate interest while her mind raced. "I suspect this will turn out to be nothing, but you were right to bring this to me," she said. "This matter is no longer your concern. My office will take it from here." She waved dismissively.

"I am my Emperor's servant, Magister Summis."

Willem Skimlok bowed low, smiling to himself as he backed away from the desk before turning to leave.

Imperial Chief of Security, Chalwen ap Gwynodd, prowled the State Balcony, eyeing the preparations and the crowds gathering in the plaza below. Guards in full ceremonial uniform stood motionless every few feet along the balustrade. Forests of flagpoles at either end of the balcony trailed limp pennants, flags of the eighty-three worlds directly ruled by the Family Skamensis.

With the toe of a gleaming boot, she smoothed out a wrinkle in the rich carpet that covered grey stone. She turned and scanned the towering walls of the Palace. Rows of windows gazed back. A sniper's paradise. She resisted the urge to re-check the inspection reports from the security squads patrolling the Palace corridors. Her staff knew their job.

Chalwen plodded up broad steps to the central dais where deeply cushioned loungers and armchairs awaited the Emperor and his guests. A phalanx of servants stood in readiness behind. Several rows of chairs stretched on either side for less exalted guests of His Imperial Majesty. A few were already occupied, and more people trickled from the depths of the Palace behind, ushered to their places by uniformed attendants.

A muted commentary murmured in Chalwen's ear, status reports from the security operations center. Long years of experience told her that the reports were routine, everything as it should be. And she knew that her security team watched from the operations center on the other side of the Palace. Nothing would escape the dozens of pairs of eyes and ever-vigilant electronics.

Alongside the standard trappings, Chalwen noted some new touches. Tall urns of ancient Chensing pottery, simple but elegant, stood in the gaps between rows of seats. They overflowed with exuberant cascades of fuchsia, crowned by tall stands of golden iris and clumps of orchid.

*Sunrise Splendor?* She looked closer in surprise. *The old Emperor's favorite.*

As she neared the Emperor's lounger, she entered a zone of blissful cool. She luxuriated in the unexpected relief from the humid stillness of the early afternoon. Another new twist. The Emperor's heat sensitivity was a minor weakness not widely advertised. Most people ascribed the cool of the Palace buildings to simple whim and a display of Imperial extravagance. This new Master of Circuses had done her research.

She turned where she stood, reluctant to leave the wash of cool air, and looked out over the plaza. In the distance on either side, she could see signs of festivities, carnival sideshows and long marquees serving food and drink. She'd had very little report of trouble. The crowd was being kept well-ordered and entertained.

Dignitaries now filled the seats on either side of the balcony. Bright robes and official insignia offered a dizzying kaleidoscope of color. Excited chatter masked an undercurrent of anticipation.

Everywhere across the plaza, larger and larger knots of people stilled and gazed towards the Palace.

She took up her position at the back of the dais. Admiral Kuvar approached and stood alongside her. He bobbed his head curtly. "Commander ap Gwynodd, I hope you know what you're doing. The Navy is stretched thin indeed, trying to police the outworlds."

"Admiral Kuvar," Chalwen murmured, "I believe the threat on Magentis is serious. We will talk further in private, but I'm grateful to you for humoring me in this matter."

The Admiral grunted. "You can thank the Emperor for that. It's always easier to bend his ear when you are on the same planet than from a hundred light years distance."

"I have as much concern as you have for the security of *all* our worlds, and I'm well aware of the need to police our borders. The threat here is an unknown quantity, but something big is under way, something the Insurrection has gone to great trouble and unusual subtlety to hide. Georgi, I'm worried."

The rare lapse into familiarity between these two, even after so many years of working together, spoke volumes. The Admiral's gruff tone softened. "Well, two *Swords* should be able to handle anything the Insurrection can mount. We are redeploying forces to fill the gaps. Must look after the seat of Empire, after all."

"Later then, Admiral," Chalwen muttered, as they were joined by the Minister of Commerce, Malcolm Stenner.

Beyond the Admiral and Malcolm, other chiefs of the Imperial administration were arranging themselves in a line behind the Emperor's seat.

A broad stage stretched across the square directly in front of the balcony. On it stood a row of four posts, each a foot thick and taller than a man, glowing with a burnished sheen in the harsh afternoon sun. Two taller poles supported a chain of hoops twenty feet above the stage, each a few feet across, held flat so its center lay directly above one of the posts.

To the uninitiated, the whole assembly looked like some child's bizarre play equipment, but Chalwen doubted there was anyone amongst the throng in the square who wasn't familiar with this execution machinery.

For now, the stage was alive with dancers and musicians entertaining the packed crowds.

A row of heralds at the front of the stage whipped trumpets to their mouths. A fanfare rang out across the square and the stage emptied of entertainers. The rows of dignitaries on the balcony hastened to their feet.

As the last notes died away, the Emperor emerged from the Palace surrounded by an entourage of guards, servants, and honored guests. The square erupted in a wall of sound as the crowd cheered.

Emperor Julian Flavio Skamensis swept along the balcony and up the steps of the dais. Shimmering emerald robes gleamed. Glittering gold thread writhed across his back, picking out the outlines of the Imperial acacia.

He turned at the top of the steps and gazed at the expectant throng. Face impassive, he settled gracefully into the cushions of his chaise longue.

Another fanfare sounded, brusque and demanding this time. A summons, not an announcement. Moments later, guards marched up a stairway leading from the depths under the stage. Between them stumbled four prisoners, naked and shackled, blinking as they emerged into the brightness.

A low buzz rose from the crowd, a rising groundswell of hate.

The guards led each prisoner to a post. One struggled as he caught sight of the hoops suspended overhead. The guards wrestled him into position and clamped manacles into place at ankles, wrists, and forearms.

A captain in dress uniform walked slowly along the line, examining each prisoner's bindings. The guards stepped back, then marched off the stage.

The poles extended out of the stage and propelled the shackled prisoners up through the centers of the hoops. Soon they hung sixty feet above the heads of the crowd. A couple of them groaned as the manacles bore their weight.

A third clarion fanfare cut through the air, silencing the visceral rumbling of half a million people. A dull *whumph* sounded from the row of hoops and white fire filled the circles, licking hungrily at the four posts. Angry hissing rose to a roar then faded almost to nothing. The white became blinding blue, then translucent as the heat passed beyond the range of visibility.

A deathly hush fell.

From the other side of the dais, Supreme Judge Abraham Crode stepped forward. His scarlet robes of office glowed in the afternoon sun. He unrolled a scroll and held it out at arms length.

"Italo di Flavio of Tinturn," Crode announced theatrically. His magnified voice carried clear across the packed plaza. "For conspiracy against the Imperial person, by the grace and mercy of his Imperial Majesty, quick death."

The man at the end of the row was already twitching and shaking. Blood dripped from wounds where the manacles bit deep into his wrists and trembling biceps. At the sound of the judge's voice, he started babbling and weeping.

Long seconds passed, the humid air heavy with expectation.

Chalwen gazed at the posts where the unnatural fire clawed for purchase. They should be glowing an angry red at least, but they stood unmarked, oblivious to the furnace cloaking them. She marveled at how a seemingly ordinary material could withstand the fury of the encircling plasma. The Empire had tried and failed many times to replicate materials like this, but they did not possess the necessary science. Instead, they traded for what they needed. At a price.

The first post retracted into the stage, drawing the prisoner down into the plasma. His shriek scaled the octaves, ending in abrupt silence.

The crowd roared approval.

Two more sentences were read out. Two more posts dropped.

Finally there was one left standing. One man, wretched and lonely, faced the wrath and bloodlust of the crowd.

Chalwen eyed the blackened husks clamped to the first three poles. Frustration gnawed her. The three lives just extinguished had been part of an Insurrection cell. That much was known. But they had left no clues about the *Chantry Bay* mystery. Chalwen relished mysteries, but only on the strict understanding that they yielded to investigation.

This last man was the only one they had positively linked to the sabotage, but the best of Henri's interrogation skills had revealed nothing. His execution was an admission of defeat. Chalwen's fingernails dug into her palms as she clenched her fists at her side. She would have liked to keep him in custody, seeking some way to unlock the knowledge he'd obliterated from his mind. But she knew that was a futile wish. Time to move on.

"Bernhardt Maas of Tinturn, for high treason against the Empire ..." Supreme Judge Abraham Crode paused. His eyes scanned the sea of upturned faces, grim relish twisting his features.

*Get on with it, you sadistic old goat.*

"Death by slow burning."

He rolled up his scroll with a snap audible across the packed square, and stepped back to stand level with Chalwen on the other side of the Emperor.

At first, nothing seemed to be happening. After a minute, it was clear that the pole was retracting, inch by inch. Soon only a few feet lay between Maas and the blistering flames.

He had courage. Chalwen granted him that. He faced the balcony, visibly scared, but unbowed and defiant.

He screwed up his face but made no sound as the flames seared his feet. Chalwen marveled at his strength. She knew full well that he'd been dosed with neurostimulants. The bite of the manacles alone would be near unbearable torment.

The pole quickly lifted him clear, then lowered him again. It wasn't until the third dip into the fire, his feet now nothing more than charred stumps, that he broke down and let out a strangled cry.

Chalwen knew that executioners took pride in prolonging their victims' agony. A public execution by slow burning was seen as an opportunity to display their gruesome prowess. Some were cold and clinical. Some macabrely theatrical. Some played cruel tricks, like dropping the pole quickly but cutting the flames at the last second, so the hapless victim never knew whether to expect torture or brief respite.

Chalwen was thankful that the Emperor, in a gesture of enlightenment, had decreed that an execution should not last longer than an hour. It was hot standing on this balcony, the luxury of cool air had been set for the benefit of the Emperor alone, and the collar of her dress uniform chafed her sweating neck.

Eventually the last screams died away. A synth chord pealed through the sudden hush, clear and jubilant. A plasma cannon at each corner of the square rent the afternoon sky in salute.

The Emperor reclined, arm stretched out along the back of the chaise longue, head lolling back seemingly oblivious to the grotesque spectacle below.

Chalwen's eyes met the Emperor's when he glanced her way. He returned her gaze stone-faced, then nodded imperceptibly before standing and sweeping theatrically off the balcony.

---

Shayla fought to hide her nausea at the spectacle of the executions while she watched the celebrations unfold. She sheltered in the relative calm of a thirty foot watchtower built near the far side of the square, across from the Palace. A tall fence encircled the foot of the tower, sheltering a huddle of temporary offices from which the evening's festivities were being orchestrated. The twenty-foot-square platform atop the tower gave Shayla and her squad of assistants a clear view over the plaza.

*Bernhardt Maas.* Shayla turned the name over in her mind. She had known him as Bluejay.

She knew nothing about the other three, even though they were undoubtedly Insurrection members, but the first one had left her shaking.

She was sure nobody around her had made sense of his incoherent babbling before he died, but Shayla had recognized a few words with deep dread. His mumblings, in an obscure Firenzi dialect, were far from aimless. They were a mantra against fear, part of his deeply implanted training. What shocked her was that, even at the end, he was still firmly in the grip of his subconscious conditioning. Conditioning that she shared.

But they, at least, were unknown. Anonymous. Bernhardt Maas was another matter. She had personally briefed him on how to prepare *Chantry Bay* for her, where to hide her flight pack, how to leave a maintenance port unsecured so she could hack into the ship's command system.

*Why didn't he escape while he could?* The question burned in her mind. He'd had a clear week's lead while the ship was in flight. *And why did he not kill himself when he knew he couldn't escape?* But she knew the answer. Nothing must arouse suspicion beforehand, and nothing would be done that would give the investigators an easy start in their work. A vanishing member of the ground crew would have been a giveaway. All the same, he must have understood what he faced.

And yet he held his ground and faced agonizing death with courage and dignity. What inner fire, what fanaticism, had pushed him to make such a sacrifice?

Shayla thought she knew about fanaticism. She'd pursued a murderous goal relentlessly, unstintingly, since the age of eleven.

At first, her grief and fury had been instinctive, childish, overwhelming. During her teens, Shayla learned to channel and direct her rage. With no firm plans, and no serious expectation of realizing her thirst for revenge, she seized any opportunity to equip herself for the task, anything that led her a step closer to within striking distance of the heart of Empire. She learned martial arts, armed and unarmed combat. As soon as she was old enough she joined the Firenzi military and thrived on the brutal regime of discipline and training.

Shayla's zeal was boundless, fuelled by a desire to be as close as possible to the forefront of combat. Eventually she realized that the military forces were little more than empty posturing. None of the Families posed any serious threat to the Empire. All the Families plotted tirelessly against the Empire and against each other, but direct military confrontation was never going to lead her to her goal. The real war lay under cover.

Her family was well-connected in Firenzi circles. Her mother was a minor member of the nobility, and she had contacts. She helped Shayla secure a position in the Secret Service. At last, here was an organisation that was truly dedicated to bringing down the Imperial family.

Now, after so many years, she was almost within reach of her goal.

Yes, she knew about fanaticism. The question was, what was she prepared to suffer in the name of revenge?

———•◦•———

As darkness fell, the sky above the plaza erupted into a blazing light show. Amongst the dancing beams, carefully controlled streamers of plasma flickered high overhead, dispelling the night chill. A pleasing touch, but also a subliminal reminder of the executions.

In between Shayla and the huge stage supporting the execution poles, a row of punishment cells was doing a brisk trade. These were all serious criminals. Lifers. Many had spent years in isolation cells or on routine torture. They had been offered a chance to gamble for their freedom, in return for one evening of unlimited public torment. All they had to do was survive.

Shayla knew the machinery had been carefully rigged. Some would make it through the night. Most would not.

The rows of complimentary catering tents had been busy all day. Now, the whole roast boars that had been cooking since morning were being served up.

The execution stage was cleared, bodies removed, and poles retracted into the floor. There had been a lot of argument over this point; it was a long standing tradition for executed prisoners to remain on grisly display. That was a tradition Shayla intended to break, especially when she realized that the most vocal proponent had been Willem Skimlok. With Skimlok out of the way, it became clear that this was nothing more than residual fear. She was glad now that she'd convinced them.

Kurt and one of the security observers directed plain clothes forces to someone they'd spotted pick-pocketing in the crowd. There had been remarkably little trouble so far, despite the numbers of people thronging the square. The team worked hard to keep the atmosphere light and bellies full. And Bo Branson had put out the word that any troublemakers would fill the vacancies in the punishment stalls.

"Got her," said the observer as the ground forces closed in. Everything seemed to be going to schedule. Her team was well briefed, and they had everything under control.

"I'm going to take a walk," Shayla said.

Kurt glanced around and nodded. "Keep in contact, My Lady."

A frown marred his features, deepening as Shayla donned a plain blue cloak. He stood and rested a hand on her shoulder, seeming to be struggling for words.

She smiled at him. "There will be no trouble tonight. You have things well covered. And I wish to experience the evening from a civilian's point of view."

Letting herself out of the fenced compound, Shayla walked through the crowd, jostled from time to time in the crush of people. She hadn't realized how much she'd gotten used to her robes of office clearing a path for her through even the most crowded streets.

Her wanderings were not as aimless as they appeared. She angled towards the back of the plaza, where the crowds thinned out, and found the street she was looking for.

There were fewer people here. Market stalls lay bare.

Another bump turned into a shove. Caught off guard, normally alert senses dulled by the jostling crowd, Shayla leapt with the movement to regain her balance. She was in deep shadow in a narrow alley. A dead end. She whirled around to find her way blocked by three hooded figures. Steel gleamed in a ray of light from the lamp on the corner.

They were almost upon her.

A half-seen movement under one of the cloaks. Shayla leaped to one side and heard the muffled cough of a projectile weapon.

A thin line of blue fire winked in the darkness. Three figures crumpled to the ground.

*Crap!*

While she switched off her shimmerblade, Shayla looked up the alley. Empty. People occasionally hurried by in the light a few yards away. None looked her way.

*What the fuck am I going to do with these three?*

"Looks like you've a bit of cleaning up to do." A rich, soft voice beside her made Shayla jump.

*Get a grip!* She recognized the voice immediately. "Finn?"

"I said I'd be here to assist." He looked down at the heaps on the ground, barely discernible amongst piles of trash in the dark. "Been making some enemies then?"

Shayla bent over the bodies. Finn joined her and produced a tiny glowtube. With the light set low, little more than a firefly flicker, Shayla pulled their hoods back from their faces. All men. Two were strangers, but the third …

"I know this one. Not by name, but I've seen him standing guard in the administrative offices."

"At least one guard then. The others possibly guards as well, but more likely hired thugs."

"How so?"

"They were sent to attack you, a senior official. I saw them following you from the square. The number of guards who would be trusted with such a mission would be few indeed. Sending a squad of them would be risky. They'd talk amongst themselves. High chance of being caught sooner or later. But one guard with outside help would have no-one to talk to inside the Palace. Less chance of a slip."

Shayla digested this analysis, wondering still how she was going to dispose of three bodies.

"I have your needle gun," said Finn. "Now you are established, there is little chance of you being searched. And it looks like you might have need of a more subtle weapon than a blade."

Shayla took the proffered weapon gratefully. "You mustn't be seen around here," she said. "Apart from crawling with security, the Insurrection has hundreds of agents in the city. As far as they are concerned, you're supposed to be dead, remember?"

"They're not the only ones with a presence here. I'm based in a Firenzi safe house. I have companions with me tonight. You can be sure we weren't going to let anything happen to you at this late stage. We're just waiting for your instructions now."

"I'll send word through the Palace contact soon. I still need to establish a position of trust with the Emperor to get close enough. And I need to ensure the Insurrection is suitably misdirected."

"Go about your duties," said Finn, firmly. "We'll clean up here and ensure nothing will lead an investigation back to you."

———•+•———

Shayla slipped out of the alley and continued on her way. A few minutes later she stepped through the entrance of Dognoty's coffee shop.

"Can I help you, My Lady?" The waiter was polite but reserved. Once more, Shayla realized the advantages offered by the official insignia she'd grown accustomed to wearing.

"Magister bin Covin, Imperial Master of Circuses," she said, with as much cold arrogance as she could muster. Her manner suggested it was more than his life was worth to question it.

The waiter's jaw dropped. "O-of course." He motioned Shayla to follow him. It was up to his superiors to worry about impostors. They had ways of dealing with people who were not who they claimed to be.

As she sat down, Elmer Dognoty himself scurried into view. "So good to see you once more, My Lady."

"Sit," she instructed, looking across the street as if addressing the cherry tree outside rather than Dognoty. "We have business to complete."

Shayla ordered drinks, then watched the waiter until he was out of earshot. "We need a place safe enough to discuss matters of delicacy," she murmured, turning to Dognoty at last.

He returned her gaze steadily, then flicked his eyes left and right. "See the tables around you?"

She nodded, but didn't turn her head, keeping her eyes fixed on Dognoty. She could clearly picture the people around her from memory.

"Over my shoulder to your right. Josephine ap Meradan, Minister of Planetary Development." Shayla remembered seeing the generously-built woman standing behind the Emperor earlier that afternoon. "That young man with her is one of her secretarial staff. Don't imagine they're discussing business.

"Behind you sits Lord Colwyn Marx and some Freeworld merchants. I believe their negotiations include more than rugs and fine furniture for his chateau in Solven.

"I could continue, but suffice it to say that this place is awash with personal spy jammers. No hope of untangling any kind of monitoring signal, but we add our own randomized noise to the mix anyway, just for good measure. Just keep your face turned away from the street. Some of Trixmin's monkeys still try the old fashioned snooping and lip-reading from time to time."

Shayla nodded again. This was pretty much the answer she'd expected. "So. Is everything prepared?"

"All cells have received instructions from Council. They are reaching out to their networks of sympathizers. Everything has been kept low key, but all the same I've never seen anything like it before. You can expect a planet-wide uprising on a grand scale once the Imperial family is gone." His voice and manner were calm, a far cry from the trembling wreck she had left a few days ago. Shayla could see the hand of the Council's propaganda counselors here. He seemed fired with barely-suppressed zeal.

"Good," she said. "I know the Council will be distributing orders to individual cells, but the key targets here are the Palace itself, and the Security headquarters. From there, our command team will be able to control the fleet right across Imperial space."

"One thing is troubling me." Dognoty leaned closer. "I understand you are arranging for access to the Palace, but the Council was sketchy on details."

"Some of the details were necessarily sketchy until I was able to work on the inside. I have a contact who will admit your assassin through the far west gate, behind the library. She doesn't realize who she's letting in. She'll think it's a delivery for the Captain of the Guard. Something clandestine, hence the secrecy. Your agent will need to kill her, then deal with the guard at the main portico. From there it should be easy."

Dognoty nodded.

"One more thing," Shayla said. "The Firenzi contingent will still be in residence. They have a strong force of their own guards with them. They owe no loyalty to the Emperor, so they should not interfere providing you leave them alone. However, they will fight to the death to protect the Firenzi family."

## Chapter 21

A knock at the door interrupted Shayla's bedtime preparations. She threw on a gown and opened the door, to be met by two guards, heads bowed in deference.

"Magister bin Covin, my apologies for the intrusion at this late hour," said one. "Your presence is required. Immediately."

Something about his manner wasn't quite right. Truthsense was a difficult skill, imprecise at the best of times, and not one that Shayla had ever properly mastered. She struggled with conflicting signals. She had a strong sense that he wasn't being deceitful, yet she had a feeling there was something important left unsaid.

Shayla hesitated, straining for signs of danger. She glimpsed a small movement from the corner of her eye and felt a cold sting in her neck. As numbness washed over her body she realized there was a third person, a hawk-nosed woman, hidden to one side of the doorway.

*Shit! That was neatly done.* Shayla caught sight of a tiny blowtube which the wiry woman pocketed as she stepped forwards. She reached up and retrieved the dart from Shayla's neck. Fear and dismay battled with professional admiration as Shayla recognized the skill of a fellow assassin.

Without thinking, Shayla tried to turn her head. Fire exploded in the back of her eyes.

*Trylex!* Or something similar. The same that she had used on Brynwyn. As the afterglow of piercing agony faded, Shayla emptied her mind of all thought of voluntary action.

"Deliver her without delay. You have thirty minutes before the dose wears off." The woman's voice was a whisper. The guards nodded, and she slipped behind Shayla and out of sight.

"Come, My Lady," said the first guard. The other arranged a plain cloak over Shayla's shoulders and led her by the elbow down the corridor.

Shayla was powerless to resist as they led her through the palace and down stairs, deep into territory she had never seen before. She tried to keep her orientation through the twists and turns, through chambers and galleries, echoing stairwells and long, brashly-lit service corridors. They left the staff quarters and household offices far behind, and passed beneath the public state and assembly rooms, but beyond that, Shayla couldn't tell where they were.

It seemed like they had chosen their tortuous route with some care to avoid attention. They saw only two others on their way, and those only at a distance.

At the same time her mind raced, assessing her situation. The guards still treated her with courtesy, not like some common prisoner. It seemed she still held some station here, so she guessed that she was not exactly under arrest. All the same, this was clearly not a routine invitation.

Her mental clock ticked off the seconds and minutes as they walked. She'd started counting when she heard the mysterious assassin's words — thirty minutes. They were close to that time when they emerged into a much wider corridor, carpeted and richly appointed. The leading guard murmured into a lapel microphone, then threw open a nearby door and ushered Shayla inside.

The numbness seemed to be wearing off at last, but Shayla knew it was pointless to try to fight the drug just yet. She examined her surroundings as best she could without moving her head. The guards led her through an anteroom into what looked like an office. A broad rosewood desk dominated the center of the room, sitting on a rich Monsk rug. Opposite the desk, a full wall screen showed a sun-drenched mountain meadow, with unkempt grasses and wild flowers dancing in an imaginary breeze. Other items of furniture oozed taste and restrained opulence. A polished bureau, a dresser bearing a lustrous copper coffee pot and a china tea service, a free-floating globe of Magentis, fully three feet across, with oceans and continents picked out in exquisite marquetry.

Shayla let herself be guided to a chair at a small side table. She noted, with a twinge of panic, that the chair was bolted to the floor. Her unease deepened as the second guard manacled her arms and legs to the chair.

They left. She was still helpless, but the first signs of voluntary movement were returning. Shayla was able to turn her head slightly when a voice alongside her said, "My apologies for the precautions. We're conducting routine checks on all recent additions to the Palace staff. You'd be surprised how many organizations still try to infiltrate us, no matter how often we demonstrate how pointless it is."

From the corner of her eye, Shayla could see a tiny woman with elfin features. Her heart sank.

*Fleur Trixmin? In person? What does she want with me?*

It seemed Fleur felt no need to introduce herself. Instead, she continued in the same light-hearted tone, "I always think that if you're going to the trouble of checking someone's identity, it's logical to assume the worst until you can establish otherwise. Else why bother? Don't you agree?" She sat. "So. Brynwyn bin Covin."

Shayla wasn't sure whether this was a question or a statement. She reckoned she had enough voluntary control by now to answer, but she remembered Brynwyn's proud self-righteousness and chose to remain silent.

Fleur set a scroll down on the table in front of her. She sprawled, one elbow on the table, hand propping up her head. The other hand toyed with a stylus, doodling on the surface of the scroll.

"Obviously this interview is being monitored, but there are things to be said that I don't want going outside these walls. I've taken the trouble to set a few unconventional communication aids in place. As far as any watchers are concerned, all they are seeing and hearing is a routine interview."

There was a long pause.

*What the hell is going on?*

"There was nothing on your record about training in Shohan Calinda."

Shayla tilted her chin. "I thought you were the Chief of *Intelligence*."

Fleur laughed, high and brittle. "Of course there wouldn't be anything on your *official* record. That *would* be a dumb question. I'm talking about my own records." She frowned. "Which School did you train in?"

"Another dumb question. Do you think any Novice would risk their status by discussing that?"

"True enough." Fleur waved her hand, suddenly looking bored with the topic. "No matter. I know you're not who you claim to be." She didn't look at Shayla, but resumed doodling.

A dread chill seeped through Shayla's stomach. *Discovered! Shit, it's over!*

She fought to keep control. She was a professional and she would play this out to the end. Yet the memories of the executions haunted her. There was only one penalty possible for what she was doing. Shayla realized that, for all the training she had been through, the hardships endured, she had never had to suffer real pain. The vision of the execution fires terrified her. For the first time in her life, the reality of her chosen course came clear. The burning thirst for revenge had been so much in the front of her mind for so many years that the thought of failure, the *consequences* of failure, had never truly occurred to her until now.

Then Shayla saw that terror would be a natural reaction to such an accusation, innocent or otherwise. She withdrew her self-control into a tiny corner of her mind and gave the panic free rein through her body. Her heart thumped. Her breathing grew ragged. Sweat moistened her brow and the small of her back.

She sat, silent and shivering, watching Fleur with wide eyes.

Fleur studied the scroll with interest. "*Very* good," she purred. She smiled at Shayla. "You'd be amazed how many agents give themselves away by their ..." She paused, pursed her lips and screwed her face into a caricature of sternness. "... Oh so professional self-control." She sighed. "So well trained. But then, not quite well enough."

Fleur stood and paced the room. "Of course, you'd be right to fear me. Most people I interview wet themselves before they reach my office. I've made grown men, battle-hardened soldiers, weep with nothing more than the raising of an eyebrow." She ran her fingers lightly across the doors of a plain grey cabinet just within Shayla's view. "They don't call me 'The Bitch in the Basement' for nothing," she said. "I could cause you such pain. Pain beyond comprehension. Beyond endurance."

She whirled towards Shayla and leaned close, their faces scant inches apart. "You were there for the executions." Her face was hard, all levity gone. "You thought them harsh, didn't you? Well, that was blessed relief compared to what those poor wretches had already been through.

And Henri's good but he lacks subtlety. In my hands, a minute will seem like a year, an hour like an eternity."

Shayla eyed the cabinet. Its stark plainness gave her the creeps. It was so incongruous in the sumptuous splendor of the office.

"I could ask you to drop the pretense, but you're too good for that. Shame. I'd have loved to chat." Fleur's voice was light again. Playful. "But I didn't bring you here to interrogate you. We are working for the same people, near enough. I know Josef Firenzi has placed an agent, you, in the Palace. I want to ensure you live long enough to complete your mission."

*No shit!* The revelation shook Shayla. She'd been bracing herself for an accusation of working for the Insurrection. On the surface, that was true. Only a handful of people knew she'd been placed there by the Firenzi Special Service, and those all belonged to the Service themselves.

She realized her face was reflecting her shock and indecision. She pulled herself back under control. Then she knew what she needed to say. Fully in command again, she let her features show intense inner conflict, then decision.

Shayla turned her head to face Fleur. She tilted her chin up defiantly. *Careful. Don't overdo it.* "If I truly believed one word of what you said, I should denounce you to the Emperor." Shayla's voice was quiet and reedy, but determined, with just the right amount of quaver.

For the first time, Fleur looked uncertain. This reaction was clearly unexpected. She studied the readings on the scroll again with a frown. Shayla's heart raced.

Then Fleur smiled again, but this time the smile failed to touch her eyes. "If you are who I believe you to be, then they chose well indeed. If not, well, no matter. You'd be no threat to me."

She sat opposite Shayla and leaned back, hands clasped behind her head.

"After that escapade with *Chantry Bay*, dear old Paul is tightening up security all over the place. He's a big teddy bear at heart, but he does know what he's doing, and he's very thorough. Everyone working in or near the Palace is being issued with new challenge codes. Your passkey is an impressive fake, it would have fooled existing security no problem, but it doesn't have all the hidden codes Brynwyn was given when she was cleared to work here. Right now, it's only a matter of time before you get caught.

"Luckily Paul's out in the provinces right now, checking over security arrangements for the Festival of Fountains. Don't want anyone taking a crack at all the Grand Families while they're assembled under one roof, now, do we? So I'm backfilling this essential task in his absence.

"I've had a document copied to your notepad. Only the intended recipient would be able to make any sense of it. I suggest you make use of the information before it's your turn to have new codes issued."

Fleur stood abruptly and left the room.

Moments later, a guard appeared and unlocked Shayla's bindings. She stood, still groggy from the effects of the drug.

"Wait!" she called.

The guard turned in the doorway.

"I'm free to go?"

"Of course, My Lady." His voice was gruff, but sounded surprised. "This was nothing more than a routine check."

"I am still new to the Palace. I have need of directions back to my quarters."

The guard bowed low. "As you wish, My Lady."

Back in her chamber, Shayla knew she was being watched. On first arriving in the Palace, she had surreptitiously scanned her quarters and found three spycams in the sitting room alone. Two more had appeared yesterday, after the executions.

She sat on a couch and crossed her legs, adopting a pose of meditation. She felt this would be a natural thing for the religious Brynwyn to do, to make sense of her ordeal.

Shayla had no use for the reflective calm of meditation, but she needed time to think.

*What the hell just happened?* Fleur knew something about her mission, that much seemed clear, but what was her game?

One thing she decided very quickly: she had no intention of trusting Fleur to be on her side. If she truly was with the Firenzi, she would show her hand soon enough. And the Special Service had approved ways of recognizing each other, which Fleur had not used, so whatever she was doing was probably not in the interests of Shayla's mission.

*And exactly which mission would that be?*

That was a good question. Here she was, Shayla Carver, a trained assassin in the Firenzi Special Service, working undercover infiltrating the Insurrection. And as an Insurrection agent she had infiltrated the Palace. Her mission with the Insurrection was to kill the Emperor and his family, and give the signal for their agents to take over and dismantle the machinery of Government. The Firenzi wanted much the same thing, but without the killing and dismantling. They wanted the machinery of Government intact and in their hands.

*So where did Fleur fit into all of this?*

Wherever it was, Shayla knew that Fleur would not be on Shayla's side. *She* was looking to do a whole lot more killing and dismantling than either the Firenzi or the Insurrection.

*So how would an innocent Brynwyn react?*

Mind made up, Shayla stood and walked over to her notepad sitting on the table where she'd left it. She opened it out. It didn't look like it had been tampered with, but she was sure that Fleur would have some of the best professionals in the business on her payroll. She paused, looking thoughtful, then went to the bedchamber, returning moments later with a tiny silver stick concealed in her hand.

She activated the jamming device and placed it on the table. Instruments like this were illegal but easily available, and used routinely by anyone with sufficient rank to get away with it. They were tolerated because spying on people of sufficient rank was equally frowned on, though equally commonplace.

Of course, it would take any watchers under Fleur's command a matter of seconds to decode the jamming signal and neutralize the block. But Shayla only needed a few seconds of privacy to invoke some of the tools hidden in the notepad.

She sat on the couch with the notepad in her lap, stylus in hand.

Abstract, atonal music played in the background.

She counted the seconds to the point where she judged they'd have broken the block and be watching again. She stayed motionless for long minutes, pretending to be deep in thought. Eventually she opened the document that had been placed there. She stared at it, face impassive.

Fleur was right. It would be utterly meaningless to most people. But Shayla recognized some of the codes that her software agents had stripped from Brynwyn's passkey.

*Holy shit! These look like the real thing. And in plain view!*

A subtle pattern in the music alerted her. Her own jamming mechanism was about to kick in. This was nothing that the Security forces would even be aware of. She hoped. It was apparent from Fleur's interview that they had the technology to subvert, rather than simply jam, spy signals. But would Fleur recognize when her own spies were being hoodwinked?

*We'll soon find out.*

The music told her that her window of opportunity was open. Fleur may have the resources to feed a false signal to monitors watching her office, but the best Shayla could do was to freeze the visual signal for a while. Her toolkit was designed to give her a few seconds of privacy at irregular intervals. Providing the scene remained static, like Shayla's pose of meditation, these brief periods of stillness should not arouse suspicion.

She set an agent to work comparing Fleur's document with the security codes she'd taken from Brynwyn. Then she resumed her pose. To the unseen watchers, it would appear as if she was still gazing at the open document.

One thing Shayla was certain of: if these codes were genuine, and unencrypted, Fleur did not intend to let her live. This information dropped on her notepad was like a quark bomb about to go critical.

*I want you to live long enough to complete your mission.*

Could Fleur really be a Firenzi agent? If that were so, they would have taken the Emperor years ago. Was this just an elaborate trap? More likely.

At the next opportunity, Shayla copied Fleur's document to a hidden site on her notepad for future reference.

The agents worked on. Coded messages in the music told a puzzling story. The access codes Fleur had given her were identical to those she'd pulled from the passkey. There was nothing missing. She was in no danger of discovery.

*What the hell is Fleur up to?*

Maybe she was looking for confirmation that Shayla was indeed an infiltrator. If the codes were correct, that could not have possibly tipped Fleur off, so her sources must lie elsewhere. Maybe they were not entirely reliable.

Whatever the answer, Shayla had no intention of playing her game.

She waited for the next jamming window, then gave the instructions to her toolkit to withdraw its feelers from the spy network and shut down.

When she was sure the observers had a clear view again, she leaned forward, shaking her head with a frown, and wiped the document from the surface of her notepad.

*Smile at that then, bitch!*

## Chapter 22

The Emperor's observation cruiser floated above low scrubby trees, casting a wide round shadow over the ground.

The cruiser was little more than a disc a hundred feet across, with an outcrop of superstructure in the middle. An awning shaded the viewing deck at the front of the disc where the Emperor sat.

Shayla studied him from her desk in the communications cabin a few feet away. Surrounded by screens, she listened to the chatter on the planning comms channel. Jojo and Jasmine monitored the hunt from their vantage point on the roof of the cabin, while Marcus and Kurt directed final preparations for the evening banquet back at the camp. Her team had been over the arrangements in painstaking detail a hundred times, and had things well in hand.

Alongside Emperor Julian Skamensis sat frail old Josef Firenzi, and his partner Margerite Calvolani, a striking woman with lustrous dark hair and flawless olive skin. A row of servants stood at attention behind them, ready to bring refreshments from the galley at the rear of the cruiser.

Two airbikes flashed past. Shayla recognized Ivan Skamensis and Scipio Firenzi. They were trailed by a small flotilla of hunt followers.

Shayla turned to a screen and scanned the ground below. Small shadows flitted through the trees.

She shuddered. *Hokloks!* Curiosity had led her last night to the armored fence where the hokloks were penned. Long-necked flightless birds, standing three feet tall, they looked harmless, almost cute.

The guards released an antelope into the pen. At the sight of the hokloks, the animal snorted and bolted on trembling legs. The birds let out high, whooping cries and gave chase. Hunting as a pack, they cornered the terrified antelope and sliced it apart with razor sharp beaks and talons.

Now they swarmed free beneath her. Their normally keen hearing had been blocked, their vision limited by tight-fitting hoods. They were trained to respond to instructions relayed from the hunters flying overhead. Each hunter directed a group of animals, a skilled task given that the hokloks' normal pack instincts were confused by their deadened senses.

Fifty prisoners had been released half an hour ago into the burning savannah. They were equipped with spears, and a water bottle each. After all, there was no point in them dying *prematurely* in the scorching heat.

A triumphant cry sounded over the hunt channel. Shayla recognized the voice of Lord Jerve Jamboro, one of Ivan's guests. He had separated from the group and was scouting a mile to their left.

The cruiser's pilot banked smoothly over to close in on the action. They were still too far off to see, but Shayla located the visuals from Lord Jamboro's airbike. On the screen in front of her, a muscular man with waist-length hair crouched, facing three hokloks. He held a spear in one hand, and brandished a smooth branch in the other. From the set of his muscles, Shayla guessed the branch was much heavier than it looked. The slow-growing trees on this plain produced a dense, iron-hard wood which would make a most effective club.

The hokloks closed in.

Long hair flying, the prisoner swung his club, missing, but keeping two of the predatory birds at bay. He skewered the third through the thorax and abandoned his spear, swinging his club again at the remaining two. Beaks slashing, they tried to break past the flailing weapon.

"Separate them!"

"Take him from behind!"

"Where are your other two hokloks?"

Questions and advice flooded the comms channel from the onlookers, still too far away to help. But suddenly, it was all over. A second spear stabbed out from the cover of a low-hanging tree, and the club connected with the head of the last startled hoklok. The man retrieved his spear, and he and his hidden companion raced off into the brush.

"An ambush! Cunning bastards!"

"Prisoners — three, Jamboro — nil!"

A mix of admiration and derision echoed around the cabin.

Lord Jamboro whirled his bike around to follow, but the Emperor's voice cut through the commotion. "Jamboro will return to camp imme-diately to replace his fallen hunters."

Jamboro turned and saluted the Emperor, his face dark with fury.

"Ha! That'll teach you to keep your hokloks together!" Scipio's laughter added to Jamboro's humiliation.

The Emperor rose from his armchair and left the shelter of the awning, crossing the few feet to the cooler comfort of the circular lounge in the center of the cruiser. He took a drink from a waiting servant, then seemed to notice Shayla for the first time, seated in the adjacent cabin.

Shayla stood, head bowed, as he stepped through the open door.

"Master of Circuses," he said. "I sense you are bringing your own style to bear on this ancient and honorable office."

Shayla gazed down at the desk, uncertain how to respond. But Julian continued. "Some amongst my guests paid great compliments to the hospitality my Family has extended them so far. I trust Administrator ap Terlion conveyed my token of appreciation?"

*Did she heck!* But Shayla simply nodded. She hoped this 'token' wouldn't prompt Mad Mabb to try more sabotage.

"These are no ordinary prisoners, are they?"

Shayla looked up, keeping her expression neutral. "All prisoners were drawn from the Prandis Capital House of Correction."

"Drawn? Carefully chosen, I think. Those two were trained fighters."

Shayla searched anxiously for any signs of admonition in his voice. "I hear the odds are overwhelmingly with the hunters. I understand my task is to entertain our guests, not bore them with tame distractions."

A hint of a smile played around Julian's mouth. "Hmm. It will be interesting to see how this plays out. Lord Firenzi enjoys a challenge, but Grand Duke Ivan can get tetchy if he is tested too far."

———•———

Several hours passed. Shayla studied the master display spread out on the desk in front of her. The constellation of red dots marking the prisoners' whereabouts had dwindled. Only a dozen of the original fifty were left. The blue dots denoting hokloks had also thinned slightly, but not enough to make a difference. The Emperor was astute in his earlier questioning. The prisoners were all hand-picked by Kurt. When Jojo had explained the nature of the hunt to Shayla, she struggled to conceal her disgust. She gave Kurt careful instructions. Ostensibly to present a fitting challenge, she told him to pick people who knew what they were embarking on and who would have a fighting chance.

As the afternoon wore on, Julian spent more and more time in the lounge, looking increasingly distressed.

On one such occasion, he caught Shayla's eye. She regarded him through the door with a slight frown on her face. He grimaced. "The heat is troubling me," he snapped, before returning to the observation deck.

The pack of riders had also thinned out as the afternoon progressed. Many of the hunters — casual participants, or merely curious — returned to the comfort of the encampment. Ivan and Scipio still led the hunt, closely shadowed by Lord Jamboro, eager to make up for his earlier embarrassment. The formidable matriarch Charlotte di Brugui followed proceedings from the edge of the pack, nominally taking part but scoring no kills. She kept a fond eye on her twin daughters, Emily and Annette, both fiercely competitive and skilled hunters.

Emily shrieked in triumph as she spotted a fleeing figure in the distance. She wheeled her airbike around to give chase. The other riders turned to follow, each one eager to bring their hokloks to bear.

Jamboro was quickest to respond and closed in, trying to head her off and distract her.

"Fuck off Jamboro! This one's mine!" Emily di Brugui followed with a stream of invective in a dialect unfamiliar to Shayla, although the meaning was clear enough, as Emily battled to maintain her lead.

Jamboro's derisive laughter turned to a scream of outrage, then fear.

Shayla looked up at the console beside her to see what had happened.

Two airbikes spun through the air. Emily soared high into the sky, wrestling to bring her craft back under control. Jamboro tumbled downwards, clipping the trees. His bike ploughed through a scrubby crown then rolled and slid along the ground.

Jamboro struggled, trapped in the twisted frame of the bike. A dozen hokloks closed in.

"Jojo!" Shayla shouted into her microphone. "Get them off there!"

In the distance she heard Julian's voice. "All hunters! Pull back!"

At first it looked like the frame of the wrecked craft would offer him protection, but the hokloks swarmed over it, beaks slashing, worming their bodies into the heart of the debris.

"Jamboro's pack are without a controller," Jojo muttered.

"Jojo!" Shaya yelled, "Use the master command net. Override the hunters. Return them to camp!"

She heard Jasmine summoning a medical crew and a squad of guards. *Good thinking!*

But it was quickly clear the medics would not be needed. Jamboro's screams over the comms net were frantic but mercifully brief.

"Thank Space for that!" Ivan drawled into the sudden hush. "Is this what nobility's come to, when they can neither hunt nor die like men?"

A few nervous laughs rejoined him.

Julian rushed into the lounge, face white, staggering to the bathroom.

After a few minutes, Shayla stood and peered through the door. Three servants waited nearby, expressions unreadable. She looked from one to the other. They avoided her gaze, but she saw a flicker of fear in the eyes of the nearest before he looked away.

"Jojo," she murmured into the microphone. "Wind up proceedings and get everyone back to camp. Have the guards round up the surviving prisoners. The hunt's over."

She crossed the lounge to the bathroom.

She pushed open the door.

The Emperor was bent over the wash basin, panting, steadying himself on outstretched arms. He looked up as Shayla entered, his face dripping with water.

*I know this man!* For an instant, Shayla saw a long-dead ghost in his face.

As she glanced away in confusion, from the corner of her eye she noticed specks of vomit spattering the toilet pan in the corner.

*Set this aside. Process later. Right now, get back to the mission.*

Julian Skamensis whirled around as Shayla shut the door behind her. For a moment, they stood in silence facing each other. Then, "You saw nothing of this," he hissed, eyes blazing.

"I see that My Lord is unwell," she whispered.

"The desert heat upsets me."

"This turn of events is distressing."

Julian spat into the basin. "The hunt is a dangerous pursuit. Everyone knows the risks, and they've all seen accidents in their time. Some of them fatal."

"But I sense that this entertainment is not to My Lord's liking," she countered, her voice firm. "I take what guidance I can from those who have served you longer than I, from records, from tradition. Please forgive me if I have strayed from your wishes."

"Tradition is good," he replied at last, steadying himself against the basin. "But tradition can get twisted by more recent demands put upon it."

He gazed at Shayla while she cleaned the toilet. "My family and guests have certain…expectations. I am obliged to meet those expectations as modestly as prudence allows."

As Shayla stood and turned to face him, their faces inches apart in the confines of the room, he said, "Your predecessor knew all too well the tightrope we walk here. If you seek guidance on tradition, look to my father's example."

———•◦•———

Shayla pondered the Emperor's words as she sat on the entrance ramp of her cruiser. She cupped a mug of tea in one hand and watched the circle of figures ranged around the roaring camp fire in the middle of the clearing. Fingertip feelers of warmth on her skin warded off the deepening chill of the desert night. Alongside her, and all around the encampment, cruisers of all sizes hulked like a circle of predatory beetles. Myriad dancing reflections of firelight glanced off their skins.

The Emperor's face still haunted her. She had last seen that look in her father's eyes, many years ago, after a freak fire had destroyed their stables. Once the embers had cooled, he'd personally seen to the burial of the former inhabitants. All beloved family pets. Though young, Shayla could tell that the task had sickened him to the core. She had risked Mother's wrath to keep vigil from the front porch long past her bedtime while he completed his work.

How well she remembered his face in the last glow of evening, nauseated but determined. The flicker of likeness had been brief but uncanny.

Shayla shivered.

Through the doorway of the command deck, she heard Marcus Halley readying the wrestlers who were due to follow the troupe of stilt-dancers currently performing. The main courses of the feast had all been served up. The rest of the evening could virtually run itself now. Most of her team were seated in the cabin behind her, helping themselves to food brought over by the kitchen staff. A rich aroma of spices dispelled the desert tang of burnt flint.

Shayla nodded her thanks to Luke Frendis as he ushered a pair of porters past her on the entrance ramp. She pressed a coin into his hand as he passed. She had kept in mind Kurt's advice from her first day in the Palace. She doubted if anyone bar the Emperor himself ate better than her own staff now.

She turned her attention back to her notepad, where reams of Imperial history unrolled across the screen. Her stylus guided the flow of information, following events and lines of thought as they caught her eye.

The old Emperor, Paul Skamensis, had ruled for barely three years before he and Julian's siblings had died in an accident, leaving Julian to be proclaimed Emperor. One of Julian's earliest acts had been to order the destruction of Eloon. It seemed he was intent on following his family's bloody tradition.

When Shayla examined the history more carefully, she realized how little she knew about those three years. The Empress Florence Skamensis, Paul and Ivan's mother, had presided over the most savage rule in a dynasty characterized by brutal repression. Shayla knew it had caused a stir when she had nominated her younger son, Paul, to succeed her instead of Ivan. It seemed a bizarre choice. Ivan was stamped in the same mold as his tyrant mother, but Paul was everything they were not.

As she read, she realized that those three years were almost missing from the histories. Nothing much happened. No acts of savagery. No uprisings quelled.

Then it all started again with Julian.

*No. Not quite.*

Something was amiss. Eloon was an anomaly. The last twenty five years had held the Empire in an iron grip, but compared with the oppressive century before Paul's brief rule it was muted.

*Someone close to Government has been keeping the worst in check.*

The insight was a shock to her, but it changed nothing.

*Look to my father's example for inspiration.*

What could he mean by that? His father's example seemed to be one of gentility. Of peace and justice. Was Julian wishing to recant the tyranny of his dynasty? Maybe he was simply mocking her?

*No matter. This changes nothing. This Slayer of Worlds will fall!*

But Shayla needed to know his mind in order to gain his trust. She had taken a gamble this evening, to test this new-found knowledge.

She closed the notebook and watched the flames dance in the distance.

A roar of outrage stilled the revelry. A terrified servant rushed from the clearing and bowed in front of Shayla. "My Lady, you are most urgently summoned to his Imperial Majesty's presence."

Shayla nodded. This was what she had been expecting.

She took a moment to compose herself, then stepped into the fire-light and stood in front of the Emperor, head bowed.

"His Lordship, the Grand Duke Ivan Skamensis, wishes to discuss a matter regarding this evening's entertainment," Julian said mildly.

Shayla looked up.

The Grand Duke's expression suggested he had something stronger than discussion in mind. "Where are the remaining prisoners?"

"They have been returned to Prandis Braz and released. As is the custom."

"Custom my arse! They were supposed to be held here. I promised My Lord Firenzi more sport with them."

Shayla met his eyes with a cool and unflinching gaze. "Forgive an ignorant Provincial, My Lord. I could imagine nothing more *sporting* than to grant them the prize so bravely won today."

Ivan's face contorted with rage. His mouth worked, but he managed nothing more than breathless panting.

Josef Firenzi threw back his head and wheezed with laughter. The short sibilant bursts cut through the deathly hush, breaking the spell that bound the onlookers. "Well spoken, young lady. Julian, I am pleased to see old traditions of honor still hold sway."

"But ..." Ivan seemed to have found his voice again.

Julian silenced him with an upraised hand. "It is done, My Lords, and it has my blessing."

His voice was matter-of-fact, his face solemn, but Shayla could have sworn she saw the briefest wink as she bowed and backed away.

Back straight, head held high, Shayla cut a swathe through the streams of people thronging the great domed vestibule, the meeting of the ways at the heart of the Palace.

The vast Throne Room sat two hundred yards behind her, at the far end of the Flamingo Gallery with its spectacular mosaic floor depicting a thousand birds in flight. Other long passages and galleries led to the Ballroom, the Banquet Hall, and the Legislative Assembly Room. Ahead, a sentry in ceremonial uniform held a heavy oak door open for her.

She entered a haven of calm from the echoing clatter and chatter of the vestibule. Carpeted floors silenced her footsteps. Rich hangings softened the walls. Another set of doors opened into the Imperial Library.

Asked to name the largest room in the Mosaic Palace, most people would say either the Throne Room or the Assembly Room. The Green Throne Room, an unencumbered circular hall a hundred and sixty yards across, with a proportionally lofty fan-vaulted ceiling, was the most imposing. The Assembly Room, only fractionally smaller, was more well-known from newscasts.

Both answers were wrong. The Imperial Library was relatively unknown, but in Shayla's eyes outshone either of them in size and splendor. From her vantage point on a wide balcony at one end, she had a clear view down nearly a quarter mile of sun-dappled benches and shelves. A temple of learning holding the accumulated wisdom of eight millennia of Empire.

Shayla descended into the silence of the main library floor, and made her way towards a circle of desks a quarter of the way down the room. She glided past tables and lecterns surmounted by a constellation of ornate lanterns twinkling into the distance. Every few yards, life-size statues of Emperors past stared down at her from shoulder-high plinths.

In the impenetrable quiet, Shayla seemed all alone, but the illusion of solitude was misleading. She estimated that, lost in the vastness of the library, there must be hundreds of patrons seated at desks, or silently prowling the labyrinth of shelves and balconies climbing the walls on either side.

She approached the nearest library attendant. "Where would I find Beatrice Mueller?" Her voice was hushed instinctively in the supernatural quiet of the library, but it barely carried to the attendant, seeming to be swallowed immediately by the air itself.

He opened his mouth to reply, but a cheery woman next to him called out, "That would be me, My Lady. How can I help you?" A row of dazzling teeth flashed at Shayla from a round face with flawless ebony skin.

Shayla leaned close, fingering the silver clasp at the neck of her robe. "I need some help with a line of research I wish to pursue."

A slight frown creased Beatrice's brow. She rubbed a finger thoughtfully over an emerald ring on her middle finger. "I suggest we take a walk and discuss this…line of research."

A moment later, Shayla felt her clasp heat sharply and tingle against her skin as the chemical recognition signal released by Beatrice reached it. Only another Firenzi agent would possess such a device, or know how to use it.

Beatrice led her deeper into the library. The wall to the left opened out into a cavernous semi-circular bay. "The Founder's Reading Room," she said, as if giving Shayla a guided tour. They climbed stairs to a gallery running around the edge of the reading room.

"It's quite safe to talk here," Beatrice said. "Sonic damping. It's damned near impossible to hear — let alone overhear — anything in this place. Handy, in our line of business, don't you think?"

Shayla glanced down at the long rows of tables below. Three men sat at the nearest table, not thirty feet from them. Books and scrolls littered the table around them, and they were clearly deep in animated discourse, not troubling to hush their voices. Yet barely a sound reached Shayla's ears.

"How long have you been here?" Shayla asked.

"Fifteen years, six of them as head librarian."

"Would you know all the Special Service agents working here?"

"It's not unheard of for the Service to run a parallel network, but I'm sure I know all our people here."

Shayla decided there was no point skirting the question. This woman was her contact in the Palace, and was bound to help her in any way she could. "Is Fleur Trixmin one of ours?"

Beatrice's ample cheeks danced as she shook in silent mirth. She sobered when she caught the expression on Shayla's face. Shayla recounted her interview with Fleur a few nights previously.

"I understand you had specialized help with your passkey."

Shayla's face settled into an unreadable mask.

Beatrice peered into her eyes, then sniffed. "So your contact is confidential. I won't pry. But am I to understand the key is okay?"

"As far as I could tell. I wondered if she was simply testing me. Maybe looking for confirmation of something gleaned from an unreliable source?"

They walked on in silence for a few moments, then, "I hear Willem Skimlok's dead."

"What?" The news jerked Shayla from her thoughts.

"Been missing a couple of days. His body turned up in the river this morning."

For a moment, Shayla struggled to tie the pieces of information together. *No, he wasn't one of the three I killed after the executions.* But then, could he have had something to do with that attack? Maybe someone else had been tidying up ...

"Finn?" she ventured.

Beatrice shook her head emphatically. "He's been in touch. Denies all knowledge, but says it was a messy job very cleverly done. Made to look like thugs."

"Made to look ..." *So someone* had *been tidying up. But who?*

Although Shayla was glad to have Skimlok out of the way, this was troubling. There was too much going on here out of her control. "I don't know what to make of that. Regardless, it could be that Security is getting too close for comfort. We must assume that time is now short."

"I hear rumors that Chalwen's team expects something to happen around the Festival of Fountains." The corner of Beatrice's mouth quirked upward. "They've been chasing an unknown visitor all around Traplinki."

"Good. So when the Festival goes without mishap, they will be off guard. Are the preparations here ready?"

"We are ready. You asked for a distraction to draw the Guard to the main gates and the Plaza."

Shayla nodded. "I have summoned some specialist help there. You will need to admit someone into the Palace to assist. I'll provide the details and call signs later, but he will help secure the gates and distract the guards."

"So, our Lord Josef and his entourage will assemble near the Concert Hall, between the Throne Room and the Emperor's quarters. Once you have the Emperor in your hands, we will be ready to force his abdication."

Shayla marveled at the fierce joy in Beatrice's voice. "Then we act the evening after my return from Henriss Garden."

*So many people to disappoint!* She felt a pang at the thought of those of her own Family who would soon die, but the price was small for what she intended to do.

---

Shayla sat back, trying to stop a grin spreading across her face. "So, the Secretary won't meet with me until after the Festival of Fountains, and only a week before the quarterly expenditure audit."

Colin nodded. His mustache drooped, mirroring his downturned mouth.

"It's a clear signal," said Kurt. "They don't want you to have a chance of negotiating anything until it's too late."

The scent of cumin, rich and earthy, wafted from a dish on the table.

"That's what I expected." Shayla speared a meatball from the dish and popped it into her mouth. She looked around the table, meeting each person's gaze. Kurt, Colin, Jojo, and Marcus. What she was about to propose was heresy in this bureaucracy, and these people would need to have absolute faith in her.

She nodded to Kurt, who went to the door of the conference room and spoke to someone outside. He returned to the table, accompanied by a short, round man in plain black robes.

"Truthsenser-Master Terrent Ali-Jefferson," said Kurt, with a slight tremor in his voice.

The truthsenser bobbed his head, and his face wrinkled in cheerful greeting, but his dark eyes gleamed like carbon steel.

It seemed the introduction was superfluous. At the first sight of his robes, the others in the room showed flickers of fear, quickly masked by neutral expressions. Jojo looked like he was trying to disappear into his chair as the truthsenser sat next to him.

"I am about to give you very specific instructions," Shayla said, "which I need you to follow without question, and without fear of consequences to yourselves." She paused to let the words sink in. "I've invited Truthsenser-Master Terrent to attest to the truth of my words." She looked at Jojo. "He is here to reassure you, not to question you."

Shayla clasped her hands on the table in front of her. She had chosen and rehearsed her words, to eliminate all falsehood from what she was about to say. She was playing with fire. One mis-placed phrase could reveal darker meaning to this master of the art of deception. "We have a temporary lack of the necessary budget to discharge our duties to the Emperor." She looked around the table. "My instructions are that we will run a deficit."

She waited, expecting an outburst, some expression of outrage. The silence was more eloquent than the loudest dissent.

A chair creaked. The truthsenser looked at Shayla, his face unreadable.

She gazed back. *Give them time.*

Marcus Halley recovered his voice first. With a pleading look at his colleagues, he whispered, "What you just said is close to treason."

The others simply nodded, open-mouthed.

"We have a duty to perform for our Emperor. The Secretary is obstructing that duty. One could well argue *that* to be treason."

Kurt snorted. "I hardly think *that* reasoning will keep our feet from the fire."

"Nor will it need to." Shayla radiated confidence.

Truthsenser Terrent leaned back in his chair, eyes half-closed, lips pressed into a thin line.

"The Emperor cares not for office squabbles," Shayla said. "However, he *will* care if we fail him." From the corner of her eye, she saw the truthsenser tilt his head a fraction. *You understand the truth of* that, *then.* "When we leave this room, Jojo will seal this office's accounts so that only I can access them. I will be the only one accountable for our budget. Spend what you need to. I will personally sign all expenses. None of you will ever know which, if any, takes us into deficit."

"But, the audit ..."

"My commitment to you is that by the time of the audit, our budget will not be an issue." Shayla put every ounce of conviction into her words. They would assume she was counting on successful negotiations with the Secretary. She had no such intent, but that didn't alter the truth of her statement. That was all that mattered.

The truthsenser squinted at her with a frown.

Shayla met his gaze, pulse pounding in her throat.

He pursed his lips. "I am not here to judge the wisdom of what I've heard, only the truth of what is spoken." He took a deep breath, eyes nailed to Shayla's. His expression said that he disapproved deeply. "I attest to the truth of your words."

Shayla kept silent for fear of giving away her relief, and inclined her head in acknowledgement.

As he stood, he turned to the others around the table. "If the need arises, I will also attest that you took no part in this gamble."

While Kurt escorted the truthsenser to the door, Shayla closed her eyes and recited a quick litany to calm her nerves. *By Space, I hope Kurt was right in his trust in this man.* If a whisper of this reached Mabbwendig, she'd bring the auditors down on them in an instant.

"Needless to say, this discussion stays between the five of us," Shayla said. "You have your instructions. Go. Make this a Festival to remember."

---

Shayla sat on her couch, pretending to meditate, in keeping with what she knew of Brynwyn's routine.

She usually spent this quiet time in the evening reflecting on her mission, reviewing progress, anticipating obstacles. But for once, her mind was almost blank, very close to a meditative trance. The music playing in the background, which she listened to every evening, had been subtly modified. Brandt had found her tunnel into the Palace and had posted a message.

The message in the music troubled her.

*Fortuitous intel [ reliable source ]: Mother here [ Chevinta ]. Purpose unknown.*

Brandt's *Chirple* language possessed no inflection to convey emotional nuances. It was designed for discussing military and covert operations: strategy, intelligence, orders. Any references to states of mind were purely objects for discussion, for manipulation, not for feeling. All the same, Shayla sensed deep unease in the curt factual tones.

She forced her mind back from the numbness his words evoked.

*What does this mean?*

More to the point, why had Brandt chosen to tell her?

*Nothing to cause concern. He said he'd tell her if he managed to trace Mother. And he did.*

So why did she feel so uneasy?

*Fortuitous intel!*

It was said that the local dialect in Prandis had fifty different words for sunshine. The brazen midday sun in a clear sky. The caress of a spring dawn. The umber glow through an afternoon dust storm.

*Chirple* had equally subtle distinctions to denote varieties of intelligence. Shayla pondered Brandt's choice of wording. Fortuitous. Arrived at by chance. Neither knowingly revealed by the target, nor specifically sought by the recipient. So Mother had not contacted Brandt and he had not managed to follow her. *Reliable source.* She must have been noticed by one of Brandt's extensive network of contacts.

She was on Chevinta in secret. What could she want there?

Chevinta. Freeworld. Owing homage to no Family. Seat of learning, and Brandt's reclusive home for the last thirteen years.

Shayla forced her mind back to practicalities.

*Is there anything I can do?*

*From here?*

There was not. Shayla had her own mission to deal with, she could not afford to worry about her mother's mysterious movements now. They would follow up later — if there *was* a 'later' — meanwhile she knew that Brandt would keep an eye on Mother.

## Chapter 24

Shayla gazed at the Palace of Butterflies, spread out below like a giant cartwheel. At its center a white tower rose half a mile into the air, fanning out near the top to offer an open trumpet mouth to the sky. An apron of buildings spread out from the base of the tower, dominated by four massive ziggurats. Symmetrical spokes of buildings and avenues radiated out from this core, enclosing a luxuriant patchwork of greens, yellows, and ochres.

The palace straddled a narrow peninsula bounded by the open ocean on one side. Sparkling turquoise and white mackerel streaks of sandbanks merged into a band of deep ultramarine which ended abruptly in heaving windswept slate.

The other side of the palace looked across a bay to the sprawling city of Henriss Garden. Shayla could just make out jumbled cliffs of white, laced with strands and patches of green. The many waterways of the Wasanni delta encircled the city and carved glittering paths through the buildings.

Shayla sat in the cockpit next to the pilot. Grey metal glinted high overhead. Only a few flashes here and there in the morning sky, but the comms screen showed a dense umbrella of military craft surrounding the city.

*Shit, they're jumpy!*

Shayla knew that security would be tight, but this was getting close to scary.

*Will my passkey stand up? What if I missed something?* She suppressed the irrational twinge. She was now on the inside, and Brynwyn bin Covin had been thoroughly vetted and registered.

*Fleur?* No. She could have denounced Shayla any time in the last four days, or however long before that she'd suspected her. Whatever Fleur's game, it was out of Shayla's control.

The accompanying fleet of cruisers banked away one by one and made for the landing field on the perimeter of the palace. Shayla's staff and the hundreds of members of the Family entourages would be checked in, and assigned quarters in one of the buildings that made up the rim of the cartwheel.

But she was in the Emperor's personal cruiser. The Emperor himself traveled in luxury on the lower deck, surrounded by aides and servants. The smaller, but still extravagantly comfortable, staff cabin behind Shayla held an assortment of Ministers and senior officials. Several of them had been summoned for last minute briefings during the hour long flight. Shayla recognized the ominous figure of Magister Chalwen ap Gwynodd amongst them, and elected, as casually as possible, to keep the pilot company.

The pilot aimed for the top of the tower, slowed and circled once, before dropping into the opening at the top. A handful of craft followed them.

———————

The next three days were an exhausting blur. Armies of palace servants bore the brunt of the unremitting demands from the phalanx of Imperial guests, but Shayla's team had the thankless task of keeping them entertained around the clock, dealing with last-minute hitches, and accommodating an endless series of unplanned and idiosyncratic requests.

The first evening brought everyone together at an informal feast. The planned events began in earnest the following day with a parade and carnival on the Henriss waterfront. Throughout the day, the two mile stretch of water between the city and the palace formed a glittering stage for a jetski tournament, where contestants displayed their skills and courage in races, stunts, and furious games of ski lacrosse.

"Not bad," Marcus Halley commented at the end of the last match. "Only three fatalities this year."

A lavish fireworks display at midnight marked the official start of two days of Conclave.

Although the Family heads were now cloistered in the Temple of Reflection, the workload increased rather than diminished as the lesser Family members and minor nobility whiled away the hours. They seemed determined to test the boundaries of Imperial hospitality. There was the di Brugui twins' penchant for early morning hunting, Georgia dom Calvino's request for the Henriss Ensemble to stage a full operatic production on the lawns in front of the Hall of Music, Ivan and Scipio's appetite for gambling companions and female entertainment, and ensuring the palace temple was filled with suitably deferential worshippers whenever the Lord Habradim and his family went to prayer.

And the whole time, Shayla fought to keep her focus through a clinging veil of weariness.

---

*Matiki screamed as Shayla sawed at his leg with the rusty blade. She had to take his paw off, but she couldn't remember why it was so important. Her heart broke with the pain she was putting her beloved pet through, and at the look of betrayal in his eyes.*

*I have to do this! It is the only way to put him out of his torment.*

*But the worm of doubt gnawed at her.*

*Then certainty broke like dawn on a mountaintop. Shayla could see the awful folly of her actions. She was wrong. Doing the wrong thing.*

*Matiki's blood made the handle of the saw slippery. He didn't struggle. He was silent now, looking at her with hurt and reproach. But she had no choice now, she couldn't stop. She had reached the point of no return. The damage was done and she had to go on ...*

Shayla vaulted out of bed and leapt to the bathroom. She barely made it before she started vomiting. She heaved until her ribs ached.

She turned at last and leaned back against the wall, gasping for breath.

Finally she pulled herself upright, almost fainting from the effort, and washed her face. She composed herself and took stock, automatically charting the positions of the hidden cameras that she knew infested her suite. She began rehearsing excuses for her actions in case anyone commented. *Can I blame it on food? Water? A local infection? Hmm. Two gardeners were reported ill yesterday ...*

While Shayla let her subconscious mind work on her story, she puzzled over the reappearance of childhood terrors. *These were nightmares from times of uncertainty.* The thought brought dark memories, memories twenty years submerged in deadly purpose. *Why would I have uncertainty now?*

She'd been taken aback by the sheer ordinariness of the planet she was about to demolish, the lives she was about to take. *Magentis isn't what I imagined.* True, everything Shayla *had* imagined was indeed here. Strutting soldiers, arrogant bureaucrats, the whole corrupt and incestuous machinery of Imperial government. But that was such a small part of it that it was almost incidental, insignificant when seen alongside the mundane majority. The inn at Skerrin Brethwyn could just as easily have been on Eloon, or any one of a hundred worlds. The people mostly lived such petty and commonplace lives. Farmers, fishermen, builders, artists, merchants ...

*And the ever-present poor.* The image of the young mother at Hawflun haunted her, and those pitiful children. *What future might they have? What am I denying them?*

Shayla felt acid rising again and furiously suppressed the thought.

She instead studied her reflection in the mirror, noting subtle mottling under her skin where the pigment in her implants battled an unnatural pallor. She breathed deeply, closed her eyes, and recited a calming litany. When she opened her eyes again, natural color once more tinged her cheeks.

———•◆•———

The summons had been quite unexpected. Shayla paced the southwest promenade, where she'd been instructed to wait, hands clenching and unclenching at her sides. She glanced up and down the promenade, overlooking a garden slowly coming to life in the early morning light, and directed a spray of nicodyne into the back of her mouth.

Shayla grimaced as the drug took effect. Desperation measures. She knew the energy debt would have to be repaid. Soon.

A light and tangy fragrance filled the air. Dense knots of Evenian lemonwood bordered the path, sporting exuberant clusters of blossom, from rich golds and russets, creamy yellows, to milky opalescence.

The rising sun had already dispelled the cool of dawn, and pre-saged another tropical day that would soon grip the palace in a foundry furnace.

From her vantage point, Shayla surveyed the garden, one of many enclosed within the palace perimeter. Although it hadn't been obvious from the air, from here she could see that the tower and imposing zig-gurats stood at the top of a shallow but perfectly symmetrical hill. The grounds fell away in front of her to the perimeter buildings half a mile away, blinding in the sunlight creeping over the walls behind her.

A maze of beds and paths cut through stands of abstract topiary. A whole regiment of guards could easily lie hidden in the bizarre laby-rinth. Shayla blinked. The layout of this garden played tricks on her eyes. Appearing random at first sight, tantalizing hints of some deep geometrical order hovered on the verge of discovery, only to evaporate on closer scrutiny.

Movement caught Shayla's eye at the end of the promenade. The Emperor walked slowly into view, surrounded by his bodyguards. She turned towards him and stood, hands clasped in front of her, head bowed, as he approached.

Julian signaled to his escort to stay back. The captain opened his mouth as if on the verge of protesting, then he saluted and backed away, delivering a flurry of hand signals to his squad. The guards spread out along the promenade on either side, watchful, fingering weapons nervously.

Shayla had already noted patrols stationing themselves discreetly in the garden below. She'd passed a gardener earlier. He'd appeared to be inspecting a flawless box hedge, but the bulge under his tunic was the wrong shape for pruning shears. *They really are expecting an attack here this week.*

She had gotten some sense of their state of anxiety from Kurt, who'd been working almost around the clock liaising with the depart-ment of border security at the Palace, but nothing had prepared her for the tension here.

She bowed low as Julian approached.

"Bin Covin," he said, voice close to a whisper. "Walk with me a while."

Puzzled, Shayla fell in step alongside him. She studied his face from the corner of her eye as they descended a broad flight of steps into the garden labyrinth. His tone seemed cordial enough, but his expression was stern.

"Did you know that the technologists in my Security branch have developed remote spy devices that can listen in on a conversation from over a mile away?"

"Spying is not my province, My Lord," Shayla lied.

"They can focus a beam onto a hard surface, such as glass or metal, and detect vibrations in the reflected radiation." He waved his arm expansively. "Look around you. What do you see?"

*Lots of plants, of course!* "No such surfaces," Shayla said. Her throat constricted when she thought of her last meeting at Dognoty's. Had his spying countermeasures included this kind of eavesdropping?

The Emperor nodded. "You have excelled in your duties, bin Covin. Palace Administrator ap Terlion made a good appointment." He sounded thoughtful. Almost surprised.

*Am I supposed to respond to that?* Shayla sensed that the familiarity with which they'd spoken during the desert hunt was unlikely to be repeated. There, Julian had been in distress, reaching out for some human contact. Here he was the Emperor again. In command. Any familiarity now, she decided, was strictly one way.

All the same, Shayla began to feel giddy elation. *I've done it! When the time comes, in the panic to come, he* will *trust me.*

She hastily checked the feeling. The time for triumph would come soon enough, but for now, concentration and discipline could not afford to slip.

They walked on in silence for a minute. A heady scent enveloped them as the last shadows slipped into hiding for the day and the morning air came alive with fluttering jeweled wings. The Emperor seemed engrossed in the antics of two iridescent blue butterflies spiraling about his head.

"The Conclave was difficult and tiring, but worthwhile," he said at last. "Proceedings have been greatly eased by the hospitality you have arranged. Now we conclude with the State Banquet tonight, and the Festival of Fountains tomorrow."

Julian Skamensis paused, as if unsure whether he should be saying this. Shayla walked alongside him in silence. Eventually he stopped and turned to face her. "The Empire has many faces, bin Covin. For most people, the Military, Security, or Judiciary are the most obvious ones. Many underestimate the power of your office. Yours is a more subtle face, but it reaches into the hearts and lives of people in a way that raw might can never do."

He frowned. "A few people close to me understand this all too well, and wish to see this power leveraged to their advantage. I am telling you this because there are some amongst my Family and Household who hold conflicting views. I suspect that you have little idea what a perilous position you hold."

*You have absolutely no idea!*

"No matter what you do," he said, suddenly earnest, "it will be impossible to avoid making formidable enemies in some quarter or other."

*I think I already have, but I don't suppose you'd know all that goes on under your nose.*

"You have a tightrope to walk, as I'm sure you will soon discover. I want you to understand that your preparations meet with my approval. The question is, do you have the courage to steer a firm course?"

## Chapter 25

S hayla and Jojo sat in a staff car behind the Emperor's open ground cruiser. Behind them, assistants muttered into a battery of communicators, orchestrating the battalions of bands, gymnasts, and dancers standing ready along the route.

The Emperor's words yesterday had surprised Shayla, yet left her elated. It seemed that she had gained his trust to an extent she had not dared hope for. When she dwelled on it, Shayla found the thought slightly disquieting. The openness with which he'd spoken, the trust he'd shown, was dangerously endearing.

*Focus! Remember why you're here.*

She could hardly remember anything of the formal State Banquet last night, and had fallen asleep during the long and exquisitely dull performance of traditional theatrical dance. "A painful necessity," Jojo had said with a grin and a wink when they'd discussed the program of events the week before. When Kurt shook her awake at the end of the concert, Shayla had only just stopped herself drawing her pistol on reflex.

She struggled to stay awake now, and concentrated on the festival around her.

On either side, dazzling white walls rose to support towering terrace gardens. Trees and shrubs fought for height, while hanging baskets overflowed, and honeysuckle cascaded down the walls.

The scene seemed to shimmer, clouded by the ghost of a memory. A young Shayla sat in a ground car alongside her father, peering out at the luxuriant greenery decking the whitewashed avenues of Trayn, one of the oldest cities on Eloon. A city now dead, burned off the face of the planet. Shayla fought for breath and squeezed her eyes shut, forcing herself back to the here-and-now.

Crowds lined the streets, hung from balconies, and thronged terraces high overhead. Everywhere, stern-faced guards stood, weapons at the ready.

Watching over all the proceedings, the menacing outline of the flagship *Wrath of Empire* lurked in the stratosphere, casting fleeting shadows over the city. Despite the tropical heat, a chill ran down Shayla's back.

The Emperor's procession wound slowly through the teeming avenues and plazas. Each of the major squares in the city vied for supremacy in putting on a dazzling display to be judged by the Emperor. At the end of the three mile long Via Magentis, they emerged first into the Empress Florence Plaza. The fountains in each corner that normally sent jets of water two hundred feet into the air had been joined by rows of lesser spouts. Together, they sent shimmering curtains cascading in time to the orchestra playing in the center of the square.

In the normally-bare North Plaza, a hundred and fifty life-size bronzes of Haro's Dolphins had been erected for the occasion, riding foaming torrents and spouting high into the air.

In between the squares, the major avenues were dressed with streamers and garlands. "I remember my grandmother telling me about the Festival of Fountains, years ago," said Jojo. "Before Florence's time. I don't believe there's been one such as this for sixty years."

"I've never actually seen one before," Shayla said, truthfully. "I understand they've been rather grim affairs in recent years."

"I've only been involved in two before. In my time with the M of C office. Very military affairs. Show of strength. Old Scottin was trying to move on from the rather bloody displays of earlier years, but it was slow going. Lot of resistance."

*Was he walking a tightrope too?*

Jojo gazed around, smiling. "Now *this*! Right out of the history texts."

Avantis Plaza was home to some of the oldest fountains in the city—elaborate sculptures of plants, fish, and mythical creatures, age-worn and crusted with salt from the ocean. The normally restrained streams of water were now all colors of the rainbow, splashing and mingling into multi-hued swirls in the pools beneath.

*These plans had the Emperor's approval. He went out of his way to tell me so.*

In the Field of Blossoms, wide pools frothed with eruptions of bubbles which danced and floated around their heads, scattering glittering shards of light from the fierce sun.

*If this is what the Emperor wanted all along, why did he not simply order it so years ago?*

Looking around her, Shayla felt a cold emptiness at the thought that this would soon all be gone.

———•◆•———

"My nephew is young still. He has much to learn about the ways of Empire." Grand Duke Ivan paced in front of the windows which spanned the far wall of the office, floor to ceiling and so flawlessly clear that it was difficult to be sure there was anything of substance there. Ivan turned and gazed out, oblivious to the thousand foot drop a few inches from his toes.

Beyond the window, the white walls of Henriss Garden gleamed across the water. He gestured towards the city. "See! Out there! Seventy million people within our view." His arm swept in a wide circle above his head as he turned on his heel to face Shayla. "Hundreds of other towns and cities. Thousands of villages on Magentis alone. Dozens of other worlds and billions of people." He clenched his fist. "It takes strength, and an iron grip, to keep all those worlds under control. At any one time, half of them are on the verge of slipping away from us."

Shayla stood in the middle of the room, studying the Grand Duke. His voice was patient, a tutor explaining a complex matter to a slow pupil, but Shayla detected undertones of tension. He was simmering with barely-controlled anger. Was this a residue of his fury with her after the desert hunt? Possible, but it seemed there were deeper matters on his mind.

She scanned the room from the corners of her eyes. The wall behind her bordered the corridor circling this level of the tower. Ahead was the clear and seamless expanse of armored plastic. The walls on either side were more interesting. Pillars alternated with heavy drapes suggesting spaces beyond. Subtle sounds and movements, almost beneath the threshold of her senses, betrayed the presence of hidden onlookers.

*What does he want with me?*

"The Emperor needs constant reminding of the strength needed to rule. And the populace needs reminding too. Shows of strength. Demonstrations that we *will* prevail. Yesterday was supposed to be just such an occasion. An opportunity to remind the Heads of Family where their interests lie."

"I understood that the Emperor had already done the necessary reminding. In the Conclave." Shayla spoke for the first time.

Ivan stared back, momentarily silenced by her uninvited comment. He took a deep breath. "Nevertheless, you have traditions to uphold."

Shayla thought back to her briefing notes on past Festivals. "Mass torture of prisoners and fountains of their blood were a late addition by the Empress Florence, entirely contrary to earlier tradition."

"Pah! Details!" Ivan looked irritated, then reined in his anger once more. His tone became more pensive. "But you have a point there, I must concede. My mother's approach lacked subtlety. We can be infinitely more creative than that. Nevertheless, this Empire was founded on values of devotion to duty, strict discipline, and unquestioning obedience. Need I remind you that you were appointed to uphold these values? Something your predecessor found increasingly difficult to manage?"

*Oh crap!* It was clear that Brynwyn was supposed to be working somehow with Ivan. *He arranged to have Brynwyn appointed.* Mabbwendig's comment days earlier now made more sense. *But to what end?* Well, Ivan's motive would have to wait, but at least that would explain his patience with her. He must have invested considerable effort in putting her there. This interview sounded like her own personal reminder.

*So…the Emperor is not the only one I need to impress. Shit, this is going to get messy.*

Shayla gazed at the floor while she thought.

*What sort of correspondence did Brynwyn and Ivan have before she left for Hawflun?* This had not been any part of Shayla's briefing. The Insurrection's ignorance she could understand. Their intelligence was limited, to say the least. But why had the Firenzi masterminds who'd threaded this plan together not noted Ivan's interest in Brynwyn?

This complicated matters. *But maybe they had known!* The thought was a shock. Maybe they'd chosen not to brief her, confident that it would either not become an issue in this short space of time, or that she could handle it on the fly. What touching faith!

She recalled Julian's words. He was expecting Brynwyn to have a balancing act to perform. With any luck the same would be true from Ivan's perspective. She had some task to perform for him, but presumably she also needed to be effective in her duties in order to establish her position. What use could she be to Ivan if she failed to please the Emperor?

"I am bound to perform my Emperor's bidding," Shayla answered, with just the right emphasis to give the impression that this was not entirely to her liking. "And if my Emperor should wish my replacement, I'm sure he will not hesitate to order it so." *And you would then lose your investment. I hope!*

When there was no response, Shayla bowed low. "I must prepare now for an audience with our Emperor."

———·•·———

Once Brynwyn had gone, Grand Duke Ivan Skamensis stood a long while, then addressed the empty room. "I am not happy. This seems not to be the woman I arranged to have appointed. Either she is playing a more subtle game with the Emperor than I had expected, or she is playing with *me*."

His slightly pensive tone hardened. "She must be tested."

Silence answered him. But he knew the unseen watchers had left to carry out his bidding.

## Chapter 26

Shayla strolled along the balcony, taking a last look at the city across the water. The open funnel atop the Palace tower rose above her, overhanging the balcony and casting a welcome shade over this wind-swept eyrie. Two thousand feet below her, the northern quarter of the palace lay spread out like a map.

"Our cruiser is ready," Kurt said behind her. She turned to follow him.

The official proceedings were now at an end, and the Emperor's guests had started to take their leave. Everything was now low-key and informal. No need for Shayla's office to involve itself in details. The rest of her staff returned to Prandis yesterday. Kurt arranged a small craft to carry himself and Shayla back. She needed time alone to think and ready herself for the final part of her plan.

A chill ran down her neck. *I am treading more tightropes here than I care to think!*

Without a word, they entered one of the elevators ringing the tower like the sapwood of a gargantuan tree. Kurt seemed unusually preoccupied, not his usual talkative self, but Shayla had enough on her own mind and welcomed the silence.

They emerged onto a balcony deep within the wineglass funnel of the hangar. A blinding circle of blue opened out far above them. Steep walls climbed to meet the sky, with ledges holding an assortment of craft.

Kurt led them to a cruiser nearby. Small, about fifty feet in length, its polished copper skin was blazoned with the Imperial crest, reserved for Palace staff on official business.

As they climbed into the tiny passenger cabin, Shayla recalled her last tiring journey to Prandis with Kurt. "I assume travel restrictions have been relaxed since the panic over that starhopper?"

"A little," he answered over his shoulder as he settled into the cockpit. "But your name carries weight now. People here are well tuned to a person's standing with the Emperor."

The sky deepened to indigo as they looped high into the outer reaches of the atmosphere. From where she sat, Shayla could just see Kurt in the pilot's seat. She poured a drink from a compact dispenser in front of her and returned her attention to her notepad.

She was supposed to be preparing a briefing for her team on the planet-wide holiday to coincide with the opening of the late session of the Imperial Legislature. Palace schematics unrolled before her eyes. Nothing to do with the Imperial Legislature. Shayla's eyes drank in details of the subterranean labyrinth, patrols and sentry positions, security, checkpoints. Every detail settled into place in her memory.

Kurt turned from the controls and stepped back into the main cabin. Shayla looked up from the screen and was shocked to find herself gazing into the aperture of a military issue beam pistol.

*Shit! Why was my guard down?*

"Kurt! What are you doing?" She allowed her very real surprise to register.

"Following orders." His voice was level, almost conversational, but the snout of the pistol never wavered.

"Whose orders? Is this treachery?"

"That's what I intend to find out. The Imperial Family appointed you to perform certain duties."

Shayla reached for her drink. "And I *am* performing my duty. The Emperor himself has commended me on my work thus far."

She reckoned she could disarm Kurt without too much difficulty, but not in front of the ever-present cameras. The only one she could detect was at the front of the cabin, facing her. She'd been careful to seat herself so that the surface of her notepad was hidden from it.

It seemed that Kurt was also being cautious, shielding the pistol from the camera with his body. "I'm not talking about the *Emperor*." All geniality was gone from his voice. "Be charitable in thought and deed. Do duty with humility."

*What?* Some memory stirred deep in Shayla's mind. "And give thanks for the blessings of Empire divine," she responded. *Where the heck did that come from?*

Kurt's eyes narrowed to slits. His fist tightened on the hilt of the pistol.

*What's going on? This sounds like a pre-arranged recognition exchange. Fuck!*

Her response had been automatic, yet she sensed it was what Kurt expected her to say. *But where did that passage come from?* Not from the Pillars of Duty, she was sure of that. One of the companion volumes maybe?

"Treat your brethren with patient compassion," Kurt said. "Atone tenfold for misdeeds."

*We're not finished yet. Everything hangs on this response.* The words were on the tip of Shayla's tongue. She recognized the passage at last, from an obscure book. She was about to respond, but Kurt's wording was slightly off. *From an earlier time?*

Her mind raced.

*Got it!* "On these pillars we stand firm against the tide of time."

At last, Shayla could picture the shrine in the history texts she'd read in the desert a few days ago. A small and simple memorial, in the grounds of a little-known Imperial residence in Cravel Braz. The Empress Florence's real resting place, a far cry from the gaudy official memorial in Prandis.

"Tell My Lord Ivan that Madre Florence's memory will endure." Instinct told Shayla to use the title inscribed on the memorial above the passage she and Kurt had just quoted.

She'd also gambled on the connection she had just glimpsed. Ivan had Brynwyn appointed to carry out some mission for him. It sounded like Kurt was also working for Ivan. *Was that why he'd been selected to escort Brynwyn?* No matter. Shayla readied herself for action in case she'd misjudged.

Kurt relaxed, although he still had his weapon trained on Shayla. "The Grand Duke feared you had forgotten your purpose here. He was concerned that your recent behavior seemed out of character. He wondered if this was the same woman he spoke to in Toomin."

*No fucking kidding! I need to end this conversation.* Shayla's heart raced. *I could kill him, but that would leave awkward questions to answer. He would soon be missed.*

"I am the woman I've always been. There is much in my life that is unknown to any in the Palace." *Keep close to the truth. This simple guard is no simple guard after all. He may have truthsense training.* "Tell My Lord Ivan that I intend to uphold the values this Empire holds dear, but all in good time. My only concern right now is to do my Emperor's bidding and to earn his trust." *Close enough to be credible.*

Shayla kept her expression and tone cold and commanding. "Now I have work to do if I am to remain in office long enough to be useful."

Kurt's eyes widened slightly, but after a moment he nodded. His pistol vanished into the folds of his robe.

Shayla settled back into her seat and kept a watchful eye on Kurt as he returned to the cockpit. She was confident that he posed no serious threat to her, not physically anyway, but she fervently hoped that she'd managed to satisfy him. Well, as long as she'd sown enough seeds of doubt to keep him out of the way for a little while, that was all that mattered. By tomorrow night it would all be over.

At one o'clock in the morning, the palace was eerily quiet. Service corridors deep under the courts and buildings were almost deserted. Shayla moved silently, cloaked in the drab robes of a maintenance inspector. There was no uncertainty in her progress to alert the ever-watchful agents filtering the thousands of visual feeds from all corners of the Palace. Even if human eyes chose to view her, she shouldn't arouse suspicion. Inspectors worked everywhere and followed no set schedule. Her presence should go unremarked.

When Shayla had first planned this route, it had seemed almost like overkill. Now she realized that her first instinct had been prudent. Brynwyn bin Covin was under too much scrutiny from too many quarters for comfort.

Using a surveillance dead zone, Brynwyn had dropped out of sight back in the administration buildings hours ago. Nobody would notice an extra inspector mingling with the hordes of Palace staff leaving the dining hall.

Her route led her on a tortuous path towards the labyrinth under the Emperor's quarters. She stopped and spent long minutes surveying a piece of machinery. From the catwalk where she stood, a tangle of pipes plunged into dark depths and soared upwards through layers of ladders and gangways.

Shayla climbed, stopping here and there to peer at hatches and valves as she had seen inspectors do. She checked the time. She needed to be in position soon, but this part could not be hurried. The areas around the Imperial family quarters were watched especially closely.

Close to ground level, she stopped on another balcony and took out her notepad. She leaned against the railing, head down, an inspector making notes. Careful to keep her movements slow and small, she twiddled her stylus under the cover of her cloak, scanning her surroundings for the cameras she knew would be present.

*There. And there.* Soon she found what she was looking for. At the back of the catwalk, in between two bulky cabinets, was another dead zone, free from surveillance. Satisfied, Shayla readied her jamming agents. She strolled over to the cabinets, pausing to examine the nearest. She slipped in between and activated the jamming signal, freezing the view of whoever might be watching.

Now there was need for haste. Shayla whipped off her cloak and swapped it for her official robes of office that she'd carried in a satchel slung over her shoulder. Satchel and inspector's cloak she stashed out of sight.

Shayla hurried out of hiding, momentarily invisible to the confused cameras. She climbed the remaining flights of stairs and into an ancient cellar, dry and dusty. As she went, she scanned ahead for more cameras, switching the jamming signal from one to another, and freeing those behind her when she was out of range.

Back in more traveled corridors she could no longer risk freezing the cameras. Interfering with spycams like that was risky enough anyway. She was banking on the limitations of automated agents' ability to spot continuity errors between cameras, but a figure suddenly appearing or vanishing from one camera's view would signal disaster. She found another dead zone, then stepped into the open once more as Brynwyn bin Covin.

She made her way up through the building. The Imperial Master of Circuses, always at her master's beckoning, summoned to a late night briefing. That's what she hoped any watchers would conclude, anyway.

She passed two guards, who stood to attention at her approach. Another staircase. More guards.

Finally, Shayla came to a dimly-lit landing, with a heavy oak balustrade, silky with age and the oils of hands from a hundred generations. Rich tapestries adorned the walls. Thick curtains half concealed the passageway beyond.

A guard patrolled slowly back and forth. He nodded in recognition as Shayla approached. She put her hand to her mouth and coughed. The guard stopped, stunned.

"Keep on walking as you were," Shayla murmured, pocketing the tiny blowtube concealed in her palm. "When your comrades join you from the Emperor's quarters, go with them."

That was a complicated instruction to give to a person under the influence of trylex, but it didn't matter much what he did as long as he was out of the way.

Shayla entered the cover of the cascade of drapes and paused to survey the corridor. Two more soldiers stood guard outside the Emperor's chamber.

*Nearly time.*

Shayla knew Dognoty's agent was inside the Palace. He waited for her signal, which would be relayed instantly to the Insurrection around the globe. She felt a momentary pang for Beatrice Mueller, who would be dead now after letting the agent into the Palace.

*Don't go soft! They are all dead anyway.*

She counted down the seconds.

Her coded signal sped through the communications network, the herald of destruction.

She steadied her breathing, then jammed the watching cameras once more. This would eventually catch somebody's attention, but the Security forces would soon have more than enough to keep them occupied. All that mattered was that her actions went unseen for as long as possible.

She took two more darts from a pouch and settled them on her tongue. The slightest scratch from the needle points would spell disaster, but this was a trick she had practiced and perfected. She palmed the blowtube and walked up to the guards.

"Is the Emperor expecting you, Magister Summis?"

Shayla's clenched hand rose to her lips. The guards froze as the drug took them.

"No, I don't believe he is." She smiled. "Go to the Green Throne Room. Collect the guard on the top landing. He will come with you. Shoot anyone else you meet along the way."

A muffled rumble in the distance told her the Insurrection's attack had started. With a bit of luck her drugged guards would clear the way for her. At the very least they would sow confusion.

She turned to the door and eased it open, peering around the opening. A servant snored in an easy chair nearby. She located and disabled the omnipresent cameras, then slipped inside.

The dozing attendant struggled awake as the door closed behind Shayla. He died, neck broken, before he could make a sound. She heaved him onto her shoulders and bundled him quietly into the nearest closet.

A series of archways led from the outer chamber to the bedchamber. More archways led to a study. Shayla peered around one of the pillars to where the Emperor slept.

## Chapter 28

Imperial Chief of Security, Chalwen ap Gwynodd, flew out of her office door, a feat which her staff would have sworn defied the laws of inertia if they hadn't been so engrossed in their own problems.

The railing on the upper balcony, overlooking the security operations room, creaked as her bulk came to rest against it. She gripped it, knuckles turning white. Her eyes flicked from display to display across the room.

The nearby duty officer jabbered a stream of instructions into a microphone. He stuttered to a halt when he saw Chalwen. He recovered and saluted. "Main Palace gates breached. Fighting in the state rooms. Barracks alerted and guards responding."

He broke off, listening to some private report. "Bring that up on the wall screen," he muttered into the microphone. "This is not just the Palace. Trouble across Prandis…wait…reports confused, but there's more."

"Get Commander Malkin up here," Chalwen barked to a nearby clerk.

"He's on his way, Magister," the duty officer answered, signaling the clerk to return to her duties.

The usual displays spanning the front of the crowded room shrank and shifted to make way for new schematics. The Palace appeared in detail, then a smaller scale map of the city. Starbursts speckled the new diagrams to join the constellation of trouble spots sprinkled across the planetary display. A patchwork of visual feeds sprang up. Explosions flared in darkness. Daytime images from elsewhere on the planet showed columns of smoke and fleeing crowds.

Chalwen's head turned as screen after screen lit up, showing scenes of violence. "Holy fucking shit," she whispered, struggling to take in the picture they painted.

Her eyes narrowed as she studied the regional reports in more detail. She scanned one page after another with a frown.

Paul Malkin appeared through the lower door, skidding as he cornered and bounded up the aisle to where Chalwen stood.

He also surveyed the information flooding the status screens. He steadied his ragged breathing, and took time to straighten his collar and button the front of his tunic as he read. "What do they hope to gain from this?" he muttered. "This is nothing more than civil unrest. On a global scale, well co-coordinated, but it's surely nothing that the local forces can't handle given time. And we have the navy standing by, and reserves of ground forces to send to reinforce any serious trouble spots."

"You're right. This will be all over by morning. Unless ..." Chalwen blinked tears of frustration from her eyes. "We're missing something. There's got to be more to this than a bit of rabble-rousing. I've sensed all along that something big was going on. But what?"

"What I want to know," a soft voice interrupted, "is how could this have been orchestrated without our knowledge?"

Chalwen jumped. "Henri! I didn't see you coming."

"People often don't," he said, with a sly grin.

Then Chalwen caught up with Henri's words. "You're right. How could we have received no intelligence whatsoever ..." Her voice tailed off in disbelief. Her mouth twisted.

Henri nodded. "Fleur."

"Any word on the whereabouts of Commander Trixmin?" Chalwen asked the duty officer. Her voice was an oily and murderous calm as she fought to stop blackness creeping into the edge of her vision. If the whole of her intelligence division was compromised, what else had they missed?

The duty officer talked with his clerks, then turned back to Chalwen white-faced and perspiring. "She's not responding, and hasn't been heard from in over three hours." He swallowed hard. "Regardless, you need to look at this." He pointed to a screen in front of him. "Look here. The Concert Hall and the Throne Room. Those are Firenzi fighters holed up in there. They seem to be fighting both our own troops and the Insurrection."

"What are they doing there?" Paul said. "They should all be in the guest wing."

The duty officer scanned more screens. "They've secured the gate house to the Imperial garden, and we've lost all transmission from the security monitors in the Imperial quarters."

Chalwen and Henri looked each other in the eye. "The Emperor!" they shouted in unison.

Chalwen's fingers clawed the air in front of her as if trying to strangle an invisible opponent. "Screw the Insurrection," she gasped. "They were nothing more than a distraction. All this ..." she waved her hands at the scenes of carnage "... just a diversion."

She lumbered down the aisle. "Paul," she called over her shoulder, "manage the security situation from here. Henri, you're with me."

"Take a cruiser," said Paul. "I'll send a detachment from the barracks to meet you."

"Damned right I'm taking a fucking cruiser. You don't see me *running* there, do you?"

———————

Emperor Julian Skamensis stirred as a distant explosion rattled the windows. Shayla held her breath until he settled again. Then, flitting like a ghost through his quarters, she went searching.

A glint of emerald green on the desk in the study caught her eye. The Emperor's personal scroll lay amongst a pile of ornaments, books, and pictures. She opened it and set her notepad down alongside. The Imperial crest on the open surface confirmed its identity. It was pointless trying to crack its security. Not that she couldn't, given time, just that it wasn't necessary. Not part of the plan. She pointed her stylus and dropped a software agent onto the Emperor's scroll. It sat on the surface for a few seconds, then faded from view. She snapped the scroll shut, and turned her attention to the sleeping Emperor.

She selected another needle from the pouch, and cupped it between two fingers. She approached the Emperor, took a deep breath, then shook his shoulder, pricking his skin with the needle. At the same time she slapped his face, and sobbed, "Please wake up, My Lord."

Julian Skamensis woke, startled, and shoved Shayla away.

"What the devil's going on?"

"Oh, thank the Almighty. I couldn't wake you. I feared you had been drugged. Or worse." Shayla backed from the bed, bowing and taking the opportunity to flick the needle out of sight under a nearby table. "My Lord, the Palace is under siege. Your guards have deserted their posts. I fear some kind of betrayal. I must get you to a place of safety, quickly."

Shayla talked rapidly, barely stopping to draw breath, knowing the Emperor would be disorientated. The drug she'd administered was distantly related to trylex, but much more subtle in its effect. For a while, Julian would be confused, easily led, normal rational judgment confounded. As long as she took the lead and kept him under pressure and unbalanced, he would be powerless to question her actions.

Another explosion rumbled. Julian's eyes darted from Shayla to the windows, and back again.

"When I heard the commotion and saw the scenes from the gates I feared for your safety." She threw him clothes and grabbed a robe from a closet.

He dressed automatically, his mouth hanging open.

"I don't know what is going on, but I must get you out of the Palace." Shayla thrust the robe into his hands. "Please, My Lord. Please hurry."

Julian hesitated, rubbing his eyes with balled fists, then rushed to the desk and grabbed the Imperial scroll.

*Thought you might have the presence of mind to remember. Just as well I disabled it!* Shayla tugged at his arm. "My Lord, we must leave the Palace. I will take you to a place of safety."

She pulled him into the deserted corridor. At the balcony, she held up her hand and paused. She peered around the curtains leading to the landing. All quiet. She beckoned the Emperor to follow. Past the windows opposite, beams flashed in the darkness. Screams and shouts drifted up from the courtyard outside.

"My Lord," Shayla hissed, "this uprising may be more widespread than the Palace, or even the city. I've heard rumors of a big plot. The Security services have been talking about it the whole time I've been here."

"Yes," he murmured, "Chalwen has been warning of such."

"My Lord, call in the navy. They may be needed to quell this uprising. They need direction from their Supreme Commander."

"Yes, of course." Julian looked around. "Back in my quarters ..."

"No time," Shayla shouted. "Your life is in danger." She knew the conflicting priorities would confuse him, compel him to seek her guidance. She could see the anguish in his face as the drug robbed him of his faculties.

"There is an access port." She pointed to a panel on the wall, half hidden behind the curtains. "Send the signal from here under your signature."

He nodded. Brow furrowed in concentration he unrolled his scroll and scratched at the surface with his stylus.

"It's no use," he cried in frustration. "It won't work. Bin Covin, what is happening here?"

More shouts and sounds of fighting echoed up the stairwell.

"Use mine!" she said, quelling the pounding in her chest. "Hurry, we must get out of here."

He took the proffered notebook and wrote on it. Shayla kept watch over the balcony as he scrawled a series of codes, then signed off with a flourish.

"It is done," he said.

"Good. Now I must get you off the planet."

Shayla led the way down the stairs, then across the landing below. She pointed to a door opposite. He looked puzzled for a moment, then nodded. Before he opened the door, Shayla put a finger to her lips. He nodded again, then pushed the door open.

Together they peered out into the darkness.

"Keep behind me," Shayla whispered, drawing her beam pistol.

Cool night air enveloped them as they crept out onto a bridge high above a narrow courtyard. The walls of the Emperor's Residence loomed behind them. Ahead rose the circular tower of a hangar. Shayla peered over the edge. Sporadic gunfire flashed beyond the kitchens in the distance. Shadowy figures milled in the courtyard by the administrative offices, and the murmur of confused voices reached her ears.

Shayla beckoned the Emperor to follow her, and signaled him to keep low. She crossed the bridge in a running crouch.

A frightened guard stammered a challenge as she reached the cover of the doorway.

"It's the Emperor, you idiot," Shayla hissed.

The guard swallowed hard, but recovered himself when he saw the figure of the Emperor in the dim light of the entrance. "Magister Summis," he whispered, drawing himself to attention. "You are alive. There were rumors…what is happening?"

Julian looked blankly at Shayla.

"There's been an uprising," she said. Julian's face was a comical picture of relief and gratitude that she was taking the lead. "The Palace is being overrun. I must get the Emperor away from here." She thought for a moment. "Who else is in this building?"

"Four guards at the ground level entrance," he answered. "I stand watch here. There is no-one else."

"Are the guards downstairs still manning their posts?"

"When I last checked a few minutes ago, yes. With the fighting outside we don't know who's who out there. They've sealed the lower entrance. I was about to do the same here."

"Good. Do so now. I'm taking the Emperor off the planet for safety."

Shayla led Julian through the entrance tunnel and into the central chamber of the hangar. They emerged onto a narrow catwalk circling the inner wall. Below them sat four air cruisers, small and sleek. Above them was a starlit circle of sky.

Julian pointed to the nearest craft. "We'll take *Amethyst*."

Shayla nodded. *So, you're starting to regain your sense of direction.*

A strangled cry from the tunnel behind made her whirl around. A beam flashed in the still-open doorway, momentarily blinding her. She pushed the Emperor to one side under cover and peered around the corner just in time to see the guard pitch backwards to the floor. Wide and sightless eyes were the only recognizable features in the charred remains of his face.

Acting on little more than subliminal signals in the darkness of the far opening, Shayla shot a shadowy figure who made the mistake of approaching.

She sent more shots through the opening, more to dazzle any others out there than in any hope of doing damage, and turned to the Emperor. "Go get *Amethyst* fired up. I'll make sure there are no more gatecrashers."

Julian placed a hand on her arm. "Be careful, Brynwyn."

Shayla grimaced, checked the entrance again, then slipped around the corner into the tunnel. Another shadow appeared in the gloom, and didn't quite live long enough to regret it.

She hurried to the far end, keeping under cover of the half-closed door. She was a trained fighter and a marksman, but above all she was an assassin. Gun fights were not her forte. She was far more at home in close combat.

She reached out to push the door closed, but snatched her hand back as a bolt sizzled off the metal, singeing her fingertips with a crackling discharge.

*Crap!* The control panel across from her had been fried. She had no way to secure the door against intruders.

Shayla's foot nudged something hard. She glanced down. The guard lay beside her, his pistol lying alongside him. With a wary eye on the doorway, and all other senses straining, she stooped to retrieve it. This was military issue, much better than the civilian weapon she carried.

Another beam lanced down the tunnel, then another.

Assessing her situation, Shayla used her own weapon to knock out the few lights in the tunnel. She was now in deeper darkness than the assailants outside. She backed half way down the corridor, crossed to the other side, and flattened herself on the floor against the wall. Just in time. A furious barrage from outside incinerated the door she had just been sheltering behind.

A wave of heat washed over her.

She now had a clear view past the glowing wreckage. Figures moved on the bridge. She waited until the nearest was in the doorway before she opened fire. Three shots in quick succession. Bodies slumped to the ground. Nothing else moved.

To be sure, Shayla opened up the butt of her beam pistol and slid out the tiny power pack. She tossed it over the bodies and onto the bridge. She aimed and fired with the more powerful pistol.

The mid section of the bridge collapsed in the blast as the power pack detonated.

Shayla turned.

A sound just on the edge of hearing made her dive and roll. Someone cursed. She continued the motion and sprang to her feet to face another assailant.

She brought her pistol up, but a heavy blow sent it skittering out of sight down the tunnel. Only quick reactions saved her arm from joining it. She blocked another blow and fought back, to be blocked in turn.

A flare lit the near doorway, revealing a familiar profile and braided hair she'd last seen in the forests of Horliath.

"Cobra!" The word was torn from her lips in shock.

He paused, also shocked. "Shark!" he spat. "What the fuck are you doing? The Emperor should be dead."

"He soon will be." The words rang with truth.

"Not good enough. This wasn't the plan. We were ambushed by both Palace and Firenzi fighters. You set this up. You betrayed us!"

The last words were accompanied by a vicious lunge which Shayla barely parried. The ferocity of Cobra's attack took her by surprise. The two fought in near darkness, sensing rather than seeing each other's presence.

At home in the jungle, Cobra had been an outstanding guide, now Shayla realized his fighting skills were an equal match.

She quelled a tide of panic. *I can beat him!* She reached deep into herself and found her inner sanctum of calm certainty. Even in the dim light, augmented by sporadic gunfire outside, it seemed she could see Cobra clearly. Time slowed. His movements appeared measured and more predictable.

Now at least she could hold her ground, but only just.

Then Cobra yelped, a cry cut short as he recovered himself. Something metallic clattered across the passageway. He must have slipped on the guard's pistol. He was off balance for only a fraction of a second, but Shayla seized the advantage, forcing him back down the tunnel and out onto the bridge.

He was now on the defensive, trying to rally himself just as Shayla had done.

It was all over in a moment. A long moment stretched in time by Shayla's heightened state of awareness. The damaged paving of the bridge crumbled, slabs falling away in slow motion. Cobra teetered on the edge of safety, then fell backwards. In desperation he launched himself towards the far side of the gap.

Shayla didn't wait to see if he made it. She raced down the tunnel and onto the catwalk. *Amethyst* waited. A low thrumming filled the chamber. She vaulted the railing and landed in the open hatchway. "Go!" she yelled. The cruiser tilted under her feet as Julian angled towards the sky. She slapped the controls to shut the hatch, and scrambled to join him in the cockpit.

As she strapped into her seat, light flared in the cockpit. *Amethyst* shuddered and canted to one side. Smoke and ozone pricked her nose.

Julian wrestled the controls of the cruiser, lifting them out of the hangar. Another beam glanced off the hull. Through the cockpit window, Shayla glimpsed Cobra leaping into one of the remaining cruisers.

The buildings of the Palace wheeled close in front of them. The windows of the senior staff quarters loomed large before the Emperor brought the nose up.

A deadly shape lifted above the walls of the hangar behind them.

"I'll take the controls," Shayla said. "We've got company."

They barely cleared the roof of the staff quarters, then dropped below the eaves on the far side.

Masonry exploded behind them. Slates shattered on the cockpit canopy. Shayla hugged the wall of the next building then banked around the corner.

The cruiser responded sluggishly. That first shot as they were taking off had done some damage. If Cobra was half as good a pilot as he was in unarmed combat, they were finished.

Shayla eased the controls, taking the craft as fast as her reactions would permit in the maze of narrow alleys at the back of the Palace. They hurtled between store rooms and barracks, grazing the corner of a building as they went. Shayla fought for control before the next building threatened them.

*I'm over-steering!* Shayla's reactions were being confounded by an unexpected luxury. *Who the fuck bothers with a grav field in a small cruiser?* She swallowed acid as the scene outside wheeled and pivoted past the canopy contradicting her other senses. *I'm used to feeling the maneuvers in this sort of combat!*

Then they were out over the eastern portico and across the Plaza. She kept low, twisting and turning all the while. With a damaged craft, Shayla chose the confines of the city squares and streets where wit and reactions were all-important, rather than exposing herself to a straight dogfight out in the open.

Bolts of liquid lightning streaked past their nose, raking a swathe through the crowds fighting in the square below. Buildings closed around them once more.

Shayla dodged down one street after another. The glass frontage of Dognoty's exploded as they flashed past. Cobra clung to her rear, reeling her in. She couldn't shake him off.

Buildings became a blur as Shayla pushed the cruiser and her own abilities to the limit. Although she was dodging and weaving too fast amongst too much background clutter for Cobra to get a proper lock on them, it was only a matter of time before a random strike downed them.

This time she found the rising panic impossible to check.

More bolts lit the cockpit.

*What? Those were way off!*

These were not aimed at *Amethyst*. Shayla pulled up almost too late as the street ahead filled with tumbling masonry.

She was high in the air. An easy target. She flung the cruiser around to regain the cover of the streets, waiting for the strike she thought was inevitable.

Nothing happened.

Shayla risked a glance behind her, and saw a third craft had joined the fight. Cobra had broken off his pursuit. The hunter had become the hunted.

She didn't bother to question this turn of events. She seized the opportunity and lifted the cruiser high into the night sky, still jinking from side to side. After a few moments, it was clear they were no longer being pursued. She opened the throttle, heading for the upper atmosphere.

She tapped the communications panel, and scanned down the list of names. "You'll be safe on one of the warships until this is over. Let's see. *Hawk, Brazen, Merciless, Relentless* ..."

"Make for *Merciless*," Julian slurred, gazing out at the lights of the city falling away below.

Chalwen relaxed her grip on the controls and circled the street where the stricken cruiser had crashed. It had come to rest half buried in an apartment block. The building looked to be on the verge of collapse.

"You're sure the Emperor was on board?"

"That was definitely *Amethyst* on the run," Henri replied. "Reserved for the Emperor's personal use alone. Only he has the passcodes to free the controls. Draw your own conclusions."

Chalwen growled, torn between the fast-vanishing craft above, and the wreckage below. "How soon will ground forces get here? Whoever was piloting that cruiser was trying to kill the Emperor. If he — or she — still lives, I will wring out the truth with my bare hands."

## Chapter 29

Shayla glanced at Julian. He slumped against the window, gazing at the darkness below speckled with the retreating lights of humanity. She turned her attention back to the controls, and sealed the cruiser for sub-orbital travel.

Up ahead, the sun burst above the horizon. It was an achingly beautiful sight.

Shayla looked away from the sunrise and scrawled the call sign for *Merciless* on the comms screen. She waited for a connection, knowing they would recognize the significance of her own call sign. What sort of reaction had she just stirred up at the receiving end?

"*Merciless* here…*Amethyst*," came a startled reply.

"*Amethyst* requesting permission to dock," Shayla announced. "The Emperor is aboard. Please arrange for a fitting reception party."

There was a long pause, then another voice sounded in the cabin, calmer and firmer. "Good morning *Amethyst*. I am sending co-ordinates for a rendezvous in fifteen minutes. The captain and crew of *Merciless* welcome His Imperial Majesty. You may dock in the forward starboard hangar." Another pause. "Is the Emperor well?"

"Thank you, *Merciless*, he is unharmed. Please make private quarters ready immediately."

Shayla turned back to the controls. The co-ordinates from *Merciless* scrolled across the comms screen. She transferred them into the cruiser's command system and locked in the course.

The blinding line of the horizon tilted as the craft banked and climbed. Shayla looked over at Julian again. "We'll be a while. I need to attend to some things before we dock."

Julian gazed at her with dead eyes, and nodded.

Shayla busied herself with her notepad, with an occasional sidelong glance at Julian. She hadn't known how he would react. He seemed stunned, unable to take in the events unfolding around him.

At last, she put her notepad away and scanned the blackness above for signs of the approaching warship. *Dammit! Where the hell are they?* The navigation screen showed exactly where to look. They had to be close, but she was coming up from the dark side of the ship.

*There!*

A sliver of white showed a partial outline ahead. Shayla gasped. A black shadow eclipsed a swathe of stars above. Now she knew what to look for, details became clearer in the waxing light from the planet beside them.

They hung motionless below *Merciless*, level with the bristling communications pod dangling below the warship's belly. The pod alone dwarfed their craft.

She jumped as the comms screen pinged.

"*Amethyst*, turn your craft over to our control for docking."

"Acknowledged, *Merciless*. *Amethyst* is in your hands."

Shayla relinquished control, heart pounding as the tiny cruiser lined itself up fore and aft with the gaping doors of the hangar overhead. The massive dome of the lower beam battery slid into view outside the cockpit. She took a deep breath as the craft lifted itself into the bowels of the hulking warship.

The hangar was unlit, its size impossible to discern. There was a jolt and muffled clang as they docked. A rectangle of stars below narrowed to a slit, then disappeared.

Pale light flooded the hangar. The walls pressed in on all sides. Although the hangar could have held at least a dozen such craft, it seemed claustrophobic after the freedom of the skies and planetary space.

Julian sprang to his feet and opened the outer hatch. The blank and shocked expression he'd worn since Shayla had roused him was gone. He was the Emperor once more. He led them up a steep companionway and through a dazzling white and clinically bare chamber.

As they stepped into the corridor beyond, a heavy thrum of machinery and conversation enveloped them. A small group of uniformed soldiers snapped to attention.

An officer in front of the group smoothed her uniform and close-cropped hair, and bowed low. "Captain Stihl, at your service Magister Summis."

"Thank you, Bernadin. I'm glad you were on hand to help." The Emperor's voice held an unexpected warmth and relief.

The captain straightened and flashed a smile.

*Rodent.* The thought came, unbidden, into Shayla's mind at the sight of uncomfortably large front teeth.

"Always an honor, My Lord." The captain reverted to a more familiar mode of address, and Shayla knew that these were old acquaintances. Captain Stihl glanced at Shayla with a frown, but Julian didn't offer an introduction. Shayla locked eyes with her, doing her best to radiate confidence and authority. *I am here to accompany the Emperor.*

"I need quarters, and a command post," said Julian.

"Of course." The captain led them at a brisk march through the ship's corridors, followed by the soldiers. Shayla stepped smartly to keep up with the group, staying close to the Emperor. Nobody tried to stop her.

They passed a steady stream of people in the narrow passageways, armed and uniformed soldiers, ship's crewmen and women, overalled engineers, all moving swiftly and purposefully.

Heart pounding in her chest, Shayla studied her surroundings. The floor was the only smooth area of any size, tiled in a non-slip checkerboard of red and grey. The walls — *bulkheads*, she reminded herself, *you're in the navy now* — were ice blue, broken by doors and buttresses, displays and communications panels, and an unblinking row of harsh white lights. A maze of wiring and machinery, ducts and conduits, gleamed white overhead.

The corridor was little more than the space left over by the partitioning-off of compartments on either side. It meandered and stepped its way through the ship, around spaces defined for other purposes, connecting them together seemingly more by accident than by design. Lots of corners for cover, if it came to a fight.

Glowing signs labeled each door. Shayla memorized the layout, planning for her eventual escape. On one side lay engineering offices and workshops. On the other, a pharmacy. Next to it, an open door revealed intense activity as nurses and orderlies hauled tote boxes from the medical stores and laid out instruments and dressings on long tables.

A broader thoroughfare branched off, echoing with a cacophony of shouted conversations. Crewmen hustled around a long row of lockers, pulling protective overalls over their uniforms.

*Merciless* was preparing for war.

They continued aft into the relative calm of a much narrower passage. Purser's office…stores office…mail room…chapel…identical doors each announced their purpose.

An armored door opened at the captain's approach, admitting them to the seething twilight world of the Imperial warship's command deck.

The skin between Shayla's shoulders crawled as they passed a sentry, weapon drawn, who fixed her with a cold stare. She hurried after the Emperor onto the bridge.

A railing separated them from a warren of pits crammed with equipment and personnel. Her mind reeled from the assault on her senses, the dizzying kaleidoscope of lights, the bedlam of shouted orders and curt responses, and the cloying smell of hot rubber.

The captain led them into a small anteroom, a haven from the bustle of activity outside, and gestured ahead. "The Admiral's day cabin is ready for you."

Emperor Julian Skamensis swept into the room, followed by the captain and two guards. The remaining soldiers took up posts on either side of the door. Shayla followed.

The Admiral's day cabin was a relic of an era when *Merciless* was a fully equipped flagship. Far more than a cabin, it was a lavishly appointed suite.

Shayla took in details at a glance: a desk, chairs, a dining alcove. Three doors would need further examination to secure the room from unwanted interruptions. She surreptitiously scanned the suite with her stylus, checking the results on her notepad. She was linked into the ship's systems. Faked security codes accepted. Good.

She turned to where Julian listened to the captain reporting on movements of the fleet surrounding Magentis.

"Magister Summis, I must speak with you. In private." Shayla's voice was low and urgent. She struggled to keep it steady through a sudden tightening of her throat. She'd hoped the drug would last this long, but

Julian was clearly recovering from its effects and she didn't know how compliant he'd be.

He frowned at the interruption, and opened his mouth.

*Dammit. He's resisting.* Shayla's mind raced. She had to get him alone. Her mind was already calculating the odds, planning the movements needed to take out the guards, muscles ready to act. She could clear the room, but could she secure the door in time?

One last try, all or nothing. Summoning every ounce of conviction, she said, "You need to know how I reached you so quickly. I knew you were in danger."

Captain Stihl's eyes narrowed. Her mouth formed a thin line. Truthsense, maybe? Good job Shayla's words were true to the letter.

The captain nodded and straightened. "My Lord, if you'll excuse me, I need to return to my post."

Julian gaped, but said nothing as the captain and the guards left.

As soon as they were alone, Julian said, "You have information about this." His voice was sharp.

Shayla held up a finger to her lips. She pushed open doors leading to a sleeping cabin, bathroom, and a tiny galley and servery. She noted another door at the far end of the galley, likely leading to the main kitchens.

She sat at the desk and scrawled on her notepad. Julian's jaw dropped at this flagrant breach of etiquette. He cleared his throat, but choked back the rebuke at Shayla's cold glare and curt "Yes?" Shayla held his gaze. "Sit down," she barked.

He hesitated, but must have seen something dangerous in Shayla's expression which compelled him to obey. He settled in an easy chair, facing her.

One wall of the room darkened. The dazzling face of Magentis swam into view, now an almost perfect semicircle. The western coast of Traplinki was just visible on the horizon under a tattered veil of cloud. A graphic appeared alongside, charting nearby planetary space. Magentis showed as a plain blue disk, surrounded by a constellation of glowing symbols. Two in particular stood out, flaring an angry red.

"*Wrath of Empire* and *Shield of Mercy* are moving into position," said Shayla, struggling to quell the emotion in her voice.

"At last," said Julian. "They'll soon bring this nonsense to an end."

*You don't know the half of it!*

Other sections of the wall showed transmissions from the ground. Scenes of fighting, fires and explosions.

"Admiral Kuvar has been trying to contact you for a few minutes now, but all communications to this room are sealed off, other than those that I've expressly permitted."

Julian's mouth hung open. "What do you mean? What—"

"Your orders have been confirmed and locked in." The admiral's voice quavered. "We will be positioned to commence planetary cleansing in fourteen minutes."

Julian whirled to face the wall.

The admiral gazed back, eyes unfocussed, his graying moustache quivered. "Magister Summis. Julian. I beg you. Recant this madness. The fleet can deal with this uprising without such drastic measures. I most anxiously await your orders and the command codes to divert from this course of action."

"Cleansing?" Julian's jaw dropped, he staggered to his feet. "I gave no such order! Admiral Kuvar, stand off immediately!"

"He can't hear you, *Emperor*," Shayla said. "I said *I* controlled communications here. And now it's time for you to take a more passive role in the proceedings."

He whirled around, but stopped, stunned, as Shayla's dart buried itself in his neck.

"Now be a good boy and sit down. I want you to have a clear view of your planet being wiped clean the way mine was." Shayla tried to sound fierce and determined, but she almost choked on the words. *What's wrong with me?*

The Emperor obeyed, drugged and helpless. Shayla turned back to the wall screens. She had penetrated the ship's command systems and set safeguards against detection. She could control anything she wanted to from here. All ways into this cabin were secured against intruders. The instructions for planetary annihilation were locked into the command systems of two of the heaviest warships in the known galaxy. They were now under automatic control. There was no way anyone could intervene, other than the Emperor himself. Or, of course, Shayla. All she had to do was wait and watch.

This should have been a moment of keen anticipation, of ultimate triumph. This was what Shayla had spent her whole adult life working towards. She should be elated. But she felt cold and sick.

All her life, ever since she had lost her home, she had been inured to death. At the impressionable age of eleven, her mind had tried to encompass the sudden deaths of a hundred million people. Tried, and come close to madness in the effort. As an assassin, Shayla had killed many times. Always with purpose, and with care and precision. But always without feeling. Even the deaths of one hundred and ninety seven people on *Chantry Bay* had left her untouched.

Almost.

But this was many orders of magnitude more than anything she had done before. She tried to convince herself that it was only natural for her to feel nervous. She had to be strong.

But a young girl gazed at her. Terrified eyes. *Innocent* eyes. How many more like her lived below Shayla's feet right now? Sleeping, playing, laughing, crying?

Memories of childhood nightmares clamored for Shayla's attention. A wrenching sense of something wrong.

She fiddled with the controls, directing the ship's remote senses to home in on the two behemoths bearing down on the unsuspecting planet. While she did so, she talked to keep her mind off the see-sawing emotions threatening to drown her. "You didn't give the order. I did. I loaned you my notepad to send an alert under the Imperial seal. Your completed message should have self-erased, but this is no ordinary notepad. It was programmed to intercept and copy the message for analysis. While we were on the move, decryption agents unraveled your seal. I sent the orders in your name before we boarded *Merciless*. Ah! Here we go."

Two more images formed on the wall. Tiny. Blurred. But menacing.

A sudden movement alerted Shayla to danger. She whirled in her seat, needle gun drawn. Two guards dropped in the doorway before it was fully open, but there were more behind. Shayla didn't stop to wonder how they had managed to break the door codes. Right now she was only concerned with empirical fact, not perceived impossibility.

Hellfire lanced through her shoulder.

She dropped the gun, stunned and paralyzed by unbearable agony. *That fucking shoulder again.* As she fell to the ground, Shayla struggled to keep a grip on rational thought through the abuse her tormented body shrieked at her.

While she was dealing with the intruders at the main door, she'd been ambushed from behind. Through the ebbing mist in front of her eyes she could just make out a large and shadowy figure lumbering towards her. The figure came into sharper focus.

"You really think your paltry door blocks could keep out the Commander in Chief of Security, did you?"

The pain in Shayla's shoulder faded. She was still partly paralyzed and sat, arms and legs manacled, on the floor in the corner of the cabin. Four guards stood over her, weapons drawn, hate in their eyes.

The desk was a few feet away, polished surface level with Shayla's eyes. On it, she could see her needle gun and knife. Two crewmen, sleeves emblazoned with the insignia of the communications corps, pored over her notepad.

*They'll get nowhere with that.* Brandt himself had devised the hiding places for the features she needed to keep hidden.

Through a forest of legs Shayla saw a doctor examining the Emperor.

"Drugged," he said flatly.

"My apologies, Magister Summis. Please stand up." Shayla recognized Henri Chargon speaking. The Emperor stood.

"Sit down."

The Emperor complied.

"My guess would be trylex," said Henri.

"Good choice," Chalwen grunted, shooting Shayla a poisonous look. "Puts him completely out of the picture. We can instruct him to do anything physical, but nothing involving fine control. Like giving an order."

Chalwen stared at the wall screens. The two warships loomed ever larger, finer detail coming into focus as they drew closer. "Bernadin. Henri. Who's in line of command in the Emperor's absence?"

They all looked at each other for a few moments. Henri broke the silence. "The next in line in the Skamensis family would be—"

"Assuming they are out of the picture," Chalwen interrupted. "Emergency measures in force."

"Oh, I see. Toss up between Admiral Kuvar, as head of the armed forces, and you."

"You sure?"

"I wouldn't like to call it without checking the protocol guides. Depends whether this is deemed a military or a security emergency."

Chalwen took a deep breath. "Security. I can argue that case. Okay, let's give it a try."

She pulled a screen out from the desk and scrawled rapidly. Her conversation with the approaching flagship's command system rolled up on the wall in front of them.

*Chalwen ap Gwynodd, Commander in Chief of Imperial security services, hereby declaring a state of emergency under security provisions. I am assuming control of all Imperial forces for the duration of the emergency, or until a legitimate claimant from the Imperial line supersedes this order.*

There was a long pause. The response rolled up. *Instruction acknowledged. State of emergency confirmed. Chalwen ap Gwynodd recognized as interim Supreme Commander of Imperial forces.*

"Hah!" Chalwen gave Shayla a triumphant look.

On the main wall display, *Shield of Mercy* loomed large then dropped below them towards the planet. From above she looked like a glittering grey beetle against the distant field of green and white.

*Rescind order for planetary cleansing of Magentis.*

Another pause, then: *Instruction lodged, pending confirmation of Imperial succession.*

"What?" Chalwen's voice thundered across the room.

It was Shayla's turn to smile. "The order was delivered under Imperial seal. Direct from the Emperor himself, with a stipulation that only the Emperor in person can rescind it."

Chalwen's face turned purple. Her mouth worked silently, then snapped shut as she swallowed hard and brought herself back under control.

"I won't ask how you managed that. I don't suppose I'd get a sensible answer anyway."

She paced back and forth across the cabin. Sweat rolled off her forehead and into her eyes. She shook it off. "Bernadin, close with *Shield* and engage in battle."

The captain's jaw dropped. "But ..." The color drained from her face.

"Yes?" Chalwen looked at her. "Follow that thought through." She spoke with uncharacteristic patience.

"It'll be suicide. We can't scratch a *Sword*. And if we open fire ..." Bernadin's face lit up. "Of course!"

"Send the command to all available units to engage *Wrath* and *Shield*," Chalwen said. "Keep them busy. Draw them off. Hit and run."

Bernadin Stihl hurried from the cabin, shouting orders as she went.

Chalwen smiled, lips pressed thin, and nodded. She turned to the screens and toyed with her stylus. Admiral Kuvar's face reappeared on the wall, and another woman in a captain's uniform. Both looked worn and scared.

"Admiral Kuvar, captain bin Terallini," Chalwen said, "you will shortly come under attack from the rest of the fleet. The locked-in instructions should be suspended while your command systems respond to the threat. Take every opportunity to disrupt the command systems while they're busy. See if you can break the lock."

The admiral's moustache bristled, and a hard gleam lit his eyes. The captain pursed her lips and nodded.

"Make sure your shields are set to protect environmental spaces and bring all crew into a shielded area. We'll be coming at you as hard as we can. If we can disable you, that will end the threat, but let's minimize damage and casualties."

The two officers acknowledged, and vanished from sight.

"Do you really think we can manage that?" Henri whispered. "Those ships are more powerful than everything else around Magentis put together."

Chalwen's face sagged. "I don't know, Henri. To be honest, the best I can hope for is to buy time to think."

She turned to Shayla. "Now Missy, you and I need to talk."

"I have nothing to say."

"Very well. Listen then. I don't know what you think this action will achieve, but you have no hope of seeing any good come of it."

"My mission is complete. I had no plans to escape this alive."

*Not quite true.* Shayla had intended, with Brandt's help, to flee on this warship while she still had control of it, with the Emperor as hostage. Her plans from this point were less well-formed, but now immaterial anyway. She had lost control, and Brandt could no longer help.

But her goal was still within reach. Why, then, did she feel so numb? So empty?

"How can the deaths of two billion people benefit you, or anyone you may be working for? This is mindless evil. Nothing in the galaxy will change. The Empire can lose a dozen planets and still be strong enough to survive."

"This Empire is evil!" Shayla spoke as much to convince herself as anything. "I have struck at the root of this evil."

"That sounds like the Insurrection speaking, but they would be intent on bringing the Empire down once and for all. This won't achieve that." Chalwen glared furiously at Shayla, brow creased in thought. "And none of the Families would stoop this low. They want power for themselves. The slaughter of civilians is not part of their agenda. Unless, of course, it has a higher purpose." She paused, mouth hanging open. "This is *personal*, isn't it?" Her voice and face showed amazement.

"Almost in range," Henri interrupted, before she could pursue the thought.

Shayla watched in fascination as the huge battleship filled the screen. They were closing in fast from behind.

"*Shield of Mercy* is warming up her plasma cannon," one of the captain's orderlies said. "She's targeting the Solven Plateau."

"The command system will follow standard procedure," said Chalwen. "Disabling military installations first, then wiping out cities."

"Shit! We're still too far away." Henri's suave calm broke.

"What have we got down on that rim?" asked Chalwen.

"Two heavy batteries. One more to the north. Command center. Training camp. Observation posts." Henri reeled off the inventory.

"It's Mount Skavo," shouted the orderly.

"The main command post? And five thousand cadets. Shit!"

"The tactical system's calculated it can take out the shields," Chalwen muttered.

They watched, aghast and helpless, as a gout of fire erupted from the lower dome of the warship.

The communications orderly located a visual feed from the besieged base just in time to see the skies light up. The flare blinded Shayla for a few seconds. She retched and gagged, overwhelmed by childhood memories of the blast that had killed her father.

When her eyes cleared, the display showed the buildings of the base still standing. The field of view panned to show an ocean of glowing rock starting just a hundred yards from the perimeter fence.

"Their shields held!" The orderly was jubilant.

Shayla's head swam.

The screen showed a swarm of distant figures racing from the parade ground to the cover of the buildings.

"Don't hold your breath," said Chalwen through clenched teeth. "Time to intercept?"

"Eight seconds. Firing again!"

The screen flared a second time, then went dark.

The room was silent. Shock etched in every face.

*Holy shit! What have I done?*

For the first time, Shayla understood the reality of what she'd set in motion. Understood in terms of human lives. People she'd seen and lived amongst for a few short weeks. Ordinary people. *Innocent* people.

*No! This regime has done far worse in the name of the Emperor. Be strong! The rest of the galaxy will thank you!*

*Merciless* swooped like an avenging angel. Her plasma cannon, little more than a toy compared to the city-wrecker carried by the mighty *Swords*, belched fire. The secondary batteries of particle beams lashed lightning, clawing and raking at *Shield of Mercy*.

A cheer echoed from the command deck beyond the open door to the cabin. The attack had been completely ineffective, but the lumbering warship had changed course.

*Merciless'* beams flashed once more as she sped away. She started wheeling around for another pass.

"Returning fire!" the orderly squawked.

The deck shuddered under Shayla's thighs.

"She's distracted. Now get us out of here, Captain," Chalwen muttered.

But all they could do was watch, helpless passengers carried on a tide of fury as *Merciless* lined up for another attack run.

"What's Bernadin up to?" gasped Chalwen. "She's taking us right over the main weapons platform."

"But away from that damned plasma cannon," the orderly whispered. "And it's a known blind spot of the *Sword* class."

"That so?" muttered Chalwen, clearly unconvinced, as they approached.

Bolts from *Shield of Mercy* whipped at them. The deck bucked again, and ozone laced the air.

"Damage reports coming in," said the orderly. "Superficial only. The shields handled most of it, but that cannon would finish us."

Even as he spoke, *Shield* rolled, trying to present her deadly underbelly. *Merciless* looped around in an ever tighter arc to keep in line with the upper carapace. All the while, she kept up a furious bombardment, all efforts focused on a single spot in the center of the weapons housing.

But it was a losing battle. The carapace slid away under them, exposing them to the full might of the beam batteries around its rim. And the aperture of the plasma cannon was rolling into view.

A low vibration ran through the ship's structure, and the lights dimmed briefly.

"That one hurt," Henri whispered.

"Bernadin's disengaging," said Chalwen flatly. "But here come *Osprey*, *Hawk*, and *Relentless*!" Her voice changed pitch, hope and excitement registering for the first time.

*Merciless* fled at full speed, drawing *Shield* away from the planet.

*Shield* spat a last salvo at *Merciless* then turned her attention to the new threat.

*Relentless* came full on, beams blazing. She ceased fire, then a cluster of firefly sparks sped from her snout and rapidly closed the gap between her and *Shield*.

"Torpedoes!" Chalwen crowed. "That'll keep them busy. Shields are no good against them, they'll have to pick them off one by one."

The battleship had already identified the threat and turned her beams on the swift, madly dodging missiles. One by one, they succumbed. *Relentless* loosed another salvo of torpedoes, but her captain wasn't as battle-trained as Bernadin. He let himself pass beneath *Shield*. The plasma cannon belched, enveloping *Relentless* in a glowing shroud.

"*Relentless* is damaged. Disengaging," stuttered the orderly.

Shayla realized she'd been holding her breath along with everyone else in the cabin.

*Merciless* closed for another attack, giving *Relentless* time to escape.

Tiny *Osprey* swept in from behind. Shayla wondered what such a diminutive craft hoped to achieve when the larger cruisers could make no impression.

"What's she trying to do? Get in behind the shields?"

"I don't believe it," gasped the orderly. *Osprey* had tucked herself right under the mushroom spread of the upper carapace, out of reach of *Shield's* weapons, and was directing all her firepower at the base of the tower supporting the weapon platform.

"What are they up to?" Chalwen said.

"The barrel of the plasma cannon runs right through the height of the ship," said the orderly. "If they can penetrate the hull shielding there, they could disable the cannon." He shook his head. "It's something that gets talked about in tactical school, but only ever idle speculation. Nobody's damn fool enough to actually try it."

"And that's why!" yelped Henri, pointing at the screen.

*Shield* responded, trying to maneuver herself away from the hornet stings of tiny *Osprey*. They watched, helpless, as the massive warship twisted and turned. *Osprey* matched her every move.

*Shield* accelerated, hurtling away from the planet. "She can't hope to outrun *Osprey*," the orderly said, uncertainly.

"I thought *Swords* were the fastest ships around," said Henri.

"In open space, yes, but she can't hop in this gravity field. And under conventional drive, the small ships have the edge."

*Shield* wasn't running. Without warning, she reversed thrust. *Osprey* slammed into the central tower, and span away. Out from her protective cover.

A blinding flash flared silently across the screen.

Chalwen studied the graphics, face grey. "We lost *Osprey*." There was a break in her voice as she spoke.

The orderly stared at the screen, face a mask of incredulity. "Where did the command system learn *that* maneuver?"

Captain bin Terallini appeared on the wall. Tears streaked her face. "Chalwen, we can't override the commands. It's no use. The system's programmed to respond with lethal force and we can't disrupt it."

Chalwen nodded. "We can keep them away from the planet, but only until we run out of ships. This is not a battle we have any hope of winning."

She sighed deeply. "Everyone, leave the room." The guards and crewmen looked uncertainly at each other. "That's an order." Her voice was little more than a whisper, yet it carried more weight of authority than the loudest parade ground bellow.

As the room emptied, she murmured, "Henri, you stay. I need a witness for my actions here."

Shayla watched, heart thudding, as Henri closed the door behind the last guard.

"Captain Iona bin Terallini had a son serving on *Osprey*." Chalwen's voice was flat.

*What's she planning to do?* Shayla had always considered herself tough. She'd been trained to resist interrogation. She knew her training would kick in automatically, whether she wanted it or not. Now she was terrified of where that training would carry her. What agony would her inner self force her to undergo before the subliminal conditioning broke? These people had turned torture into an exquisite art form. The things she had seen, the pain, was something training never prepared you for. And she knew she couldn't face it.

But Chalwen ignored Shayla and turned to where the Emperor had sat, unmoving, throughout the whole battle. "Julian, I beg your forgiveness for what I have to do." Tears ran freely down her face.

She drew a beam pistol and checked the magazine. Hands trembling, she placed the snout against the Emperor's temple.

Chapter 31

S hayla struggled to understand what was happening.
Pistol trained on the Emperor, with her free hand Chalwen brushed the tears from her eyes. "Henri, do you have contact with the Grand Duke?"

Henri nodded. Teeth set in a death's head grimace, his hands clenched and released the butt of his pistol.

"He's next in line of succession." Chalwen's voice grew harsh. "As soon as the Emperor's death is certified, he will have the authority to call off the attack." She swallowed hard. "He will be the new Emperor. Heaven help us all."

Julian did something Shayla would have sworn was impossible in his state.

He nodded.

A fractional movement of his head, but a clear voluntary movement nonetheless. Shayla couldn't begin to imagine what force of will it had taken, or what torment he'd undergone in fighting the drug.

"Stop!" she screamed. "Wait. This is…insane." *Yes, it is. What am I doing?* "How can you show such devotion to this man? This monster?" Her voice tailed off, her words felt like little more than empty rote.

"You know nothing of this man!" Chalwen thundered. "You know nothing of the evil he has spared the galaxy. I can't begin to tell you what life will be like under Grand Duke Ivan Skamensis, but I will not stand by and watch you slaughter two billion people."

"He cleansed my home planet," Shayla whispered. But even as she spoke, the nagging doubts in her mind gave her pause. *Look to my father's example for inspiration.* The Emperor's words haunted her.

"He did not! He has never given any such order." Chalwen's denial was emphatic. And oddly credible.

"I think she's referring to Eloon," Henri breathed, eyes wide in wonder.

Chalwen's mouth opened in an 'O'. "But that was over twenty years ago," she said at last. Then more briskly, "I can see your thirst for vengeance, but it is directed at the wrong person. There is much you don't know about that episode, and no time now for explanations. You cannot win. Either call off the attack yourself, or I will ensure a legitimate heir is in place to do so. One way or another, this attack stops now."

The certainty that had guided Shayla for so many years crumbled. Nothing made sense.

On the wall behind Chalwen, *Shield of Mercy* lashed out in eerie silence as more craft joined the fray. Another scene showed *Wrath of Empire* bearing down on the defenseless capital city, Prandis Braz, and the Mosaic Palace.

Shayla's shoulders sagged. "Free my hands and give me my notepad." She almost choked on the words. *I can't believe I'm doing this.*

Henri's eyed widened in panic as Chalwen went to the desk. "This could be a trick," he said.

"You don't get to be head of security without some measure of truthsense." Chalwen's tone was firm. "I sense she wants to hear more."

Chalwen nevertheless pushed Shayla's weapons to the far end of the desk before Henri bent down to remove the magnetic clamps from her wrists. Chalwen kept her pistol trained on Shayla the whole time.

Shayla took her notepad from Henri's hands and worked hurriedly with the stylus. "You have thirty minutes to convince me," she said. "At the end of that time, the attack resumes. You will instruct the fleet to stand off. Furthermore *Shield of Mercy* and *Wrath of Empire* will take position over Prandis Braz and Henriss Garden. Any sign of hostility and you can say goodbye to both cities. They will be gone before you can possibly intervene, and this time they will not be distracted."

"I said it was a trick!" Henri yelled.

Chalwen raised her hand to quiet him. She didn't take her eyes of Shayla. "Understood," she said. "And as we are working from a position of mutual mistrust, you understand in turn that at the first resumption of hostility, the Emperor dies and the Grand Duke issues the instruction to cease. Henri will be preparing the necessary communications for immediate implementation. After he has replaced your bindings, of course."

Shayla nodded, and offered her wrists for the manacles. "In which case, we will both have lost."

She saw Henri looking longingly at her notepad as he replaced it on the desk. "Don't try repeating what you saw me do. It's a cyclical code. You can't reuse it. And the hidden functions will self-destruct if they detect a forced intrusion. I *really* don't think you want that to happen."

———•◦•———

The hard wall behind her chafed the raw wound in Shayla's shoulder. Burning pain echoed the mental wounds Chalwen's words had opened. Everything she'd lived for lay in ruins. But someone had ordered Eloon to be cleansed. Only the Emperor could give such an order, and yet ...

Chalwen's words, the harmonics revealing her inner conviction, taunted Shayla. If she was not convinced, the Emperor would still pay, somehow. But she had to know the truth.

On the other side of the cabin, Chalwen gazed at the wall screens, watching the massive warships wheeling into position over the two leading cities on the planet. She seemed in no hurry to talk.

"May I sit more comfortably?" Shayla asked.

Without looking around, Chalwen nodded and motioned her to one of the chairs at the coffee table, next to the Emperor. Shayla struggled to her feet and hobbled across the room. As she sat, she noted that Chalwen had positioned her where Henri could still cover her from his seat at the desk. He smiled, lips pressed thin, and stared at her over the snout of his pistol.

"So," said Chalwen at last, "I have to convince you we are not the monsters you imagine." She stared hard at Shayla. "The question is, are you willing to open your mind to truth? Or at least to reason?"

"I am willing to hear what you have to say. The truth of it, I will judge for myself."

"Good enough." Chalwen grunted. "The heart of the matter is, I believe, revenge. Yes?"

Shayla hesitated, then nodded.

"Good. I want to be sure I am addressing the right issue." Chalwen paced in front of the wall screens. From their vantage point, *Shield of Mercy* glittered far below, menacing the white walled gardens of Henriss. "So, would it be fair to say that your anger is rightfully directed at the *person* responsible for the cleansing of Eloon?"

Chalwen seemed to be choosing her words carefully. Shayla found herself waiting impatiently for whatever she had to say, and her hesitant manner was becoming irritating. "Of course," she snapped.

"And what of the people of Magentis?"

The question caught Shayla off guard and it was not something she wanted to think about. "What of them? You promised me the truth about Eloon."

"Well, let's break this into easy steps." Chalwen seemed to ignore Shayla's outburst. "Do you bear the *civilian* population any malice?"

The civilian population? The room seemed to dissolve before Shayla's eyes. The armies of arrogant strutting soldiers, fat bureaucrats, corrupt officials, were all here just as she'd pictured. All part of the machine. All fair game.

But nothing had prepared her for the *other* population. Close up, behind the impenetrable security, the secretive world of Magentis was so damned *ordinary*.

Shayla grimaced and blinked away the darkness crowding her vision.

"Well then." Chalwen stopped pacing. She folded her arms and nodded as if Shayla had revealed some deep truth. "I'll take that as a 'no'. I think you do have a conscience after all. Small and miserly, repressed and underused, but still alive somewhere in there." She resumed pacing. "If the Emperor is your target. Would it be fair to describe the world of Magentis as nothing more than a means to an end?"

Shayla felt exposed in the glare of her gimlet gaze. She wet her lips. "An eye for an eye."

Her reasoning, her justification, stated so simply seemed as substantial as gossamer. Shayla braced herself for an outburst of anger or scorn, but Chalwen simply nodded and lowered herself into the embrace of a chair the other side of the coffee table. "That is something I can understand. And it gives me reason for hope."

*What?*

But Chalwen was still talking, her voice mesmerizing. "There is reason in you. Blind rage, yes, but cold calculation too. So I'm thinking it would trouble you to learn that your rage is misplaced. That you are exacting a terrible revenge on the wrong person."

"So you said already."

"And that brings us to the crux of my argument. Let us suppose for a moment, that the Emperor is not the person you seek. Would you then have any further need for this course of madness?"

Chalwen held up her hand as Shayla started to protest. "That is something I still have to prove. I realize that. I just want to be sure that you are open to rational persuasion." She leaned forwards, sweat rolling down her cheeks, voice suddenly low and earnest. "If I can convince you that this man is not responsible for your home's destruction, will you spare Magentis?"

"I ..." Shayla struggled to manage the roiling tumult inside her as Chalwen's words corroded the single-minded goal that had consumed her for so many years. *This is just hypothetical. Where's the harm?* The way Chalwen had put it, it seemed blindingly obvious. Too obvious. Where was the catch?

At the same time, Shayla found the possibility strangely enticing. She recalled the cold dread she'd felt while alone with the Emperor. The emptiness, the sense of something horribly out of place.

The possibility of an escape from this awful destruction beckoned.

"Yes," she whispered. "If you can show me I'm wrong then I would have no further need to kill this planet."

Chalwen nodded, face serious, and settled back into her chair. "So, just who do you think holds the power in the Empire?"

"I'll say 'the Emperor', but I sense this is a trick question."

"No trick, just an illustration. The question seems to have a simple answer, but in reality it's far from straightforward." She leaned close again. "The truth is, the Emperor only rules with the support of those around him, and that support is fragile, fickle, and divided.

"You've lived in the Palace a short while. You must have observed the factions at work." Chalwen didn't wait for Shayla to answer. "Ranged against the Emperor, and against each other, there are obvious figures like Ivan Skamensis and some of the more powerful nobles. Then there are the political factions within the Legislature and the Judiciary, the navy, and the Merchant Guilds on which the Empire depends. Everyone brings their own agenda and their networks of spies and supporters.

"So, we go back now to Eloon, twenty five years ago."

"Twenty three."

Chalwen grunted. "I suppose you'd know." Her face clouded. Her features set like granite. "But I also remember those days all too well. Fear and suspicion were everywhere. People think things are bad today, but they have such short memories."

She grimaced and shook her head. "Time is pressing," she muttered to herself. "The order to cleanse Eloon was issued under a state of emergency. It appeared at the time that an all-out assault on the Cutler Drift was about to be launched, orchestrated from Eloon. The cleansing was supposedly a pre-emptive move to head off a major catastrophe." She sighed deeply. "It turned out that our intelligence was flawed, and much of the evidence was flimsy, exaggerated, or fabricated. There was no assault in the making. Eloon was destroyed for nothing."

Chalwen stared long at the floor. When she met Shayla's eyes again, her face seemed haunted by the watching ghosts of a vanished population. "The order was issued by Grand Duke Ivan, not by Julian."

Chalwen stopped and gazed at Shayla, as if trying to gauge her reaction to this news.

Shayla sat, stunned, unable to take it all in. In her whole life, truth-sense was the one skill she'd tried and failed to master fully, yet now her senses seemed sharpened beyond anything she'd ever experienced. She heard the tell-tale harmonics in Chalwen's voice so clearly. She believed what she was saying. But to accept the truth would mean abandoning everything Shayla had devoted her life to.

"The order came direct from the Emperor," Shayla protested. "Under the Imperial seal. That is a matter of record."

"As did *your* order to cleanse Magentis," Chalwen snapped.

Shayla blinked, feeling foolish.

"At that time, Ivan was in the habit of issuing orders under the Imperial seal. Remember that Julian was just thirteen years of age, Emperor in name and little else. Ivan was really the one in charge, although that balance of power was a closely guarded secret within the Palace. But Julian was furious when he found out." Chalwen chuckled. "That was the first time I saw him assert himself and stand up to Ivan."

She sobered quickly. "That was a very dangerous time. Ivan had been happy to have a young and impressionable teenager as a figurehead. Someone who looked up to him. Someone he could control. But now that figurehead was showing a mind of his own." She shook her head. "The balance of power was precarious indeed. We were lucky to survive those years."

"Why hadn't Ivan simply proclaimed himself Emperor? Surely he could have dealt with Julian?"

"I said the Empire hung in the balance. Ivan was and still is a powerful figure, but Julian too had many followers, even at that age. All the same, the attack on Eloon was deeply unpopular. I'm sure it crossed Ivan's mind to denounce Julian at that point, but if it ever became known that the attack was for nothing, the Skamensis dynasty would have fallen. Even Ivan would not have survived that."

Pieces of the puzzle clicked into place in Shayla's mind. "None of this was ever recorded."

"Not even in the *secured* archives." Chalwen narrowed her eyes at Shayla.

Shayla's stomach lurched. With knowledge like this, her life was surely measured in hours rather than the days a trial would take.

"And obviously they kept the truth out of the public eye," Chalwen continued, "but Ivan now needed Julian more than ever, which meant Julian had to be retained as a credible ruler. Publicly, he proclaimed the cleansing as a necessary measure to protect the Empire. Within the walls of the Palace, it was clear that he was no longer a dumb figurehead." She hesitated. "The Chief of Intelligence at the time took his own life shortly afterwards, or so it appeared. We never got to the bottom of where the false evidence came from." Chalwen's mouth twisted in distaste at what seemed to be an unwelcome admission of defeat.

"So," she said slowly, "I put it to you that Ivan is the one you want. The young Julian was ignorant of what was happening around him, and has worked ever since to curb Ivan's excesses."

She waved her hand around the room. "More than that, in this room you see the leading members of a movement to preserve some light in the Empire. This movement was started by the old Emperor Paul, and his mother Florence in her dying years.

"They had — we have — to work in secret. The machinery of Empire is even now riddled with powerful people who waxed fat on the old order. They are not going to give up without a fight.

"But Ivan has to move carefully, too. The few years of Paul's rule showed a groundswell of support for a better way of life. There are powerful factions on both sides. The Empire is balanced on a knife edge. Oh, we will band together against any outside threat. We are all loyal to the Family Skamensis, after all. But look inside, and the divisions run deep."

"But if Julian is truly in power now," Shayla interrupted, "why is the Empire still so rotten? If he has the upper hand, why can't he clean out the wrongdoers and establish a better rule?"

"That would mean dismantling much of the machinery of the Empire. It would not go without many years of bloody conflict. We've chosen a gentler path. Longer, but surer. Furthermore, the direct way has been tried. It failed. And Ivan has a hold that we must break first."

"What was tried? And what hold can Ivan have to make Julian tolerate these atrocities?"

"Both those answers are intertwined, and both rest with the old Emperor Paul Skamensis."

"Julian's father?"

"And Ivan's brother. Yes. Do you know what happened to the old Emperor? Don't suppose you even remember it. You must have been young then."

"I read the histories. He died in an accident. Along with most of the family."

"That's what they reported." Chalwen hesitated, chewing her lip. "He died, but it was no accident. He paid the price for trying to move too quickly."

She stood and leaned her face close in to Shayla's. "But the rest of the family still lives."

The words stunned Shayla. It took a few moments even to understand what Chalwen had just said. Shayla stared at Chalwen long and hard. The words were truly incredible, and yet the truth in Chalwen's voice could not be denied.

Chalwen must have seen Shayla's confusion. "Yes. They live. Julian's brothers, sisters, and the Lady Miriam. They have been held hostage by Ivan for the past quarter century. Julian still rules, but always with a sword hanging over him."

"But how can Ivan keep them hidden like that? Surely someone would know something about it. You have all the resources of the Empire at your fingertips ..."

Even as she spoke, Shayla realized what the answer would be. Chalwen confirmed it. "All the resources." She snorted. "Many of whom secretly long to see him dead and Ivan proclaimed Emperor. Who to trust? But for all those years, a small band of us have been scouring the Empire for their whereabouts."

"To no avail," muttered Henri. "We've followed lead after lead over the years. Always hints. Nothing concrete."

"Ivan holds them somewhere out of our reach," added Chalwen. Her face sagged.

"How do you know they're even alive?" asked Shayla.

"We get communications. Every year. On the anniversary of their capture. A reminder of what is at stake."

Shayla looked from the corner of her eye at the Emperor, still seated impassively beside her. A single tear clung to his cheek.

Without a word, she held her hands out towards Henri. He glanced at Chalwen, who nodded. He unlocked her manacles and passed her the notebook.

———•••———

The walk back through the ship seemed to last forever. Clean blue and white corridors utterly alien. Shayla was marched by a grim-faced escort of a dozen hand-picked guards. "For your own protection," Chalwen explained.

Head hanging low, from the corners of her eyes Shayla nevertheless saw the expressions on the crew's faces as she passed. Talk stilled as she approached. Eyes followed her. Hatred, anger, contempt.

But nothing hurt more than the emptiness inside her. The feeling of failure. The lifetime wasted, and a disbelieving awareness of the greater catastrophe that she'd almost enacted.

A small corner of cogency in her mind noted that they were nearly back to the entrance to the hangars, when her escort led her into a small room. A thin-faced man in a plain uniform stood as they entered. "This her, is it?" he grunted.

The door thumped shut behind her, and the warden removed her manacles under the watchful eyes and ready weapons of the guards.

"Strip her."

Shayla offered no resistance as two of the guards complied. She stood, naked and uncaring in the middle of the floor. They scanned her for signs of electronics and hidden weapons. At length, the warden threw her a lime green jumpsuit. She dressed, and allowed herself to be led into a tiny cell.

There was a small latrine and hand basin against the wall at the far end. A ledge down one wall held a thin mattress and pillow. A simple communication panel was set into the wall above the bed, nothing more than a speakerphone and a call button.

The door hissed closed behind her, a solid block of clear armored plastic. Utter silence enveloped her, although she could see the warden and guards outside talking still, casting occasional glances her way.

Thankful to be alone at last, Shayla sank down onto the bed.

Grief swallowed her.

*What have I done?*

Images haunted her. Cadets running across a parade ground. The sky lighting up. Ships burning. People everywhere. People with friends, families, lovers, lives to live. People like her. People who had lost everything they held dear. Because of her.

*I did this.*

## Chapter 32

"Shayla." A small voice hissed. Insistent. Nearby. "Shayla."

Shayla's eyes snapped open. "Brandt?" *I must be dreaming.*

"Lie still. The guard outside mustn't see you move."

"Brandt! Where are you?"

"At home, on Chevinta. You don't want to know how many comms nets I had to hack to reach you." The voice came from the comms panel above her head.

"How did you manage to track me down here?" Still sleep-drugged, Shayla fumbled for meaning in a thousand random snippets of thought.

"You followed your standard procedure. Heck, you must have been on autopilot." The tone was admonishing. "When you breached this ship's system, you left a back door open."

"Of course. Standard practice." Blinking away the last cobwebs of restless sleep, Shayla felt a glimmer of hope for the first time since getting caught. *Always leave another way in, in case your primary access gets compromised.* "And you traced my signature."

"That's what it's there for."

"Things didn't go as planned." A chill washed over Shayla.

"I felt so helpless when I saw you'd been taken."

"You were watching?"

"Too late to help. I realized you weren't going to be killed immediately, so I spent time rummaging through the ship's archives to catch up on the details."

"Can you get me out of here?"

"Electronics not a problem, but I can't do anything about the guards. I eavesdropped on a few conversations. They're just itching for an excuse to shoot you. The only thing stopping them is the prospect of seeing you burn."

*I can't blame them.* The chill deepened.

"But I think you can salvage something from this."

"What do you mean?"

"No time for explanations."

Shayla caught the edge in his voice.

"You'll have to figure this out yourself. Someone's betrayed me, and I don't have much time left."

All senses alert now, the trained agent again, Shayla listened.

"Remember what the fat one said about the Emperor, his family, his uncle? It makes sense to me now. I've spent the last three hours checking some details, and I believe her. The person we really want is still out there. Ironic, isn't it? We're now on the same side as the Emperor. You must speak to them. You can help them. Remember the black hole. That's the key."

"How can I speak to them? I'm a prisoner and they won't listen to me."

"No time! Listen! I've sent an order for you to be taken to her. Shit, they're coming for me." This last comment was a muttered undertone. "The black hole. That's where they'll all be."

"What ..." But the connection was dead. "Brandt?" No answer.

*How can I help them? And what's happened to Brandt?* Shayla felt more alone and more afraid than ever. *Somebody's betrayed him?* The Freeworld of Chevinta took its neutrality seriously. If the authorities knew how Brandt had been helping her, he would be treated severely. How could they know? Only a very few people even knew of Brandt, let alone of his connection to her.

A movement outside the door caught her eye.

The door opened. A stocky guard, a woman who had led the escort earlier, said, "On yer feet, bitch! Magister ap Gwynodd wants to see you."

Shayla didn't need to wonder how Brandt had managed that. Once inside the ship's systems it would have been a simple matter to fake such an instruction. The guard could not have received her orders in person.

So Chalwen would not be expecting her. Shayla might have a few seconds of surprise, but nothing more than that, in which to say her piece.

But what was she going to say?

She puzzled over Brandt's instructions, trying desperately not to get distracted by worries about Brandt himself. They both shared a lifelong thirst for revenge over the destruction of their home world — Shayla's stomach knotted as the pang of defeat gnawed at her. She had chosen the direct route, equipping herself physically and mentally for combat. But Brandt was an intellectual, an academic. He waged his war from afar. He had never been in physical danger before, and now he'd been taken.

They approached the command deck. Shayla thought furiously about what she should say.

*You can help them.* How could she help them? Help them with what? She reviewed her recent conversation with Chalwen about the Emperor, the Grand Duke, and the missing family.

*The black hole?* What in Space did Brandt mean by that? *That's where they'll be?*

A memory tugged at her. This was no stellar phenomenon. There was only one thing Brandt had ever called 'the black hole'.

Chalwen looked up from the remains of a meal as Shayla entered the cabin. The Emperor sat with his back to Shayla, eating ravenously. The drug had worn off at last. She must have been out for hours. He turned as Chalwen struggled to her feet, her eyes widening. He looked tired and grey, aged beyond his years.

"Get her out of here," yelled Chalwen.

The guards hesitated, confused.

Shayla saw the tiny window of opportunity about to slam in her face. "I know where the Imperial family is held." The words came unbidden.

The effect was electric. A deathly silence gripped them. All eyes were on her, faces a mix of shock and disbelief.

It was suddenly blindingly clear to her. All the pieces fell into place. "I listened while you explained things to me. Things that changed my mind about you. All I ask is for you to return the courtesy."

Chalwen's face darkened. "I've been searching for their prison for nigh on twenty five years now. How can you possibly ..."

She spluttered to silence as the Emperor held up a hand. "I think the merest possibility is worth a few minutes of our time." His voice was mild, but his eyes flashed danger.

*So, I do wield a big lever. I wonder how far I can push this.* "First, I would bargain for my life." Shayla ignored the volcanic rumblings from Chalwen and addressed the Emperor directly. "I have done things I am not proud of, but I don't ask forgiveness for an act of war. What I ask is for your understanding that I am no longer fighting you. We have a common enemy and I wish to play my part in his downfall."

"You seek to bargain with me for an alliance," he rasped. "That is a privilege reserved for nobility."

"You have already bargained with me, by proxy," she countered, nodding towards Chalwen, who seemed to be holding her silence by the most strenuous effort. "That argument is spent."

The Emperor sat back, looking bemused at being answered back.

"I am prepared to admit to a mistake," Shayla said. "If that were not so, you would be dead now. Nobility or not, I spared your life to avoid a great evil. I now bargain for my life with the offer of a great good."

The Emperor looked thoughtful. "All people are Imperial subjects. Regardless of motivation, your actions constituted high treason, not an act of war, and treason is not something to be forgiven." His voice was firm, but seemed to contain no malice. "I cannot bargain on that point. Do you throw yourself on my mercy?"

Shayla's shoulders sagged. She had run out of arguments. *All I want is vengeance for my home world. I had no serious expectation of living beyond that. What's changed?*

"Very well." She kneeled, arms outstretched. *Let's do this properly.*

"My Lord Emperor, I have information that is of surpassing value to you, and skills that you could use. I gift you my service. I ask on your honor to judge me by my actions in your service rather than past deeds."

"You pledge me your service? Your loyalty?"

"I do."

"Without reservation?"

"None."

A long minute passed in silence, save for the all-enveloping hum of the warship.

"I accept your gift and the burden of honor it places on me."

"And my life?" Shayla prompted.

"You know," he said sharply, "that your fate hangs in the balance. You have information. I will judge when I see its worth."

"Very well." Shayla turned towards Chalwen. "You've been looking all over Imperial space for a hiding place. You've not been able to find it because it was not there to be found."

*By Space I hope I'm right about this!* As she phrased the explanation in her mind, Shayla realized how thin her supposition was. The clear certainty she'd felt a few minutes before, in that moment of blinding insight, now seemed impossibly fragile.

*Oh shit! Here goes.*

"When I last visited Eloon the whole planet was still bare." She struggled to keep the bitterness out of her voice. "But I know there's a small outpost on the north polar cap. There are some very subtle countermeasures in place which make it impossible to approach. I tried to find out more about it. There's indirect evidence, movements to and from, but the trails all disappear. I called it 'the black hole'. It doesn't officially exist, which makes me sure it's of the most vital importance."

That was only half the truth. Brandt had known for years of a secret facility, where all records ceased to exist. He had named it 'the black hole'. It was only when Shayla revisited Eloon all those years ago that they had speculated on it and the polar base being one and the same.

But these people didn't need to know about Brandt.

"Someone has gone to a lot of trouble to create a place of concealment. And what would be worth hiding so thoroughly?"

"Eloon is in Firenzi territory," Chalwen protested. "How would Ivan have access to such a base?"

"Someone close to the Emperor is working with someone in the Firenzi hierarchy," said Shayla. "Fleur Trixmin knew something of my mission. Not enough to be sure of the details, or even to be sure I was the agent, but enough to know the plot against the Emperor was led by the Firenzi Service and not by the Insurrection." She recounted her interview with Fleur. "My orders came direct from Josef Firenzi himself." She turned to Julian as he made a strangled squeak of outrage. "By his instructions, you were not to be harmed. This was all within the long-standing rules of chivalry between the Families." Shayla grimaced and looked away. "I had my own agenda. The point is, there was another player in the game, with feet in both camps, who wanted to turn this to their own ends."

Chalwen thought for a few minutes. The silence lengthened.

"Bernadin," she said at last, "where is *Wrath of Empire* now?"

The Captain glanced at an orderly, who consulted a notepad. "*Wrath* reported they were chasing Firenzi rebels who broke away from Magentis while we were suppressing the uprisings."

Chalwen arched an eyebrow. "That's what they reported. Can it be verified?"

The Captain and her orderly pored over the screen. Eventually, face white, Bernadin looked up. "It wasn't just a rebel ship. It was *Wildfire*."

"The Firenzi family cruiser?" Chalwen didn't sound surprised.

"There's more," said Bernadin. "We've located Josef Firenzi, or rather, his body. His partner, Margerite Calvolani, is dead too."

Shayla felt a wrench in her gut.

"Scipio Firenzi is missing. And so is the Grand Duke." Bernadin turned back to the orderly. "Has there been any word from *Wrath* since then? They should have caught and overpowered any escaping ship long ago."

The orderly worked for a few moments. "No word." He frowned. "That's strange. Please excuse me for a moment." He left for the command deck, reappearing a few minutes later. "Communications report they cannot raise *Wrath* at all. No tracer showing on the net, and not responding to calls."

"Henri," said Chalwen, "I assume you have agents on board?"

Henri smiled. "On every ship, as you well know."

A minute later the smile faded. "The larger ships all have an official investigation unit on board. Neither they nor the undercover agents on *Wrath of Empire* are answering. They're all out of touch." He looked at a loss. "Chalwen, what does this mean?"

"It means there was no chase. It was a rendezvous. *Wrath* has turned against us."

"Admiral Kuvar?" Henri's incredulous tone required no elaboration.

"No. And I trust Captain Cormie, too." Chalwen's voice was thoughtful. "But *Wrath* is a ship steeped in the old traditions. With Ivan Skamensis on board, a mutiny is entirely possible."

She heaved herself around in her chair to face the orderly. "When you said there was no trace of *Wrath*, I assume you have tracking stations between here and Ploorbellin trying to pick her up?" She didn't wait for a reply. "You might be looking in the wrong direction. Try casting your net out towards Eloon. Bernadin! Make arrangements to rendezvous with *Shield of Mercy.*" Chalwen glanced at Shayla. Her expression was a curious mix of hope and irritation. "We need a faster ship to give chase."

Shayla tried to control the hammering in her chest. *They really do believe me!*

"Do you hope to find *Wrath*?" Bernadin asked. "Without a tracer signal?"

"I do not. But we need to reach Eloon before they do."

Bernadin nodded, and conversed with the orderly.

"Do you think the Imperial family will still be alive after this night?" asked Henri.

"Ivan will be going to collect them. I'm sure of it. He knows the game is up, and he will want some bargaining chips. He has no idea we have some insight into his intent."

Shayla kept quiet, eyes darting from one speaker to the next as the discussion unfolded.

"We'll need to move without giving our own intentions away," said Henri.

"We'll let it be known that we are making for Ploorbellin. That would be a natural thing to do in retaliation for this treachery. We'll shut down our own tracers and communicate directly through your staff units, Henri."

Bernadin interrupted, her face grim. "It seems we managed to inflict some damage on *Shield* after all. Primary drive, of all things. She can't assist until they complete repairs."

"How long?"

"A day, maybe two."

Chalwen cursed. "We can't afford to give them that kind of a lead, even with surprise on our side."

Bernadin sighed. "*Wrath* is faster than us. Not by much though." She grimaced. "They have five hours head start now, so just how important is it to beat them to Eloon?" She held up a hand as Chalwen spluttered for an answer. "I thought so. I have some tricks up my sleeve Chalwen, but there will be a heavy price to pay. I just want to be sure you are ready to pay it."

## Chapter 33

S hayla returned to her seat on one side of the crew dining hall. She gazed at the remains of her meal, wondering whether or not she felt up to eating anything more. The permanent guard shadowing her every move was becoming embarrassing, especially with her increasingly frequent visits to the bathroom to be sick.

Although Shayla was free to move, with the provisional blessing of the Emperor, Chalwen had insisted on continued guard.

For her own protection.

And Shayla could believe it. The hostility amongst the crew had abated only slightly in the last five days. When she dined, she dined alone. She was surprised now to see Bernadin's orderly sitting opposite the space she had momentarily vacated. He looked up as she sat, nodded, and continued eating.

"Most people move away when I approach," said Shayla, toying half-heartedly with her fork. "Either afraid of me, or afraid to be seen with me."

"Lady bin Covin, your name has become synonymous with treachery and murder. And then in the blink of an eye, you offer to realize the one hope that has held this crew together for many long years. What do you expect people to think?"

"You are not afraid to speak with me. What do *you* think?"

When he didn't answer, Shayla continued. "I tried to destroy a planet. I made a huge mistake, and I'm not asking your forgiveness, but my own planet was destroyed in the name of this family. Now I find I've been chasing the wrong enemy all my life. I don't know what to think any more either."

Another thought occurred to her. "My name is Shayla Carver, formerly of Eloon. Brynwyn bin Covin died a loyal servant of the Emperor. Don't let her name be sullied by my crimes."

He grunted. "Marcus Corrin." He held out a hand. "And, given what you've managed to do, I think I'd rather have you fighting with me than against me."

As she clasped the outstretched hand, he looked closely at Shayla for the first time. "You look rough."

"I don't understand what's happening to me. I'm throwing up every few hours, and I've noticed others getting sick as well."

He nodded again.

"You don't seem surprised."

"It's the hops," he said. "We're racing *Wrath of Empire*. The Chief's screwing every last cycle and mile of reach he can get out of the drive. He's pushing *Merciless* beyond the bounds of sanity."

Marcus must have seen Shayla's blank look. He pushed his plate away and sat back. "Every time you hop, there's a chance of things reappearing in realspace slightly out of alignment. Quantum relationships, chemical bonds, things like that. It's all subtle, but the human body is fragile. Right now, your body is getting riddled with shredded DNA, cell proteins fragmented, and broken synapses."

"What about electronics?"

"You're right. The systems will be picking up damage as well, especially quantum gates." He lowered his voice. "Nobody wants to talk about it, because those systems are critical to the hopper drive. Most of it's redundant and self-repairing, but on the bright side, if the wrong part dies we probably won't know about it."

"So why don't we get sick every time we travel?" Shayla asked, with a frown.

"Thing is, the further you reach, the greater the chance of problems. Ships normally work well within safe limits. Let's just say, we're operating kinda outside of safe limits. And at a million hops a second, the crap adds up." He shook his head. "This ship will likely be scrap by the time we reach Eloon, and the crew will be in little better shape. I'd expect some deaths before we're through."

Shayla pushed her own plate away, brow furrowed. "So, would you say this is a bit like radiation sickness?"

"Similar. We have drugs to help with the worst effects, but still the damage piles up. I said we'd expect some deaths in the next few days, but even those who survive will mostly die young after this journey."

"And the crew are aware of this?" Shayla glanced at the guards on either side.

They averted their eyes, refusing to meet her gaze.

"All members of the crew are aware of the hazards," said Marcus. "They were given the chance to transfer to *Shield* before we left. None took up the option. If it means bringing back our Royal family from the dead, this crew will follow the Emperor to the ends of space. In fact, a full contingent of marines volunteered to join us for the ground assault."

"I don't recall being offered that choice," Shayla said dryly.

"I think the Emperor felt entitled to choose on your behalf."

She pursed her lips. "If it's any help, the Firenzi have more effective drugs against this kind of ailment. I can do nothing to help until we reach Firenzi space and a proper medical facility, but after that, there is no need for anyone to die from this sickness."

Marcus hesitated. "Thanks. I'll pass that on to Captain Stihl."

———•————

"Not a chance in hell!"

"Absolutely out of the question." Bernadin echoed Chalwen's emphatic denial.

"I am a fighter," Shayla protested. "I can't just sit here. I wish to accompany the landing party, and I'll seek the Emperor's permission directly if necessary."

"He will look to us for guidance," said Chalwen. "And this will happen only over my dead body."

"You would deny me the chance to prove myself? To be useful?"

"Well, where do you want me to begin?" Chalwen retorted. "You may have pledged your service to the Emperor, but in my eyes that proves nothing."

"I'm leading you to the Emperor's family."

"Which we still only have your word for. It's something we have yet to establish." Chalwen shook her head. "I'm not ready to allow a weapon in your hands."

"Besides, the soldiers and crew still hold you in deepest suspicion," Bernadin added. "How can you expect them to fight alongside someone they don't trust?"

Bernadin's face softened at Shayla's obvious distress. "If your information turns out to be worthwhile, that will put things in a new light. And on top of that we will all thank you for directing us to good medical aid."

Chalwen pursed her lips. "We had suspicions that the Firenzi were far advanced in such matters. Materials generally, in fact. We know what is openly traded, and what secrets can be bought or otherwise acquired. But covert intelligence has yielded little new for the last fifty years. The Firenzi family guards its secrets well." She studied Shayla. "I detect a measure of self-interest in your offer to secure us aid."

Bernadin nodded. "Another reason not to let you land. You're in no condition to fight."

This was partly true, but only partly. In the week since her talk with Marcus, many crew became seriously ill. Three died in the last two days and another eighteen were confined to the sick bay in critical condition. Shayla herself had found the effort of maintaining her disguise too much for her weakened body, but the mimetic implants were something she had no intention of revealing. She'd welcomed the excuse of sickness and spent much of the last few days in self-imposed isolation in her bunk, allowing her features to return to normal.

The woman standing in front of Chalwen and Bernadin was pale and thin. Shayla had excused her unrecognizable features as — truthfully enough — the absence of any further reason for disguise. She fervently hoped that the disparity between her former and present appearance would be masked by illness and fatigue, and that they wouldn't question her further on how she'd disguised herself so effectively.

Shayla looked around as a murmur of excitement ran through the crowd in the dining hall. She, Chalwen, and Bernadin stood to one side of a makeshift stage. The long tables and benches had been pushed against the side walls and the far counter and closed shutters of the servery. Tables, benches, and the floor in between were thronged with uniformed marines, crew, and officers.

Guards appeared in the door leading from the officers' quarters, followed by the Emperor himself. This was the first time Shayla had seen him since leaving Magentis. His appearance shocked her. He was no longer the tired ghost of a man she'd last seen recovering from the effects of her drugs, but the grey and haggard face was replaced by translucent waxy skin, glistening under the harsh lights of the dining hall. Deep lines framed his mouth. Lips drawn into a thin line curled as he walked, as if each step pained him.

He didn't acknowledge Shayla as he brushed past her and took the only seat on one side of the stage.

He gestured to Bernadin. "Proceed."

Bernadin saluted and stepped to the center of the stage. "We are presently sitting twenty nine light years from Eloon. Tomorrow, we will land and attempt a historic rescue."

A deafening cheer echoed around the packed room.

"We have stopped hopping for a total of four and a half hours while we adjust our natural velocity in preparation for entering the system."

A low mutter sounded here and there. People exchanged puzzled looks. "That sounds a long time," Bernadin called across the buzz of speculation. "It is. We are not establishing a matching velocity. We are pushing our secondary drive to the limit to build up a relative velocity of two percent light speed."

This time she let the startled hum run its course. While Bernadin waited, she signaled to Marcus Corrin on the other side of the stage. A schematic of the planetary system filled the wall behind her.

She stood patiently until silence reigned and all eyes were fixed on her once more. "I'll hand over to Colonel Jimi Kant to brief you on the details."

As she stepped down, the colonel strode forward from the front row, and took a position on the far side of the stage from the Emperor. When he spoke, it was as much to address Julian as the assembly.

"We have a tough challenge," he began. "With just one medium-sized warship we intend to take on a planetary base of unknown strength.

"We have some advantages which we will use to maximum effect. The main one is surprise. All communications on the Imperial net have been designed to give the impression the fleet is heading for Ploorbellin. Nobody beyond the walls of this ship, and of course *Shield of Mercy*, is aware that we know about Eloon.

"According to Magister Carver," he nodded towards Shayla, face expressionless, "the base is heavily concealed under the north polar ice cap."

*Magister Carver? I must still have some rank then.*

"Our hope is that the base is staffed by a minimal crew. They rely on secrecy to stay hidden. Our biggest concern is to effect a rescue before any harm can come to the Imperial family."

Across from Shayla, the Emperor leaned forward in his seat. His fingers half-buried themselves in the fabric where he gripped the armrests.

The colonel paused, as if waiting for the Emperor to say something, then continued. "We are making preparations to maximize surprise and conceal the true nature of our strength. If they realize they only have one solitary warship to deal with, they may choose to fight until *Wrath of Empire* arrives."

He surveyed the sea of faces surrounding him. "I think we all understand what that would mean. But if we can convince them they face a superior force they are likely to capitulate before they realize the truth.

"We will enter the system and hop to a point one hundred fifty million miles above the northern orbital plane. At this distance, we can expect to escape detection. We will be running with no comms and under minimal power.

"Our relative velocity will be set to carry us straight towards Eloon. We will release a string of communications relays, then hop out of the system again."

The display on the wall illustrated the movements as he talked.

"The relays will remain dormant and will fall unpowered towards Eloon. They will be rigged to wake up after ten hours and begin a standard attack pattern of communications jamming. We hope to create the illusion of a large invasion fleet approaching.

"As soon as we've deployed the relays, we move out to just over one light year." The display changed to show nearby interstellar space. "We will adjust velocity again, this time to match Eloon. We will be out of range of any ground or orbital-based observation, and Commander ap Gwynodd is sure that we'd have noticed any attempt to create a deep space surveillance net, especially around a dead planet and a base that is not supposed to exist."

Shayla grimaced.

"We will close in to Eloon under primary drive, to coincide with the drones' wake-up. We drop off the landing party under the south pole, then hop around the planet and reveal ourselves. We hope that *Merciless* and the comms drones will divert attention enough for the landing party to approach and storm the base with surprise on their side. Exactly how much will depend on how good their ground-based watch is."

He paused. "So, any questions before we go into detail?"

There was a deathly hush, then a young marine raised her hand.

"Yes. Sergeant bin Merrin."

"Exactly how close to Eloon will we be hopping?"

A sigh like a distant seashore hissed across the room. *That's what is on all their minds!*

"Too close. Next question?" Colonel Kant made a show of scanning the crowd for more questions, then turned back to bin Merrin with a twisted grin. "OK. You got me. I'm not kidding when I say 'too close.' We aim to get within a planetary diameter at superlight speed before dropping off the landing party."

The colonel continued above the shocked gasps, "This is risky, but no more so than what we've been doing already. And I believe the chief engineer has had plenty of practice now in screwing the best out of our drive."

A tall, sandy-haired man standing at ease in the front row raised his hand in acknowledgement at the ripple of nervous laughter.

The mood in the room became more subdued as the colonel continued his briefing. Shayla glanced sidelong at Chalwen and saw she was sweating heavily, her mouth working silently as she chewed the inside of her cheek.

She scanned the room and saw grave faces, fear, and businesslike determination.

*Inside a planetary diameter!* Even Shayla understood how dangerous this was. She'd done her research since her conversation with Marcus. Gravitational fields distorted the hop field. Forget about gradual sickness, the slightest miscalculation here and the entire ship would disintegrate around them.

## Chapter 34

S hayla buried her head in her hands and groaned. She opened her eyes a crack and focused on the wall screen showing the dizzying approach to Eloon.

It was no use. Whenever she opened her eyes, the room danced before her. When she squeezed them shut, blinding flashes pierced her eyelids.

One minor detail that Colonel Kant hadn't mentioned in his briefing was the perilously close approach to Eloon's sun on the way in. The tiny, blinding white disk of Chevin Chenga looked like an old friend ten hours ago, when they stopped to drop the communications drones on their long plunge towards Eloon. Now it wheeled close, bloated and dangerous. The heat of the sun posed no threat, but its invisible fingers of gravity tugged on the particles of ship and crew as they flung themselves across a fractal labyrinth of inter-dimensional chasms.

Pain lanced through Shayla's temples and acid soured her throat. A faint crackling filled the air. Ozone bit her nostrils.

"The drones have started singing. Right on time!" Joseph Herrin, senior operations controller, called across the room.

Henri Chargon sat next to Shayla on the tiny viewing balcony of the operations room, fidgeting and looking almost as bad as she felt. That he wasn't pacing the deck spoke volumes for his state of health. Chalwen was nowhere to be seen.

Joseph gave terse instructions to a team of communications technicians that would be orchestrating the assault on Eloon. Hangar doors open. Landing craft ready to drop. Shayla could hear confirmations from the cruiser pilots and from Colonel Kant in the lead ship.

The pounding in Shayla's head eased as the sun receded. A tiny spark separated from the spinning starscape, and flew at them. Unable to control herself, Shayla pressed back into her chair, knuckles cracking with the ferocity of her grip on the railing in front.

The outline of the southern ice cap, familiar from childhood, flashed into view then stilled abruptly in the center of the screen.

*We made it!* Almost overcome with nausea, Shayla leapt to her feet and ran from the operations room to be sick. As she raced down the corridor to the nearest washroom, she was relieved to see she wasn't the only one to succumb to the effects of their suicidal sprint. A trickle of men and women, faces drawn and pale, was entering and leaving.

*This is crippling us!* But she knew all critical posts on the ship were double-manned, with backup crews ready to take over from incapacitated colleagues.

Shayla gagged on the sweet stench as she stumbled through the washroom door. She retched painfully, stomach dry and empty, then rinsed her face in a basin and leaned back against the counter. She checked the medipatch clamped to her wrist, and thumbed a tab on its edge. Everyone on board wore one now, but some responded better to the drugs than others. Shayla had long since discarded safe dosage guidelines. The potent cocktail it dispensed was the only thing keeping her alive.

Metal shrieked. The deck bucked beneath her feet, slamming her into the counter. The overhead lights flared then winked out. Shayla tried to ignore panicked cries, and felt her way to the door, vision adjusting to dim red emergency lighting.

Out in the corridor, smoke pricked her eyes. She blinked, and paused to picture the route back to the command deck.

A brighter glow flickered into life. *We still have power.* Shayla smacked her forehead with the palm of her hand. *Of course we have power. Your feet are still on the floor aren't they?*

Only just, though. The usually-steady gravity wavered. The sensation reminded her of being on a boat. Shayla stumbled along the corridor, past ghostly figures in the eddies of smoke. She felt her feet lift from the deck. She hung, weightless for a few heart-stopping seconds before thumping back to the floor. She rolled with the impact and regained her feet.

A scream nearby told her someone else hadn't landed so well. Shayla peered through the gloom to where a figure lay huddled on the floor, moaning. She knelt, and recognized the guard who'd escorted her to and from her cell what seemed like a lifetime ago.

Along the corridor, half-seen people sprawled, stirring, struggling to their feet.

Squinting through tears, the guard held a hand out to her. "Help me. Please."

The red and grey of the floor swam out of focus. Shayla needed to return to the operations room. Her scalp crawled at the thought of unseen assailants out there, of unknown strength. She needed to find out what was happening.

Swallowing the sickening feeling of helplessness, she placed a hand on the guard's shoulder. "Where are you hurt?"

The guard's eyes widened. She must have finally recognized Shayla. She brushed Shayla's hand away and hissed through clenched teeth as she tried to pull herself upright. She gasped and slumped back to the floor. "My leg," she groaned.

"Can you stand if I help you?"

The guard grimaced, then nodded. She held out a trembling hand.

A shriek of pain told Shayla this was not going to be easy. She thought a moment, then reached under the guard's tunic. "Hold still," she said as the guard struggled. "This will paralyze you down one side, but will also deaden the pain."

Her probing forefinger found the pressure point. The guard gasped and swore. But she was able to stand, leaning on Shayla, shattered leg trailing behind her.

Shayla turned towards the command deck, struggling under the weight.

"No. This way," said the guard.

"But the sick bay's this way, isn't it?"

"The dining hall becomes the main field hospital in battle."

They limped down the cramped corridor, joining a line of people helping injured colleagues. The smoke cleared and the deck under their feet steadied, though Shayla was sure she felt lighter than usual.

"We must hurry. That nerve block will wear off in a few minutes."

The ship shuddered around them.

"That was the plasma cannon," the guard said.

"You can tell that?"

"You get to know the sound and feel of a ship. We're hurt badly, I can tell you that much, but we're still fighting."

Shayla helped the guard into the crew dining hall where the briefing had taken place the day before. A team of nurses scurried around two huddled heaps on the row of tables in the center of the room. One was screaming, one ominously still. An expanse of burnt flesh disappeared under a blanket of sterifoam spray.

A medical orderly glanced at them, then motioned them towards a row of stretchers against one wall.

Shayla helped the guard down onto the nearest empty stretcher. "I must return to the operations room now." She paused. "Good luck."

As Shayla turned to leave, the guard gripped her wrist. "Please tell me you haven't led us into a trap!"

Shayla tried to keep the fear out of her voice. "If I have, it is not one of my making."

———•◆•———

Shayla returned to her seat in the operations room. "What happened?"

Henri glanced up from the wall screens across the room.

Shayla blinked as a silent explosion lit the room with ghostly light.

"Good. Got them at last!" Henri turned his attention back to Shayla. "We have company, in case you hadn't guessed."

"No kidding!"

"We dropped the landing party then spotted two warships in orbit. We mopped up the scout ship before they knew what hit them, but that frigate—" Henri waved at the fading afterglow "—got off a salvo of torpedoes. One of them got past our beams. That's what did the damage. They didn't manage to catch us again but they did lead us a merry chase around the planet."

"Where's the landing party?"

"Closing in on the pole now. The base will know something's up, but they won't have the decryption codes to communicate through the muck thrown out by those drones. With a bit of luck, all eyes will be on what's going on up here, and not on their near horizon."

The starscape on the screens wheeled. A distant speck showed at extreme range, difficult to make out near the blinding sun.

"A freighter," said Henri, suddenly tense. "That's what we were afraid of. Someone making a run for it. We can't let them get clear of the jamming signal to send a message."

"Why haven't they hopped out of the system by now? They could have escaped."

"For all they know, there could be a cordon around the system. They have no idea what sort of force is out there. And they could be under orders from Ivan to stay put."

"Until *Wrath of Empire* arrives to finish us," Shayla muttered. "So they must hope to escape detection from the invasion force they think is coming. At least that part of our plan seems to be working."

The view jumped. The freighter loomed large. *Merciless's* beams lashed out, clawing at the hull shields.

"Wish the captain would stop doing that," Henri sighed. "We've been lucky so far, hopping so close in."

The freighter vanished.

"Shit! They're hopping as well!" Henri's yell carried into the shocked hush.

"They're desperate," Joseph called over his shoulder.

Nausea forgotten, Shayla's heart hammered as one of the techs struggled to regain contact with the craft.

"There," the tech called, pointing at a miniscule dot on the screen. The dot turned into a streak, shining with the brilliance of a second sun. "Guess they hadn't quite mastered the technique."

———•◆•———

"Primary drive's fried. That last hop finished it." Captain Bernadin Stihl swiveled in her seat to face them. Her over-large teeth gnawed at her bottom lip.

"How long do you think we have before *Wrath of Empire* gets here?" Chalwen had joined Shayla and Henri on the command deck. Her face was swollen, eyes red raw. Her normally immaculate uniform hung off her like a sack.

"Anybody's guess. At their nominal maximum speed, another three days. If they've been pushing their drive, they could be here any time. For all we know, they might have come and gone already."

Shayla's heart sank. What if the landing party found the base empty?

The white disk of Chevin Chenga hung close, unmoving against the endless night. *Merciless* raced towards Eloon, progress too slow to see in the unbroken grip of normal spatial dimensions.

"What word from the landing party?" Bernadin addressed Joseph's image on a nearby screen.

There was a long pause. "They've located an entrance. Moving in."

"Dammit!" Bernadin muttered. "We should have been overhead to support them."

"We couldn't let that freighter escape. We have a strong enough force on the ground, providing the base is as small as we've been led to believe." Chalwen glowered at Shayla. "We can do nothing to help them, but we do need to give thought to how to get away from here afterwards. We do not want to encounter *Wrath*."

"Under conventional drive it'll be ten hours before we are back in orbit around Eloon," Bernadin said. "You're right. The landers are on their own. Lieutenant Herrin, is Colonel Kant aware of the situation?"

"He is. Shouldn't be a problem. He's reporting minimal resistance."

"Small mercies," growled Chalwen. "So what can we do to evade *Wrath*? The longer we spend, the more likely we are to meet them."

"All we can do is get away from the planet, and find some background clutter to hide against," said Bernadin.

"What about repairing the drive?"

"Commander Brasch is working on that. He has worked miracles before, but he doesn't sound hopeful."

"So, hiding places then." Chalwen chewed a stylus while she and Bernadin studied a schematic of the system. "If we are pressed for time, somewhere on the surface of the planet itself?"

"We can't set down on land," Bernadin answered. "We'd have to run our drive to hold position, so we'd be conspicuous. No better off than up in orbit." She looked thoughtful. "Only possibility would be a very deep canyon with a high ferrous content to soak up emissions. Even that's pretty slim." She gazed at the system. "Sizeable asteroid belt. Any idea of the mineral content?"

This last was addressed to Shayla, who shook her head. "I was only young when I left here."

"All the same, that looks more promising."

"If we have time to reach it," Chalwen said. "And what if we are caught by *Wrath* out in open space?"

Bernadin simply shook her head.

———•—•———

"Sir, Colonel Kant's reporting in." Joseph Herrin's voice, from the adjacent operations room, broke the anxious hush that had cloaked the command deck for the past half an hour. Worry lines creased his face. "I'm putting him directly through to you."

The colonel appeared on another screen. "Captain Stihl," he said, throwing a hasty salute. "We've completed a first search of the base. It is small. Only twenty-seven crew."

"Any sign of my family?" The Emperor had emerged, unnoticed, from his cabin.

"No, My Lord."

Shayla's stomach lurched. The command deck blurred in front of her.

The colonel's voice seemed distant. "This place doesn't look like a prison."

Chalwen and the Emperor turned to face Shayla. Julian was expressionless, but Chalwen's expression was murderous.

"In fact I'm not actually sure why this base is here." The colonel's words cut through the deathly and unaccustomed silence on the command deck. "There's quarters for the crew, equipped for a long term stay. Landing facility, if you can call it that. Maintenance. But there's nothing military here. No warehousing for a waystation. No science. No obvious purpose."

*Nothing there?* Shayla felt alone and exposed, all eyes on her.

"We'll go over everything more thoroughly. We may have missed something, but right now the only thing of any note here is this communications room." The colonel seemed oblivious to the fact that no-one was paying him any attention.

The remnant of the assassin in Shayla noted one of the guards sliding a pistol from its holster, but she knew her death wasn't going to be that easy.

"On your feet." Chalwen's tone was gruff, but more tired than angry.

Shayla swung herself off the bunk. For once she was grateful for the impassive guards at the door of the tiny cabin she'd been given. The renewed hostility of the crew, however understandable, was impossible to face. "Commander ap Gwynodd—"

"Save it! I've been thinking of little else for the last eight hours. However hard I try, I can't dispel a strong sense that you acted in good faith. You really did believe they'd be here, didn't you?"

Shayla chewed her lip. "To be honest, I couldn't be certain. I was acting on deduction rather than hard fact." She looked at Chalwen, trying to gauge her mood. "It was a lifeline I had to grasp."

"Humph! Good old-fashioned honesty?" Chalwen sighed. "People always expect answers. Certainty." Her tone became distant and wistful. "So many decisions I've had to make based on nothing more than deduction. Sometimes with lives or whole planets in the balance."

"What will happen now?"

"That is for the Emperor to decide. I can't begin to tell you what a bitter blow this is to him. Luckily for you he's not disposed to rash judgments."

She handed Shayla a thickly lined and hooded overall. "Anyway, you're coming with me."

Shayla pulled on the overalls and a pair of boots. "Down to the surface?"

Chalwen nodded. "I wish to retrieve something from this disaster. We still have people sickening and dying. The ground force reports a well-equipped pharmacy, but they can't make sense of the drugs. There is nothing there familiar to us. We're preparing to drop down there while they bring the prisoners up." She fixed Shayla with a cold stare. "Pray that you can help."

Shayla's heart lifted. "Drugs are something I know."

Chalwen grunted and motioned Shayla out of the cabin. "Doctor Benthari ap Miskin," she said, gesturing to a tall woman standing alongside the guards in the corridor.

Shayla bowed, noting dark skin contrasting with the camouflage white of polar overalls. The doctor inclined her head only fractionally in reply.

They walked in silence to the aft hangars.

The passageways around the officers' cabins were mercifully free of traffic. Shayla was still numb from the crushing disappointment, but helping save some lives might buy her time. The slight hope loosened her frozen mind. She could feel thoughts turning over once more, assessing, calculating.

Brandt was still out there. He must be in trouble or he'd have found a way to contact her.

And Ivan! Shayla's old rage kindled again. The Emperor may no longer be her focus, but she still had a job to do.

All she had to do right now was survive, and trust that opportunities would present themselves.

They crossed an antechamber, similar to the one by which Shayla had entered the warship nearly two weeks ago, and climbed down a stairway. Chalwen pointed to a small air cruiser waiting in the hangar. Shayla clambered into the hatch, followed by Chalwen, the doctor, and one of the guards.

The pilot readied the controls. He glanced at Shayla as she took the seat next to him, then turned to Chalwen. "Captain says we'll be overhead in three minutes. Ready to drop."

The guard closed the hatch. The hangar lights dimmed and the outer doors opened. They waited in awkward silence, hanging in darkness.

At last, the cruiser dropped clear of the warship. Shayla's heart thudded in her chest as she watched the planet, her home, grow beneath them. They plunged towards a wrinkled landscape cloaked in green, giving way to fields of snow in gathering twilight.

The sky darkened around them. An ocean of ghostly white unrolled below. As they descended, starlight revealed a jagged wilderness of mountains and ice.

The pilot reached down and switched off the navigation computer. "This thing's useless until we work out how to disable those defenses. When we came in first time the leading ship had veered off ten degrees before we realized what was happening."

All that was left on the display was a simple chart and a cluster of cross-hairs. "Homing beacons," the pilot said, noticing Shayla's curious gaze. "Strange," he mused. "To say what little there is there, it's surrounded by state-of-the-art defenses. Most craft on standard navigation would steer themselves right round that base without anyone noticing. We only found them when they tried to punch a distress signal through the blanket. We switched off navigation and followed their transmission."

A pool of light appeared in the distance. As they came closer, Shayla saw it came from floodlights on the landing craft. They flew low over a blackened outpost. "They had some ground to air ordnance," the pilot explained, pointing to the shattered remains as they passed. "Luckily we caught them on the hop. Could have been bad news if they'd had a chance to bring that to bear."

They landed alongside one of the ground assault cruisers, a looming shadow in the arctic night.

On Chalwen's command, Shayla, the doctor, and the guard sealed their overalls and climbed out into the darkness. A bitter wind keened around them. A guard sheltering in the lee of the cruiser signaled to them and pointed towards a narrow cleft in a low cliff of ice opposite.

They struggled across a rough and windswept slope to be met by another guard. As they reached the base of the cliff, the wind slackened off enough for a shouted conversation. "Through here," the guard yelled. "Twenty yards in. Bear right. You'll see a nightlight on in the top reception chamber. Wait there for an escort."

They entered the welcome shelter of the gap in the cliff. Bright stars overhead, eclipsed occasionally by driven flurries of snow, showed the line of the fissure cutting into the depths of the shelf.

Dim ruby light spilled across the path, and they filed into a circular domed chamber carved into the ice. Their breath formed clouds in the air, but Shayla felt her cheeks flush warm after brief exposure to the glacial winter storm.

"Wait over there." Another camouflaged marine stood at the top of a staircase cut into the floor and waved them to one side. Moments later, more marines appeared, weapons ready, leading small groups of men and women out. Shayla counted nineteen prisoners. Sullen, defiant, scared. Shayla recognized the young sergeant, bin Merrin, commanding the escort.

Once the way was clear, they climbed down the long and narrow staircase. Every thirty steps or so it opened out into a small chamber, leveled off, then continued downwards. The walls showed they still descended through solid ice. The steps were covered in thick matting for traction. Above their heads, a series of lights set into the ice gave steadily brighter illumination as they went.

After five flights, the glistening ice gave way to stark white plastic. Blackened scars bore evidence of some resistance. Three more flights, and they found themselves in a rectangular anteroom. A heavy door lay twisted and shattered to one side.

A corridor led them into a larger guard room. A marine sitting at a desk looked up as they entered. He conversed with their escort and made some notes on a scroll. Moments later, Colonel Kant appeared through a doorway behind him.

"Magister ap Gwynodd, Doctor ap Miskin." He bobbed his head. "This way please."

They followed the colonel along a curved corridor. As far as Shayla could tell, it looked like it would lead them around full circle back to the guard room. "Please be quick," the colonel said. "We have completed a search of the base and are bringing all personnel back up to the cruisers."

They passed an open doorway on the inner wall. Stairs led down to a lower level. Just past it, on the other side, the colonel led them into a medical examination room.

Shayla prowled round the tiny pharmacy at the back of the examination room, opening cabinets, rummaging through drawers. It was no wonder the marine medic could make no sense of it. The Firenzi pharmacopoeia was so far in advance of anything the Empire possessed. Some of their medical knowledge was shared and openly traded, but much was reserved for their own military. Many of these drugs would be unknown to the Imperial medical community, and these were all labeled in Firenzi military argot, incomprehensible to an outsider.

She soon found what she sought.

"These are still pretty basic," she said to Doctor ap Miskin. "We need a full planetary medical facility, not an outpost, but they are a one hundred percent improvement on what you're using right now."

Shayla set out cartons on the counter top.

"Promotes genetic repair. Cell membranes. Neurological balance." While she reeled off uses and discussed dosage, the doctor scrawled notes on the cartons. She was thankful that no-one but her could make sense of the writing. She was drawing on creative ingenuity and pre-scribing uses way beyond the bounds of their official purposes.

She tapped the last box. "This for the worst cases. Metabolic retar-dant. This will put them into a deep coma and slow the damage until we can reach proper care."

Chalwen watched her curiously. "How do you know so much about drugs?"

"An assassin must know all about the human body. To kill or disable someone with the greatest economy, it helps to know how the body functions. I am a fully qualified medical doctor."

Chalwen grunted. "Colonel Kant. I think we're done here," she called. "You said there was a communications room? I'll let *Merciless* know we're on our way."

Shayla watched the doctor pack the drugs into a bag, then hurried to follow.

The colonel led them back to the main corridor and through a door on the far side of the guard room. Chalwen strode to the console and tapped on the panel. While she waited for the warship to respond, she turned around, surveying the room.

"*Merciless* here."

The call went unanswered. Chalwen stood, mouth hanging open. "I know this room." Her voice was quiet. Awestruck.

She whirled back to the console. "*Merciless*! Any sign of *Wrath* yet? We need more time down here. Get Commander Chargon. Quickly!"

She turned to Shayla and Colonel Kant, eyes shining. "They *are* here. Somewhere." She waved at the room the colonel had remarked on hours earlier. Opposite the communications console, a clear wall divided them from what looked like a comfortable and richly furnished sitting room.

"Looks like a recording studio?" Shayla ventured, noting the lighting rigs and equipment on the near side of the room beyond the window.

"All these years, we've had communications from the Emperor's family. Every year. Reminders that they still live. How often have I studied those transmissions, looking for some clue, some tiny detail, that might lead us to them?" Chalwen placed balled fists against the dividing glass. "This room here is as familiar to me as my own quarters."

"Chalwen?" Henri's face appeared on the screen.

"Henri! We need information out of those prisoners. Fast."

She directed the visual feed towards the far room. Henri's mouth formed a silent 'O'.

"You understand what we need from them?"

He closed his mouth and nodded, eyes glinting with determination, then vanished from sight.

"Colonel, get as many craft and troops as you can scanning the area. There must be a second facility somewhere nearby, or some corner of this base you've missed. See if you can find it before Commander Chargon extracts the information."

<hr />

In the crew dining hall on *Merciless*, Shayla, Bernadin, and Marcus nursed mugs of tea. The tea cooled. Nobody drank. Every wasted minute brought them closer to a deadly encounter, but still they sat, helpless, waiting.

Shayla wondered just how long they would sit here in orbit, exposed and defenseless, before running for cover. Would they ever give up? Would they continue to wait, their goal tantalizingly out of reach, until the mighty *Wrath of Empire* showed up to end the game?

Around the room, men and women watched the far door. There were few words, but the expressions on their faces told the anguish they felt, some rage, some fear, a good measure of distaste, and endless frustration mirrored again and again in their eyes.

Even the armored walls couldn't quite stifle the screams emanating from the room next door. The officers' dining hall had been turned into a makeshift interrogation room. Shayla had glanced in to see the nineteen prisoners strapped to tables. With a cold, determined look in her eye, Chalwen shut the door in her face before Henri started work.

Every sound of anguish tore at her. These were her countrymen. But she couldn't bring herself to leave. She felt the urgency of the Imperial crew. The fading hope. The Emperor's family was here, some-where close. These people held the key and they knew it. They knew also that a warship was on its way.

'Wrath of Empire'. How fitting.

Henri and Chalwen were desperate. Too desperate for subtlety. And they would show no mercy, she knew it.

She also knew that these Firenzi would have been hand-picked and well trained. They would likely die before they betrayed their masters.

Maybe they wouldn't need to. She tried to buoy herself with the hope that the interrogations would become redundant. All available crew and craft were scouring the surface around the base, and scan-ning the depths of the ice with every instrument at their disposal. But it was slow going, and the winter storm on the surface showed no signs of abating.

At last, Shayla broke the painful hush. "You realize this interroga-tion is hopeless."

Bernadin grimaced, then shrugged. "What would you have us do?"

Shayla hesitated. Another long wail sent featherlight fingers up her spine. She swallowed, deciding how best to express the idea forming in her mind. "Have I been true to my word?"

Bernadin sat back, chewing the inside of her cheek, gazing at Shayla. "I can't say I trust you, but it seems you have led us true after all. Magister ap Gwynodd certainly thinks so. Enough to keep us here like a fly on a lure when *Wrath* might turn up at any moment."

"And the landing party reported twenty seven personnel," said Marcus with a twisted grin. "Eight are dead, and nineteen currently wish they were."

"The point?" Shayla asked, distracted from her train of thought.

"Colonel Kant is thorough. He reported thirty two billets on the accommodation level that were evidently in use. That leaves five people still unaccounted for."

"Five ..." Shayla hesitated. "The Imperial family?"

Marcus snorted. "Unlikely. These were regular guard bunks. Military issue kit, uniforms, and weapons."

"The family are prisoners, not guests," Bernadin added. "These missing personnel must be guarding them somewhere away from the main base."

"Yes. Fair enough," Shayla said. "But the point is, these prisoners will not lead Imperial forces to them."

"You have another suggestion?"

"Yes," she said slowly. "I believe I do."

———•+•———

Shayla stood in the center of the room, waiting for the last of the guards to leave. On her instructions, and over a protest from Chalwen that the Emperor himself had struggled to quell, the prisoners had been unshackled and clothed. The same standard issue green jumpsuit she'd worn while in the cells.

While they eased themselves, groaning and wincing, off the tables she couldn't help surreptitiously looking for indications of torture. Apart from livid bruises where they'd struggled against their shackles, there were few outward signs of their ordeal. A few red patches of skin, a few hair thin scratches. Shayla had studied interrogation techniques, modern, ancient, and some steeped in legend. Nobody practiced gross physical mutilation any more, other than out of on-the-spot necessity. Most tortures were more subtle. Drug-enhancement could make the touch of a feather unbearable, or could conjure demons from the depths of the mind more terrifying than any amount of real pain.

But the screams had been real enough. Shayla gritted her teeth.

When she was alone with the survivors from the base, she turned slowly to survey the room. She was surrounded. She felt all eyes on her, assessing her. She knew the thought, unspoken, ran through nineteen minds: *There is only one of her!* All her senses strained for sounds of movement, of a threat. None came. Her self-assurance held them in check.

She addressed them in the Firenzi military tongue. "I am Shayla Carver, undercover agent with the Firenzi Special Service."

She continued turning, locking eyes with anyone who would meet her gaze.

Faces showed shock and betrayal. One man, thick set with long sandy hair, stood and stepped forward. "Traitorous whore!" he spat. His face beet red, twisted with fury.

With little more than a glance in his direction, Shayla straight-armed him in the sternum. He staggered backwards into the table, wheezing blood.

"Just one minor housekeeping note," she said conversationally, as if nothing had happened, "any further challenge of that nature will prove fatal."

She stood still, gazing at the floor.

Vulnerable.

A tempting target.

Nothing happened. The psychological moment passed. She knew she had the upper hand now, her supremacy acknowledged by their tacit compliance.

"So. You find me on an Imperial warship, assisting the Emperor, and you question my loyalty." Her tone was matter-of-fact. "Maybe you've been out of contact with civilization, but you must be aware that His Excellency Josef Firenzi only recently renewed an oath of allegiance to the Emperor. In doing so he bound us *all* to His service."

She looked around the room once more. "My question is, where do *your* loyalties lie? You are holding members of the Imperial family. For that, your lives are forfeit by Firenzi law, let alone by Imperial retribution."

Nobody challenged her assertion.

"The truth is, we have all been betrayed. Josef Firenzi and the Lady Margerite are dead. Murdered by Scipio Firenzi." Shayla paused to let the shocked outburst run its course. *So! Scipio elected not to reveal that little item yet.* A tiny gamble had paid off. While she waited, she studied their reactions carefully. A small handful were genuinely outraged. Many were clearly faking. Some had trouble concealing their glee.

*Scipio chose his crew carefully. But not quite carefully enough. And he didn't trust them with this news.*

"You are holding out, waiting for relief. You believe that Scipio is coming on board an Imperial *Sword*-class battleship. That hope is futile. The Imperial navy is waiting overhead to capture him. Those of you who might, by some slim chance, escape the Emperor's wrath will stand trial for treason in the Firenzi courts. Scipio cannot help you. He is a renegade, and any allies he had in the Family hierarchy are rushing to disown him."

She paused again to let her words sink in.

"Your role as jailers is over."

———•——

"He insists he will speak to you, and you alone." Chalwen was breathless, her voice thick with suppressed excitement.

Shayla's heart leapt. She had left the interrogation room with instructions that the prisoners should be separated and confined in isolation from each other. With no opportunity to converse amongst themselves, each was left to their own thoughts.

Shayla knew she had sown the necessary seeds. Most would stand firm. Scipio had selected the most loyal people he could find. But some amongst them would be rooted still in the old Firenzi code. It was those few she had addressed. She had given them a clear indication of where their duty lay under that code, something nobody in the Imperial hierarchy could have done.

Since then, all they could do was wait. Minutes ticked by. The ground parties still quartered the inhospitable surface, but their task was next to hopeless. The entrance to the main base had only been given away because the base crew had tried to fight off the attackers.

Now, one of the prisoners wanted to talk.

Chalwen led Shayla to the infirmary. With a shock she recognized the man who'd tried to attack her. He sat with his chest strapped, eyes bloodshot but alert.

"I hope they are making you comfortable," Shayla said.

"Jevin Colt," he wheezed. "Is it true that Josef is dead?" He spoke in the Firenzi tongue, with a suspicious glance at Chalwen and the guards around him.

"Yes," Shayla whispered past a lump in her throat.

He nodded. "I felt the pain in your voice when you said it." He hesitated, frowning. "The Lady Margerite too?"

Shayla nodded.

He sighed. "Years ago, I thought we were doing this for Josef. We were an elite team, doing something great for the Family. Something that would bring them power in the galaxy. Years passed. Nothing happened. It seemed like we'd been forgotten." He looked Shayla in the eye with a wry smile. "Josef knew nothing of this venture, did he?"

"He would never have consented to it. He'd have had no qualms about overthrowing the Emperor at any opportunity, but not at any price."

"We were all fools." He switched back to the Imperial tongue and spoke to Chalwen. "I will lead you to them."

———•✦•———

Shayla fingered the collar of her uniform. It felt strange wearing the Firenzi colors again. They'd landed and returned to the base, where Jevin scoured the store room for a spare lieutenant's uniform. It hung slightly loose off her, but it would do for her purpose.

They stood in front of an armored door at the bottom of flights of stairs similar to the ones that led down to the main base. A crevice a mile from the base concealed the entrance. It would have taken days for the ground forces to find.

Jevin thumbed the tab on a comms panel next to the door. "Elly!" he called. "They're here." He gestured to Shayla standing at ease behind him. "I'm coming in, please clear me, I don't want to get my ass burned off now."

"You're okay to enter." A pause. "Is it really over?"

Shayla leaned forward. "Lieutenant Gabrielle Carver," she lied easily. "Second Division of the Special Guard. My Lord Scipio commends your fortitude. Assemble your personnel quickly. We're abandoning this base."

Jevin scrawled an entry code on the door's control panel and it swung open.

*You must get them all. Any sign of trouble and the family will die.*

Shayla marched through the door ahead of Jevin. She returned salutes thrown by the occupants of the room.

*Only four! Where's the last one?*

Another figure appeared in a far doorway.

Shayla's needle gun appeared in her hand as if by magic. Chalwen had not been happy about that, or any aspect of this plan for that matter, but she'd not been able to propose a workable alternative. Shayla knew that Colonel Kant and his marines were waiting out of sight, and would be on their way as soon as she signaled them. They would be here in less than a minute.

A lot of bad things could happen in less than a minute.

She dropped the most distant figure first, then two more before anyone could react.

A beam sizzled past her head, accompanied by a clatter and a cry of pain. The stench of burning plastic caught at the back of her throat.

Shayla whirled round to see a chair sliding into a corner of the room. Jevin had thrown it to disarm the woman who'd let them in. The woman stooped to retrieve her pistol while Jevin leaped across the room to wrestle the fifth guard, who was drawing his weapon.

One more needle dealt with the woman. The fifth guard, struggling in Jevin's grip, went still when he felt the snout of Shayla's needle gun pressed to his neck. His eyes flicked to his fallen compatriots then back to Shayla.

Shayla pressed her lapel transmitter to summon the colonel, then fixed the guard with an icy stare. "You will lead us to the Emperor's family."

He swallowed hard, then nodded.

Jevin glanced at the paralyzed guards, and leaned close to Shayla with a frown. "You said they'd be unharmed."

"Trylex," Shayla said. "It'll wear off in a few hours, but right now they're helpless." She grinned. "Best bit is, they'll obey simple instructions so we won't have to carry them up those stairs." The grin faded from her face. "You shouldn't have fought in your condition."

Jevin grimaced, and wiped a fleck of blood from the corner of his mouth. "I'll live."

---

Shayla and Chalwen reached the command deck on *Merciless* to rapturous applause.

"Everyone on board?" Bernadin asked Joseph Herrin. "Then secure for flight. Lieutenant Stone! Get us out of here."

"Captain!" a voice called suddenly urgent across the sounds of jubilation. "I have a ship on my screen."

"Holy crap," Bernadin muttered. "That's a *Sword*."

## Chapter 36

The warship hung right in their path, no more than a distant blur on the screen, but her menacing outline and bulk was unmistakable.

At last, Henri's calm voice broke the silence on *Merciless's* command deck. "We cannot hope to escape them, nor to fight. Let us pray the presence of the Emperor on board can bring Ivan to his senses."

"Comms!" Bernadin called. "Bring us back onto the Imperial net." She turned in her seat, expression grim. "I don't think our location is a secret any more."

The communications watch officer acknowledged. More anxious seconds ticked by.

Then ...

"This is *Mace of Terror*. Nice to see you are on speaking terms again *Merciless*."

———————

The jubilation that accompanied the release of the Emperor's family last night, and the relief at meeting a friendly battleship, had faded. Frustration now gnawed at Shayla, a feeling she knew she shared with many on the command deck.

"Ships always put out an encrypted tracer on the comms net." The young communications chief, Frances Jokko, paced the floor of the bridge. Her startling white hair glowed in the perpetual multi-colored twilight. "That's standard procedure, but *Wrath* has shut off all contact. They are out of reach and untraceable."

Henri pursed his lips. "If they're out of contact, they would know nothing of our presence here. They should have shown up by now."

"They're not stupid," Chalwen said. "They won't give themselves away, but they must have other channels of communication."

"So we must assume they know the Imperial family is now safe."

"Why didn't they just take us on?" Bernadin wondered. "This ship wouldn't be a match for *Wrath* at the best of times."

"Depends how good their intelligence is," said Chalwen. "If they have good information, they know we've been joined by *Mace of Terror*. And *Shield of Mercy* will be here within the day."

"But if they have scant knowledge," added Henri, "they may assume we are in fact *Shield of Mercy*. As far as they know, *Merciless* should not have been able to outrun them."

"In either case, they must have diverted elsewhere." Chalwen's breath hissed in through her teeth, then out in a gust of exasperation. "Where are they running to? What do Ivan and Scipio hope to achieve now?"

Shayla lounged in the watch officer's chair, only half listening to the discussion. She swiveled around to survey the command deck below her feet. A few faces turned her way from the crew at their posts. The unremitting hostility of the last two weeks had evaporated. Their contact was guarded still, but people acknowledged her, met her eyes, spoke to her.

"It's unbelievable!" Henri's tone was a mixture of exasperation and resignation. "There has to be some way to find them." He leaned back against the railing of the bridge. He seemed to have regained his health, but after a few near collisions he'd curbed his own habitual prowling and conceded the cramped floor to Frances's youthful energy.

With a frown, Shayla returned to her thoughts. All Imperial forces now sought the Grand Duke and *Wrath of Empire*. She would bide her time and look for an opportunity to deal with Ivan personally, but meanwhile she'd still heard nothing from Brandt. If he was so much as within spitting distance of a communications terminal, no matter how guarded, he would have found a way to track her down and send word to her. She knew it.

Not for the first time, she toyed with the thought of enlisting help from someone on *Merciless*. She chewed her lip. Her position was still fragile. She had traded her service against the chance of salvation, but Brandt had made no such pledge, and may not be given the chance. No. Best he stay out of the Empire's eye.

Despite the frustration, Shayla reveled in the change in mood throughout the warship. Sometime during the celebrations last night, she realized she was no longer followed by an armed guard. Even though a more discreet shadow still lurked in the background, most likely on Chalwen's orders, she had greater freedom of movement. If only she could retrieve her notepad and its treasure trove of illicit software, she could search for Brandt without help.

Shayla looked up as Marcus Corrin leaned against the railing next to her. He handed her a steaming mug of spiced tea.

She smiled, and cupped her hands around the mug. She gazed at the steam curling into the air, lost once more in her own thoughts.

*Standard procedure ...*

Shayla toyed with the thought. Something tugged at her memory.

She whirled in her seat, slopping scalding tea over her hands.

"I've got it!" she yelled. "Shit!" shaking drips from her hand. "I think we have a way to track them."

"You do?"

"You're kidding!"

"How?"

"I need my notepad," said Shayla above the wave of incredulity.

Chalwen and Henri exchanged looks in the sudden hush. Eventually Chalwen grimaced and nodded to a waiting orderly, who saluted and scurried away. "But I want to know up front what you intend to do. And Henri and Frances will supervise."

Shayla arched an eyebrow at Chalwen. "What will it take to earn your trust?"

"This from a woman who devoted a life to deception?"

"If I still meant harm, I could have taken *any* life on board this ship in the last week. Don't imagine your guards or the lack of a weapon would have posed any serious obstacle."

"And this from a woman who's shown she can pass up easy targets in favor of bigger prizes?"

Shayla snorted and shook her head.

"Relax, missy. Deception is your profession. Suspicion is mine. Nothing personal, but my instructions stand."

Shayla ground her teeth. *These are your masters now. Remember that.* "While I was taking over *Merciless's* command system I used the Imperial net to plant trapdoor agents on *Wrath* and *Shield* as well, just in case."

"Just how much of our security have you compromised?" Chalwen's eyes narrowed. She exchanged glances with Henri.

"Point is, they may have shut down all normal channels, but they wouldn't know about these agents. They're designed to stay hidden."

Frances's face lit up. "They'll be leaving their own signature out on the comms net. If we have the signature we can trace them." Her face fell. "Erm…Just how complicated is this signature?"

"It's derived from a graphic, and encrypted. I have it on my notepad. Why?"

"Thing is…your notepad …"

"You messed with it?" Shayla's voice shook with rage.

"No, nothing more than a standard examination. But the hops…a lot of equipment got junked on the way here."

The orderly returned and handed Shayla the notepad. She grabbed it and opened it out. At first, everything seemed okay, but…"The notepad is still functional," she said at last, "but it has been damaged."

"How bad?"

"The hidden layers must have interpreted the damage as a forced intrusion, and self-destructed." The words seemed to stick in Shayla's throat. She forced them out, trying to keep her voice level. "There's nothing left. It's just an ordinary notepad now." Her shoulders slumped. The Empire would catch Ivan eventually, but how was she ever going to find Brandt?

"So tracking *Wrath* is not going to be that easy. Can you reproduce that signature from memory?" Chalwen's voice was tight.

Shayla hesitated. "It's complicated …" *Complicated, and painful to recall. But pain sharpens the memory.* "Yes. I can do it."

"Let's do this down in the comms den," said Frances, beckoning.

Shayla followed Frances down from the bridge and into the warren of pits crowded with crew and equipment. They picked their way through a maze buzzing with controlled activity.

Shimmering hair framed dark skin and a sudden flash of teeth as Frances turned to Shayla. "Welcome to my lair, My Lady."

Two communications clerks looked up as they entered the cramped enclosure. "Shift yer ass, Stevie," Frances called to a heavy-set woman chewing on the end of a stylus.

Stevie turned, brow furrowed, and surveyed Shayla over the tip of the stylus. She sighed and heaved herself upright. Shayla slipped into her seat and reached for a stylus from a nearby tray, ignoring the chewed instrument proffered by Stevie.

Shayla gazed at the desk surface. She cleared her mind then formed an image of her childhood home. She pictured the house, the meadows, the layout from above, every detail etched sharp in her mind. Her knuckles whitened where she gripped the stylus. The desk blurred in front of her.

She swallowed hard, and blinked to clear her eyes. *This will lead me to Ivan.* Cold fury swamped the grief. She tried again, focusing just on the details, shutting out the memories that went with them. She started sketching, letting her unconscious mind guide her hand.

Finally, Shayla circled the image she'd sketched, and scrawled an encryption key alongside it. She took a deep breath and looked critically over her work. "That's it. Run this through a standard Boor-Skam algorithm and reduce it to a fully normalized matrix of topological invariants."

"That's your signature?" Frances sounded impressed.

"And it sounded almost like you understood that bit about the algorithm too," grunted Stevie, dumping herself back into the seat Shayla vacated. "Standard B-S on the way. I'll put out a search for a tracer with this signature. Follow it back through the network. That should lead us to *Wrath.*"

Shayla was unsurprised that Stevie had seen through her pretence. All the technical stuff was Brandt's province. She knew how to use the formidable toolkit he'd given her, but knew nothing about how it worked. Her world lay in human life, and the taking of it. Technical theory held no interest for her, but she was thankful he'd drilled her in how to recreate the signature.

After a few minutes work Stevie looked up at Shayla still standing expectantly at her shoulder.

"What?" She sniffed. "No point hanging around here. This'll take hours."

They gazed long at the plot, puzzling over its message. The five hundred and twenty three inhabited systems of humanity sparkled across the wall of the operations room. A narrow green cone stemmed from a point in space near Eloon, spreading out deep into Firenzi territory.

"This is the best projection we can make so far," said Frances. "It will take a few more hours of tracking to narrow it down."

"But it's already clear they are not heading for Ploorbellin," muttered Chalwen. "So the seat of Firenzi government is not their target, and nor do they seem to be heading for the independent territories."

"But they could change course. Who says they're making straight for their destination?" asked Shayla.

"A possibility," Chalwen grunted. "But they went to some trouble to avoid being tracked. For now we have to work on the basis that they believe they've been successful."

"We'll see soon enough whether or not they're holding a true course," added Frances.

"Maybe they're looking for somewhere to make a stand?" Henri suggested. "It's possible Ivan's grip on the crew is not so secure after all. They may not follow him into exile."

"If that's true," said Chalwen, "then time would be of the essence. Their course would be the most direct they could take while avoiding detection."

Shayla looked at the star chart, familiar names reeling off in her mind. One in particular stood out, alongside a tiny orange disc, just on the edge of the green swathe. "If I were looking to stand and fight, I'd make for Jemiyal," she said.

"Jemiyal?" Chalwen snorted. "From my recollection there's nothing there but a mining colony. Not even a habitable world."

Shayla laughed. "Your recollection is right, up to a point. It *is* a mining colony. There's no habitable world, but the system is rich in ores and heavy metals, scattered amongst many asteroids and planetoids. The main Jemiyal base was built around a small moon. It's an artificial world now. None of the moon's surface is left exposed."

"So why would Ivan go there?"

"Ivan wouldn't, but *Scipio* would. It's an open secret in Firenzi circles that Jemiyal is a fortress to rival anything the Empire can muster."

Chalwen's eyes widened. "How did they manage to fortify it without our knowledge?"

"With all the engineering needed to create a moon-sized artificial habitat?" said Shayla. "And all the mining equipment being shipped there? A few more specialized shipments were easy to hide. Plus with all the industrial plant established there, they could manufacture much of what they needed on site."

She had another thought. "And where would your intelligence have come from, anyway?"

"Fleur!" Chalwen spat. "Of course."

## Chapter 37

"A fleet support ship from Cendithor arrives in two days." Captain Bernadin Stihl stood at ease at the front of the operations room addressing the Emperor. "Temporary repairs will take another one or two days to complete, then I recommend returning Merciless to the nearest naval base for a complete overhaul."

The Emperor nodded. "So be it. *Merciless* is a brave ship. I would like to see her returned to full combat readiness."

"I've summoned *Slayer* and *Vanguard* to escort *Merciless*. There are reports that the Firenzi navy is assembling a force. I don't believe they are likely to threaten us, but I don't want to invite an attack."

"So…Are we sure we know *Wrath of Empire's* destination?"

"We can track her, thanks to Lady Carver's information." Bernadin inclined her head towards Shayla where she sat at the back of the room with Chalwen, Henri, and Marcus. "Her movements are consistent with a course to Jemiyal.

"Nobody beyond this ship knows we are tracking *Wrath*. Until she settles in orbit somewhere, all we can do is track and follow her. We can't hope to engage her in open space. Our best hope is to let them believe we don't know where they are, and catch them when they reach their destination."

"Why can't we fight them?" Shayla whispered to Marcus. "We out-number them. Surely we can take them on?"

"How many battles do you know that took place away from a planet?" Marcus asked. When Shayla shook her head in irritation, he continued. "All our weapons operate in realspace. No use against a hopping ship. The only way to force a fight is to catch your enemy in a gravity well where they don't dare hop."

"What units do we have available?" The Emperor and Bernadin were still discussing their plans.

"*Shield of Mercy* has joined us. *Sword of Might*, *Staff of Justice*, and *Spear of Retribution* are all near this frontier and within a week of Jemiyal."

"With *Mace of Terror*, that gives us five *Swords*." Julian looked thoughtful. "Will that be enough?"

Bernadin frowned. "If Jemiyal is as heavily fortified as Lady Carver says, we might not have the firepower for a direct confrontation. The other *Swords* are two weeks or more away. I'm discounting them for now, but they may come into play if this draws out into a siege. Our hope is that the colony leaders will not want a fight."

"If they really are heading for Jemiyal, how long before they reach it?"

"Five days. We will be two days behind them."

"Very well." Julian's voice hardened. Questioning over, it was time for decisions. "We transfer to *Shield of Mercy*. You will accompany us, *Admiral* Stihl. Turn *Merciless* over to your second in command. Make arrangements to rendezvous near Jemiyal, but be careful not to reveal our ultimate destination. We don't know what spies Ivan has reporting to him still."

⸻

Shayla watched the scroll in her lap. She had connected to the external visuals on the assault cruiser that was transferring her, Chalwen, Henri, and some of Bernadin's key personnel across to *Shield of Mercy*. The Emperor was at the controls of *Amethyst* up ahead, with his family and the newly-promoted Bernadin on board.

Even though she was growing accustomed to working for the Empire (*Shayla Carver — Imperial lackey?* She smiled at the memory from a lifetime ago) the sight of the warship's profile inspired a visceral dread.

A glint of reflected sunlight betrayed the presence of *Mace of Terror* fifteen hundred miles away, but *Shield of Mercy* loomed ever larger ahead of them. Her long and slender body, with pairs of drive pods nestling close to her hind quarters, looked out of proportion against the hulking spread of the upper weapons platform. But the lower pod held Shayla's attention as they swung beneath *Shield* and slowed to line up with the lower hangar.

The dull bronzed aperture of the plasma cannon gaped at them, wide enough to swallow their transport and *Amethyst* side by side. The Empire's decisive weapon of domination. The city-burner. The planet-leveler.

Shayla squeezed her eyes shut against hot tears as memories resurfaced, from long ago but etched in raw fire on her young mind. She had held Brandt close in the crowded passenger lounge of the fleeing starhopper, staring in horror at the screens showing live broadcasts from the doomed planet. The Empire making a point to anyone who dared follow the path of rebellion.

A hand on her shoulder brought Shayla out of her contemplation.

"We're here," said Marcus Corrin.

Shayla took a deep breath before opening her eyes and looking up. Most of the cruiser's occupants had already gone. Shayla stood and followed Marcus out onto the floor of the hangar. The true scale of the warship became apparent. This, she knew, was not the main hanger, but it was still a cavernous space. Their cruiser was just one of many craft lined up in long rows down each side.

"Stick close," said Marcus. "You don't want to get lost here."

He led the way across the hangar to a door in the near wall. A glowing orange circle on the door blinked rapidly then turned green.

"A ferret?" Shayla gasped, as the door opened.

Marcus smiled. "Not many ships are big enough to warrant their own transit system. But the *Swords* are over four thousand feet in length, and half that in height. That's an awful lot of climbing to do."

They entered the tiny capsule and the door closed behind them. Shayla felt movement underfoot as the capsule moved away from the pickup point and waited for direction. Marcus tapped a code onto a screen by the door. "I'll show you how to get at the ship's schematics later. The ferret is standard enough, so you'll have no trouble using the visuals here to find your way around, but it helps to know the codes for the places you most need to get to."

A few seconds later, the door opened again and they stepped out into a brightly lit corridor.

"This is the main administration deck. The living quarters go down a few levels below us. Someone will show you to your quarters, but right now I believe we're expected on the command deck."

The corridor bore some similarities to those Shayla had become accustomed to on *Merciless*. The walls were the same ice blue, the floor the same non-slip checkerboard, but green and grey instead of red. The ceiling was white too, but smooth and unobstructed, and the lighting was less harsh. Shayla noticed other differences. The uncrowded width and sense of space. The corridor ran straight and true into the distance on either side. Here was a vessel with room to spare. No need to cram people and machinery into every available nook and cranny.

Marcus led the way. Shayla struggled to regain her confounded sense of direction. *That's the trouble with enclosed transit systems.*

They passed clear double doors leading into a stairwell. *That must go down to the living quarters.* All the accommodation on *Merciless* had been on a single level, running the length of the ship over the top of machinery and storage spaces. *Welcome back to the world of three dimensions.*

Fifty yards along from the transit entrance, they turned down a side corridor. From the labels on the doors either side, it was clear they were nearing the nerve center of the battleship. They passed briefing rooms and operations rooms, then turned a corner and emerged at the back of the command deck.

*Shield of Mercy's* command deck was a little larger than the one on *Merciless*. Once again, some common themes of Imperial naval architecture stood out. The floor of the deck was set down a few feet from where they stood, and was a similar maze of crew and equipment. It was overlooked by the balcony of the command bridge bulging out into the room from the center of the rear wall.

The sweeping wall opposite the command bridge sported a jumble of images and schematics. There was Eloon, with *Shield*, *Mace*, and *Merciless* in orbit. A broader spread showed a large slice of Imperial and Firenzi space. There was *Wrath*, unaware she was being tracked. There were Imperial craft converging on Eloon and on the rendezvous point, and Firenzi warships massing nearby. An outline of the ship itself was surrounded by labels and status lights, all glowing green. All stations at full readiness.

The bridge platform was overlooked by a second balcony, where Shayla could see Bernadin and the Emperor in deep discussion. Stairs to her left led up to this higher level, but Marcus led them along instead to the central bridge. He stopped and saluted a tall woman with short black hair drawn up into sharp spikes.

"Lady Shayla Carver requests permission to board."

Grey eyes surveyed Shayla from either side of a thin nose.

"Captain Iona bin Terallini, at your service." The words were polite, but eyes of flint sparked fire.

## Chapter 38

The orange disc of Corvin Prime separated from the dusting of stars on the monitor screen and swelled rapidly. The star stopped and hung there, a bloated furnace in the distance. Nearby, a tiny crescent became visible as the viewing filters dimmed the glare: Breth, a huge and lifeless ball of rock and iron beneath a crushing and toxic atmosphere. The moon, Jemiyal, was too small to be seen yet.

"Good choice for a base," Bernadin remarked. "A heavy star, and a massive planet nearby. Any ship has to approach in realspace from way out here. There's no way they can be taken by surprise."

"Also means they can't get away quickly," said Chalwen under her breath.

"We'll be in position above Jemiyal in just under two hours."

"Thank you, Admiral. I'll inform the Emperor."

Chalwen watched as the giant planet Breth filled a quarter of the screen. Luminous bands of sapphire and cobalt dusted here and there with streaks of milky white.

A dark blemish appeared just off-center, a tiny shadow against the glare, growing minute by minute.

Jemiyal.

They approached and swung alongside the moon. Away from the dazzle of the planet, Jemiyal glowed with a light of its own. Skeins of lights like dew-strung spider webs encircled the moon. Delicate traceries of geometrical brilliance clothed every quarter of its surface.

A familiar shadow eclipsed the jeweled lights of the base.

"Is that *Wrath of Empire?*" Chalwen called down to Captain bin Terallini where she paced the floor of the command bridge.

"It is."

"So. At least we know we're in the right place."

"Captain!" An orderly stepped forwards. "We have some odd readings from down there." He hesitated. "*Wrath's* weaponry is ready for firing."

"Any other hostile signals?"

He consulted the scroll in his hands. "They are holding position in the docking basin, but they are targeting Jemiyal itself."

Captain bin Terallini looked up to the admiral's bridge, frowning. "What do you make of that?"

Chalwen laughed. A short, barking noise. "Insurance!" She chortled. "My guess is that the terrible twosome may not be welcome there."

"Get the base Governor on this screen," Julian called across the bridge. To his nearer companions he muttered, "I don't imagine our approach will have gone unnoticed."

A white and worried face appeared on the screen. "Governor Cuthbar Mantro, Magister Summis." He bowed. Lights glistened off his polished scalp.

"A party of renegades has landed at your facility," Julian said. "You will turn them over to me, and we will trouble you no further."

Cuthbar Mantro gulped. His eyes bulged. "I — I cannot comply, Magister Summis."

Julian's face settled into a mask. His voice was icy. "This is your Emperor speaking. You understand the penalty for harboring traitors."

Cuthbar's voice quavered. The words were difficult to make out. "I am hosting a member of the Firenzi Noble Family. He and his guests are protected by the Trown Plains Accord."

"I will determine what protection they are due," Julian breathed.

The poor wretch looked ready to faint. His eyes darted between the Emperor and some point to one side of the screen. His hands twisted in front of him. "I…They have claimed sanctuary. I'm sorry, My Lord. I am compelled to honor their request."

The screen went dark.

"Not entirely unexpected." Chalwen broke the shocked hush. Her voice was resigned.

"A telling choice of words though," said Henri. "I suspect he would turn them over in an instant if he didn't have *Wrath* pointing a cannon at him from inside his shields."

"Nevertheless," Julian said calmly, "we are left with no choice. Admiral Stihl! Position the fleet to begin bombardment."

———— • ————

Shayla sat at the back of the admiral's bridge, away from the railing and the baleful gaze of Captain bin Terallini on the command deck below.

A ball of ice settled in her stomach. She watched the fleet approach the moon with dread and anticipation. The menacing warships wheeled in formation closer and closer, bringing echoes of Eloon and, more recently, her aborted attack on Magentis itself. At the same time, she knew her quarry was down there. Somewhere. Amongst the lights and shadows, deep in the maze of many-layered buildings that cloaked the moon's surface.

The Emperor would exact a heavy price for Ivan's treachery, but she would prefer to make him pay in person. All she needed was one chance to slip off this ship and to the base. The middle of a bombardment was not it. She would wait.

She'd briefed Chalwen, Henri, and Bernadin as best as she could on the layout and defenses of Jemiyal. Her knowledge was sketchy though. Jemiyal was not such a secret as Eloon had been, but it was a world with two faces. There was the very public army of miners, the vast industrial processing yards that covered one side of the moon, and the supporting infrastructure that made up a rough but vibrant community. Interwoven with all of this, nestling amongst the processing plants and warehouses, docking yards, accommodation blocks, schools, hospitals, and administration, the moon was dotted with a network of large silos of less certain purpose. Nominally labeled 'defense', their true strength and capability was carefully guarded.

After the rescue on Eloon, Shayla had managed to retain her needle gun. In the heightened emotion of those hours, nobody asked her to return it, and she didn't feel like raising the subject. She also still had in her possession the carefully doctored Book of Unity, the last relic of her impersonation of Brynwyn. Chalwen examined it when she'd been captured, but failed to understand its importance.

Whilst on board *Merciless*, Marcus had found her a uniform. Devoid of any insignia of rank, it marked her out as a guest on board. Outside the official hierarchy. Obviously he'd not issued her with a sidearm. No matter. She felt more at ease with bare hands and her chemical armory than with such crude instruments. She had all that she needed to deal with Ivan when the time came.

All five battleships fired at once. Shayla remembered how the deck on *Merciless* had quivered when the plasma cannon fired. Here, there was no sound, no vibration, but the nape of her neck crawled at the controlled discharge of stellar energies a few hundred feet behind her.

The ten mile globe of Jemiyal vanished from view. When the screen cleared, seconds later, the moon was unscathed.

They fired again, and again, to no avail.

"Close in," Bernadin ordered. "Concentrate all fire on one spot."

Jemiyal grew larger on the screens.

The five *Swords* fired as one.

This time, Jemiyal returned fire. A massive bolt lashed out at *Staff of Justice*.

Pandemonium broke out on the bridge below. Commands, questions, and answers clamored for attention. Bernadin leaned on the railing, gazing from screen to screen, listening. "Fall back," she called. She leaned over to consult with the captain and a communications clerk, then turned to face the Emperor. "*Staff* is damaged. Outer shield overloaded and primary cannon disabled."

"A fortress, eh?" Chalwen cocked an eyebrow at Shayla. To Bernadin she said, "That was a warning. With a battery that size, they could have picked us off by now if they'd a mind to it."

---

"So," said Bernadin, "we can't break that outer shield. We'd have to get behind it, but they have the firepower to hold us off."

She swiveled back and forth in a chair near one end of the table. She seemed to address the ceiling more than the other occupants of the conference room. Julian sat opposite her, elbows on the table, hands steepled in front of him almost hiding the deep frown on his face.

Chalwen, Iona, and two naval tactical officers sat near Bernadin and Julian, gazing at the screen showing the moon and surrounding ships, which had pulled back to a safe distance. Henri and Shayla kept to the shadows at the other end of the room.

Uniformed catering staff refilled mugs of stimulant-laced tea, and removed untouched plates of food.

"I thought these ships had enough firepower to overcome any shield." Julian's voice expressed the frustration felt by them all.

"Normally true." Bernadin diverted her gaze from the ceiling. "There's a limit to how big a shield a ship can mount. Ground-based shields can be much heavier, but they need that extra strength to absorb the blast rather than simply deflecting it off into space. If you deflect too much into the rock you're standing on, you sink into your own personal volcano."

Shayla shuddered.

"Either way, we've never met a shield we can't overpower. Now, here we have something as strong as any ground base, but able to deflect efficiently like a ship."

"And on the offensive front," Iona added, "they don't have to deal with an atmosphere that normally limits the effectiveness of ground-based batteries."

Bernadin sniffed. "That clout hurt *Staff of Justice*. Enough to show they are not to be trifled with. I wouldn't want any of our smaller craft to get in the way."

"So…It seems we are at a stalemate." Julian said. "We either need more firepower to overwhelm the shield, or some way to get past it."

"Right now, we know they can hold off the combined efforts of five *Swords*," said Bernadin. "*Hammer of War* will be here in another week. *Dagger of Fate* and *Fire of Revenge* were patrolling the far side of our borders. It will be three weeks before they can reach us."

"Even then," Chalwen growled, "there's no guarantee that will be sufficient. From what I've seen I'm not sure the combined efforts of the entire fleet could take them down."

"I assume you're discounting the smaller units?" said Iona.

"We have four *Implacable* class in position, and lots of smaller craft. They will keep an effective blockade, but their combined firepower is trifling in comparison to the *Swords*, even assuming they could get close enough."

"Are we preparing for a siege then?"

"Unless we can come up with some other offensive possibility, or a negotiated settlement," Bernadin said with a sigh.

"Is there any possibility that some of *Wrath*'s crew could still be loyal?" Henri asked. "They are holding Jemiyal hostage right now. Could they be turned to our side?"

"*Wrath of Empire* is still out of contact," said Iona.

"A wise move on their part," Chalwen grunted. "The game would be over if we could get into their command system."

Chalwen froze. Her mouth hung open and she looked like she was struggling to breathe. "You still have an agent planted in *Wrath*'s command system don't you?" she gasped, looking around at Shayla.

Shayla nodded, glancing at the Emperor. She remembered Chalwen's outrage at her intrusions into Imperial security.

"You took over the system once. You could do it again."

"Not without my notebook," Shayla said bitterly. "I've been trained in the use of my tools, but I'm not a technical wizard. I don't have the know-how to breach the system's security."

Julian half-stood, leaning across the table, eyes wide. "But can you set up a channel to the command system?"

"I guess so. But what good would that do? I can't get past the barriers."

"Who am I?" asked Julian.

"The Emperor," said Shayla, puzzled.

"And?" He smiled.

Shayla shook her head, not sure what he meant. "And lots of things, I guess."

"Commander in Chief of the armed forces," said Chalwen with an unaccustomed grin.

Julian nodded. "I don't need to breach *Wrath*'s security. I *own* it! All I need is to make contact."

## Chapter 39

S hayla's heart thudded in her chest. She could almost picture Ivan down there, somewhere, oblivious to the havoc she was about to unleash on his world. And if this worked, maybe she could risk enlisting Chalwen's help to find Brandt.

She sat near one end of a row of screens in the darkened operations room. To her left, two members of the communications corps managed the complex web of tracers that hunted her unique signature across the cosmos, maintaining the tenuous link between this room and the docked warship three hundred miles below. Julian Skamensis sat next to her, clenching and unclenching his fists. Beyond him, a full command crew stood ready.

They had spent all night planning the necessary movements and rehearsing them a hundred times. They would only get one shot at this, before the crew of *Wrath of Empire* realized what was happening.

First Lieutenant Alexander Binikov, senior operations controller, marched up and down the room in front of them, grilling them once more on their task. He stopped to face them, arms held above his head.

Shayla reviewed her notes one last time. She held up her right hand, thumb and forefinger forming an 'O' to signal readiness.

Every station in the room, she knew, would be indicating go or no-go. Lieutenant Binikov scanned the room, face impassive. Seconds passed, feeling like minutes. Shayla resisted the urge to turn her head to see what the hold-up was. She kept her eyes fixed on the upraised hands.

At last, fingers ticked off the seconds. The lieutenant fixed her with a stare. "Trapdoor, execute!"

Shayla opened up her end of the link. Her agent responded. *Good.*

Using the language only her covert agent understood, she checked both it and her trapdoor for signs of intrusion. Just a precaution, if the crew had discovered it they would surely have shut it down long ago.

Careful not to do anything that would give away her skulking presence inside the battleship's systems, she scanned for signs of surveillance, then looked for a port into *Wrath's* central command system.

She checked and re-checked each step of her way through the ship's electronic architecture, securing her path from detection and intrusion.

*Dammit!* She wasn't used to directing the agent without the supporting tools on her notepad. When she took control of *Merciless*, so long ago now, her notepad handled all these routine precautions for her. This was like walking a narrow catwalk without safety railings. One mis-step ...

She found the portal she needed, and sent the agent's feelers forward.

And she stopped. There had to be more to it than this. She dredged her memory for details of the security protocols Brandt had programmed into her notepad.

She wiped the palms of her hands on her tunic. There were more subtle traps she should have been looking out for. She backtracked, alert for any signs of alarm, then resumed watch on the portal.

The silence in the room deepened.

Shayla waited, chewing the inside of her cheek. There was one more thing nagging in the back of her mind.

The portal flickered. Shayla scanned reports from her agent and exhaled, a long drawn out breath. A security monitor was recording all access to the command system from inside the portal, out of her reach. The flicker showed a periodic audit collecting data and checking for abnormalities. If she'd proceeded, she would have been seen.

She waited once more, counting the seconds.

When she saw the flicker again, she held up her hand to show she'd hit a problem. "I'm at the portal. There's a monitor inside collecting audit data on a one-minute cycle."

Lieutenant Binikov frowned, then glanced at a systems technician at the back of the room.

"A moment," the woman said. She pored over her screen. "Got it. It's a standard procedure. We've got the same in our command system. It'll report any access from physically outside of the command deck. They'll be on high alert so my guess is they'll check that report."

"So," said the lieutenant, "we will have a minute to enter, turn control over to us, and lock them out. My Lord?" He looked at Julian.

Shayla held her breath. All the practice runs had taken at least two minutes through this stage. But...they'd been rehearsing for care and accuracy, not for speed.

Julian's face set like flint. "I have a renegade to bring to justice. Barring a miracle of diplomacy, this is the only way to avoid a prolonged siege. We proceed."

"I'll wait for the next cycle, then give you a countdown and let you in," Shayla said.

Lieutenant Binikov signaled for attention and checked for readiness once more, then nodded to Shayla.

Shayla resumed her vigil. The portal flickered. "One minute." She counted in the back of her mind, rehearsing her next moves. "Ten seconds." Her hands poised to send instructions to her agent.

There was the flicker.

Shayla's agent connected to the portal and secured the conduit back to the operations room. With the tools on her notepad, she could have broken through the portal. Without it, only the Emperor had the necessary codes to subvert the command system. She handed the link over to Julian, and sat back, hands trembling. Her part in this was done.

Counting the seconds, Shayla watched her screen as Julian's instructions unfolded to establish his authority and secure the link against interference. Shayla let out a breath she didn't realize she'd been holding once that crucial milestone was passed. With a flourish, the Emperor locked out *Wrath's* own command deck and turned control over to his crew next to him.

"Good work, My Lord." Lieutenant Binikov saluted Julian then turned to the command crew standing ready. "Navigation. Execute."

On the main wall screen, the outline of *Wrath of Empire* showed clear against the luminous basin of the docking bay. A cheer rang around the room as the shadow shifted against the background.

"Responding. Lifting her up."

"Slowly. Environment? Fire control?"

"Shields engaged. Umm...Pressure loss in the starboard transit tubes. Sealing off."

"That'll be where they were docked," said the lieutenant.

The main dock of Jemiyal was built into a mile-deep crater that spanned half the moon's near face. Docking stations, hangars, and repair shops rose in terraces from the floor up the shallow slopes. The battleship drifted out of the crater until her weapons platform showed above the rim.

"Targeting the southern power plants," the fire control officer reported.

*Not too far!* Shayla's attention was focused anxiously on the defensive batteries encircling the rim. If they had a wide enough arc of fire, Jemiyal could finish the warship in seconds.

*Wrath's* beam batteries lashed out at either end of the power plant. They kept up a furious bombardment, careless of burnout, for long seconds.

"Cease fire. That's enough of a demonstration. Now let's have *Wrath* look menacing."

*Wrath of Empire* settled back into the safety of the crater, away from the moon's deadly batteries. Her silhouette on the screen shifted as she rolled, presenting her underside to the moon's command complex on the northern rim. Battle graphics alongside the images showed that her primary battery was ready to fire.

Shayla knew the unseen watchers on the moon below them would be all too well aware that they were being targeted.

Captain Iona bin Terallini appeared on the wall alongside the image of the moon. "Jemiyal is signaling. They wish to discuss terms."

## Chapter 40

Governor Cuthbar Mantro knelt in front of the Emperor.
Shayla watched him from one end of the line of officials
standing to attention behind Julian's throne. Cuthbar was short and
rather stout. A long black moustache stood out against his pale and
glistening face.

A small escort of Firenzi soldiers and senior administrative staff fidg-
eted at the back of the room, flanked by a stony-faced guard of Imperial
marines in full ceremonial regalia.

The Governor's cruiser was docked in the main hangar, which,
along with the ship's weapon systems, made up a large portion of the
upper pod. From here, Shield of Mercy could launch a sizeable army to
invade a troublesome planet.

Shayla could imagine the impact on the Firenzi party as they
entered one of three launch bays, each larger than an entire hangar on
most capital ships, then passed into the cathedral space beyond. She
knew they had been escorted down deliberately to one of the more distant transit points on the main deck, then made to walk through long
and empty corridors to this throne room.

All moves calculated to impress on the visitors the size and scale of
the ships surrounding them.

The throne room alone was a formidable statement of power.
Portraits of Imperial nobility looked down from the walls, in between
drapes and banners. In the center of the polished stone floor, a magnifi-
cently crafted mosaic forty feet across depicted a map of Magentis.

A hundred feet above their heads, a clear armored dome looked out
onto the blackness of space. From where she stood, Shayla could see, far
above, the sweeping front edge of the weapons platform. But Cuthbar's
eyes kept darting up to where he could see his home, Jemiyal, hanging
defenseless in full view.

"Admiral Stihl," Julian said over his shoulder. His voice dripped ice. "I am growing concerned either for my eyesight or my memory. Please help me out here. I'm sure my instructions were to bring Ivan Skamensis and Scipio Firenzi before me in chains, and we would discuss the terms of their surrender."

Governor Cuthbar Mantro squirmed, a forlorn and solitary figure in the middle of the floor. He looked on the verge of saying something, but held himself in check, mindful of protocol.

"That is so, Magister Summis," Bernadin answered.

"So. My memory is clear. And yet I cannot see them." His gaze skewered Cuthbar. "Does my eyesight fail me, Governor?"

Cuthbar staggered to his feet. "It does not, Magister Summis. I offer you the unconditional surrender of Jemiyal ..."

"I want Ivan!" Julian thundered.

*So do I!* Shayla might yet have the chance to hunt him down herself.

Cuthbar recoiled at his outburst. "And we will find him, Magister Summis, and My Lord Scipio. But they are not mine to deliver to you. They have fled into the depths of Jemiyal, and Jemiyal is a big place."

"I'm through bargaining with traitors," Julian snarled. "I've spent a lifetime in their thrall! Admiral Stihl! Finish them."

*He can't mean that!*

Cuthbar broke the shocked silence, his voice quavering. "My Lord! The base is now defenseless. There are three million people in there. Miners, families, children. They have no part in this!"

"The terms of surrender were for you to deliver me Ivan and Scipio. You insult me by coming here without them." Julian's face was purple. Cuthbar backed away step by step, cringing at each new crescendo of wrath.

Julian turned to Bernadin. "Signal all units. Burn out Jemiyal, layer by layer."

"Hold!" Shayla yelled. She stepped from behind the Emperor and placed herself alongside Cuthbar. "You cannot do this."

"I am the Emperor!" he roared. "Do not presume to tell me what I can and cannot do!"

"I presume nothing. These people have surrendered. Your position as Emperor obliges you to honorable conduct."

"You are my servant. How dare you challenge me like this!"

"I gifted the Emperor Julian Skamensis my service. I pledged him my undying loyalty," Shayla agreed. "But this is not that man speaking. *This* is not the Emperor who earned my loyalty. I hear Ivan speaking, not Julian." She paused to control her breathing, to bring her voice down to a conversational level. "I am addressing the Emperor Julian Skamensis who earned my trust. That man would not slaughter innocents in pursuit of his goal. It is from loyalty to that man and his values that I now speak."

Julian's face darkened. His eyes flashed danger. But before he could say anything Chalwen stepped past him and stood alongside Shayla.

"You too?" he gasped.

Henri followed, then Iona. One by one, some firmly, some hesitantly, everyone ranged behind the throne joined them and stood silently facing Julian.

Chalwen spoke softly. "Magister Summis. For once, the assassin speaks more sense than she knows. This is not the path we have spent so many years planning."

While the Emperor faced them, slack jawed, she continued. "We will find Ivan and Scipio. We will bring them to justice. With Cuthbar's help there will be no place for them to hide. The fleet will ensure there is no escape."

Cuthbar nodded eagerly. "My Lord, the resources of Jemiyal are at your disposal. We've heard what happened to My Lord Josef and the Lady Margerite." His expression hardened. All subservience gone, replaced by a ferocious determination. "The renegade Scipio has no place here. He and your uncle will be hunted down. My people know this rock inside and out."

"You're right. It's the same signature as the one from Wrath we were tracing, but what's it doing coming from those co-ordinates on Jemiyal?"

"I don't know what to make of it, but the wording of the message suggests a family connection."

"Hmm." Captain Iona bin Terallini read the message on the scroll in front of her once more. "The ones we want are here. They plan to use you to help them escape. Don't come. It is a trap. You cannot help me. Leave it to the Fat One to handle. She will do our work for us. B."

She leaned back in her chair, gazing through the one-way windows of her day cabin to the command bridge beyond. When she finally spoke, her voice was slow and thoughtful, as if she were speaking aloud to herself. "What do you imagine Milady Carver would do with this information? I *sincerely* hope she wouldn't consider anything rash." Her finger tapped her teeth absently while she thought. "Let's see. I know full well how busy Commander ap Gwynodd and her staff are right now. But at the same time, I know this is something they will want to pursue. I need to draw it to their attention, and make sure they understand its importance, but I am reluctant to send the full text of this message anywhere other than directly into her hands. It is too sensitive. I'm sure she will agree."

She sat up straight. Her tone became brisk. "Transfer the envelope information, just the signature and co-ordinates, to a message capsule for the attention of the Security services. Leave out the text. That will be enough to inform the right people of its importance. Be sure that this is presented to Commander ap Gwynodd," she smiled slyly, "either in person or via a *trusted* member of the Imperial staff."

She gazed into the eyes of the young communications technician standing on the other side of the desk. "Do we understand each other?"

"Yes, Mother."

"That's 'Captain' to you," she said fondly.

———————•—•——————

Shayla pulled heavily insulated overalls over her uniform, followed by a military traveling cloak. She looked around her tiny cabin one last time and checked her pockets. Glowtubes, food concentrate and water. Nothing but bare essentials. Scroll and stylus. She badly missed her old notepad, but she still had her needle gun and the cunningly doctored Book of Unity. She frowned, then also pocketed the pencil-sized communicator she'd been issued along with her uniform. It would look suspicious if she left without it. She'd ditch it when she didn't want to be reached.

She had been alone in the operations room when one of the communications crew had found her.

"I need a message to be conveyed direct to Commander ap Gwynodd," he'd said.

"She's on Jemiyal, directing the search operations from their civil administration center."

"Captain bin Terallini has information which she will release only to the Commander in person." The young rating had looked troubled. "This message capsule should inform her as to the importance of this information. Are you a member of her staff?"

"Yes," Shayla had lied. *Well, close enough.* "I'll sign for it and deliver it in person."

The look of relief on the rating's face had been comical.

Shayla entered a transit capsule and scrawled a code on the screen. There was a brief pause. She knew it would be checking her identity and confirming her clearance to leave the ship.

A few minutes later, she stepped out into a wide concourse clinging to the side of the docking crater on Jemiyal. Windows looked across the crater and arced high over her head. The vast shadow of *Shield of Mercy* loomed above, eclipsing the dazzling starscape.

She returned the salute from the sergeant at the head of the squad of Imperial guards surrounding the transit terminal. "I understand Security has set up a search headquarters in the civilian admin center."

Of course, she knew exactly where to find it. She had spent the last few hours studying schematics of the base, taking in its layout, its unique three dimensional topology. Smaller than a planet, but bigger than any ship.

The sergeant gestured to an elevator tube on the far side of the concourse. "Up to level five. Follow the perimeter walk north a quarter mile, until you see signs for the civil administration block."

Shayla walked with a slight bounce in her step. *Gravity field. Obviously artificial on a rock this small.* She'd grown accustomed to the Imperial navy standard. Slightly higher than the natural pull on most habitable planets, and ten percent above the interstellar standard used by most space craft. Now in the moon's field, she felt like a load had been lifted from her shoulders.

An elevator capsule whisked her up a slope that grew steadily steeper as it climbed the uneven ramparts towering above her. The walls of the capsule, and the tube in which it rode, were clear, giving Shayla a dizzying view across the floor of the crater. Hundreds of craft clung to docking posts around the walls. All were dwarfed by the threatening bulk of *Shield of Mercy*. Soon she drew level with the weapons platform, ringed with blisters of particle beam batteries. Seconds later she was above the carapace, looking down on the warship in all its functional ugliness.

The elevator slowed and stopped. *Level five.* From her research, Shayla knew this meant five levels below the mean surface of the moon. She stepped out into a wide corridor stretching into the distance on either side.

The concourse more than half a mile below had been quiet and empty, cleared of all civilians by the Imperial troops. This corridor was alive with activity. Businesses lined the perimeter walk, shops selling supplies and equipment — everything you would need to prepare yourself for months in space — cafes, bars, and an endless variety of entertainment. From the signs enticing customers, it seemed that sophistication was not a hallmark of this mining colony.

Shayla turned north and started walking.

Crowds of people lined the windows overlooking the crater. Curious onlookers. Most of them had never seen such a vast warship up close. For those who had, it was unlikely to have been a happy experience.

Now here was the Imperial navy, in all its might, working alongside them to hunt down a common enemy. A curious sight indeed.

As she walked, Shayla overheard snatches of conversation. There were hints of uneasiness at Governor Mantro's pledge to assist the Emperor, and anger directed at the Empire for the siege. But the news of Scipio and Ivan's perfidy had been spread far and wide. The Imperial communications team had done their job well. *And the Firenzi are no strangers to propaganda either!*

Covert glances in her direction as people recognized the Imperial uniform. Voices hushed as she approached, but not too much. She was a foreigner. They spoke the Firenzi tongue and blithely assumed she could not understand.

The outrage at the murder of their Family head was clear, and engendered some sympathy for the Emperor's pursuit in revenge for his own family's imprisonment. But suspicion of the Empire was never far away. Warships *here*, in their territory! And everywhere, speculation was rife. The traitors had vanished. They were here. Somewhere.

The signs for the administration center were clear enough. Shayla turned in that direction, but after a short distance she slipped through a brightly-lit door leading into a bustling clothing mart. She emerged on a balcony running around a domed atrium. Stars glowed above, almost invisible in the glaring multicolored lights. Tiers of balconies dropped hundreds of feet down. She rode an elevator into the depths of the complex, then hurried to the nearest transit station.

*Now you see me, now you don't.*

Safely alone inside a transit capsule, Shayla scribbled a long series of instructions on the screen.

*Let's see what you make of these clearance codes.*

She gave her Special Service identity. This was a Firenzi community, it should recognize her status. With this identity, she should be able to travel freely, and secretly. She would be able to pass, unseen and unchallenged, through the cordons set up by the search teams as they scoured the moon, layer by layer, mile by mile.

The capsule moved away into the transit tunnel and stopped while it absorbed her instructions. For now, she had become invisible to the world outside while the capsule talked on a private channel to the moon's command network. A code like hers would need to be verified.

After an anxious wait, the screen acknowledged her.
*You can run, Ivan, but not far or fast enough to evade me!*

---

Chalwen loomed over Captain Iona bin Terallini's desk, balled fists planted on the desk surface, knuckles white.

A full transcript of the message lay on the desk between them.

"If I thought for an instant that you had planned this, I would not hesitate to have you flogged in Prandis Square."

"Lady Carver vouchsafed the delivery of this message direct to you. If she is no longer a trusted servant of the Emperor then I should have been notified."

Grey eyes gazed coolly back into smoldering brown.

After a long minute, Chalwen blinked and straightened up with an irritated shake of her head. "I know you are hurting. Osprey was a sore loss to us all. Jason was your eldest, wasn't he?"

Iona nodded.

Chalwen sighed. "We have all suffered at this assassin's hands, in one way or another. But her fate belongs to the Emperor. No-one else. You would do well to remember that."

"And the Emperor has also benefited beyond measure." Iona spoke after a long silence. "That will no doubt erase a great many *unimportant* deaths."

"An understandable concern." Chalwen eased herself into a seat opposite Iona. She kneaded her eyelids with one hand then reached into her pocket for a nicodyne spray. "Our Emperor has a difficult line to tread with that one. He has yet to pronounce judgment on her." She met Iona's gaze again. "I have faith that he will reach a just verdict, weighing *all* considerations."

She drew the spray into her lungs. "A part of me wants to rejoice that you may have spared him an awkward decision. But this is not the right path."

"So. We are preparing a force to scour that zone." Iona said. "We have detailed schematics from Governor Mantro, and his staff are helping to plan a search pattern. They will be equipped and briefed, and ready to move within the hour."

"They will have to move carefully. As far as we are concerned, Lady Carver is on her own. She has made her own path. Our priority is to take Ivan and Scipio alive."

"The message says that Lady Carver will be contacted. That they will try to draw her into a trap. We've had no such communication yet."

"You bloody fool!" Chalwen snapped. "Don't you understand? This message *is* the contact. They *have* drawn her in."

---

Shayla sat in a deserted service corridor hundreds of feet below a sprawling industrial complex near the south pole of Jemiyal. She pulled her cloak more tightly around herself. The air was bone dry, but chill.

With her scroll unrolled on her lap, she nibbled on a food bar while she checked her location once more against the origin of the message. She'd not been able to open the message capsule she'd been entrusted with, but the signature alone was enough. Brandt. Somehow, he was here. It must have been one of Ivan's or Scipio's agents who'd taken him from his home.

Still working under the privilege bestowed by her Special Service identity, she scanned her surroundings for signs of life.

Nothing.

*Bad news! Where the hell are they hiding out?*

An unsettling thought occurred to her. She was working under a cloak of secrecy. What if Scipio had similar codes? That would explain how they had evaded detection up to now.

In hindsight, it seemed obvious. Only a Firenzi would be able to travel freely around this base, but a member of the nobility would automatically be monitored closely. There was no other way Scipio could have avoided revealing himself to a member of the Special Service.

Shayla sat and thought. At length she reached a decision. This would ring alarm bells back in the Governor's office and bring the security forces down on her. On the plus side, she was too remote for them to reach quickly. And by the time they arrived, she would have moved on again under cover of privileged invisibility.

Eyes closed for a moment, Shayla dredged her memory for forbidden knowledge. Her stylus moved across the face of the scroll scratching out a new set of clearance codes, signing her in with a new, highly privileged, stolen identity.

*Bless Brandt for his terminal curiosity. The cerebral magpie!* How many treasures had he unearthed over the years? Glittering shards of knowledge, presumed safe by their owners. He had passed on some gems to Shayla, anything that might help her in their quest, but she knew this was only the tip of the iceberg.

There was a long pause, then the surface of the scroll cleared. New information unrolled across it. A new and exalted perspective, revealing hidden secrets.

*There you are!*

Stripped of their protection, the tiny pocket of habitation showed clearly in the depths. Shayla hastily marked the location, already noting paths and obstacles. She copied other details from the ever-present monitors while she had the chance. There were at least twenty people down there. Ivan and Scipio must have some loyal followers with them. This was not going to be easy.

All the same, while she broke the connection and dropped once more from ordinary surveillance, she smiled to herself. *I wonder what I've just stirred up a few miles away? What would Governor Mantro be making of the sudden resurrection of Josef Firenzi?*

———•—•———

Half an hour later, Shayla leaned over a balcony at the end of a long and unlit passage hewn from bare rock. She breathed heavily, recovering from a sprint through the labyrinth, a combination of anxiety to remove herself from the tell-tale signal she'd revealed, and eagerness to complete her long quest.

She composed herself. *Don't blow it now!*

The balcony overlooked a shaft which dropped away into the darkness, one of hundreds like it that honeycombed the rock. A relic of the days when this moon itself had been mined, before being enveloped in buildings and industry and becoming a base from which the rest of the system could be plundered.

At the bottom of the shaft, nearly a mile beneath her feet, lay Ivan's hiding place.

This part of the moon was all but abandoned. On the surface in this zone, some old refineries were still in use, but down here there was no sign of life. No elevators. No transit system. There were stairs, lots of them of course, but she knew all approaches would be under close watch.

Shayla did what she figured any moderately sane woman would do in her situation.

She jumped.

Chapter 42

Governor Cuthbar Mantro strode up and down his office, hands wringing, footsteps muffled in deep carpet. "How can this be? The system must be screwed!"

The two security clerks standing to attention in the center of the room glanced at each other. "The signature was unmistakable, Sir," the senior clerk said.

"Are you sure His Excellency Josef Firenzi is dead?" This question was directed to Chalwen, who was seated in the most comfortable chair she could find.

She narrowed her eyes. "Entirely sure. My staff, *trusted* staff, identified his body in the palace on Magentis."

Governor Mantro frowned and shook his head, resuming his pacing and hand-wringing.

Chalwen rolled her eyes. "Calm down, Mantro. This will be the doing of that bloody assassin. She seems to have access to surprising resources. I would put nothing past her." She pursed her lips. "This means she is still alive and still on Ivan's trail. How close are our marines?"

Governor Mantro consulted a display on his desk. "They have reached the southern zone and deployed, but they still have three thousand feet to descend on foot. They will have to move carefully. Those mines are a haven from a defensive point of view."

---

The walls of the shaft glided past, glistening in the light of the glowtube. A few seconds after dropping from the balcony, the artificial gravity in this zone had cut out on Shayla's instruction. Jemiyal's command network had quietly acquiesced to her authority leaving her virtually weightless. Rushing air slowed her descent until the moon's feeble gravity exerted its own influence. She drifted down, seeking the bottom of the shaft.

She had chosen a shaft a little way away from the network of chambers where her quarry lay in hiding. She hoped no-one would venture into this zone and discover the suspicious loss of weight.

At last, the floor of the shaft came into view. It appeared so quickly in the pool of light that Shayla barely had time to tuck and roll with the impact. She bounced, and found herself high in the air again, floundering for balance. *Oh crap! Didn't think of that!* She fumbled for her scroll, tumbling in the feeble gravity, and instructed the command net to restore a small pull to bring herself down again.

Safely on the ground, Shayla looked around. The cold shiver down her back had nothing to do with the pervasive chill. She shook her head, dismissing the uncomfortable feeling of being watched.

She checked the schematics for this zone once more and orientated herself against the shadowed openings yawning on either side.

*That's the one.* She located a dark passageway cut into the side of the shaft about twenty feet above her head. She gathered herself and leapt lightly into the opening, before restoring full gravity once more.

"Shayla Carver."

Shayla jumped, scalp crawling at the familiar voice. Light. Mocking.

"I think the time is ripe for a family reunion."

She looked around slowly. Her needle gun had appeared in her hand. Fleur Trixmin sat with her back to the rough wall of the passage, cloak pulled around her, blending into the stone.

"I'm unarmed," Fleur said, standing. Shayla trained her gun on Fleur, who was careful to keep her hands in sight. "That oaf Scipio has all his guards watching the stairs and approach passageways. I wagered you would find a less traveled route."

"You said 'a family reunion'. What did you mean?"

"I guess you'll just have to let me show you." When Shayla didn't move, Fleur continued, "You are wondering if this is a trap. Of course it is. We are all waiting for you. I've already alerted the others to your presence. You'll come with me if you value your brother's life."

*Brandt?* The words hit Shayla like a blow. All thoughts of Ivan fled her mind. If the Bitch in the Basement had anything to do with Brandt's capture, things were serious. *If he's hurt...* Shayla pushed the thought aside. Now, more than ever, she needed cold focus.

Fleur grinned, then, seemingly oblivious to the pistol menacing her, she sauntered down the passageway. "Nice trick with the grav field," she called over her shoulder. "To have that level of authority you must have been a highly trusted agent. Once."

Shayla hesitated, furious at having the initiative wrested from her so effortlessly. But it was clear that all attempts at surprise were now futile. She had no choice. She followed, senses straining for signs of danger.

The rough-cut passage bored straight through the rock of the moon. Here and there other shafts led off from it, some horizontal, some angled steeply down into the core of the tiny world.

After five minutes the walls became smoother. Light glowed in the distance ahead.

A shadow detached itself from the wall and stood, silhouetted against the brightness of a half-open doorway.

"Shayla Carver." The rich tones of Finn Probey echoed from the walls. Shayla felt a cold knot in her stomach. "The Special Service is most disappointed with your performance on this mission."

She kept her needle gun trained on Fleur while glancing at Finn. It was difficult to tell in the shadows, but he appeared to be unarmed. At least, his hands were empty.

"There is much about this mission that didn't proceed to expectations," Shayla muttered. "Lead the way, Finn."

He bowed low with a mocking grin, and stepped aside with a gesture towards the door.

"Uh-uh!" said Shayla. "You both stay within my line of sight and five paces ahead."

Finn shrugged and walked down the corridor, with Fleur following a few feet behind.

They stepped through the door. Shayla paused at the threshold to let her eyes adjust to the relative brightness, and to assess the room.

A row of free-standing glowtubes lit the room. A pile of crates threw the far corner into shadow. Through the crack of a door opposite, Shayla glimpsed more glowtubes lighting another corridor.

Finn led them to the left and into yet another corridor, floor tiled and walls lined. This area looked like it might once have been part of modest living quarters. Doors led off from either side.

Finn walked through the nearest door. "Jasmina Skolax, I give you Shayla Carver."

"Mother?" Shayla almost dropped her needle gun in shock at Finn's words. She recovered just in time to lock eyes with Fleur who'd whirled around to face her as she entered the room. Fleur's face was inscrutable as she froze on the spot, raising her hands slightly to show compliance.

With a small movement of her gun, Shayla waved Fleur and Finn to one side of the room. She also moved aside so she no longer had the door at her back. This had once been a dormitory. A row of bunks and lockers had been pushed carelessly aside. A helmet and a solitary boot gathered dust under the nearest bunk.

Having scanned the room for threats, the only other occupants now drew Shayla's attention. Her mother, Jasmina, stood behind a chair with the snout of a military pistol pressed to Brandt's skull. Brandt, strapped to the chair, regarded Shayla through bloodshot eyes. A yellow bruise marred his cheekbone. A smear of blood stained the corner of his mouth.

"Hello Shayla."

Shayla's eyes snapped back to Jasmina. *How does she pack so much disapproval in two tiny words?*

Shayla glanced at Fleur and Finn as she trained her gun on Jasmina. "It must be a surprise to find me here."

That same matriarchal sneer, lecturing a wayward child, brought a red haze to Shayla's eyes. *Focus!* "Why did you kidnap Brandt?"

"I was following your work on Magentis. I didn't realize how far you'd planned to go. You were only supposed to finish the Emperor, not the whole planet, then we were going to pick up the pieces."

*So, this explains Mother's excursions. Friends in high places indeed.*

"I was rather relieved when your mission *failed* ..."

Shayla gritted her teeth at the scorn Jasmina poured into that last word.

"... but Ivan and Scipio had already shown their hand. If the Emperor survived, they were finished, so we needed an escape plan."

"Why not just run? Why take Brandt?" *And if you've hurt him...* His bruised face was one thing, but Shayla had already seen how torture could be inflicted leaving no visible marks.

"Anyone else would have died by now in Imperial custody, but I know how resourceful you are, and how rash. I decided I needed some insurance. Your presence here proves I was right. I didn't want you doing anything foolish before I'd had a chance to be heard. Ivan, Scipio, and some followers are waiting nearby. Once you've calmed down you will help us leave this rock."

"Over my dead body! Or rather, Ivan's."

"We have a fast cruiser in a shaft nearby," Jasmina continued as if Shayla hadn't spoken. "The shaft has an undocumented access lock on the surface. In their wisdom, the Firenzi hierarchy built a number of secret escape routes in the early days of Jemiyal."

"You have half the Imperial navy camped out on your doorstep."

"And, with the trust you've established with Imperial security service, you will get us through the blockade."

"Brandt and I have spent the last twenty-three years of our lives hunting the man responsible for destroying our home. You don't imagine I'm going to help him escape?"

"The Emperor Julian was responsible for that. You had him in your grasp and you let him go."

The harmonics in Jasmina's voice jarred Shayla. "Ivan is the man I'm after. I'm convinced of the truth of that."

"You are so much like your father," Jasmina said. "In your own way. So very different, and yet so much in common."

That much was true. *Pappi!* Shayla grimaced at the memory, the loss.

"Your father spent years waging war on the old Empire, when Florence started getting soft and finally named Paul her successor instead of Ivan. When things got too dangerous for him within the borders of Imperial space, he escaped to Eloon and established an underground movement to continue the fight from there. In a way, he sealed the fate of that planet long before you were born. The Empire couldn't let him live. You never knew that I was once a Firenzi Special agent, just like you. Working under deep cover."

This confirmed what Shayla already suspected. It explained why Brandt had always failed to track her when she wanted to stay hidden.

"The Family Firenzi sent me to make contact with your father before the Empire got to him. He was a powerful figure working against them, so an alliance seemed possible."

"You *married* him! You had children with him!" Shayla was aghast. "Are you telling me that was just part of your *mission?*"

"You know what it means to be dedicated to a mission." Jasmina sneered. "How is this different?"

"So why didn't you leave us on Eloon, to be destroyed along with all your other loose ends?"

"I saw the potential in you and Brandt. I didn't want to lose some useful assets." She sniffed. "You came so close to living up to my expectations." Jasmina looked thoughtful, then she smiled at Shayla. A predatory smile. "You never knew your father's name."

"Lorenzo Carver," Shayla answered, puzzled.

"Lorenzo Carver Georgi *Skamensis*," Jasmina snarled. "He is Ivan's brother. An outcast by his own choice, all trace of him erased from official records, nevertheless you are a Skamensis like Ivan."

The words pierced Shayla. From the corner of her eye, she saw Fleur's eyes widen in shock.

Jasmina nodded in satisfaction at Shayla's stunned expression. "I can't imagine what lies you've been fed while in the custody of the Emperor. Your father was working with Ivan to restore the rule of order in the Empire. To bring it back onto its rightful path. That is why Julian had him destroyed. He cared little that a whole planet lay in his path."

"No!"

*Truthsense. A difficult and imprecise skill to master. The sensing of truth in the spoken word. But the highest mastery of all is to recognize truth from your own lips.*

As she spoke, Shayla *knew* the truth, the insight, with which she spoke. "My father worked with Paul and then with Julian to thwart the likes of Ivan. You snared him in order to distract him, to subdue him with family ties. Then you betrayed him."

Her mother looked like she'd been slapped. "You cannot know that!"

"I know." The words were quiet, but final.

The room was still. The tableau frozen in time.

Shayla's needle gun was trained on her mother, whose finger was on the firing stud of the beam pistol at Brandt's head.

Finn was poised, blade drawn.

"Finn," Shayla said, "this is a family matter now. My family. You owe these people no allegiance."

"You can't win this, Shayla," Jasmina said. "Finn is loyal to the Firenzi Family. You turned traitor. Shoot me, and your beloved brother dies. This is a sensitive trigger, the merest twitch will bring death. But get us through that blockade and you can spare his life and save him unbearable pain."

"Finn," said Shayla, "I know your history. This is not what you pledged your loyalty to."

Fleur stood next to Finn, unfolding a roll of linen. Sinister metallic glints flashed in the folds of the cloth.

"Fleur doesn't have the resources of an interrogation room at her disposal," Jasmina continued. "But I understand she is quite good at improvising with a small pocketful of tools."

"It's pointless, Mother. I can't get you past the blockade. Imperial security has Brandt's transmission. They know I'm here."

Jasmina's face dropped. "You ..." she spluttered to Brandt. "You were supposed to contact Shayla directly. She would have found a way here without them knowing."

Brandt's face twisted in a lopsided grin. "You think I didn't realize what was happening when I found myself within reach of a comms port? I knew you were expecting me to contact Shayla, and I knew exactly what she'd do. I made sure it got intercepted instead." He pursed his lips at Shayla. "You're not supposed to be here."

Shayla snorted. "Someone else came to the same conclusion and made sure the message got back on course. Regardless, I'd have heard about it sooner or later and I would not have done any differently." She felt her heart was about to burst with pride at Brandt's act of defiance. "And of course I knew what I was getting into."

"How bloody touching," Jasmina snarled. "This changes nothing. Lay down your weapon. You're coming with us whether you can be persuaded to help or not."

"Finn," Shayla murmured, "she killed Pere Josef and Margerite."

"I know. And I am facing the most difficult task of my career." Finn's voice was flat, yet carried deadly resolve.

"Finn!" Jasmina barked. "Disarm her."

Fleur ran the tip of her tongue along her lips.

Finn Probey raised his hand. The blade flashed blue. Fleur's chest blossomed red. For a moment, she looked surprised. She turned stunned eyes, already draining of life, towards Finn as she slumped to the floor.

Finn turned towards Jasmina. She turned her pistol on him.

The beam lit the room, blinding Shayla. With a jolt she understood the sacrifice Finn had just made. She fired, aiming purely from memory.

Jasmina shrieked, a sound choked off as paralysis gripped her. Her eyes widened and her face contorted in agony.

"Nacrolin," Shayla snarled. "This dart I had reserved first for the Emperor, then for Ivan. It has now found a more fitting mark."

She glanced at Finn. Lifeless eyes stared back at her from where he lay.

She turned her attention back to her mother, sinking slowly to the floor, hands scrabbling feebly at her chest. "The dose was set to give a full day of unbearable torment before the release of death."

Shayla stepped forwards, face close to her mother's. "You know well what this poison does. The pain will grow, hour by hour, as your nervous system disintegrates. There is no hope for you, save that someone might show mercy and finish it more quickly."

Jasmina's hand flashed in an arc past Shayla, inches from her face. The movement caught Shayla by surprise. So quick was it that she leapt back only just in time.

*Crap! Where did she get the willpower to move like that?*

But that effort spent Jasmina's last reserves of resistance. She fell backwards, writhing slightly and moaning under her breath. She was fully in the grip of the poison now, paralyzed, submerged in her own private hell.

Heart thudding, Shayla noticed that someone else was screaming her name.

"Brandt!" She turned.

He gazed at her, eyes clouded with tears, face a rigid mask of pain and terror. In mounting horror, Shayla's eyes followed his right arm down to where his hand clutched his leg. She knelt, and carefully drew out the dart. The dart her mother had plucked from her chest and tried to scratch her with.

"Oh Brandt, I'm so sorry." Tears ran freely down Shayla's face.

"Shayla," he whispered, "what's happening to me?" He grimaced at the effort of speaking.

"It's a poison. Part of my armory. One of the rarest and most feared." Her voice seemed to belong to someone else. Someone speaking from another room. Another world.

"There could only have been a tiny amount left on the needle. It will take longer to work. Longer to paralyze. Longer to kill."

*But kill it inevitably will!*

She nearly broke down, consumed by grief. *I must stay focused. I must detach myself from my actions.*

"The most frightening thing about nacrolin is that the tiniest dose is fatal." *Please understand what I must do.* "The smaller the dose, the longer and more agonizing the death. And there is no antidote."

Shayla spoke gently, trying not to look at the gathering pain clouding her brother's eyes. She directed her actions on autopilot, trying not to think about what she was doing. Trying to defer judgment.

"I love you Brandt. Please forgive me." She cradled his head in one arm. His face lit briefly as the beam drilled his heart. Jasmina's pistol dropped from Shayla's hand and clattered to the floor as she hugged Brandt.

Her head arched backwards, sightless eyes gazed at the ceiling, her mouth hung open. A long howl pierced the air.

Shayla sat, the sole survivor amongst the dead and the terminally damned.

She didn't notice the thud and whoosh of demolition charges in the distance. She didn't hear the crackle of beam discharges, or the sounds of fighting growing closer.

She didn't look around when the troops burst into the room.

## Epilogue

"Lorenzo Skamensis," Chalwen said for the third time, gazing through the clear dome of the throne room at the sunlit rim of the docking crater. "She kept repeating his name. Over and over."

"Lorenzo *Carver* Georgi Skamensis," Henri whispered, voice full of awe. "Also known as Lorenzo Carver of Eloon after he fled the Empire. A figure of legend. Among those in the know."

"It all fits. His marriage and children are a matter of record."

"Ironic, really. The assassin restores a ruler's family to him, and loses her own in the process."

The throne room was filling with people around them. Speculation was rife. The Emperor had set the time for judgment, but he had given no clues as to how he planned to deal with this conundrum. The traitor, the murderous assassin who had wrought such damage, but who was now celebrated for undoing Ivan's grip on the Empire.

"Do you think she has any idea who her father really was?" Chalwen mused.

"She has the same spirit, there's no question of that. And, in a rather roundabout and misguided way, she has continued the work he started at the height of Florence's rule."

"The same work we picked up with Julian, years later."

"Do you think this news will make any difference to the Emperor's pronouncement?"

———— •◆•———

Emperor Julian Skamensis regarded Shayla for long minutes. The packed throne room was silent. All eyes on the Emperor, resplendent in green robes, or on the lonely figure standing, head bowed, in the center of the map of Magentis.

"Shayla Carver," he said at last, "you have helped restore the Imperial family from twenty five years of imprisonment. For that single act, we are in your debt. Further, you have led us to the capture of the traitors Ivan Skamensis and Scipio Firenzi. However," his voice was firm and stern, "you plotted against the Empire, and against the person of the Emperor and his family. You have, as a specimen charge, the murders of the passengers and crew of *Chantry Bay* laid against you."

He took a deep breath. "I could continue, but I think you get the idea." He looked at Shayla, his face unreadable. "Do you deny these charges?"

Shayla gazed at the ground, fighting back welling tears. The room, and the Emperor's voice, seemed miles distant. All she could think of was Brandt's pleading eyes as she killed him. *He did understand, didn't he? He knew she had no choice.* At length, she composed herself and looked up. "I do not."

"Shayla Carver, high treason cannot be forgiven. The very foundations of civilization demand a fitting punishment." His voice echoed across the room like the knell of Death itself. Do you have anything to say in your defense before I pass sentence?"

A thousand pleas of mitigation flew through her mind. The injustice inflicted on her own world. The years of anguish. The indoctrination — after all, the Grand Families were constantly plotting against the Emperor and against each other, why was this any different? None of it seemed to justify her actions now.

She took a deep breath, and quietly said, "No."

"Very well." He nodded in satisfaction, as if this simple act of humility was what he had been waiting for. "Shayla Carver, in full and complete reckoning for all crimes committed in this realm, I sentence you to lifelong exile and confinement to a planet of my choice."

*So, no execution then.* The thought should have brought relief, but Shayla's mind was numb with grief. Life no longer held any meaning.

"You will spend the rest of your days on Eloon."

The words electrified Shayla, bringing her out of her torpor. She wondered if she had mis-heard. It made no sense. Eloon was dead. *Fitting, I guess.*

"I am declaring Eloon a Freeworld. It will live as a protectorate of the Empire for a term of fifty years before transitioning fully to Freeworld status."

*Where is this leading to?* Shayla hardly dared believe the words she was hearing.

"I hereby appoint you, Shayla Carver, as first Governor of the Freeworld of Eloon."

*Holy crap!*

But the Emperor was still speaking. "This will be no small undertaking. You will have a suitable budget and resources at your disposal to rebuild a world."

He smiled, and the lines of fatigue seemed to wash from his face. "This alone would be an ample task to keep the most dedicated and single-minded person occupied for a lifetime. And enough to keep even you out of trouble, I think. But there is more. In order to hold your status as a Freeworld you need a purpose and a Charter that other forces in the realm of humanity will be prepared to honor and respect. You will establish a refuge for the dispossessed and the victims of conflict. You will accept and rehabilitate broken lives. You will refuse no-one entry who needs it."

He looked Shayla steadily in the eye. "Do you have anything to say?"

"I...no...I mean, yes, far too much, but this is not the time."

All thoughts of loss had been pushed from her mind. They would be back, she knew, again and again in the years to come. But right now, a new glimmer of purpose kindled deep inside and burned, still small, but intense.

Shayla had spent so long pursuing a single goal, that she had given no thought to what might come after. Now she realized that the emptiness that had eaten her soul since the battle of Magentis would have consumed her, even if she had succeeded.

She still had to take it in. It seemed unreal. She had no idea what might be involved, what the future might hold. But that didn't matter. For the first time since childhood, the future beckoned with a sense of purpose and hope.

She was going home.

The end

31378136R00176

Made in the USA
Charleston, SC
15 July 2014